THE
SCARLET
CODE

Also by C. S. Quinn

A Revolution Spy Series
The Bastille Spy

The Thief Taker Series
The Thief Taker
Fire Catcher
Dark Stars
The Changeling Murders
Death Magic (short story)

THE
SCARLET
CODE

C. S. QUINN

CORVUS

Published in hardback in Great Britain in 2020 by Corvus, an imprint of Atlantic Books Ltd.

Copyright © C. S. Quinn, 2020

The moral right of C. S. Quinn to be identified as the author of this work has been asserted them in accordance with the Copyright, Designs and Patents Act of 1988.

10 9 8 7 6 5 4 3 2 1

A CIP catalogue record for this book is available from the British Library.

Hardback ISBN: 978 1 78649 846 5
E-book ISBN: 978 1 78649 849 6

Printed in Great Britain by TJ International Ltd, Padstow, Cornwall

Corvus
An imprint of Atlantic Books Ltd
Ormond House
26–27 Boswell Street
London
WC1N 3JZ

www.corvus-books.co.uk

For Simon, Natalie and Ben

CHAPTER ONE

Lisbon, 1789

𝓘T IS NIGHT. THE DOCKYARD IS STILL, SAVE FOR THE CREAK of masts and tap of wood as boats knock against one another. From the crow's nest of an empty ship, I survey the shore. Guitar sounds and the occasional shout float on the air. A scent of garlic and frying fish from grills outside sailor taverns. As I watch, the last torch on a quay flutters out. The land guard is asleep. There is no time to lose.

I draw my knife; a great curved black blade. Placing it between my teeth I drop silently from the crow's nest to the deck, landing feet apart, balance perfect, taking the weapon into my hand. I wear assassin's garb – soft-soled dancing slippers, loose Arabic-style clothes, black silk trousers, a long-sleeved kurta cut short, tied with a thick scarf at the waist. My dark hair is braided up.

I slip across the deck, barely making a sound, step on to the prow, and jump easily across to the next ship. I assure myself the vessel is deserted, the crescent darkness of my knife invisible in the moonlight.

Looking out on to the water, I count the ships. Three to pass over until I reach the one where the captive is held. Her kidnappers have hidden her well: in an empty floating prison bound for Africa, to be filled with slaves.

Since there is no cargo yet loaded, there is a scant guard, but still I am careful. Assuring myself all is clear, I cross the deck, leap to the next boat. I'm in a rhythm now, running, jumping, checking for threats, knife held tight in my fist. I traverse a ship destined to take wool to England, a lumber transporter from Sweden, the smell of cut pine still fresh on deck. I arrive finally on *The Saint Jose*. A gilded diplomatic ship, old-fashioned, with a broad belly and shapely rear rising to a duck's tail of decorative carving and small windows.

Now my pace slows. There will be guards here. Quietly, I pad towards the captain's quarters at the back. As I suspected, the door is tightly secured from the outside. I need to open the padlock.

The first attack comes swiftly from behind. Feet strike the deck, then someone grabs my shoulder. My own hand sweeps back, locating my attacker's jugular, and I turn to face him. For a moment our stance is almost romantic, my fingers lightly at his throat, his grip still on my shoulder. With our faces only inches apart, his lips part in surprise. He hadn't been expecting a woman, and other instincts are befuddling him. Before he can resolve his confusion, my knife arrives at the artery my fingers have located. He drops soundlessly, blood filling his lungs.

The second man is only half-awake, a strong smell of drink pouring from him as he staggers to his feet. My eyes log the keys swinging at his hip. I close in before he can point his gun, since silence is imperative. His hand shoots out, grabs my chin. My knife is under his armpit, up and out before he realises. As he loses his grip on me, my knife comes up and around the base of his skull. The right eyelid spasms and he drops. I catch him before he thuds to the deck and lay him softly down.

I stand watching his twitching eye, still trained on me in disbelief. When the dying gaze clouds, I unhook his set of keys, then take the pistol from his belt and launch it through the air. It lands loudly on the deck of the lumber ship and a flurry of footsteps rings out on the adjacent deck. I listen, tense, making sure that any other guards are headed away. Then I approach a magnificent cabin door with its gaudy lock.

Always the way with Catholic countries, I think to myself as I fit the golden key, *to keep captives in finery.*

The door opens to reveal a woman, fashionably dressed in the latest French style of blousy muslin. She is sat at a table with a carafe of red wine and a silver plate before her. To her right is a bread basket and she holds a torn piece of its content half to her mouth as she stares at me in surprise.

'Am I being abducted?' she asks finally. 'How droll. Did the Duke send you?' she adds hopefully.

Naturally, as a noblewoman, she reads a good deal too many romance novels.

'You are Fleur de Lucile?' I confirm, as she adjusts her dress to expose more of her shoulders.

She nods.

'You have already been abducted,' I tell her. 'It is only that you haven't noticed.'

She looks around the decorated captain's cabin.

'It is a jest?' she suggests, the slightest frown of puzzlement crinkling her smooth, white forehead. 'As you can see, I am very well cared for.' She gestures by way of explanation to the spread of food and wine, the finely set mahogany table.

'Silver forks do not ensure a host is trustworthy.' I walk to the window of tiny glass panes, assuring myself no warning torches have been fired on the docks. 'Your husband's stance against slavery has gained you powerful enemies.' I turn back to her. 'Did you ever question why your door was bolted from the outside? Why you are here alone, with guards placed to keep watch?'

'They said it was for my own protection,' she says slowly. 'The Portuguese ambassador—'

'Is in the pockets of the slave traders,' I say, moving closer to her table. 'You are aware how much money is made by slave trading every year?'

'Oh yes,' she says, rolling her eyes. 'My husband's friends are tiresome on the subject. But what has this to do with me?'

'Your husband is due to address the King and convince him to sign the Rights of Man.'

Her mouth moves slowly, trying to match the words to a memory.

'The document written after the Bastille was stormed,' I explain patiently. She smiles in polite confoundedness.

'Agreeing that all men are equal,' I say, keeping my frustration in check.

'Oh that!' She claps her hands together. 'Why should plantation owners care if commoners and nobles are equal?'

'If the King signs the Rights of Man,' I tell her, 'he accepts that all men are equal. *All* men. Including the blacks in the French colonies.'

She does the thing with her mouth again, as though sounding out difficult words.

'Your captors are ruthless men; plantation owners, who will do anything to protect their business,' I tell her. 'Believe me, they have done worse than cut the throat of a lady and toss her in the sea.'

Understanding finally flickers over her features. She stands in shock.

'Who *are* you?' she manages. 'Are you Portuguese?' she adds, taking in the shade of my skin and my black hair. I reach into my kurta and remove a letter from her husband. She takes it wordlessly.

'My name is Attica Morgan,' I say, as she reads. 'I'm an English spy. I have come to rescue you.'

CHAPTER TWO

*F*LEUR STARES FOR A LONG TIME AT HER HUSBAND'S LETTER.

Her eyes dart to me, something in her mind not matching.

'How am I to trust you?' she asks eventually. 'How can I be sure *you* are a friend?'

In reply I show her the slave brand, hidden under my hair at the back of my neck.

'My mother was African,' I explain. 'We were enslaved together in Virginia when I was a girl. She died.'

Her eyes dart all over me now, looking for clues and inconsistencies. I often have this effect on people, since I am half of one continent, half of another. The medley of tawny skin and light eyes has been a great boon in my spy work, since I can pass for many nationalities.

'As soon as I got old enough to outrun my captors, I escaped to England and found my father. Lord Morgan,' I tell her.

'You are Lord Morgan's *daughter*?' She says it that way people always do, when they know rumours of my bastard origins. 'I have heard of Lord Morgan,' she says slowly.

'Everybody has,' I say, unwilling to have the same tired conversation about my brilliant, yet erratic, father, and his brief awful decline into laudanum addiction. 'He is better now,' I add. 'Remarried. We should go.'

My family history has been enough to convince her. Fleur follows me on to the dark deck, and then grips my arm tight at the sight of the slaughtered guards littering the floor outside her cabin.

'They're dead,' I assure her, but it doesn't have the effect I hoped. I wonder briefly if I should have brought smelling salts, but Fleur manages to collect herself.

'This way.' I draw her to the prow, looking out on to the inky black water of the docks.

We creep along the edge of the boat. Moving to the side of the deck, I pull out my tinderbox and strike it. There's a pause and then across the docks another light flickers in reply. I count the flashes. Three.

'That's the signal,' I tell Fleur, identifying the ship. 'Our rescuers are near. We will sail by night, and you shall be back with your husband by morning.'

'You surely will not attempt to sail us out of these docks?' says Fleur, panic rising. 'They are guarded. As soon as we raise anchor, they will gun us out of the water.'

'You must keep faith, madame.'

I unwrap the scarf from my waist and begin fashioning a makeshift grappling hook, tying the end to my knife handle.

Fleur watches the black curved blade in amazement.

'It is a Mangbetu,' I say proudly, 'awarded to the fiercest fighters of the African Congo. My mother gave it to me.'

I send the blade winging over the side of the ship to lodge in a little yacht bobbing adjacent to us. Walking to the ship's wheel, I attach the other end of the silk and begin turning. Gripping with both hands, I haul on the scarf, winding it in.

There's a creaking sound as the little yacht begins drifting towards us. It's hard work and sweat beads my forehead, but I manage to pull the vessel close.

I allow the scarf to slacken. Our boats bob naturally against another. I put one leg over the prow and begin climbing down the rungs of the side of our larger boat, with Fleur following above me.

Once aboard I strike the tinderbox again. There is a pause, then a rope at the prow lifts clear from the water and tightens, and, slowly but surely, we are pulled silently between the enormous ships until we reach the hull of a large vessel waiting at the edge of open water.

A grappling hook spins from above and lands loudly on the side of our yacht. Fleur starts back with a cry of fear, then clamps her hands over her mouth. I can see the whites of her eyes in the moonlight, wide and frightened. A pack of swarthy men can be seen from the higher deck, winching our boat close to theirs.

'You mustn't mind their appearance,' I tell Fleur. 'They are here to help us.'

A dark figure slides expertly down one of the ropes and lands nimbly on our deck. He steps from the shadows. Jemmy Avery, almost invisible in his black shirt and trousers, only his sword and flashy set of pistols glinting in the moonlight. He makes me a mock bow.

'Your Ladyship.' Jemmy winks.

I give him a wide smile. 'Good to see you, Captain Avery.

'This is Jemmy Avery,' I tell Fleur, noticing the fear in her eyes has deepened. 'He is …' I decide to omit the word 'pirate'. '… a good sailor,' I conclude.

'Best sailor this side of the South Sea,' corrects Jemmy.

'And only that because we know of no land beyond it.'

'A humble man, as you see,' I murmur.

To Fleur, Jemmy bows low, taking off his broad-brimmed hat and rolling it smoothly along his forearm. I notice Fleur's shoulders relax, her expression soften.

'And this must by Fleur de Lucile? Do not fear; you are quite safe with me.' Jemmy is the very devil for charm when he needs to be.

He offers her his hand. 'May I? There is a ladder along the side of my ship.' He points to where nailed planks can be seen, picking a route up the side to the top.

Fleur's blue eyes widen. She is smiling coquettishly.

'It looks very dangerous,' she says, her voice suddenly breathy and low. 'I am afraid.'

'Madame, I shall climb beneath you,' Jemmy assures her. 'If you slip I can break your fall. You are quite safe.'

Her smile broadens. I roll my eyes. Jemmy hands her to the first rung, and we all three ascend to our ship, Fleur moving faster than I might have thought possible for a woman so afraid of heights.

As we reach the top, Jemmy leaps to a nearby rope and pulls himself up the final distance on to deck, so he might reach down and hand Fleur up.

'Welcome to my ship,' he tells her.

'My saviour,' she says, batting her lashes. 'How can I ever repay you?'

'A word, Captain Avery?' I interject, heaving myself up unaided and swinging my legs on to the deck.

'Thank you kindly,' mutters Jemmy, raising a dark eyebrow at me and glancing back at Fleur. 'Anyone would think you were jealous.'

'Everything is as we planned?' I ask.

His eyes meet mine, their mongrel mix of green and brown masked by the moonlight. The teardrop-shaped burn at the side of his face looks more livid in the shadow.

'It is all as you wished it,' he says. 'The boys have been working hard. Lining below deck with barrels of pitch and brimstone, honeycombed. Brush and straw across the top. It goes against my boys' nature, to be sure, treating good ships that way. You're certain this will work, Attica?'

'I'm certain there's no other way out of this dock.'

His lips press together.

'I made a great study of naval warfare in my youth,' I assure him. 'So long as you can sail us where we need to be, it will work.'

'I can sail a horse trough through a hurricane, Attica, you needn't worry about that. She'll be where you want her.' He pats the prow then glances to Fleur, who is standing a little apart from us now. Jemmy runs a hand over his shoulder-length black hair. 'Ready to blast the slave traders all to hell?' he says.

'Ready.'

Jemmy strides to the ship's wheel, calling orders to his men. We are all action now, with no time for silence. Sails are trimmed, yardarms swing. The night breeze fills the sail. Shouts come from the shore. A torch lights.

'They've seen us now,' mutters Jemmy, turning the wheel expertly. 'Let's hope this old girl doesn't fall apart on us. There's a good tide once we're clear.'

The crew are cutting away the wrapping ropes, severing our connection to the smaller yacht as we drift free. We pick up the wind and begin a slow course off shore.

Men are running along the quay, their voices raised as they near us, climbing aboard a man-of-war bristling with cannons.

Fleur is shaking her head, hands gripping the side of the boat.

'We'll never make it,' she whispers. 'They'll blow us to pieces.'

In answer, I strike a flint. It sparks on a little puff of cotton-flower kindling. I pick up the flaming material, lean overboard and drop it straight through the opening of the smaller yacht, drifting away from us. There's a silent moment before a crackling of ignition. Then smoke begins pouring up.

Moments later, flames lick upwards. The vessel continues to drift, headed straight for a cluster of moored boats that Jemmy's crew have already packed with tar and brimstone.

'We're not going to escape these docks,' I tell her, as Jemmy and his crew manoeuvre our rickety boat expertly towards the open ocean. 'We're going to burn them. Every last ship.'

Jemmy spins the wheel and the sails catch fully. Our boat begins to pick up speed, sailing fast from the Lisbon docks.

When I look behind us, all is blazing fury, as the fiery boat bobs benignly against the other moorings, spreading flaming cinders on everything it touches.

We enter the cool night air of the ocean with nothing but smoke and flames behind us.

CHAPTER THREE

Paris, one week later

𝒥EMMY AND I APPROACH A SMART TOWNHOUSE – ONE OF THE newly built edifices of cream-coloured stone. All along the street the carved façades are designed to echo ancient Greece, with stucco shaped like temple thresholds and half-pillars.

'The most soulless part of town,' murmurs Jemmy. 'Not a wine shop in sight.'

'No stink of overflowing gutters,' I point out, though I am inclined to agree with him. My own apartment is in a neighbourhood of multi-generational buildings.

'You have to admit this is getting more risky,' says Jemmy. 'Since this Rights of Man, the plantation owners are out for blood.'

'They're afraid,' I say. 'It's a good thing.'

'Think the King will ever actually sign it?'

'We can only hope. And continue to rescue those the plantation owners threaten.'

I raise my hand and knock on the door.

'You might have worn something French,' he says wistfully,

looking at my rigid clothing as we wait. 'Floaty gauzy things are all the fashion now.'

'I wouldn't expect an American to understand,' I tell him. 'But I have loyalty to my country. Not to mention, thick corsetry hides all manner of lethal things.' I pat the sturdy confines of my stays.

'Patriotism extends to fashion, does it?'

'Of course it does. It's the only way women can be political. You were born in a country that is not a country,' I tell him. 'There is a code to it all that is lost to you.'

I glance up at the house, wondering why it is taking so long to answer the door.

'As you well know, I live to my own code,' says Jemmy. 'Be loyal to your crew, defend those who need defending—'

'And don't kill anyone you like,' I finish. 'I know. You are tiresome on the subject of pirate honour.'

'And what is your code, Lady Morgan?'

'I am English.'

He throws his hands up in frustration. 'You were born illegitimate to an African slave mother, and spent the first five years of your life in America.'

'My mother was Queen of her Congo tribe,' I say, insulted. 'And my parents were married in the sight of the elders—'

'My point is, you're no more English than I am.' He shakes his head. 'Perhaps less,' he adds, 'if my mother's claims about my father are true. Though when my mammy's not lying, she's drinking, and when she's not drinking, she's whoring,' he concludes philosophically, rubbing his nose and glancing up at the townhouse.

'It isn't about where you're born. It's a code, like yours. Keep your promises. Behave honourably.'

'Qualities of a decent person, to be sure. Never knew England had the run of them.'

I think of my illegitimate uncle, Lord Pole, struggling always to be recognised as noble.

'I am a spy,' I tell him. 'It is a low-down, dirty thing. If I don't do it for the love of my country, it would make me … I don't even know.'

'A murdering criminal with integrity,' beams Jemmy. 'Like me.' He leans forward and pounds aggressively on the door. 'Manners aren't always helpful,' he adds with a wink.

I smile back at him despite myself. There is noise now inside, like someone coming down the stairs.

Jemmy makes an elaborate show of using the mud-scraper.

The door is opened by a maid who looks to have been caught halfway through eating. She takes my card, chewing violently, then swallows with effort before directing us to the first floor.

I can sense Jemmy mentally recoiling from the high hubbub of female voices in the room beyond, as the maid sails forth to deliver our card. An expensively dressed perfumer walks past us, his tray of little bottles tinkling, blazing a trail of his strongest stock in his wake.

'You're certain I need to be with you?' tries Jemmy, edging back, waving away the scent.

'Absolutely.' I grab his arm. 'We get our best information here. The salon ladies pay me no mind at all with a real-life pirate to paw at. Not even to bore me with their high views on Rousseau.'

'It's a poor business to be used as bait, so,' says Jemmy, looking morose. 'Not a single girl here cares a fig for their marriage vows.'

'You cannot be as romantic as you pretend. You should go out in the city with me. See the sights.'

'Oh no.' He straightens his coat. 'You'll never see me in any of those bathhouses, Attica.'

'It's Paris. Everyone is doing it.'

'Not me.' He sighs, looking warily at the pack of decadently dressed women. 'A little lapdog,' mutters Jemmy miserably. 'That's what I am to those harpies.'

'Don't be so provincial. In any case, you love the macarons.'

CHAPTER FOUR

*J*EMMY AND I ARE WAITING FOR THE HOST, ABSORBING THE perfumed decadence of the salon. There are almost as many servants as guests, and women chatter animatedly as their dainty glasses are filled. A little band of musicians plays chamber music at a discreet volume in a far corner.

To his great delight, Jemmy has spotted the obligatory tray of macarons. His eyes follow the approaching maid, who now carries a silver salver of the pink delicacies. He takes four in a closed fist, then seeing my expression returns one, then another, awkwardly following after as the maid tries to take the tray away again.

'Oh, let him take as many as he likes!' says a shrill delighted voice. A cherub-lipped girl whose face holds the familiar hallmarks of noble descent bears down on us. She has a short, slanting forehead and a weak chin already giving way to fat, characteristics the French nobility have bred in over the last century. Combined with large brown eyes and thick, rather mannish brows, she reminds me of a friendly horse, right down to her hair, styled naturally, as is the fashion, but curled and ribboned as though she can't quite go through with the lack of artifice. She smiles as she sails towards us, clapping her hands with glee, eyes only for Jemmy. 'I'll dare say they're better than ship's biscuits, Mr Avery.'

Jemmy, macaron halfway to his mouth, enacts some magic trick of vanishing it into his hand and bows deeply.

'Madame du Quenoy,' he says.

She curtseys in response, never shifting her eyes from his face, then notices me as an afterthought.

'Mademoiselle Morgan.' She curtseys politely. 'I hope your translations are not keeping you up late?' And without waiting for an answer, 'Is this what they wear in England nowadays? Your people are becoming fashionable here, if you can believe it. Your unaffected country style.' The words don't match her open disdain for my rigidly panelled dress.

'We're simple people,' I reply, eyeing her translucent muslin dress. 'And as you see, I am traditional.'

'Very good. Of course you are unmarried and must dress for an English husband.' She gives a light laugh, then frowns a little, barely lining her sloped forehead.

'Is there anyone you might like to be introduced to, Mademoiselle Morgan?' she asks hopefully, eyes tracking between Jemmy and me in naked desperation to get him alone.

'I shouldn't be so bold as to suggest it,' I say, as her face drops in dismay, 'but I did hear Madame Pinochet's husband might be in need of a translator.'

She brightens. 'Allow me to take you to her.' She links her arm in mine. 'Don't imagine you shall escape so easily,' she adds, seeing Jemmy attempt to shuffle back out of view. 'I must hear of your latest adventures.'

Madame du Quenoy marches us to a baffled-looking woman and all but throws me towards her.

'Madame Pinochet, this is Mademoiselle Morgan. From England.'

The woman, thin as a rake with watery eyes and a beaky nose crusted with snuff, peers at me over a glass of wine. She makes the strange smile of an older lady who has learned not to crack her paste make-up, which has been applied liberally. Her ageing body, unaccustomed to the flowing liberty of the latest fashion, stoops and bulges as if yearning for support.

'Mademoiselle Morgan,' she says, not managing to hide her dismay as she curtseys. She looks around, hoping to find someone to foist me on. 'Still working?' she manages, her long finger trailing distractedly around the rim of her wine glass.

'Oh yes.' I smile. 'I am making some very interesting Latin translations.'

'Really?' Her face strains with the effort of polite interest.

'I'd love to tell you all about them,' I add, as Jemmy is spirited away by our host. 'But where are my manners? I should hear your news. Your husband travels to Versailles with the other plantation owners?'

'Next Tuesday,' she confirms guilelessly, relieved to be granted a reprieve from my academic discourse, as I mentally log the day. 'Even nobles must fear the customs gates nowadays.' She takes out a highly decorated snuffbox, turning it affectedly so I might notice the intricacy of the pearl enamelling.

'Oh?' I enquire politely, sipping wine. I glance across to Jemmy, who is now deep in the clutches of the young host. She has him backed against a wall whilst she leans in, head tilted, inviting him to give his opinion on a musk and rose oil behind her ears.

'Of course, you are English,' says my beaky-nosed companion. 'You do not know how terrible things are here.' The snuffbox makes another whirl through her fingers like a magician's trick. She lowers her voice and leans in.

'Since the Bastille fell, the King has put a customs guard on every gate out of the city.'

'His Majesty wishes to tax the goods?' I suggest, feigning ignorance.

'Oh no, my dear. He wants to stop seditious books and papers. These filthy revolutionaries would spread their poison anywhere they could.'

I nod sympathetically.

'But,' she continues grandly, opening the snuffbox, 'His Majesty is all the way out in Versailles. He has no idea what *really* happens in Paris.' She shakes her head solemnly and I copy the gesture. 'The *men*,' she spits the word, 'who guard the gates are open revolutionaries. They take it upon themselves to search everyone. Even their betters!' She pauses to sprinkle snuff liberally on to the side of her hand and sniff violently. Her long nose goes into a kind of spasm and her bloodshot eyes shed a line of salty tears that slice through her paste make-up.

'Last week my husband was detained for an hour while an upstart rifled his possessions. The guard even had the affront to wear the tricolour cockade in clear view.'

'How very dreadful. I had no idea the city was in such disarray,' I tell her. 'I must be careful, for I wish to leave myself next week.'

'Take the Porte Saint-Denis,' she advises. 'The King still had a few loyal men there.'

'I am grateful to you,' I say truthfully. 'And I shall pray for your husband's safe journey. You must be certain his carriage is well stocked,' I prompt. 'I am told there is no food to be had at the palace, for all the finery.'

'Oh, they shall travel at night,' she says, confirming my suspicion. 'They mean to confound this dratted English fellow. The Scarlet Poppy, or some such, they call him. He seems to know all their plans even before they do.'

'The Scarlet Pimpernel?' I suggest.

'Yes?' The beady eyes settle on me in surprise. 'How did you know that?'

'Only by chance,' I reply. 'They say he is everywhere nowadays.'

Her eyes widen in alarm, imagining English villains lurking in every corner.

'Allow me to fetch you more wine,' I add. 'You mustn't concern yourself with the Pimpernel, madame. There is no question that you French nobles will find him out sooner or later.'

She nods vaguely as I depart, a small smile on my face.

CHAPTER FIVE

*R*OBESPIERRE ARRIVES AT THE CHEAP BROTHEL, HIS PRESSED lawyer's suit of striped frock-coat with matching breeches and box-fresh wig entirely out of place. He is a diminutive man, a slip of laundered linen and polished leather in a byway of broad-shouldered sailors and loud-mouthed drunks.

With an expression of extreme distaste, he picks daintily around the animal droppings and rotting litter that have mulched into the mud of the streets, and looks in vain for a mud-scraper to clean his silver-buckled shoes.

The building was once a bishop's house, but the low-ceilinged style has fallen out of favour, and the church leases it cheaply. The carved oak door now stands perpetually open. Through it is a broad staircase, on which sailors stand in line, elbowing one another out of the way. On the landing above, a door opens and a man exits, rearranging his clothing. Behind him a tired-looking girl tilts her head at the long queue.

'Next,' she shouts, without enthusiasm.

Breathing in, to protect himself from the disease that must surely run rampant in the air, Robespierre pushes his way up the stairs, trying not to touch anything.

'Hi there, city boy,' says a drunken old salt, eyeing Robespierre's neat clerical style. 'There's plenty of girls for you on the Champs Élysées. These cheap whores are for the sailors.'

'I am not here for that purpose,' mutters Robespierre.

'Of course not,' leers the old man, as the lawyer passes.

Robespierre ignores him, walking along the landing to the furthest door. A rabbit's foot hangs on the handle. The symbol that the girl inside is not available.

'She'll not take kindly to being disturbed!' shouts a man from midway on the staircase.

Ignoring him, Robespierre pushes open the door. A dark-skinned woman is squatting over a tin pot of dirty water, cleaning herself with a rag of strong-smelling chemicals. She pulls her skirts down hurriedly and stands, but not fast enough to disguise a rainbow of bruising along her flank.

Robespierre's lips press tight together.

This is the famous Centime. He knows her. Or of her, rather. Has always pitied her at a distance. Even more so, now her brutal master has returned.

'I have a keeper again now,' she says fiercely. 'You want a black girl, you must go elsewhere.' Up close she is younger than he imagined, and her face is lovely. Large doe-like eyes, long-lashed and almost black. In contrast, her full lips are the softest, lightest pink, like a rose yet to bloom.

Robespierre is not generally a connoisseur of such things, but even he can see she is far too attractive for this low-rent place. The colour of her skin has counted against her. Probably, she believes herself lucky not to be walking the streets. He wonders which plantation she was shipped from.

'He is in there?' replies Robespierre simply, pointing to the door on the far side of the room.

Centime's hostile expression drops away, replaced by several successive emotions.

'He sent for you?' she asks, fear twisting her face.

Robespierre crosses to Centime. His eyes dart to the door.

'You must not fear,' he says. 'I mean you no harm.' He remembers the bruises she tried to hide, thinking there are a hundred, a thousand, just like her, all over France.

'His work?' suggests Robespierre, gesturing at where the bruising lies.

'He is a good and kind master,' she says in a quavering voice. 'You may not go in if you were not sent for.'

'All this will soon be over.' He sweeps a hand to encompass the brothel, perhaps France itself. 'A new world is about to be born.' Behind his glasses, his blue eyes are earnest. Something about his fervour calms her.

Without waiting for a reply, he turns the handle on the door, which has been partially covered by curtains. Despite his reassurances, his hand shakes as he enters the room.

It is far larger than the exterior might suggest, muggy with pipe smoke, and fashioned like an office with a large old desk. Sat behind it is a dark-haired nobleman with strong features – thick broad lips and heavy-lidded eyes with deep brows. They flick to the intruder, then narrow.

'Who the devil are you?' he demands. 'I told that damned whore I was not to be disturbed.'

'She is blameless. The fault is mine.' Robespierre is taking in the spray of expensive lace at the man's neck and cuffs, the golden threads that pepper his silken clothes.

'Then you shall pay for it.'

'The Marquis de Salvatore, I assume?' says Robespierre, ignoring the threat, his lips tightening at the honorific title.

When the man's face registers rage, Robespierre gives a thin smile. 'You are more difficult to find out of the Bastille than inside it.' He pulls a chair, hesitates for a moment, then sits with a brief glance at the seated marquis.

'You dare sit before me?' whispers Salvatore. 'I shall have you whipped for your insolence.'

Robespierre gives the barest frown, his round glasses slipping fractionally down his nose.

'Perhaps you should first ask yourself what kind of man has located you, here in this most secret of places, known only to your very closest of criminal companions,' Robespierre pushes his glasses up with the tip of his finger, 'before issuing the summary stock of threats you nobles aim at us commoners.' Another frown sends the wire frames back down his nose.

Salvatore opens his mouth to reply, but Robespierre, perhaps sensing a second volley of displeasingly unoriginal denunciations, talks on.

'You communicate with your colleagues in code, of sorts,' says Robespierre, answering his own question without emotion. 'I would suggest you look to something more sophisticated. Your current missives are very easy to break.'

He stands, and makes a short bow. 'Allow me to introduce myself. I am Monsieur Robespierre. A lawyer by trade. I have a business proposition for you.'

Salvatore leans back in his chair, dark features fathomless.

'Well then,' he says, 'I shall hear it, before I have you beaten.'

Robespierre gives no indication he is afraid. Instead, he removes papers from his coat and wordlessly passes them across.

Salvatore stares at the papers for a long time.

'These routes are real?' he demands finally.

Robespierre bobs his head, birdlike. 'I am adept at breaking codes. This is only a small part of what I have translated.' Emboldened, Robespierre takes a step forward. Salvatore shoots him a fierce look.

'With my help, your arms smuggling operations will double their profits. Perhaps even triple them.'

Salvatore doesn't disagree, only stares at the routes.

'Three hundred livres,' he says finally. 'That is a high payment considering your impertinence. You shall have it in gold, and once you have given me the routes I shall never see or hear of you again.'

Robespierre's mouth compresses very slightly.

'I do not ask for money.'

'Then what? A title?' There is an open sneer on Salvatore's face.

'I want no titles,' says Robespierre smoothly. 'Such things are of no interest to a man such as myself. As you can see, I am a person of humble means.' He gestures to his plain suit, immaculate but of a common cut. 'There is only one thing I should desire in payment.'

'Which is?' Salvatore lets the paper drop now, as if expecting a price beyond his abilities.

'A small thing only. A boon. Something that is well within your power to grasp.' He gives a strange little smile, and Salvatore, who deals daily with murderous smugglers, recoils. 'It is all a question of killing the right people.'

CHAPTER SIX

*J*EMMY AND I WALK IN COMPANIONABLE SILENCE FOR THE few minutes it takes to reach our favoured tavern.

The preferred spot is directly in front of Porte Saint-Martin, with tables on the street that allow drinkers to enjoy all the drama of the city gates. A girl with a jug of wine emerges as soon as we sit.

'We've doubled our money these last weeks,' she tells us, nodding to the gates. 'Best seats in town to watch the aristos get their just deserts. They even threw one in the lock-up last week.' Her eyes drift to an expensively clad man and wife, arguing in high outraged voices as a man in a tricolour cockade carelessly searches their carriage, making no effort to keep his muddy boots from the satin interior.

'About time they got treated like the rest of us, stuck-up pigs,' she opines. 'No offence,' she adds offhandedly, noticing my and Jemmy's clothing.

'I am no aristo friend,' says Jemmy, offended. 'An Irish boy raised in America is what I am. There are New York gutters that consider themselves too fancy for the likes of me.' Her eyes drift to me, clearly deciding that whatever the reason for my dress it isn't nobility.

She bobs a little curtsey and retreats, her eyes lingering a little too long on Jemmy's face.

As soon as Jemmy and I are certain we are out of earshot and ensconced in the tavern we both speak at once.

'Tuesday.'

'We discovered the same, then,' I confirm. 'It will be Tuesday. By night.'

Jemmy nods, raking dark hair back behind his ear. 'You were right about one thing,' he says. 'These bored girls will spill all their husbands' plans without a second thought. But it's become too dangerous, Attica.'

'Why do you say so? The plan is working perfectly.' I frown. 'They tell us the plantation owners' plans to sabotage the abolitionists. We protect those who need protecting. It can't be more than a few weeks before the King gives in and signs the Rights of Man. All equal.' I raise my cup in toast. 'Whites and blacks included.'

Jemmy joins the toast uneasily.

'We're becoming known for only rescuing English people. It makes us vulnerable. I think we should mix our rescues. There's a French lieutenant in danger, spoke out about the King ...'

'Atherton will never approve it.'

Jemmy's face adopts a pained look. 'Must we always do what Atherton says?'

I pause, glass halfway to my lips. 'We need Atherton. He grants us inventions and tools we could not be without. We cannot ask him to go against his principles.'

'You would say that. You're in love with the fella.'

I chew my fingernail. 'I have ... a great affection for Atherton. But he is a married man.'

27

'And the two of you fancy yourselves so high-minded, you won't act on your feelings for one another. All this simmering unrequited business is bad for the blood. You'll get overheated. If you want my advice, jump in the sack together and be done with it,' Jemmy continues, rubbing his chin. 'You might realise after all this green sickness, you're not suited at all. A girlish fancy you never grew out of, if you ask me, falling in love with your teacher.'

'He was never my teacher.'

'He taught you all the code breaking, did he not? Arranged for you to train as an assassin in Sicily. It's not just the difference in age.' Jemmy's face contorts, with the abrasive rum or something else. 'He's your spy-master. It's ... peculiar.'

'Speaking of peculiar romances,' I prompt, opting to change the subject. 'Did our plump young host share anything else with you, besides a full view of her figure in that see-through dress?'

To my surprise, Jemmy hesitates uneasily.

'She did, as a matter of fact,' he says, something like an accusation in his tone. 'Apparently Robespierre has been asking about the Scarlet Pimpernel. He gets everywhere, you know,' Jemmy adds pointedly. 'Just like you.'

I hesitate. 'Oh? Robespierre doesn't suspect you, does he?' I ask.

Jemmy snorts in reply. 'It is well known that the Scarlet Pimpernel is an educated man, a genius of phenomenal intelligence and singular mind. I only learned to write my name in order to win a bet.'

'Then what is the problem?'

Jemmy is sat at an awkward halfway angle on his chair, one booted foot splayed out, face creased in consternation.

'The tokens, Attica,' he says pointedly. 'Little cards in the shape of red flowers?'

I sip wine a little too quickly. 'What about them?'

'You've been using them when I told you not to. And now it seems Robespierre has gotten hold of several. I warned against it. Those things are an arrogance. A foolishness. A robber doesn't leave a calling card.'

'We are not robbers,' I tell him. 'This is entirely the reason we should be known. It is important the Scarlet Pimpernel is not some highwayman vigilante or plunderer. We are freedom fighters.'

'Anyone would think you want to be found,' says Jemmy.

'Now you are absurd.'

'Well, whatever you were wanting to gain by your little flourish,' decides Jemmy, leaning back more easily and crossing one ankle over the other, while considering me over his silver tankard, 'you succeeded in deeply aggravating Robespierre. And I have the strangest feeling that just might have been your intention.'

'Since when were you so concerned with my anonymity? I thought you were in this for the gold.'

Jemmy shrugs. 'Perhaps I am a little converted. All this do-gooding rubs off on a man. I grew up a little gutter rat. I never dreamed I could have any impact on the world besides staying alive and depriving it of as much rum as I could fit in my belly. It's refreshing to have a cause. Besides, we share an oath, do we not? We are crew now.'

'Then let's get back to the plan,' I suggest, straightening my back and returning my cup to the little barrel that serves as a table. 'If they go on Tuesday, then the pamphlet writer is in the most danger. We should extract her first.'

'If you poke at a snake,' says Jemmy, ignoring my attempt to change the subject and shifting in his seat to pour us both more wine, 'do not complain when it bites you. You're playing a dangerous game is what I'm saying.'

'Who doesn't love a little danger?' I wink at him. 'Surely Robespierre doesn't frighten you? He's the same size as my eleven-year-old cousin.'

'Don't make the mistake of underestimating him, Attica.'

'Well, *I* have no fear of a murdering little lawyer,' I say sharply, looking up at Jemmy.

He sighs in a world-weary way. 'That's what I'm afraid of.'

CHAPTER SEVEN

London

THE AUTUMN AIR BLOWING OFF THE THAMES IS REFRESHING after the stench of Paris. The streets of Westminster are wide and well swept. Women carry baskets of cobnuts and blackberries, a baked-potato man fans the flames of his black barrel oven, and a peddler with a copper canteen sells the last of the elderflower wine.

Since I'm about to see Atherton, Jemmy's words keep coming back to me. I find myself wondering what would happen if we simply had an affair, as so many other nobles do. But this is out of the question. Even so, I have taken greater care of my dress today than I usually might.

I wear a riding habit – a tailored navy coat, close fitting and detailed to the bust, falling to the tops of my low-heeled boots. My hat is a jaunty bicorn in the same colour as my dress.

I approach my old friend Peter, the hot pea seller, whose battered cauldron belches contented puffs of steam from its rolling sage-green ooze. He gives me a broad, single-toothed grin when he sees me.

I remove a wrap of tobacco leaves I bought him at Wapping docks and wave the bundle.

'An apology for my long absence,' I tell him. He slips it into his coat, beaming.

'Where was it this time, then, girl?'

'France.'

'Lookin' for a Frenchie husband, was you?'

My smile broadens. 'Hardly. I've yet to find a tavern in Paris that serves beer.'

'You could do worse, Attica. I heard all them nobles out there got castles a' gold, on account of takin' all the taxes off them peasants.'

He wipes the back of his nose with his hand and sniffs loudly.

'Times are changing,' I tell him.

'Well, maybe's for the best,' he decides after a moment of thought. 'You might have a care, mind.' His eyes narrow. 'Them high-ups are always talking of who you'll marry. I hear things.' He taps his nose knowingly.

'Thank you,' I say sincerely. 'I'll be careful.'

Peter scans the middle distance with practised caution, then stands neatly aside to allow me through. Behind his stall is a secret entrance to Westminster. The underground headquarters of the Sealed Knot. A partially legal hinterland of spies, crooks and thieves that allow our honest government to win wars.

I slip through, always glad to be back. I descend to a low-ceilinged undercroft, where a long run of ancient battered tables are laid out for plans and plotting. Men pore over large maps of land or shipping routes. The merits of various new pieces of weaponry are being enthusiastically debated. At one table, dice are thrown to decide who will undertake the least prestigious missions for King and country.

I pass a table stacked with glittering gold coins, and lift one. I bite into it, then examine it wonderingly.

'Fine forgeries, Emile,' I tell the man arranging the money. 'I could not tell them apart.'

I speak in Romany, since it is a language we share. Emile, one of the many misfits who populate the Sealed Knot, is a fencing champion who is half gypsy. He glances up, then grins.

'What brings you back?' he says. 'We thought we'd lost you to the French.'

'You had,' I say truthfully. 'I came back for him.' I nod my head towards Atherton's door. 'There is something they want me to do in Paris. No doubt it will be some bloodless plot of Lord Pole's.'

The truth is, I can't wait to see Atherton. There's a fizzing feeling in my stomach at the prospect. We write to one another often, but it isn't the same. Sometimes I wonder how it would be if he wasn't married, but France is good for forgetting.

'I'll meet you at the King's Head later,' I tell Emile, heading for the thick door at the back of the room. 'Tell you all about the fall of the Bastille before I sail back.'

CHAPTER EIGHT

A THERTON'S ROOM FEELS WRONG AS SOON AS I ENTER. So much so, my hand slips automatically for my knife. The airy office, usually scattered with inventions and experiments, has been cleared of surface clutter. Several of Atherton's colourful chinoiserie furnishings have been transplanted by dark carved wood replacements. The desk is the same, but the man sitting at it isn't.

It takes me a full few seconds to identify the newcomer.

Lord Pole. He is hunched over his papers, in the black parliamentary robes he insists on wearing. As always he reminds me of a predatory, carrion-eating bird, the stench of death never quite shaken free from his bear-fur collar. His little scribe-like hat serves only to emphasise the beak-like nose.

There is a resemblance between him and my father, Lord Morgan, but to my mind it is fleeting. They share black hair and brown eyes. But Lord Pole's illegitimacy has bequeathed him the hawk-like features of his Bavarian count father, and a perpetual expression of ruthless calculation. A childhood on the peripheries of nobility does strange things to a person. I should know.

He looks up from where he has been populating a page with tiny numbers, and gives a tight nod for me to sit. I walk uncertainly to a chair in front of the familiar desk, as he finalises whatever calculation he is making with a frowning flourish.

'Where is Atherton?' I ask, as he lays down his pen.

He takes an exaggerated breath to express his displeasure at the question.

'No kind greeting for your uncle?' he observes drily. 'Atherton was called away on urgent family business.'

Since Atherton's only family is his wife, painful possibilities loom.

A birth? A son and heir? It was bound to happen at some point, I suppose. Atherton and his wife are politely estranged, but that doesn't stop most nobles from doing their duty.

Lord Pole looks as though he might say more and then prevents himself, staring intently into my face. 'So it has fallen to me to temporarily manage his duties,' he concludes.

I'm still fighting away the disappointment both of not seeing Atherton and at the reason for his absence.

'Aren't you very busy sacrificing good men to your perfect run of victories?' I say, noticing Lord Pole has populated Atherton's chaotic room with precisely arranged military maps and plans. On his desk lies a board set with little figurines and guns depicting the current American crisis. The layout suggests a heavy retreat. I imagine Lord Pole sweeping away swathes of young lives with the briefest of frowns.

He leans back, knitting his hands together. 'Ah, for the privilege of youth,' he says, with something bordering on a smile. 'I miss that time, of being so very certain wars could be won honourably.' He sits up again, waving a hand dismissively. 'But I cannot un-know what I know.' He leans forward, draws a crystal decanter of port towards him and fills two dainty glasses. 'Heavy is the head that wears the crown.' He pushes a glass towards me.

'Thank you.' I pick it up. 'A little modern for you?' I suggest with a raised eyebrow, nodding to the little vessel.

'My,' says Lord Pole, sounding annoyed. 'Larger vessels are out of fashion.' He drains his port in a single swig.

'Shall we speak now of the mission? We've work for you in France,' he says, dark eyes on mine. I have a sudden image of a whirring clocklike interior behind the predatory expression, an array of possibilities and solutions ready to be clicked into place.

'I am occupied,' I tell him. 'I already told Atherton—'

'Yes, yes, I have heard all about it.' He waves a hand curtly. 'You have made a little sport for yourself in Paris, freeing aristocrats from the hands of the mob.'

'It is slave abolitionists we rescue …'

'Aristocrats make a better story,' says Lord Pole. 'Weeping ladies with pretty hats. Apple-cheeked children in silken breeches.' I can see his mind ticking, laying elaborate plans to waylay French nobles with mobs and rescue them just in time. Lord Pole's favourite currency is gratitude. And the debt that comes with it.

'We protect commoners and aristocrats alike,' I say, gritting my teeth in annoyance. 'On merit not birth.'

'Pity,' he says. 'Still, I imagine you need a reason to stay in Paris. I'm sure you have been enjoying the French lifestyle.' Knowing Lord Pole, he has information as to my every movement, and knows exactly which taverns and salons I favour. 'In any case,' his brows lower even further, 'it is a little business, is it not, these rescues? One or two people. Five at best. All very entertaining. But your life is devoted to ending slavery, Attica. Lord knows, you have told me enough times. And I'm afraid France will not abolish the practice any time soon.'

I press my lips together, working through his possible motives for summoning me.

'If the King signs the Rights of Man—' I say.

'The plantation owners will never allow it,' says Lord Pole. 'However, you might say we would be working for the same cause in this particular case.'

I find this so unlikely I make a snorting sound into my port.

He raises a long-fingered hand. 'Hear me out. I do have some understanding of you, Attica, despite what you may think.'

I give a small nod that he should continue speaking.

'Someone has been found dead outside Versailles,' he says flatly. 'Executed in the manner of the *ancien régime*.'

My stomach tightens. France is infamous for the gruesome torturous deaths it still inflicts on criminals; a legacy of their bloated aristocracy ruling by terror, to keep their toiling peasants from demanding a fairer taxation system.

'We covered it up as best we could,' adds Lord Pole. 'The murder of a British subject in Paris has all kinds of political ramifications. Particularly the manner in which it was carried out.' He winces.

'Who was the victim?' I ask him.

'She was an anti-slaving reformer, come to Paris to sway the National Assembly.'

'She?' My stomach lurches. The idea of a woman being tortured to death is a hideous image.

Lord Pole leans back, considering my expression.

'What have you done?' I demand.

'It's more a case of what she has done,' frowns Lord Pole. 'The lady in question was part of a group of rather silly abolitionists.' He holds up a hand at my furious expression. 'No disrespect to your cause,' he says in a tired voice. 'A woman by the name of Jenny Gunnel.'

I'm silent, recognising the name.

'You knew her?' suggests Lord Pole.

'We never met,' I say. 'But her essays were getting her on the wrong side of the French nobles. We had a plan to extract her if things turned sour.'

'No need for that now,' offers Lord Pole unnecessarily.

'We didn't think she was in immediate danger,' I say quietly, guilt washing through me.

'You were precisely right,' says Lord Pole, an unexpected shade of kindness to his tone. 'Her revolutionary views could have had her imprisoned, no worse. Why anyone would want her dead at this point in time is a mystery. It's possible one of the plantation owners thought she had more influence than she did. Or just maybe she found out something she shouldn't.'

I am interested despite myself, though reluctant to share too much enthusiasm with Lord Pole.

'Tell me more.' I reach across his desk to refill both our glasses with port.

'This was found in the victim's hand.'

Lord Pole's hand slides beneath his desk and smoothly emerges with a lead musket ball rolling in his palm. It is small, the kind commonly used in lightweight continental muskets. I lift it up and look closer.

It bears a letter, scraped into the side. A flourishing 'A'.

'A calling card?' I suggest.

Lord Pole nods. 'Have you heard of a man named Salvatore de Aragon?'

I plunder my memory for French aristocrats who are of interest to the English government.

'He's an arms trader,' I say, recalling the papers, 'with a nasty habit of finding who is making the best guns, stealing them by the thousand, and supplying them to French troops.' I think some more. 'As a younger man, Salvatore joined the King's army explicitly to torture peasants. When there was a suggestion of restricting his behaviour, he began his own gun-smuggling operation, using his military contacts. Supplied a great number of lightweight Dutch muskets to French troops in America, which likely lost us the Battle of Yorktown.' My mind tracks to the last few details. 'If I remember correctly, Salvatore is half Italian, half French, hence the first name.'

'Very good,' says Lord Pole. 'His mother was an Italian opera singer. Educated her son in a near hysteria for his father's great family name – hers being very much in question. You know how people are about birthright.'

Something passes over his face and is gone. I often forget that for all his peerage robes and position, Lord Pole's lineage is not so far from my own. A bastard with only a half claim to nobility.

'The effect was to make Salvatore one of the most grandiose and entitled of his kind,' continues Lord Pole. 'He truly *believes* the French aristocracy is a distinct race. Real blue blood. But even aristocrats can be checked. Last year Salvatore was placed in the Bastille by his family for his own protection, since he was flying very close to annoying Marie Antoinette.'

'Don't tell me he tried to sell her some diamonds?' I say

with a flash of insolence, reminding Pole of the danger he placed me in with one of his recent schemes to implicate the Queen in the smuggling of a politically volatile necklace.

Lord Pole ignores the jibe. 'Salvatore exercises his noble privileges with rather too much relish. One of the nastiest of his breed. Peasant girls, that kind of thing.' He doesn't elaborate and I don't ask. 'Marie Antoinette objects. She is kind in her own way, I suppose. In any case, the irony is that when the Bastille fell, Salvatore walked free. A man who thinks the common upstarts lower than cattle.'

A flash of anger must have showed in my eyes, because Lord Pole nods with unexpected understanding.

'If he is at large in Paris, why am I only hearing of him now?'

Since I have been living in the French capital for the past few months, I have made it my business to be involved in any underground goings-on.

'He left France after his release from prison to rekindle his old business connections. The mystery is that for all his hatred of commoners, Salvatore is not a political man. His family estate includes slave plantations, of course, but he has never been vocal in defence of the practice.'

I nod, turning this information over.

'This killing, there's more to it,' continues Lord Pole. 'Someone is influencing Salvatore, and I want you to find out who. Before any more of our citizens are executed.'

'Have you considered Robespierre's involvement?' I suggest.

Lord Pole sighs. 'Be careful you do not let the French water make you as emotional as the natives, Attica. You have a fascination with this little lawyer that defies logic. Nothing has ever been proven as to Robespierre's criminal activities.

As far as the Sealed Knot is concerned, he is nothing more than a lawyer with revolutionary zeal.'

'Something is happening at the Paris city gates,' I tell him. 'Jemmy and I have been watching Porte Saint-Martin, and duties on imports and exports are being enforced with an iron fist. It's almost impossible for people to get in and out of the city without being searched.'

Lord Pole looks up, mildly interested.

'That is the King, surely? He makes some fruitless attempt to waylay revolutionary books and so forth.'

'I thought so too. But I looked into the men on the gates taking the taxes. Almost all have secret revolutionary affiliations. I'd lay money Robespierre has a heavy body of spies on those gates. It's a prime place to obtain information. And if you control movement in and out of the city ...'

'Any evidence Robespierre himself is behind the tightening of security at the gates?'

'Robespierre is careful,' I say through gritted teeth. 'Inhumanly so. You said so yourself ...'

'I said Le Société des Amis was careful – whoever they are.'

'*La* Société,' I correct him.

Lord Pole throws up his hands in apparent despair at the French system of gendering words.

'Male or female,' he says, 'they are seemingly everywhere, yet slip through our fingers whenever we get close. Even their purpose remains elusive, though we assume it to be political.'

Not knowing everything about the mysterious faction is as close as Lord Pole has ever come to failure. He looks rather ill at the mention of them.

'Certainly, I am undecided as to whether Robespierre is even involved with the Society of Friends,' he says, recovering himself. 'If he is, then it is a lowly role. In any case,' he concludes, 'Salvatore is hardly likely to work for common revolutionaries. He would see them dead before their coarse leather shoes sullied his marble floor.'

I open my mouth then shut it again. He is right.

'So if not Robespierre or the Society, then who?'

'That is what we want you to find out. I'm sure you agree our interests are mutual.'

'That is still to be discovered.' I sip port, letting the complex flavours linger on my tongue as I consider. He looks up at me and there is something in his eyes I have never seen before.

'Would it be too much to believe I value the happiness of my favourite niece?' he asks.

'I am your only niece. And yes, it would. What advantage is there to you if I kill a French arms dealer?'

Lord Pole grins wolfishly. 'Who said I wanted him killed?'

CHAPTER NINE

*I*T IS LATE AS ROBESPIERRE FINISHES THE LAST OF A TIDY pile of legal documents. He is pleased with his work and will allow himself a small indulgence, expending the cost of a full candle wax dedicated to his favourite new pastime. Straightening his immaculate lawyer's suit and locking the door of his little office, he pulls forth a slim box from under a neat stack of papers. A locked chest within a locked chest. He opens it with a small key from his pocket.

Inside is his treasure. Little boxes and trinkets from his past, worn and colourless with age. Right at the bottom, pressed carefully between two pieces of paper, is a lock of blonde hair. Sometimes, just after sunset, if his wine is stronger than usual, he takes it out – the hair so old now it is brittle and dull. The ribbon it is tied with is faded and has lost its smell. Even so, Robespierre will lift it to his nose, inhale, stroke the satin between pale fingers. As a boy he used to sleep with it clutched in his small fist, pushed up against his cheek.

Today he does none of these things. Laid atop his mementoes are an array of little flower tokens. The last was brought to him only yesterday. With each he feels closer to the unravelling, but still far away.

Robespierre lifts out the little card tokens one by one and lays them on his desk. It is a ritual he carries out often. He owns three now, and has put it out that a full franc will be paid to anyone who brings him more. A few people have tried to trick him with badly attempted frauds, but they are easy to see through, Robespierre knows each of his three tokens by heart. Understands they are part of a code he has not yet broken.

Each thick piece is cut in the jagged shape of a flower. A pimpernel. Red paint has been – to his eye, at least – rather artlessly washed across the fronts. He lifts the first, turns it face up. It has been cut from a playing card. A queen of hearts. Next is a jack of the same suit. Sometimes Robespierre finds himself stiff with cold, pained with hunger, having sat until his candle burns out, examining these mysterious tokens. He is certain they are a message from his adversary. A little game they play between the two of them, while the serious business of saving France plays out.

CHAPTER TEN

I STARE AT LORD POLE, WORKING THROUGH WHAT HE IS suggesting.

'If you don't want me to kill Salvatore,' I say eventually, 'what do you want?'

'We need him to stop assassinating bloody republicans and get on with dealing arms,' says Lord Pole smoothly.

This doesn't make immediate sense. 'But that would weaken your position in America,' I say.

'That thing is long done,' says Lord Pole, looking tired. 'We shall not retrieve those territories now. Better we try to salvage a trading relationship. Besides, the French King has lost interest in being America's hero now that he has problems at home. *But,*' Lord Pole fixes his dark eyes on me, 'with all the upheaval *someone* will start a war with France. Prussia, Austria, Spain …' He spreads his hands in a way that says, *I don't care who.*

'You want to be sure the French have enough good guns to put up a decent fight,' I say, catching his drift. 'Weaken another country.'

'*Certainement,*' agrees Lord Pole in perfect French, glancing at the diagrams of trading routes laid out on his desk. 'The

French cannot win it, of course. But they might do a lot of damage with the right weaponry and save us a good deal of work acquiring several lucrative trading routes.'

'If attack comes, France will be in chaos,' I say, thinking aloud. 'The people are already driven to fever pitch.'

'I fail to see how that is a *concern*,' says Lord Pole. 'I hope you are not forgetting you are English, Attica, for all the delights of the French Marais. They eat frogs, you know,' he adds, waving an admonishing finger.

'I work for King and country,' I tell him, insulted at the suggestion I have gone native.

'Then you have a fine opportunity to show your patriotism.'

'And how do you suggest we persuade this Salvatore fellow to stop murdering revolutionaries? Marry me to him? That is your usual solution to problems of this kind, is it not?'

'Very funny, Attica. You will be pleased to know I have given up on bettering your position, since you show such truculence in the face of eligible suitors. You know my thoughts on the subject. If you are so intent on helping abolish slavery, your ambitions would be better served with a suitable husband. It seems you would rather play around with your pirate friend, rescuing one loud-mouth radical at a time and grossly under-achieving your potential. So be it.'

I wonder if he can see from my face that his barb has hit home. My guilt at not doing more for the slave cause burns me. But just for now, helping the French people achieve freedom and ensuring the Rights of Man is signed seems more tangible. A traitorous part of my mind flashes an image of Jemmy. I dismiss it.

Lord Pole reaches to a neat pile of documents and retrieves something from the bottom.

'There is a weapons fayre in Paris this week,' he says, waving an expensively produced card. 'All the latest weaponry by the finest rifle makers in Europe. Mostly selling jewelled pistols to ladies, but there will be an underground trade for the more military minded.'

'There always is.' I nod.

'Salvatore will be in attendance. We found part of a document suggesting he plans to meet his influencer there.'

'You want me to find him, discover who is putting him up to the murders?'

Lord Pole smiles insincerely. 'You see, Attica? We can occasionally be on the same side. Find out who Salvatore is working with. Sever the association.'

He makes a sharp cutting motion with his hand.

'What about Atherton?' I ask.

'What about him?' The question seems to wrong-foot Lord Pole so entirely I wonder what I've missed.

'Weapons, equipment,' I explain patiently. 'Have you anything for me in his absence?'

'Ah!' Lord Pole is himself again. He opens a drawer. 'I have a few things here.'

A silken handkerchief emerges, inscribed with a map of Versailles, and a set of old dice carved from bone. As an afterthought he produces a necklace with an amber stone locket.

I lift the little cubes and smell mercury-nitrate on the six. 'Loaded dice, such as every gambler in Cheapside owns.' I lift the light silk. 'The old map-hidden-on-a-handkerchief trick.'

'Not the very latest innovations,' agrees Lord Pole. 'We're in a pinch without Atherton.'

I open the locket to reveal two white tablets. 'And poison pills? I didn't realise you had so much faith in me.'

'Every spy is required to carry them after that dreadful business in Brazil,' says Lord Pole, and it isn't clear if he means the torture of an English spy or the spilling of state secrets.

'Don't mock those pills,' he adds. 'They're of my own devising and have saved several men from a very nasty death.'

'By killing them.'

'Quickly. Cleanly. Without torture.'

'And without spilling your secrets. Do you have anything else tucked away?' I suggest. 'I have heard rumours of a device called a wheel that sounds very useful.'

'Atherton and his latest tools will be deployed at the earliest opportunity,' says Lord Pole. My heart beats a little faster at the possibility of seeing him. 'He is currently quartered outside Calais, so you may meet him on your way back to France.'

I am desperate to ask what kind of family business would take Atherton to France, but I won't give Lord Pole the satisfaction of refusing to tell me. I see him watching me for a reaction. He gives a small shake of his head when he sees I will not break with my good breeding.

'Atherton tells me there are some fascinating new developments,' adds Lord Pole. 'He has been working on a way to store strong acid, so our agents might carry it on their person without coming to harm. You might remember that fellow on the Irish crossing who blinded himself.' I nod. 'In the meantime, try a little gratitude, Attica. In my day, we spies had a garrotte and our wits.'

'Very good, your Lordship.' I curtsey. 'Outmoded equipment notwithstanding, I dare say it shouldn't be too difficult for us to discover who is leading Salvatore.'

'Us?' Now Lord Pole frowns deeply.

'The pirate,' I explain. 'Jemmy Avery. The weapons fayre is smuggler territory, and he knows contraband. I need him.'

Something flashes across Lord Pole's face.

'Have you asked him to accompany you when you return to Paris?'

'Not yet.'

'You seem very certain he will.'

'Jemmy has a great love of showy pistols,' I say with a shrug. 'And he works for gold.'

'Are you sure it isn't only gold he works for?' enquires Lord Pole. 'Atherton seems to think him quite in love with you.'

I laugh at the idea.

'Atherton thinks every man within fifty foot of me is petitioning for my hand. He has an excessive idea of my bridal value. Outside of your political schemes, I assure you a half-breed bastard is not so prized.' Lord Pole winces. 'Not to mention Jemmy Avery loves only his ship and his crew.'

'Yet he'll desert them so readily?'

'As I say, he works for gold.'

Lord Pole looks ready to say something, then changes his mind and instead taps his knuckles on his desk.

'Very well then,' he says, selecting a sealed document from his drawer and passing it to me. 'Permission from His Majesty to join the flying mail coach to Dover. With a fair wind you might even be back in time for a dish of roasted snails in one of those dingy taverns you favour.'

'I'm not so French yet.' I smile at him. 'But I am learning a great deal about brandy.'

CHAPTER ELEVEN

*I*T IS MORNING WHEN ROBESPIERRE AWAKES, HIS HEAD ON the hard desk, body stiff with cold. His candle is burned right down to its wick from working through the night. The tokens are laid out neatly on his desk, implacable in their inscrutability.

He hears movement from outside; most likely the market women, he thinks. They have taken to gathering by his office to offer him little gifts in gratitude for the speeches he makes.

Robespierre sighs to himself, glancing for one last time at the tokens, willing them to give up their secrets. His ink bottle is almost empty, he notices, and lifts the bell on his desk.

A few moments after the ring, his housekeeper enters.

She curtseys. A look of pain flashes across his face.

'No need for deference, Madame Bouvay,' he reminds her. 'We are equals. Might I have fresh ink? Be sure to smell it for turpentine,' he adds. 'Some of those merchants are still selling thick summer-ink that clogs.'

She only narrowly prevents herself from curtseying again.

'A little breakfast?' she suggests. 'You haven't eaten since yesterday morning.'

'I will take a little fruit later on. Is there any news from the pamphleteers?'

'Nothing from France. Only something from Lisbon. A dockyard set afire last week.'

Robespierre tilts his head, only half interested. 'Why?'

'No one knows. These merchants sabotage one another all the time.'

'They are docks which launch slave ships, are they not?'

'I couldn't say, monsieur.'

Robespierre almost dismisses the thing, then decides against it. Better to have every small pieces of information, no matter how inconsequential it might seem. He makes a note to undertake further enquiries.

Madame Bouvay makes to leave, this time forgetting not to curtsey and then apologising. Her petitions to have him eat a breakfast roll have fallen on deaf ears.

As she heads for the door, she runs squarely into Georges Danton, who has appeared unannounced in the doorway. Danton is a great wall of a man, already earning fame for his bravery and great booming orations on the revolutionary cause. His outsized head, scarred and pockmarked, is stupendously ugly and incongruous atop his lawyer's suit of smart black velvet and white linen with only the occasional grease stain. It is generally agreed Danton is the man you would want at your side in a battle. He enters with his usual heavy-footed charisma and an ever-present miasma of last night's wine.

Robespierre glares through his small round glasses as Danton pats the housekeeper on the bottom with a lascivious grin as she passes.

'Don't look at me like that, Max,' Danton says, addressing Robespierre, as Madame Bouvay makes a hasty retreat. 'She

51

loves a little male attention. They all do.' He stamps his feet against the autumn chill, dropping a spray of city mud on to the immaculate floor.

'God's teeth, Max, mightn't you even have a small fire? It's cold.'

Robespierre begins tidying his hobby aside. 'November the first,' he says, 'the fire is lit.'

'Did you know there's a gaggle of market women outside your office?' Danton asks.

'They like my speeches,' explains Robespierre. 'No one takes the trouble to speak with women. Yet they will form one half of our new virtuous society. Equals.'

'Whatever you say. Perhaps you'll even marry one day.'

'Perhaps.'

Danton shakes his head, then approaches the desk before Robespierre can sweep his current occupation away.

'Hoping to divine the true identity of the Scarlet Pimpernel, eh?'

'Decode. God is an illusion perpetuated by the clergy, so they might rob hard-working peasants of one tenth of their income.'

'Yes, yes.' Danton waves a meaty hand. 'I am no Catholic, as you well know. No need to lecture me.' He peers closer. 'You might as well read tea leaves. They are nothing but calling cards, Max. A little flair, that's all. Our traitorous Englishman is flamboyant.'

Robespierre lifts the little tokens and lets them drift through his fingers. 'There is something here. Something to be unpicked that will determine the identity of this fellow.'

'Still nursing a grudge against this Pimpernel?' observes Danton easily, saying the name in heavily accented French.

'You always did love a war of intellect. But can you be so certain the Englishman is a problem? After all, he rescues men of our own cause.'

'He is *the* problem.' Robespierre turns on Danton, his eyes flashing. 'These poor peasants believe in a God who sits on a golden throne. This Pimpernel perpetuates that. A hero who is noble. It is the very definition of the system we must smash.'

Robespierre's mouth has pressed very thin.

'Very well,' says Danton. 'You explain it decently enough.' He waves a thick hand. 'I don't think you will ever find him, mind. He is too clever.'

Robespierre looks up in annoyance. 'Why did you come?' he says shortly.

Danton adjusts his waistcoat again. 'Ah, yes, let us get to the heart of the matter. There is a girl. A sister of one of the lawyers. It has been suggested she would make you a good wife.'

Robespierre shakes his head. 'I have no time for such distractions.'

'A man must have some distractions,' opines Danton, his rumbling voice growing loud. 'It's not good for you, Max, walled up in here, staring at words, barely eating. You must have some diversion.' He leans in closer. 'Perhaps the sister was a bad idea. So go to a bathhouse, Max; it is no business of mine. God's blood, even I've staggered into the Turkish quarter after a good night's drinking. Only get some release, I beg you. Before it starts coming out of your nose.'

'The ancients believed a man's potency should be shored up, held in reserve,' says Robespierre.

'Not that again. You'll make yourself unwell.' Danton adjusts his waistcoat. 'Do not look so angry. It is the duty of a friend to tell you these things, hmm? Better that than surround

53

yourself with those who tell you what you want to hear.'

Danton stands with a casual shrug. The die is cast and it is not his business to intervene with the fates. 'Let me know if you change your mind about the sister. It could be good for you. Your career. Make you look normal. Trustworthy. Things are about to change, by the way. Reports of movement in Versailles.'

Robespierre sits a little straighter. 'The King has agreed to sign it?'

Danton shakes his head, his gaze roaming Robespierre's desk until it lights upon a decanter of thin-looking wine. Sighing, he lifts it to the light, then swigs directly from the opening, wincing at the piquancy of the contents.

'Louis cannot decide, as usual,' says Danton. 'His Bastille is a pile of rubble. The people have shown their discontent, yet continue to starve under his rule. They must have something. Louis teeters on the brink of decency. Then his ministers and so forth change his mind again. But he has agreed us politicians and lawyers can represent the people with our National Assembly at Versailles.'

'A debate,' says Robespierre wearily.

Danton nods. 'Infuriating, *n'est-ce pas?*'

CHAPTER TWELVE

$\mathcal{I}$ DOCK IN CALAIS TO FIND A WAITING COACH. ALWAYS, WITH Lord Pole, transports arrangement run like clockwork, and in under an hour the horses arrive at the scheduled meeting point. Atherton has been given the run of some kind of warehouse just outside the port. I don't have exact details, but the smell of caramelised sugar began half a mile from our destination. From the carriage window I see the tall chimney pumping sweet fumes into the air. It's part of a larger warehouse building standing alone in the countryside, with a wide, well-kept road allowing good access for deliveries. I note several wagons of sugarcane have arrived from the docks.

'A sugar refinery?' I eye the soldiers but they don't reply. I can't make sense of it, since sugarcane is always processed on the plantations to reduce shipping volumes.

As we arrive, I see an enormous wagon of turnip-like tubers being unloaded into a chute at the side of the warehouse.

It takes a moment for the deduction to unravel, and then my lips curve into a smile.

The knobbly vegetables must be sugar beet. One of my Russian operations gathered intelligence on the secret science of extracting syrup from beetroots, with a view to stealing the process and creating a rival sugar production to France's slave-traded industry.

Atherton must be testing the viability of sugar refining by alternative means.

Inside the broad stable-like doors is a hive of industry. Churning wooden wheels squelch at wet vegetable matter, sending steady torrents of yellow-hued juice into a metal vat. Towards the back of the warehouse interior, metal pots bubble over open fires, each rising to chest height. Men stir the lilac-coloured molten sugar with long paddles.

As I watch, a signal is given, and two workers take hold of a hot pot with grunting effort and begin pouring the smoking content into conical moulds, ready for whitening. On the plantations, as I remember, they call the dregs of brown sugar 'bastards'. An unfavourable comparison was once made between myself and such leavings at one of my father's society parties. I remember it, because my father, in a rare hiatus from laudanum, threw the guest out.

Breaking away from my soldier escorts, I take in my surroundings, narrowing my eyes in thought. Atherton will favour ready access to heat, I decide, my eyes falling on the large oven at the back. Also water, and some kind of mechanisation. Confident, I stride towards the back of the refinery, and smile to see a small blue wax seal on one of the doors. Atherton always did love to leave clues.

I open the door, and when I see him I can't keep the smile from my face. Atherton has his back to me, hunched over an open barrel with an attitude of intense concentration. Though I cannot see his face, I can picture it absolutely, taut in concentration. Atherton shares the same haughty features as almost every other member of his family – the long aristocratic nose, refined cheekbones and light green eyes. But his impish nature and incongruously broad mouth subvert him into something different entirely. As usual, he wears his dark blue naval coat with gold trim, though he has long ago dispensed with the wig, tricorn hat and snowy britches, in favour of more muted fashion.

Atherton straightens suddenly, and as he does so the contents of the barrel explode upwards in a torrent of yellowish water.

'Any advances in the underwater explosives?' I ask, wincing at the smell. A rotten reek of sulphur is issuing from the displaced water. Atherton turns, seeming unsurprised to find me there.

'Attica!' He gives me his familiar beaming smile. I pause, taking him in. It's never certain what state Atherton's mysterious illness will have left him in. Some days you mightn't even know he was plagued with it. Others he can barely walk and his face makes peculiar expressions.

'As you can see, my legs have been kind enough to serve me today,' he says, not missing a thing. 'Though I'm afraid I stink,' he adds mildly, as I come to embrace him.

'I don't mind.' I fold my arms around his narrow body, which seems even more frail than the last time I saw him. His sticks are resting against the wall, suggesting his legs aren't working as well as he'd like me to believe. There's another change, too: a slight twitch at his mouth, which was not there before. I find myself wondering if his wife notices such things, suspect she does not, then chide myself on the thought.

'Bloody hell,' I add, withdrawing slightly with a laugh. 'You really do smell.'

He smiles absently, wiping sulphur from his cheek. Atherton doesn't seem himself, not quite meeting my eye. I have a dread he is about to share news of his burgeoning family, so I launch into spy matters.

'Setting you to work in a secret sugar refinery was a clever choice,' I say, though truthfully sugar and cotton processing always reminds me of slaves. Since he doesn't answer, I plough on. 'You always had a genius for manufacture. Not to mention plenty of heat and power from the mill. Access to all kinds of supplies from Calais, for your other endeavours.'

'If we develop a way to process home-grown beets on a large scale, we could gain a considerable economic advantage,' he agrees. 'Half of Europe runs on sugar profits.'

He shifts about uncomfortably.

'Lord Pole didn't tell you the other reason I am here?' he asks.

I swallow, shaking my head.

'Oh.' Atherton scratches awkwardly behind his ear, causing a portion of his shaggy hair to stand on end. I resist the urge to smooth it down.

To my surprise, Atherton plunges his hands into his coat pocket and wheels away from me. He turns back, face twisted in an agony of indecision.

'Lord Pole really told you nothing about my reason for temporarily leaving England?' Atherton confirms. He looks into my face now, scrutinising.

'He said it was something to do with family business.' My heart has started a low rhythmic pounding. I absolutely do not want to hear it from Atherton. Anyone, in fact, but him. I try for a laugh but it comes out wrong. 'Your family is your own concern, Atherton.'

Now he smiles a little. I take a breath. There is no avoiding it, I suppose. It is time to accept that any fool notions of some future happening between us are about to be irrevocably rent asunder. Atherton will explain that his silly wife, whom he barely sees, has done her duty by him, or he by her. The worst would be a son, I find myself thinking, and then hating myself for it. Atherton, being the man he is, would devote a lot of time to his son.

Don't say it, I urge Atherton with my mind. *Let me hear it from someone else.*

He clears his throat and begins speaking about his wife. Explaining how she is a good person, despite what is said about her. That it is true, in part, she married him for his title, but she had always intended to be a good wife in her way.

There's a kind of white buzzing in my head. Images of the time Atherton spent with me when I was a difficult girl, stuck between the clever world of men and the unappealing expectations of young ladies. If it wasn't for Atherton's belief in my potential, I should never have solved codes, or trained with a knife, or learned Russian. Any of it at all. He was my mentor and my best friend all in one. There's a lump in my throat. A mingle of self-disgust and self-pity.

'Did you hear what I said?' asks Atherton, his green eyes earnest. I shake my head.

'It is a foregone conclusion,' says Atherton patiently, in a way that suggests he is repeating himself. 'Things are now being finalised.' He takes a breath. 'Attica, soon I will no longer be a married man.'

CHAPTER THIRTEEN

ATHERTON'S REVELATION HANGS IN THE AIR, THICKER than the sugar syrup smell wafting from the refinery.

'My wife has eloped,' continues Atherton. 'Under the circumstances I have no choice but to break the marriage.' He twists a finger in his palm in a boyish gesture and manages a little smile.

'If you want the whole sordid story, she ran away to Spain with a sailor,' he adds. 'Of course, I should be mortified.' His eyes glide up to mine, solemn. 'But somehow, I can't seem to muster much more than relief.' The ghost of a smile plays on his lips again. 'I only hope she is happy. It always was a bad arrangement for both of us. I wasn't a good husband. I should never have agreed to a convenience match. Married in haste, as they say. Only,' he moves his fingers to drum on his lips, 'I had wanted to ask someone else, you see.' He fixes me with his light eyes.

My mouth is dry. On Atherton's wedding day he admitted, in a drunken moment, he had wanted to ask my father's permission for my hand. But had thought I would refuse, since I was always so outspoken on similarities between being a slave and being a wife.

60

'Perhaps I was heartbroken,' concludes Atherton, not taking his gaze off me.

I feel my chest constrict. In all this time, Atherton and I have loosely concealed our feelings for one another. We exchange glances, embrace for slightly longer than is friendly, but neither of us would ever violate marriage vows. So to hear him say this aloud is overwhelming.

'We could be married,' he says quietly. 'You and I. If you wished it.'

An unexpected nausea grips me. I have longed for this moment, but never truly imagined it would arrive. The bloom of feelings in my chest is so intense I can hardly bear it.

'I need to sit down,' I tell him. My eyes fall on an upturned barrel and I lower myself on to it, fighting the urge to sink my head to my lap and shut out the whole confusing business.

'You are unwell?' Atherton is at my side, down on one knee, so he might look into my face without putting all his weight on his crippled legs. For a moment I think he means to propose, and the world is falling away all around me.

He must see my reaction to the stance because he tucks the second knee under, with a tight expression of pain.

'No ... I ...' I'm trying to fight back my sudden panic, which is puzzling, even to me. The knowledge I'm pouring cold water on his overtures is paralysing. I try for a smile, but can feel it isn't convincing.

'I am only a little overwhelmed,' I manage. 'It wasn't ... I thought you were going to tell me your wife was with child.'

To my complete mortification there are tears now. As if my emotions are taking free rein of my sanity. I take a long heaving breath and manage to stop my shoulders shaking.

Atherton looks up at me, his concern only slightly abated.

'I am sorry, Attica,' he says, frowning. 'I was too hasty. Too sudden. Of course a woman must be wooed …'

I raise a hand to silence him, keeping the other tight on my pounding stomach. The worst of it is I simply cannot make sense of my reaction. My body is completely betraying me, ruining what should be a longed-for moment.

'There is no need,' I tell him. 'We have known one another a long time. It was only … I was taken by surprise.'

Atherton, who knows I am regularly accosted by armed attackers leaping from shadows, looks unconvinced.

'Lord Pole approves of the match,' he says, perhaps assuming I fear my uncle's good opinion. 'More than approves, in actual fact. He believes it to be useful timing. For the Sealed Knot, that is.'

I remember Lord Pole's strange silence on the subject of Atherton's absence and deduce that, in his own strange way, my uncle was leaving an opening for romance. For Atherton to propose naturally. The shock of this unexpected emotion in my uncle adds an additionally surreal sensation to events.

'What would be the advantage to Lord Pole?' I cannot quite bring myself to say 'our marriage'.

'There's a slave ring operating off the west coast of Africa,' says Atherton. 'They're causing considerable disruption to the trading routes down there. The Sealed Knot need someone who speaks Swahili to infiltrate it. And since you spoke the language during your time as a slave …' He lets the sentiment complete itself without words.

I'm stunned into silence. My whole adult life I've been waiting for a mission of this kind. It is perfect in every way, so why do I feel so afraid?

'Lord Pole believes a trader and his wife would be the ideal cover,' concludes Atherton, rising to his feet, and I notice he uses neutral language, nothing to imply we personally will be the couple. 'I … I understand, Attica,' he says sadly. 'You were raised in captivity and regard marriage as slavery. I only hoped; I never assumed. And you have a life in Paris. We will forget I ever spoke of it.'

He looks down at his desk and begins fiddling with a portable device for sharpening knives.

I shake my head fiercely. 'I was much younger when you wed. A headstrong girl.' I look at him, feeling more myself again. 'I don't know if I would have refused,' I say, relieved to find my voice is back to normal. 'Perhaps I would have. It would have been foolish of me. I know that now.' I try for a smile.

I can't quite find the words to tell Atherton how ever since his marriage, I have kept every letter he sent. That when he sends me out with the latest equipment for spy work, I feel I am carrying him with me, like an amulet.

Atherton's frown lifts. 'Then you give me hope,' he says. 'I shall not demand an answer now.'

I find I can only nod. Relief floods through me, but it is tinged with a terrible feeling. I have been a coward and allowed a chance for happiness to steal away.

He is retreating, giving me room to think, and I find myself appreciating his cool consideration, whilst wanting to shake him for it at the same time. My hands grip into fists, willing myself to pull the situation back.

'Atherton?' He must hear something in my tone, because his expression changes. 'I don't need to think about the proposal.' I swallow hard. 'My answer is yes. I shall pack up my Paris apartment.' I pause. 'I …'

The delight on his face is such that had I not already begun speaking my next words, I should have stopped.

'I only ask one thing,' I finish.

'Anything.' He beams, striding nearer and picking up my hands in his.

'I … I have unfinished business in Paris.'

'You want to go back to Paris with the pirate?' The smile has fallen from his face. He looks devastated. I realise between us we have somehow sucked any sentiment out of the whole proposal. I don't know how to get it back, and am wrong-footed and confused at his rather strange focus on Jemmy.

'A woman is dead,' I say. 'An abolitionist. I think her death was part of a political plot. The King is about to sign the Rights of Man.'

'You are English, Attica. This is a French concern.'

'It has implications for the colonies. If the King of France declares all men are equal, then slavery must be abolished on principle.'

Atherton is shaking his head. 'It is never as simple as that. The French economy runs on slave-made goods.'

'There is a wider mission. Lord Pole's. The victim was murdered by a known arms trader. Pole wants me to discover the reasons for him being politicised, so he might get back to arming the French for a war.'

Atherton nods. 'Well, that is a worthy pursuit,' he agrees. 'Let them all kill each other. On the other side of the Channel. Better than risking our good men.'

I have the painful sensation that if I told him the full truth – how I've grown to care about justice in France – he wouldn't understand.

Atherton walks to the far side of the room to retrieve his

sticks. A moment between us has gone and, even as it evaporates, I curse the loss of it. I could have told him everything. The thing would have been done. Why couldn't I say it?

Because Jemmy would think you a traitor to the crew, whispers a voice.

'I've been working on a few items for you,' says Atherton.

The cogs have turned. We're fully back inside the boundaries of our business relationship. In the jangle of emotions still twanging in my chest, I slide back into the safety of it with equal parts regret and relief.

He approaches a large plain table with jerky movements of his legs, then places both hands on it to steady himself. 'Come and see,' he says. 'We've made some excellent advances.'

I eye the table.

Atherton lifts a round cast-iron ball.

'A grenade?' I'm frowning. It looks like the kind that has been more or less removed from military kit, due to their general uselessness.

'Five times the power!' says Atherton proudly. 'Twenty times if you drop it in water. No need for a direct hit. Even a bad bowler like you could use it.' He winks.

Atherton taught me cricket when I was fifteen – back when I thought the age gap meant he was an old man. At that time he had a devastating throwing arm. I never did improve at the game. I couldn't see the point, when I could knock the wickets over with my slingshot.

'Isn't that incredibly dangerous?' I suggest to Atherton. 'How could you be far enough away not to be included in the blast?'

Atherton's smile widens. He taps the top of the grenade, which has a strangely long neck.

'It's a new kind of ignition,' he says. 'It doesn't rely on a lit fuse. More like a tinderbox, with an internal percussion striking a flint. Works like a relay system in here.' His long finger prods at the rounded belly of the weapon. 'The spark lights a slow wax-coated fuse.'

'You could use a lot more wax to slow it,' I say, understanding, 'since it is all contained.'

Atherton nods.

'How long until it explodes?' I ask.

'Around ten seconds. I'm looking at shorter fuses for use in battle,' he adds, sensing my objection. 'The wax is a problem there.'

I take it from him. 'If it isn't a lit fuse,' I say, tilting my head to examine it, 'how does it ignite?'

'You twist the top,' says Atherton. 'Three full turns clockwise will release a spring.' He holds it out to me. 'Otherwise it's quite stable.'

'You're certain?' I take it and toss it in the air, enjoying Atherton's pained expression as I catch it just in time. 'I learned cricket from the best,' I tell him with a smirk. 'Have you anything else for me?'

'Well, I've improved the acid formula.' He hands me a glass bottle. 'Refill your hidden vials with this version. It's safer to transport and will dissolve up to an inch of metal per dram.'

I take the bottle and remove the two slim vials I keep hidden in my corsetry. While I'm refilling them, Atherton busies himself across the room.

I move closer, wondering what weaponry he has developed.

He fumbles in a box for a moment, then lifts out a small sharpened piece of wood.

'A stick?' I can't keep the disappointment from my voice.

He selects a piece of paper, and writes my name smoothly.

I lean across the page, amazed.

'It will write up to ten pages, without wearing down,' he says proudly, 'no ink needed.'

'That is incredible.' I lift the little writing tool, turning it wonderingly.

'It's the same principle as a carpenter's pencil,' says Atherton. 'But we've reduced the graphite core to a tenth of an inch by baking it with clay. Partly your idea,' he adds. 'I've been using a kiln for all kinds of things since your suggestion we bake porcelain with coded messages.'

'It's wonderful,' I say, closing my hand around it.

'Don't stab anyone with it,' adds Atherton. 'It's the only one I have and was expensive.'

I slide it into my hanging purse.

'Thank you.' I realise I'm toying with the opening far longer than is necessary.

'You must go to Paris,' says Atherton suddenly. 'Things are due another turn in France. It's on a knife-edge since the Bastille fell.'

I nod.

'Then you should go now.' He manages a smile.

Feeling more distant from Atherton than I have ever felt, I force myself to walk towards him, put my hands on his shoulders. When I kiss him, just to the side of his mouth, it feels contrived. He stands completely still, as though any movement might dispel the gesture. I can feel his breath, coming fast on the side of my cheek.

'You'll be back?' Atherton asks quietly, as I draw back.

'I always am.'

67

He unpins something from his coat. His royal cockade – black ribbons to symbolise his fealty to our Hanoverian king.

'This is for you,' he says, fixing it gently to the top of my dress.

'What does it do?'

'It will remind you of your Englishman, waiting at home for you.'

'Oh.' I touch it, abashed. 'I will be back in four days,' I say, speaking hurriedly in my embarrassment at confusing his romantic gesture.

He beams. 'This Monday, then. I'll ask your father to ready your family chapel. Unless you think it too soon.'

I try for a smile again, fingering the cockade. 'No. Not at all. I should rather keep it a simple affair, and my relatives will make it grand if we give them any notice.'

Everything is coming out wrong. I kiss him awkwardly on the cheek, then turn to leave.

It's only then I notice one of his papers has drifted to the floor. On it are the words 'marry me', written in the grey of his new pencil invention. I force my feet to carry me out, pretending I haven't seen it.

I walk out of the sugar refinery with thoughts awhirl in my brain. I have just been offered everything I've ever wanted. So why do I feel so unhappy?

CHAPTER FOURTEEN

THE SUN IS RISING ON A NEW DAY IN PARIS, AS OVETTE Campan arrives at Faubourg Saint-Antoine, with her basket of wares. Every morning she wakes before dawn and picks over what is left of the Bastille, looking for saleable pieces.

Now she arrives at the market, passing thick-armed fishwives who have owned their pitches for generations sitting cross-legged before hampers of shellfish. Less fortunate sellers with fish on the turn stalk the market with baskets on their hips, avoiding donkeys laden with fruit who nudge their way through the scant crowd.

Ovette makes her way to the peripheries, dirt tracks etched with guts and peel, where the lowliest sellers convene. Here, women have set out their aprons on the ground, rubble and stone laid atop the linen. A more enterprising woman has repurposed ironwork from prison fetters as fire pokers.

'These from the cell of the Marquis de Sade!' she bellows, holding them up to passers-by. 'These with blood stains!'

None of them look at Ovette as she arrives. She is a middle-aged woman, but life has beaten her old. Her dark hair is shot with a thick streak of grey at the temples and her face is gaunt and weathered. There is a large, livid birthmark splashed across one side of her face that has earned her the nickname '*La Deux Visages*' from the other traders.

Ovette stops to see her usual pitch is occupied and today she is too resigned to fight for it. She shifts her load to the other hip, causing dust to cascade through the wicker.

'What do you want, Monsieur Robespierre?' she asks wearily. He has been here before, and wholly disconcerted her by bowing. No one had ever bowed to her before. Not even at her ill-fated wedding to a quick-fisted fisherman, which her own relations refused to attend.

He peers in her basket.

'You have been hard at work,' he says. 'I am in awe of the ingenuity of the people.' He sweeps his hands in the direction of the vanquished prison. 'Nothing there now but a dark hole. Yet it really happened. The Parisians pulled it down only a few months ago. Here is a memory.' He reaches across, lifts a stone, and gazes at it thoughtfully before dropping it back.

She is already shaking her head. 'I cannot join your cause,' says Ovette. 'The other traders hate me. They call me Two-Faces.' She glances at the nearby sellers. 'I am not like them, raised in the marketplace. They think I am hoity-toity because I can read.'

She does not mention the other unkind tricks played on her by the low-bred market women. The dumping of stinking rubbish on her pitch. The pissing in the gutter that runs past her baskets.

A scant smile plays on Robespierre's mouth.

'They are simple women,' he says, 'bred to distrust what they do not understand. It keeps them alive, so we cannot be scornful.'

70

She shakes her head again. 'Leave me in peace, monsieur,' she whispers. 'I gave all I had. I tried to speak above the throng, and it gained me nothing.'

'You did not hire a good lawyer.'

'I spent every last sous …' begins Ovette. Robespierre holds up a hand.

'I understand your outlay was significant. I only say it was not enough to earn your son the representation he needed to walk free. For that, I am afraid you need bribes. Large ones. And someone with good enough connections to deploy them.'

'You have such connections, then?' says Ovette sadly, trying not to wish for what might have been.

'No.' Robespierre adjusts his neckerchief. 'Furthermore, I operate only within the law and could not have saved your son,' he says bluntly. 'But I was able to argue successfully against the definition of his crime, after the sentence was carried out.'

He holds up papers. She takes them, reads them slowly, her lips moving.

'They will bury him on church grounds?' Her eyes brim with tears.

Robespierre nods and holds out a hand to fend off her embrace. 'I am not of your belief, madame. It is my understanding that religion is nothing but a trick to keep poor people labouring away, giving their money to priests and kings.'

'Then why did you represent my plight?' she asks, thoroughly confused.

'It was a miscarriage of justice,' he says, frowning as though it is all wholly obvious.

She clutches the papers tight to her chest and sobs. Robespierre waits patiently, as a man might glance at the sky, waiting for rain to ease off.

'Change is possible,' he tells her. 'But not in such a small way. We must change the system. Someone in amongst the women who can read, who can lead a charge, change might come from such a person.'

'That is not me.'

'I saw you speak in court, madame. You have fire.'

'I spoke for the life of my son.'

'Madame Campan,' says Robespierre, 'your son is gone. I am not a man for gentle words, to tell you he is in heaven, for I do not believe it. We cannot change what has been. *C'est la vie.* But you can save other sons for other mothers. Will you turn this tragedy to some good, madame? Or will you let it defeat you, and starve here in the market, working until your body gives out, paying court costs you do not rightfully owe?'

Ovette's eyes drift to the huddle of women who get together every week to discuss legal revolutionary things.

She closes her eyes. 'And if I do not do what you ask?'

'I ask nothing,' says Robespierre, looking offended. 'My services are free.' He turns to leave with another tight bow.

'*Adieu,* madame,' he says. '*Vive la Révolution!*'

She watches him stride away to the meeting of the market women.

Why should I care? My son is dead.

Beneath everything – the daily grind of selling Bastille rubble to pay her court fees – this knowledge always bubbles. Ovette tries to skirt above it, to stop from sinking. Some days the effort makes it difficult to keep her eyes open.

'Monsieur Robespierre!' Her voice slices through the marketplace, above the din of hawkers. 'Wait!' She hitches up her basket. 'I will come with you.'

He slows and turns, looking unsurprised.

'If you are to join the cause, I suggest you put aside your pride, madame,' he comments. 'Tell them the truth. Your son was hanged. The tragedy of it all left you destitute. You are all equals.'

A flush slowly rises on her cheeks, blooming beneath the large birthmark.

'What can I do?' she asks.

'Read,' says Robespierre. 'Pamphlets, speeches, instructions.'

'Instructions?'

'The women have been talking for weeks about a protest, a march on City Hall. They only lack a little direction.'

CHAPTER FIFTEEN

*W*HENEVER I HAVE RETURNED TO PARIS IN RECENT MONTHS, my first port of call is Jemmy's ship, docked just upriver of the city. I like to greet the crew, with whom I have grown close, and plot with Jemmy over too much brandy as to our next grand rescue. It is the favourite part of my return. So I cannot quite explain why I walk instead to the Marais, not even to my favourite tavern, but to another infamous and low-brow affair, filled with sailors and dancing girls, opposite a bathhouse open only to men. It's one of the reasons I love Paris. The authorities turn a blind eye. Not like London.

The landlady sits on a hard chair, smoking a pipe, calling for barrels of this and that from the cellar. She fixes me with a hard stare as I shout over the din for brandy.

'You are lost?' she accuses, taking in my silk dress. 'This is no place for ladies.' I smile a little in reply. Something in my expression must assure her I can take care of myself in her den of thieving and worse, because she nods and cups both hands to call my order. A boy emerges seconds later with a small barrel.

'Brandy for the lady,' says the landlady.

'I am no lady,' I assure her, as the boy fills my held-out tankard. She seems reassured by this. I pass her coins, throw back the brandy and hold out the tankard for more. Her grim expression lifts at the sight of the money. 'Fill it to the brim,' she urges the boy. 'Don't skimp her.'

I take several deep sips, noting how the tumult in my head recedes.

'Heartbroken?' demands the landlady, eyeing my faraway expression.

I shake my head and my field of vision doesn't quite follow the motion. The brandy is strong and already taking effect. 'The love of my life has just proposed.'

She nods slowly at this. 'Wedding jitters, then. I had the same as a girl. The wedding night is all over in an instant for most; put it out of your mind.' Her head tilts. 'You look old to be first married,' she remarks.

'My family …' I say, letting my gaze sweep the room. 'Arrangements can become complicated.'

'Ah.' Her face doesn't match her words, though. She seems confused by it all. 'Well, you have your darling now,' she decides. I raise my tankard in silent toast, and notice, in an abstract way, some liquor sloshes free. I realise I usually drink brandy with Jemmy and this makes unexpectedly lonely.

'He is a French man?' asks the woman.

'He is from Irish family, born in America,' I say. Then I realise she is referring to Atherton. 'English,' I say. 'The man I will marry is English.'

She is silent for a moment, observing me carefully, taking in my tawny skin and dark hair more fully.

'I believe I've heard of you,' she says finally. 'Attica, is it not? You were a slave once. The tavern near the river, the woman there speaks of you,' she adds by way of explanation. 'She likes you. Thinks you are one of us, despite your bad dress sense.' She nods to my unfashionable clothes. 'An English girl with a French heart, that is what she says. Courageous and fierce, but you drink too much to be happy.'

'Surely a good deal of drink is just the right amount?'

She ignores this. 'You shall have to decide which side you are on when the revolution comes,' she opines. 'The English are with the cold-blooded nobles. They do not like us oddities of the Marais.'

It's the first time someone has said this aloud, although of course I knew it.

'Perhaps you shall marry this man and become one of them. But you must know where you fit,' the woman adds philosophically. 'Their world or ours.'

CHAPTER SIXTEEN

*I*N FAUBOURG SAINT-ANTOINE, THE WOMEN OF THE MARKET Hall are meeting to discuss bread prices. Without official premises, their meeting consists of a somewhat disorderly huddle. The poorly clad ladies form a circle, shoulder to shoulder, in the only venue they are entitled to: the cobbled bit by the broken fountain that smells of piss.

As usual, the main discussion is about the hated Marie Antoinette and her latest excesses.

'Madame Veto, isn't it?' sneers a fish-seller. 'That's what she is now. She was Madame Deficit. Now she's Madame Veto.'

'What's a veto, then?'

''S, like a tax, isn't it? The royals want a new tax for our National Assembly.'

'Poxed if they're getting one!'

They're interrupted by a high-pitched cough.

Smiling politely, Robespierre taps on the nearest shoulder. A gaunt woman turns on him accusingly.

''S a meeting,' she tells him aggressively. 'For the market ladies. No men. Get out of it.'

'It's all right, Eugenie,' says another. 'It's the lawyer. He's one of us, isn't that right, Monsieur Robespierre?'

Robespierre inches between the women, coming up several inches shorter than several of them. He gives the same polite smile and resists the urge to bring his scented handkerchief to his nose as he is welcomed into their fetid midst.

The women greet him warmly now. Those that know him like him. Monsieur Robespierre is gaining a name for himself speaking for the woman. He even believes they should have a vote. Those who do not know him cannot fail to be reassured by his pin-neat appearance and diminutive stature. He is like a smart little toy, their very own bijou member of the establishment. Not to mention he looks a little bit ill. That pale face and thin legs. He is in need of a good bowl of soup. The exact opposite of the brutish men they are used to encountering in their daily lives.

Then they see the woman behind him.

'Whatcha brought Two-Face for?' demands one aggressively, eyeballing Ovette's stained complexion. 'She'll run tattle to the nearest guard.'

'Madame Campan is a convert to the cause,' says Robespierre. 'She will be able to read you the pamphlets and so forth.'

Murmurs of discontent rumble around the women. They do not like the well-spoken Ovette in her too-clean clothes, who so clearly thinks she is better than them all.

'S'pose we could do with a reader,' grumbles one, with bad grace.

Ovette shuffles uncomfortably and looks at her feet.

Robespierre begins speaking, weaving tales of Bastille souvenirs winging their way across France, taking a message of freedom. The power of the people to enact such great change.

As his words fly, any illusions of his frailty fall away. It is agreed by all that he is a veritable sorcerer with words. The women listen entranced as he describes his perfect society. Where everyone is equal and hard-working men and woman are treated with respect, not scorn. At this last part a great cheer is raised.

Now he has the women in the palm of his hand, Robespierre lowers his voice, like a fireside storyteller.

'There is a legend, told by the ancient Greeks, whose societies were built on perfect virtue, of a man named Sisyphus, who was condemned to a punishment in hell.'

He waits a moment to let this sink in. The women's brows wrinkle in confusion.

'Sisyphus was made to push a heavy boulder up a hill, but the moment he was about to reach the summit, with its tantalising promise of freedom, the boulder would roll back down again.' Robespierre pauses for effect. 'It is the same for us, is it not? The Bastille was stormed, the people declared their right to liberty. The King himself agreed to sign the new constitution. Then, just on the dawn of change, *pfsst.*' He makes a noise through his teeth. 'Gone.'

Robespierre's eyes close. He looks suddenly boyish. 'We are so close … so *close.*' His eyes open, fiery behind his round glasses, his tiny hand is balled into a fist, outstretched as though to grasp something. 'Just one small push is needed and we will meet the brow of the hill. The thing will tumble into a new dawn, running on its own momentum.'

There is a long silence. The women's expressions are rapt, thoughtful.

Just one small push.

Speech concluded, Robespierre makes to leave. But the women are not finished with him. They press him with gifts

– humble things but the best they have. Apples and leeks are pushed into his white fingers. He accepts them with gratitude.

'Make it happen for us, Monsieur Robespierre,' begs a woman with missing front teeth. 'If you go to Versailles they will listen to you. Tell them our children starve.'

Robespierre bows, a faint smile on his lips.

'I will endeavour to make your woes heard,' he tells them, before glancing meaningfully at Ovette. 'But I fear the King will only listen to an army.'

CHAPTER SEVENTEEN

I AWAKE TO A THUMPING HEAD AND AN EVEN LOUDER pounding at the door. Wincing against the commotion, I get to my feet, kicking over empty wine bottles. A scuff of rouge on the adjacent pillow to mine suggests I wasn't alone last night. Whoever it was vacated early. Thoughts solidify in my head. A tavern in the Marais. Women dancing together. A dark-haired singer. I must have got there by way of the sailors' den, and have a vague memory of the landlady insisting on finding me a sedan chair to pass through the more dangerous alleys.

I press a hand to my forehead and traipse from my bedchamber, grabbing a satin chemise from a chair and pulling it over my head. I fumble around in an open trunk, retrieving a wide lace sash and wrapping it around my waist as I cross into the single large reception room of my Paris apartment. The curtains are drawn and I tread on spent candles, cursing, and scatter playing cards with my feet as I make my way to the large door.

Atherton must have sent a letter to arrive this morning. The unexpected pleasure of this blends uneasily with my queasy morning-after regret. *Only a little too much brandy*, I tell myself.

Once I'm married I shan't have cause to go out alone on the Marais.

Something unsettling tugs at me all the same. But as I open the door, it is already receding, pushed away by the anticipation of Atherton's letter. The delight of replying as his wife-to-be. A smile pulls at the corners of my lips, picturing my future husband's face, quill in hand, writing earnestly.

Instead of a messenger, however, it is Jemmy, larger than life and a great deal more grinningly buoyant than my current fragile state allows for.

'Late night or early morning?' he asks, tilting his head to take in my pained features.

'A little of both.' I am disappointed not to receive a letter from Atherton, but pleased to see Jemmy all the same.

'What in the hell is that?' He is pointing to Atherton's cockade of black ribbons, pinned limply to my dress. 'You've taken to declaring your Englishness now, have ye?'

'A little patriotism, that's all,' I say defensively, not willing to tell him about my engagement. 'How did you get in unannounced?' I add. 'There's a doorman. You're supposed to leave a card. It's protocol.'

'The fella waiting outside? He buys dockside contraband. I gave him a good price on a bundle of cloth for his wife a while ago. Aren't you going to invite me in?'

'Come in.' I lead him in, suddenly rather conscious of my apartment and its disarray. I reach out a hand and shut the door to my bedchamber, with its unmade bed heaped high in linens and silk, a half-bottle of white wine and two lipsticked glasses on the floor. A sandbag in the shape of a man lies beneath, pocked with stab marks where I practise my dagger skills.

He follows me into the large reception room, taking in the proportions and whistling admiringly.

'So this is where you've been hiding?' he says. 'Fancy. Or at least it could be.' He crosses to the thick velvet curtains and tugs them back mercilessly, letting strong sunlight spill through.

He runs a disapproving finger over a dusty windowsill. 'I've seen drunkard deckhands with cleaner quarters. I thought ladies had maids.'

'As I keep telling people, I'm not a lady.'

'Ach, you're all ladies to us common folk. Besides, even bourgeois shop-owners have a housekeeper.'

He draws up a stool. Sits.

'Make yourself at home,' I say drily.

'Don't mind if I do.' He lifts a loosely bound book.

'*Mechanics of the Ancient Greeks?*' he reads, labouring the words. 'A little light reading?'

'An interest of mine. Truthfully my passion is Italian engineering, but it's hard to get the books.'

'You're a strange woman, to be sure. Is there anything to drink around here?'

I walk to a crate of red wine bottles left untidily where the vintner delivered it, and pull one free. I uncork it. When I return, Jemmy is picking up playing cards from the floor and sorting them into a neat deck.

'I have no glasses,' I begin, but Jemmy is already pulling free a tankard.

'Didn't imagine you would.' He places the half-tidied cards at his feet. A queen of diamonds looks up at us accusingly.

I fill his cup. Sit uneasily across from him.

'So what is the grand secret?' he asks.

'I don't know what you mean.'

'Don't play me for a fool, Attica. You come over on some steam-packet crossing without even telling me you're back in

Paris. Don't show hide nor hair of yourself at the docks. Then I hear you have some mission or other. Is Robespierre up to his old tricks again?'

I consider lying to him, then decide against it. He would know anyway. Jemmy is a demon for poker.

'Atherton is no longer married,' I say. 'Lord Pole seems to think arrangements could be made for us. To be wed, I mean.'

There's a pause. Jemmy fingers his tankard.

'Ah,' he says, 'your spy handler.' He sounds strangely bitter. 'Well, that explains your ridiculous royal cockade,' he adds, eyeing my colourful ribbons. 'Not very subtle. A little tribute from the most English of English grooms.'

I realise I'm winding my finger into my hair. I stop.

'You don't approve?' I accuse, feeling unaccountably annoyed with him.

'Of dressing yourself as an English nationalist? No. Though I knew you weren't foolish enough to walk around Paris with that flag-waving nonsense pinned to your chest.'

'I meant of my engagement,' I say quietly.

Jemmy scoffs. 'You? Married to that soft-handed popinjay?'

'That popinjay has saved your life more than once. The fire sticks he invented. That exploding cape.'

'To be sure, it's a fine jest, Attica. You and … and this,' he waves his hand vaguely, 'inventor of things. What will you do as the wife of such a man? Embroider his linen?'

'I'm not so skilled at embroidery.'

His gaze sweeps the room. 'No, I shouldn't think you are. So you are to be married, then. For certain?' He looks at the floor. 'The end of us working together, then.'

'He has agreed we might complete one last mission before the wedding,' I admit. 'If you agree, that is.'

'Generous of him. An English mission?' Jemmy's face is guarded. He doesn't like anything to do with my government, as a rule.

'My uncle has an idea our schemes might ally.' I shoot him a rueful glance. Jemmy has met Lord Pole and knows his great ability for plots and schemes. 'A matter in Paris.'

'A Scarlet Pimpernel matter?' asks Jemmy hopefully.

'An overlap,' I say. 'You'd be paid in gold. I work for principle.'

'See how principled you'd be if you were dirt poor, Your Ladyship. You might have been born on a slave plantation, but you got your silver spoon back right enough.'

It occurs to my aching head that this is the first time Jemmy has visited my apartment. It can't have been easy for him to track me down, since I don't like him to carry the risk of my whereabouts. Not with Robespierre so keen to find me. I realise Jemmy must have an important reason for coming here.

'What brought you to my apartment?' I ask him. 'You bring news of your own?'

'I do, Attica,' says Jemmy, 'some unfortunate news.' He takes a deep drink, sits the bottle on a table. 'The girl we meant to rescue.'

'She made it to England?' Hot panic sweeps through me.

Jemmy waves a hand, appeasing. 'Of course she did. She was on my ship, was she not? I meant the next one. The lady who writes the pamphlets.'

'Someone has threatened vengeance?' I say. 'Rebel factions make idle threats.'

'Idle means they don't carry it out.' Jemmy's face is grim. 'She's been found dead.' He glances at me. 'Not quietly assassinated like some of the other abolitionists. Murdered in a very special kind of way.'

The way he says 'special' makes his face contort, as though remembering something terrible.

'The ancient regime had methods of executing criminals,' he says. 'The killer enacted those old ways on his victim.'

An awful certainty hits me. This is all sounding very familiar.

'The body,' I say, feeling unwell. 'Was she left with a bullet in her hand? A musket ball inscribed with a letter?'

'Exactly so. How did you know?'

I press my palm to my head, nod, trying to piece together the connection. I reach across for the bottle of wine. Take a swig. The sour flavour tastes wrong so early in the day.

'The English government want me to find a killer,' I say. 'They believe him to be working to some kind of agenda, but don't know what.' I drink more wine. It tastes better. 'I suppose that is the first part of the mission completed,' I add philosophically. 'He is assassinating those we mean to rescue.'

There is a heavy pause and Jemmy considers my proclamation.

'She is the second,' I tell him. 'The first was Jenny Gunnel. Two women. Both British vocal anti-slavers come to Paris. Both on our list.'

Both tortured to death for unknown reasons.

'That cannot be, Attica,' says Jemmy. 'No one could know our intended rescues. We never put names in writing, or even speak of them outside my ship.'

'There is no possibility one of your crew—'

Jemmy holds up his hand, a furious expression on his face. 'I will stop you, Attica, before you speak ill of one of my brothers.'

'Robespierre, then.'

'Robespierre is against the death penalty,' Jemmy points out. 'Not to mention he makes impassioned speeches against the very techniques used on those women.'

'I have a feeling that he has not retired to humble law work as he would have us believe.'

Jemmy shrugs. 'If so, he is covering himself well. Robespierre's current occupation is a drive for equality of the forgotten sorts. Jews, actors, blacks.' He casts a glance in my direction. 'I even think you admire him a little.'

'How could you say such a thing?' I stand, my anger surpassing my aching head.

Jemmy leans back on his stool, unconcerned. He's the only person I know who reacts this way to my temper.

'Calm yourself, Attica. You could not have saved your friend from Robespierre's orders. Fashioning your guilt as anger helps no one.'

The fight goes out of me.

'I do admire Robespierre's politics, how could I not?' I concede, standing and pacing distractedly. 'His ideals are excellent. Not so his manner of executing them.'

'Even so, Attica, I'd say our boy is behaving himself.'

I shake my head. 'Now he has crossed a line, it is only the start. He slowly realises what he is capable of. He will become emboldened.'

'You sound as if you know him.'

I shake my head. 'I only know killing changes a person, the same as you know it.' I raise my eyes to look at Jemmy. 'The stain is there. Even if he only orders the kill from afar, as Robespierre does, he is a killer now. Capable of more than he was before. The ends justifies the means,' I tell Jemmy. 'That is how he thinks. We only need understand what ends he is trying to accomplish.'

'What does your government think?' asks Jemmy, unconvinced.

'The same as you. Robespierre is working as a lawyer, writing laws and making speeches for change.'

We are both quiet, thinking this through. It seems both unlikely and the only possible answer.

'You saw the remains?' I am stricken for Jemmy, since I know the manner of the murder.

'I think he killed her first,' says Jemmy quietly. 'I hope he did, at least.' My stomach turns. The awful methods used by nobles to keep the commoners afraid flick through my mind. Boilings, flayings, the removing of limbs.

'I'm sorry,' I say, noting the deep horror in his eyes.

He waves a hand. 'I've seen worse at sea.' But I'm not sure he's telling the truth. Jemmy upends his tankard. I refill it. He takes another few gulps of wine. 'In any case,' he says, 'tell me about the bullet. The English know something of its meaning?'

I nod, rolling the wine bottle in my hands. 'It is a calling card of sorts. From a very dangerous man – an arms trader by the name of Salvatore de Aragon.'

Jemmy goes very quiet. 'I know of him,' he says finally. 'I thought he was dead. Or hoped he was.'

'You've never met him?'

Jemmy shakes his head. 'Nor would I ever want to. He's a monster, Attica. Thinks only those with noble blood in their veins are real people. Common men such as myself are lower than animals to him. There are dreadful tales of him starving the workers on his family estate. Men, women children.' Jemmy's mouth is set tight. 'Would that such a man had landed in New York,' he says, 'and let the street justice take him. We have no such deference to finery where I'm from.' There's an evil glint in his eye. 'What business do the Sealed Knot have with him?'

'He was imprisoned in the Bastille,' I explain, 'escaped when the prison fell. Went back to whatever weaponry dealings he had before. His recent killings don't make sense. Since he isn't a political man, the English government suspects he is being influenced. My mission is to discover the influencer and sever the connection.'

Jemmy considers. 'Out of character for your heartless Lord Pole to trouble himself with a few little murders.'

I smile. 'It's rather he wants to free Salvatore from any distractions.' I sigh, pressing a cool palm against my burning forehead. 'Salvatore is an arms dealer. My government want him to get back to arming the French.'

'Ah. So we're going to discover who is putting him up to murder? Then let him get away with it?'

'That's the plan,' I tell Jemmy, wishing he'd stop looking at me so fixedly. 'Don't tell me,' I add drily, 'the pirate does not approve.'

'I work for no king and my country is my crew,' says Jemmy, 'yet it occurs to me that since you're living in France, you might not want to see it ripped apart by war.'

His eyes are on mine, with their motley blend of deep green and flecked brown. I find myself considering the straight mouth and rather crooked nose – courtesy of his absent maybe-pirate father, who himself was likely of uncertain parentage, a jumble of dockside dalliances and foreign flings spiralling back who knows how far. I think of Atherton, whose light green eyes and narrow nose can be traced through several generations in portraiture. I have always admired his family's legacy. For the first time I realise it could also be considered rather detached and predictable.

'You might consider yourself a man of the world,' I tell Jemmy, rubbing my head. 'I am English. My country comes first.' The wine is beginning to ease my headache. I take another sip.

'Salvatore is in Paris tonight,' I continue. 'There's an arms fayre in the Louvre. All the finest jewelled pistols and rifles.'

Jemmy brightens. 'Is there so? An arms fayre.'

I smile. 'The most prestigious gunmakers in France put on an annual event so ladies can elbow one another aside for the best jewelled pistols. Even the King and Queen sometimes show up.'

'Not this time,' says Jemmy, still smiling at the idea of a gun-party. 'The King won't come to Paris. He is frightened the people won't let him leave again.'

'He is right to be frightened. In any case, Salvatore will be there. So there will be another fayre somewhere on the premises. For the illegal buyers. Smugglers. Your line of expertise.'

'I'm a pirate, not a smuggler.'

'Surely there can be no difference?'

To my surprise, Jemmy looks mortally offended.

'There is a great deal of difference, Your Ladyship, not that I would expect a noble such as yourself to understand such subtleties. Smugglers sail at night, and murder any in their way.'

'But don't pirates—'

'We fight *battles*. In daylight. There is a world of difference between an honest fight between armed men and a sneaking throat-cutter crawling around in tunnels like a worm.'

I throw up my hands, exasperated. 'Forgive my mistake. You are an honourable criminal, whatever that means.'

Jemmy nods. 'So we go together?'

'It wouldn't be a party unless we did.'

CHAPTER EIGHTEEN

*I*NSIDE, THE ICEHOUSE IS DAMP WITH AUTUMN CHILL AND the several tonnes of Norwegian ice, stacked in blocks at the base of the egg-shaped cavern.

Keeping a careful distance from the wet bricked walls, Robespierre tucks his hands into his pockets and watches Danton stamp against the cold.

'Is this really necessary?' Danton blows on his hands and eyes his small companion.

'We must take care, always,' says Robespierre. 'There could be a time, my friend, when one or both of us are asked difficult questions. We must always be sure we have not been overheard.'

He ventures a slim hand and pats the moist wall.

'Ten feet thick,' he says, 'and the entrance three feet from the surface. This is the perfect place to exchange secrets.'

Danton looks back at the doorway, tucking his hands under his armpits and shivering.

'They really use all this ice, do they? The nobles?'

'You are disingenuous,' says Robespierre sharply. 'I am sure you eat the sorbets at Café Procope.'

Danton is uncertain how to take this small attack on

his frequenting of the bourgeois café where Robespierre, naturally, is never seen, preferring a scant diet of fruit, when he eats at all.

'Well then,' coughs Danton, shivering again, 'let us get on with it. How is your situation at the city customs gates?'

'It is a lucrative source of information,' says Robespierre. 'Our men have infiltrated the guard, but the King's men still hold a degree of power. It is a slow process.'

'Control what goes in and out and you gain the Society a great deal of influence.' Danton nods. 'Ambitious if it works. Certainly it has not gained you everything, or you shouldn't have summoned me to this dank little hole.' He glances around with a shudder. 'What do you need to know?'

'Plans of Versailles,' says Robespierre. 'Can you get them?'

'Should I ask why you need them?'

Robespierre smiles thinly in reply.

'I likely know someone who can get them,' says Danton gruffly. 'But if you're thinking what I think you are, they mightn't be of use.' He pauses. 'There's a side gate at the palace,' he says. 'It leads directly to the Princes' Court, and the entrance to the royal quarters. They lock it at night. Unless you can get a key, there is no sense to any of this.' He indicates with his hunched shoulder the freezing chill of their clandestine meeting place.

Robespierre looks thoughtful. 'This should not pose a problem,' he replies. 'I know someone who might be of use.'

Danton looks suddenly wary. 'Max,' he says, 'I hear you have been making plans with the arms dealer?'

Robespierre's face clouds and Danton shakes his head.

'No, no, Max,' he says, 'do not be angry. No one has broken your confidence; I only make my own deductions.' Danton's little rosebud mouth twists. 'I have to say, Max, I don't like it. Better do it my way. Run in, sword in hand.'

Robespierre manages a small smile. 'Not all of us are born to be heroes.'

Danton's eyes rest on Robespierre's tiny frame, short and thin as the malnourished fishwives on the market square. 'They are not to be trusted, the nobles,' he says.

Robespierre smiles slightly. 'You are a little afraid of them, I think.'

'You're damn right, I'm afraid of them,' says Danton, trying ineffectually to pull his coat tighter around his big belly. 'Only a fool would not be afraid. Their cruelty. Their singular ability to see us all as animals.' He shudders, but not from cold.

'Such things can be put to good use, if channelled properly.'

'And so you hide behind this man. But be careful you do not become like them, Max.' Danton waves a fat finger. 'You think you can distance yourself from this Salvatore fellow; you cannot. I have met men like him before. Lone men. Ones who cannot work with others. Good killers, to be sure. But bad recruits. Ah, but I see you have already made up your mind. Well then! The blood is on your hands. Only be careful. You can best Salvatore at chess, but must allow for the fact he may kick the board over.'

'I am always careful.'

'Just like the Pimpernel, eh?' agrees Danton good-naturedly, failing to notice how the comparison draws a flash of rage in his friend. 'Have you discovered anything to unmask him?'

Robespierre shakes his small head slowly.

'But you thought there was a pattern to those this Pimpernel fellow chose to aid?'

Robespierre's eyes have a distant look. 'There is *something*,' he says. 'I am sure of it.' He holds up a list. 'Here are some of the people he smuggles from justice. Women. Children. I became certain there was a theme. Something to join them all together.' Robespierre taps his mouth with slim fingers. 'The children were a distraction. The women, slave reformers all. Women with powerful influence, one way or another. Money, contacts. Husbands with plantations.'

'You thought our dashing rescuer an abolitionist,' says Danton. 'The information you requested on the Lisbon docks might confirm it.' He pats his waistcoat but does not make to remove any papers. 'You may be intrigued to know that place is where the Pimpernel's last rescue was held. It is a slave ship dock. A place where the vessels depart for Africa. This confirms your own findings?'

'It does.' Robespierre's face is unnaturally still, like a mask. Then he speaks.

'It was burned down?' he confirms softly.

'Quite the statement, eh?'

'This is something,' breathes Robespierre. 'It tells us a great deal. For the setting fire to the dockyard was unnecessary by all accounts. Far easier to sail free with his prize than risk alerting guards to a fire. A reckless man, then. Flamboyant, and fond of drawing attention to his daring deeds.'

Robespierre is pacing in a small circle and seems to have forgotten Danton is there. He taps his fingers and looks alarmed when Danton clears his throat.

'Perhaps he sends me a message.' Robespierre's eyes are burning. 'A taunt. He knows I speak out against slavery. I think ... I believe a part of him *wants* to be found. Like all great men, he yearns for his genius to be recognised. It is not enough he performs his daring rescues. He wants to be admired. Even celebrated. Yet he is underestimated by those around him; belittled and passed over for some reason I can't discern.'

Danton reaches across and pats Robespierre kindly, the way one might a dog. 'You speak of yourself, perhaps, my friend.'

Robespierre adjusts his neat white wig, and eyes with displeasure the part of his shoulder where Danton's hand was moments ago. 'We are alike, I think.'

'Your cleverness will be discovered soon enough – you can be sure of it. Things in Versailles are bound to change before long. It is cold,' he adds. 'Better go before we catch a chill.' Danton gives Robespierre a long look. 'Good God, man, don't you even feel it?'

Robespierre glances distractedly around. 'They shall come for us, you know,' he says, pale fingers adjusting his glasses. 'This unforgivable audacity cannot be borne. As soon as the pressure is lifted they will find a reason and they shall execute us terribly.'

Danton lays a heavy hand on Robespierre's shoulder.

'I know it, my friend,' he says gravely. 'If we have done a little good, perhaps it will be worth it. That is how I sleep at night. That and the wine.'

Robespierre's lip twitches. 'What if I could save us, Georges? All of us? What if I could make us safe?'

There's a pause as Danton searches Robespierre's face for the slightest hint of uncertainty. He doesn't find it.

'Well then, you must do it,' he says quietly. 'You must do it.'

CHAPTER NINETEEN

*M*Y CARRIAGE PASSES ALONG THE RUE DE RIVOLI, JOLTING along the cobbles. I am out of the habit of formal clothing these past months. Since the Bastille fell, aristocratic ladies are at pains to appear meritocratic. Their salons are accordingly open for all walks of life and dress, not wishing to make their common guests feel underdressed. The fashion is for floating gauzy things with ribbons. There is a strong move to ancient democracies. Greek and Roman.

In contrast, I am feeling hemmed in, rather literally, by my heavy party wear. I'm wearing a deep red velvet over-mantle, studded along the bias-cut opening with silver buttons that run from my neck to my ankle. My elbow-length gloves are matching, as is the scarlet ostrich feather swaying atop my dark hair. Lord Pole's amber locket, with its consignment of deadly poison, hangs at my neck.

The boxy lines of the Louvre come into view, resplendent by the light of a hundred flaming torches. Carriages are rolling lazily into the open courtyard, disgorging an assortment of fabulously dressed nobles. As my horses come to a halt, the door is opened by a dark-haired man. He looks so much a highwayman that my hand is halfway to my knife before I realise it's Jemmy.

'I had forgotten your penchant for arming yourself for social occasions,' I remark, as he hands me down. 'Does all that metal play a tune as you walk?' His waistband is stuffed with both dagger and sword – with jewelled hilts, naturally – and his usual flashy pistols have been replaced with even louder substitutes.

'Even pirates know how to dress for smart occasions,' he says proudly, patting the elaborately enamelled gun butts. 'You know how to play the part, that's for sure,' he adds, letting out a long whistle as he eyes me up and down. 'How long did the hair take?'

I reach up to touch the tower of waxed and jewelled hair with its waving feather. 'Two hours,' I admit. 'It was very dull.' Even so, my hair is nothing to most of the towering constructions worn by ladies here.

'The amber necklace doesn't match, mind,' he adds. 'A little something from the Sealed Knot? Will it explode if I touch it?'

'Don't ask,' I say, shaking my head. 'You're expected to arrive in a carriage,' I add, looking around to see who has noticed. 'It's all part of being admitted. You have to put on a show.'

'Never was one for etiquette of that kind,' admits Jemmy, shining a button with his finger. 'Clean clothes, shiny boots, a few jewels on your weaponry and the rest can go to hell, so it can. Besides, you've etiquette for both of us, I reckon.'

Behind us, a steady stream of carriages are depositing splendidly dressed aristocrats, and wheeling away again. I watch a couple, dripping in silks, lace and gems like exotic birds.

'They have no idea, do they?' says Jemmy, watching their faces as they promenade towards the door. 'Their days of living off the backs of common folk are numbered. All this is already gone.' There is a hard set to his jaw.

'The French aristocracy has existed for over four hundred years,' I tell him. 'They will carry on in one form or another.'

'You see things as an Englishwoman,' replies Jemmy lightly, adjusting the sword at his hip. 'We Americans see the possibility for change in a way you cannot.'

'I thought you were Irish?'

'Depends on the arresting officer. I have been known to be Spanish, if it can get me good terms with the judge.'

My mind swings to the Bastille, now nothing but an enormous hole in the ground; lined with hawkers selling stones and hinges. I remember the mood of the people who stormed the prison, how impossible things are done when starvation is the only option.

We have neared the magnificent entrance to the palace now. Fortunately, in the maelstrom of preposterously decorated carriages, Jemmy's arrival *à pied* seems to have gone unnoticed.

A thundering of wheels close behind causes us both to turn sharply. Four enormous plumed horses, their glossy coats slick with sweat, drag a bulbous carriage on enormous gilded wheels. The weight of decorations is pushing it low on its leather suspension straps.

'That bloody dandy has near killed those poor horses,' mutters Jemmy, his hand falling to his sword. 'I'm going to have words.'

I put a restraining hand on his arm. 'I'd lay odds this is the man we've come to meet.'

Jemmy and I watch as the carriage jolts to a halt. My eyes move to the driver. He sits in front, reining the horses with cruel ferocity. My eye is instantly drawn to his outlandish dress – far too elaborate for a coachman. His coat and breeches are of aquamarine silk, brocaded a full two inches on every hem with pearls and gold. A munificent flounce of Flanders lace is at his neck, under a high snowy-white linen collar tied with a black silk ribbon. His face is wolfish, with a pronounced widow's peak to his dark hair.

Salvatore, I presume.

Through the glass window, I catch sight of a beautiful girl, her face twisted as she bounces uncomfortably on her satin seat. She's so arresting I find myself staring.

The girl's skin is black – the kind of flawless ebony you rarely see outside of the plantations. Unusually she wears no wig. Her tightly curled hair is swept high and pinned with jewels, a few tendrils free to brush her slender neck. She wears a strangely formal dress for someone of her age, thick embroidered panels holding her upright.

Is she a slave? A servant? She is dressed too finely for either.

Unlike most captive slaves she is rather slight. The rigid embrace of her corsetry amplifies the birdlike quality of her slender frame as something fragile and vulnerable. Since she sits alone, she must be a hugely wealthy lady or a courtesan. But it is almost unheard of for a black girl to be either.

I switch my eyes back to the driver, now dismounting. Two footmen almost fall over themselves to reach the carriage.

'Monsieur le Marquis Salvatore de Aragon,' mumbles one, bowing very low.

Salvatore arches an eyebrow, like a sneer. His skin has a deathly prison pallor that sets a doubly unnatural tone to his bloodshot close-set eyes. He looks like a predator.

'Find me a new driver,' Salvatore says, tossing the reins to the footman. 'The fool I just kicked into the gutter would have taken all week to get us here.'

I see the footman glance at the blown horses and then back at the Marquis.

'At once,' he says. 'What pleases you.' He glances to the carriage door where the girl sits inside, her head turned determinedly forward.

'What are you waiting for?' snaps Salvatore. 'Hand her out, man. She's no lady to wait on my noble arm.'

The footman walks quickly to the painted door, with its outsized family crest, and opens it. I watch as the lovely girl inside extends dark fingers and allows herself to be drawn out. The way she holds herself reminds me of the plantation where I spent my early childhood. It was common for slaves to lose hope a few years after capture and trudge about, heads bowed. Others retreated into themselves, queens of their own internal domain, no matter what befell their outward selves. This girl has something of that about her. As if no weapon could ever pierce her armour.

Was she once a slave? I wonder. Or did she arrive in Paris by other means?

As she passes the horses, her mask slips. She hesitates and extends a tender hand to the nose of the nearest, taking in its foaming mouth and sweat-slicked head with sorrow.

Salvatore flicks his head back. 'If you tarry, Centime, you'll find a riding crop has many uses.'

She picks up her skirts and trips nervously after him.

I turn to Jemmy, my eyes blazing.

'To hell with protocol,' I say. 'Let's go in.'

101

CHAPTER TWENTY

*T*HE ENTRANCE IS STAFFED BY TWO VERY TALL MEN, EACH holding a showpiece rifle. Part guard, part decoration.

'I'll wager those fancy things don't even shoot straight,' Jemmy mutters as we pass by. But he keeps his distance even so.

Salvatore and his lovely companion have vanished away so entirely, I can only assume they have gone to another part of the building. My eyes scan the thick crowd of painted faces and plumed wigs, but there is no sign of them.

The interior of the Louvre is breathtaking, a huge airy space of gilded walls and black-and-white tiled floors. Today the effect is heightened by the decadent showmanship of Europe's greatest gunmakers. Huge sprays of blousy white flowers line the length of the room. The sumptuously carved furnishings of the Louvre have been reconvened to display rifles and pistols. Cabinets and tables of mahogany and ebony form a loose square around the reception room.

'Bloody saints,' breathes Jemmy, staring at the flowers. 'Those blooms are hot-house. Must be worth ten francs a piece.'

His eye glides over an ivory-inlaid cabinet on which three shining rifles have been artfully displayed in a fan.

'We're not here to buy,' I tell him as we walk into a larger reception room beyond. 'This part is all for show. Salvatore will be hosting his serious trade elsewhere.'

We pass a bowl of marzipan and real fruit. Jemmy stretches out a hand, then retracts it on noticing my expression.

Inside the huge belly of the Louvre, the walls are hung with works of art from the royal collection, and grander purpose-built display cases of guns, rifles and pistols are laid all around. Even in this large space, the density of weaponry exhibited makes it difficult for the wide-skirted ladies to move between them.

Jemmy's eyes have grown round.

'There is talk that Marie Antoinette took to visiting such events in disguise,' I explain in a whisper, taking in the courtly ladies. 'Little chance of that now.'

'If you met the Queen, you would have to curtsey,' says Jemmy. 'I should like to see it. Your English pride.'

'I should never curtsey to a French Queen,' I tell him. 'I am English. We are half at war.'

'Then I should like to see the meeting even more.' He smirks maddeningly.

'And what of you?' I demand. 'Would you bow to a woman who lets her people starve?'

'My mammy taught me to bow to all ladies,' says Jemmy. 'Takes you a long way in life, good manners.'

He looks away, distracted by a sparkling gun.

'Look at the workmanship,' he breathes, gliding a hand over a mother-of-pearl-inlaid rifle displayed on a velvet cushion.

Immediately, a man in green silk with an outrageously coiffed white wig is at our side.

'Might I help you?' He bows obsequiously low.

Jemmy holds out a hand, and the man stares for a moment, unused to such egalitarian gestures in France, then shakes it uncertainly.

'Captain Avery, at your service,' smiles Jemmy.

The man's mouth moves silently.

'You are … You were … Not the same Captain Avery who was imprisoned in England?'

'The very same,' agrees Jemmy, giving no indication he is abashed by this. 'The English set me free when they realised I could out-sail their best men,' he adds, with his characteristic lack of humility. 'Sometimes I am paid to privateer, but mostly I do as I please.'

The man's attention turns to me, a sly look of admiration creeping on to his features. 'Seems you are doing very well for yourself indeed. You come along for the ride, eh?' He eyes me venally and lifts my hand to kiss it. Naturally, he thinks me a whore, albeit a fine one.

'This is my wife,' interjects Jemmy smoothly.

The man drops my hand as though it were red hot.

'My apologies,' he mumbles. His face passes through an alarming array of expressions. 'Your wife?' he asks finally, giving me a perplexed look. For a man like Jemmy to have clothed his wife so magnificently is a puzzle he cannot decode.

'She is Russian,' explains Jemmy. 'She came with a wardrobe. But doesn't speak or understand English or French.'

'You weighed her stupidity and dirty blood against good looks and fine dresses, eh?' decides the man, relieved at a feasible explanation. 'But *mon Dieu*, what a face to her! She looks ready to kill.'

I catch my expression in a mirror across the room and realise the furious glint to my eyes is terrifying.

'A Russian habit,' says Jemmy, 'pay it no mind.'

The man is looking nervously at me from the corner of his eyes. 'If you say so.'

'We are here to meet someone,' says Jemmy. 'A marquis.'

The man's eyelid twitches. 'A few such men are here.'

'I think you know the man I have in mind. He was recently released from the Bastille.'

'Perhaps I can help you,' agrees the man, a degree of cunning creeping into his expression. 'First, let us discuss your weaponry needs.'

Jemmy nods as though expecting this.

'I can pay well, for the right quality,' he tells the man, who hefts the rifle Jemmy was considering, beaming.

'The wheel-stock is walnut,' he tells Jemmy. 'Carved by the greatest craftsman in France, who resides here at the Louvre, under His Majesty's patronage.' He sweeps a hand around the palace interior. 'Much of his work is cabinetry of the finest kind,' he explains, 'but he makes occasional pieces, only for us. No other gunmaker is worthy of his art.'

Jemmy runs a loving hand along the barrel.

'We also have very fine daggers,' continues the man smoothly, his gaze dropping to Jemmy's outlandish sword hilt. 'The pinnacle of silver-work. Nothing less than marvels of engineering.'

I decide to leave Jemmy poring over the wares, and begin making a sweep of the room. That's when I see the same girl who was with Salvatore earlier. Centime, her black skin striking against the sea of white faces. She is walking quickly towards an elaborately corniced doorway. A guard moves to bar her entry and she opens her hand to show him something. He moves back and she steps through.

Curious now, I walk quickly in the same direction, arriving before the guarded entrance just as Centime vanishes from sight into the room beyond. I try to get a good look inside. It is less crowded than the main fayre and the guests seem less decorated and decidedly more male in number. Tables for billiard and shuffle games are laid out, and clusters of serious-faced gamers are leant over tables, moving counters and shuffling tokens. I can't see Centime by a table.

'This room is by invitation only,' says the guard, looking me up and down.

I trust my quick wits, and in reply remove from my hanging pocket the monographed musket bullet given me by Lord Pole.

'The Marquis has invited me personally,' I tell the guard, letting the lead ball roll in my palm, its calligraphied 'A' on clear display.

He nods and falls back to let me past. I walk through, to a very different party beyond.

CHAPTER TWENTY-ONE

*I*N FAUBOURG SAINT-ANTOINE, DUSK IS SETTLING OVER THE meagre fish market. Wares are in short supply and beginning to stink. No one can afford to buy bread. Fish is a secondary consideration.

A woman with three good-sized pumpkins and a baby strapped to her chest argues loudly with another as to her rightful pitch. A haggard old soup-seller is looking hopefully inside her empty kettle. Children methodically sweep the dirty floor, searching for scraps.

Ovette is picking through the rubble of her basket, tossing away pieces she cannot sell. Robespierre has sent her a message she does not quite understand. She carries it folded away in her dress.

It simply says: *Await the pamphleteer.*

She cannot imagine what the news pamphlets could tell the women that they don't already know. Things in Paris are dire. People starve. Bread is too expensive to buy.

Even so, Ovette looks up expectantly as the morose routine of market labour is interrupted by a pamphleteer shouting of the latest news. He is a young boy, struggling with his thick stack of printed paper, his fingers dark with ink.

'News from Versailles!' announces the pamphleteer, eyeing the women. One stands and strides towards him.

'What news?' she demands.

'One centime a pamphlet ...' begins the boy, but the woman cuffs him around the head. 'I suckled you at my teat when your mother died of the pox, Jean-Baptise,' she says. 'Tell me the news.'

'I ... Well. There is no news,' admits the boy. 'I'm not allowed to read it.'

'You mean you can't read it?' The woman cuffs him again. 'Didn't your father pay for that day at the poor school? What were you learning?'

The boy flushes furiously and turns his attention to the writing, his eyes watering with the effort.

Ovette stands.

'Here,' she says, walking towards him. 'Let me.'

The boy looks back and forth between Ovette and the other women. Seeing no other instruction he hands the paper over.

'What does it say?' demands the woman, glowering over Ovette's shoulder. 'What of the menfolk? Are they now at Versailles?'

Ovette shakes her head, looking nervously at the women sat or stood near their wares.

'It was decided to delay,' she explains.

A wave of deflation sweeps over the women. Their faces are slack with misery.

'That's that, then,' mutters one. 'What of the price of bread?' she adds, a menacing undertone to her voice.

Ovette's jaw is set tight. 'It has gone up.'

Now despair joins forces with disappointment. Their men will not make a stand. They must surely starve.

Ovette looks at the women. Poor women. Hungry women, with their starving children bound to their chests or sat on their hips. She squares her shoulders.

'Women of Faubourg Saint-Antoine,' she announces, 'we must make a stand ourselves!'

Jeers greet Ovette. The women are already turning away, back to their sad lives. She has misjudged things.

'Sit your arse down, Two-Face,' says the nearest woman. 'This isn't the fight of women like you.'

But Ovette is not to be silenced.

'Fuck this,' she mutters, raising her hands to her mouth. 'Fuck this!'

A few women stop to listen now. She is speaking their language.

'The men will not march today!' she shouts. 'The price of bread has risen.'

She waits for the horrid, furious chatter to swell into shouts, then raises her voice louder.

'Fuck those cowardly men!' she shouts. 'And fuck the King too, and the Queen's fat arse on her velvet cushions!'

There are laughs and shouts of agreement.

'The lawyer was right!' she says. 'Our men will not do it. But we can, we should!'

Ovette waits for her moment. 'I say we go ourselves, us women, to Hôtel de Ville, and we do not leave without bread!'

All around the marketplace, eyes come alight. Many women were there at the fall of the Bastille, drunk in the heady abandon of breaking the rules. They are starving and ready for change. Any change.

Several begin to stand.

'I say it too!' shouts the pumpkin-seller.

'And I!' agrees a woman with a basket of clams. 'Nothing doing now for market sales anyway, is there? No sense waiting all day in the rain for men with no money in their pockets.'

At this a few more women get to their feet, decision made.

'To the Hôtel de Ville!' cries Ovette. 'And we shall not be repelled until they give us bread!'

CHAPTER TWENTY-TWO

*R*ETURNING THE BULLET TO MY PURSE I ENTER THE ROOM, letting my gaze sweep the people. This is a very different set-up to the fine ladies buying jewelled weaponry. The air is thick with pipe smoke and a hubbub of urgent negotiation, framed by far plainer cabinetry than the public fayre. Here the guns are larger, for killing rather than adorning. The daggers are discreet and deadly. Swords come in a variety of styles, with huddles of men discussing their merits. There are crossbows and garrottes, axes and pikestaffs. Innovative bullets are being handed round, and gunpowder ignited in crucibles, to demonstrate its force.

The victuals are of a basic kind too. Fare for soldiers and sailors. Two open barrels of red wine into which the men periodically dunk their empty tankards for a refill, and a vast board of torn-up bread, sausage and cheese.

The customers are from all over the world. Russians in heavy leathers, a Chinaman in a light watered-silk overcoat and turned-up shoes, several Italians that I instantly deduce from their stance (weight shifted slightly on to the balls of their feet) attended the same assassins' school as I did. The smell of unwashed bodies and oily wool clothing is high in the air. I find myself smiling. A typical warlord get-together.

As is usual in gatherings of this kind, a good deal of gambling is taking place alongside the cut and thrust of the bartering. Louvre billiard and shuffle tables have been reconvened for the purpose, and a number of common men are playing the unfamiliar games with reckless gusto. From the piles of gold coins stacked by the players, it's a high-stakes assortment of individuals.

I see Centime. She stands, beautiful and ethereal, next to the dark-haired Marquis, whose predatory eyes are fixed on the game before him. Despite the fastidious grooming of men of his class – the powder, the wigs, the perfume – he still emanates some unkempt woodland quality. A hunter, I decide. A man who stalks by night.

He lays wooden counters on a number board. Judging by the towering mound of coins at his elbow, he is on a lucky streak. Then I see why. The dealer watches where the Marquis lays his tokens, then removes cards from a compartment concealed beneath the table. In an impressive sleight of hand, he turns them to reveal Salvatore's chosen numbers. With a little smile, the Marquis awaits his winnings.

Centime places a hand on his shoulder. She whispers something in his ear and he nods, then sweeps her forward, an arm on her small waist. She winces as he crushes her to him, causing some of the wine from her glass to spill. Salvatore says something to the assembled gamers, and a carnal sneer travels around the men at the table. Several openly leer at Centime's low-cut dress. Apparently satisfied, Salvatore releases her, and Centime walks away, back erect, to a corner of the room, upending the rest of the wine into her mouth as she goes.

She stands alone before a painting of King Louis XIV, the original Sun King, swaddled in gold-studded ermine, his white-stockinged legs poking from the bottom in a dancer's pose. When a servant fills her empty glass, she takes a jerky sip, hands trembling, face mask-like.

Alive with sympathy, I watch her for a moment, looking glassily out on to the crowds. Her gloved hand moves so that she can swallow her drink in compulsive small gulps. As I drift towards her, she looks up first in alarm, then something else. Mistrust, or trepidation.

'Small men who wish to appear larger,' I observe, 'do the worst harm, do they not?'

Now her eyes widen in fear. They are a bluish brown, I notice. Almost grey. And, I can't help but think, rather beautiful in their terror.

'The Sun King,' I qualify, gesturing to the painting. 'Those high wigs and tall shoes were compensating for something, don't you think? He made all of Versailles worship him like a God. Ceremonies, rituals.'

'You are English?' It isn't exactly a question. More an accusation. She is taking in my dress.

'I am Attica Morgan.' I curtsey very low, keeping my eyes on hers. 'I couldn't help but think you looked sad, over here, alone. I have come to rescue you.'

Centime eyes me for a moment, then breaks away the gaze. She laughs. A brittle sound.

'I assure you, mademoiselle,' she says, looking into the crowds again, 'there is nothing to save *me* from. My life is far too interesting.' She eyes me with open disdain. 'Shouldn't you wait for the host to make introductions?' Her voice seems too deep and worldly for her childlike features.

I tilt my head. 'I like to make my own rules.'

She smiles into her drink and sips with the glass pressed close to her lips. 'Then you are fortunate. Not all of us are born so.'

'You were shipped as a girl from West Africa, I think?' I let my eyes sweep her shoulders. 'Taken from any family you had and sold to one of the cheap windmill brothels as a curiosity, since you were too small to make a useful slave?'

She looks down. Her head makes the slightest bobbing nod.

'That must have been very hard,' I say. 'I heard the Marquis call you Centime. A cruel jest to a girl sold for a centime a time for millworkers waiting in a line. Branded as a whore, which is why your dress covers your right shoulder.'

Her face moves through a quivering series of expressions, then settles on resignation.

'Very good. I wish you well of your cleverness. In my experience it never does a woman any good. Even nobles.' She smiles a little.

'I was raised enslaved, like you,' I tell her. 'And I did the same as you do now. You think to withdraw into yourself, where nothing can touch you.'

Something flickers in her grey eyes. She is taking in my skin colour, not sure whether to believe me.

'What is your business here?' she demands finally. 'How did you get in?'

'Your master has taken up a new pursuit,' I say. 'He is killing women who speak out against slavery. Someone has put him up to it. I am here to discover whom, and I believe they will meet tonight.'

A movement on her features confirms my intelligence is correct. She scrutinises my face.

'The handsome man you arrived with,' she says, 'the one who was buying showy guns.'

I am surprised by her description of Jemmy. With the teardrop burn at his eye and his rugged features, I think of him as charming rather than handsome. I suppose to a certain kind of woman he must be, and the noble women in Madame du Quenoy's salon certainly enjoy his low-born allure.

'A friend of yours?' she suggests.

'I imagine if you noticed him, Salvatore has placed you to watch the guests, and you already know all about us.'

Centime nods, a certain pleasure in her distant expression.

'You told me you were enslaved,' she says. 'If that is really so, how did you escape? Did the pirate buy you?'

Foolishly, I hadn't anticipated her asking about my slave past. A familiar pain strikes at my heart, powerful for being unexpected. My hand moves to the Mangbetu blade across my chest.

'My road to freedom is a long story,' I tell her. 'And too sad for a party.'

I can see from her expression she is not fooled. But in this moment, I cannot bear to revisit the awful escape that led to the death of my mother.

Centime takes another quick sip of wine and turns slightly away. It is a dismissal.

'You are out of your depth, mademoiselle,' she says. 'And you cannot rescue me.'

I reach out and grab her wrist. Her eyes flick wide, affronted.

'And what if I could?' I demand. 'What if I could save you?' I take her small hand and open her fingers. Then I place a flower token in her palm and enclose it in my larger grip.

She stares at it for a long moment.

'What does it mean?'

'This is a promise that you will be rescued,' I tell her. 'It has never been broken. If you take it, you have my word you will be put safe. But you must help me. I know Salvatore plans something. I must know what.'

She removes her hand from mine and taps her closed fist on her chin.

'You do not know what you suggest,' she says. 'The man you speak of ...' She shakes her head and then lifts her eyes to the ceiling. When they drop back to mine she seems to see something there that makes her decision.

'Salvatore will meet with his new associate tonight,' she says, speaking fast. 'Below. In the secret bedchamber of the Sun King where he entertained his mistresses. You can find it ...'

She pauses, choosing her words, and then her eyes widen in fear. Over her shoulder I see the Marquis approaching, face like thunder.

CHAPTER TWENTY-THREE

𝒯HE MARQUIS SLIDES TO CENTIME'S SIDE, SMILING THINLY. He raises his hand. She flinches and tries to hide it. A servant arrives with a jewelled chalice. His personal cup, I assume, since it doesn't match any others here.

'I see you like to make your own introductions,' he says, looking between the two of us. 'There is something very familiar about you,' he adds, staring fixedly at me. 'Have we met before?'

'I am the daughter of an English nobleman,' I tell him, holding the penetrating gaze. 'Had you ever business in that part of the world?'

He shakes his head, frowning, as though trying to dislodge some thought. 'English,' he mutters, 'no, that was not it. Have I perhaps seen you at the hunt?'

'I do not hunt, monsieur.'

'Really? I have known women be the most bloodthirsty in bringing in the kill. And you have a determined look to you.' His fingers dance on his lips. 'Your name, mademoiselle?'

'It has not come to you?' I smile sweetly. 'My name is Attica Morgan.' I don't curtsey.

There is a pause as he assesses me. Another servant arrives with a bottle of wine, and Salvatore nods the servant might pour, but doesn't extend the courtesy to Centime or me.

'I only drink bottled wine,' he says. 'I have sensibilities above the illiterate farmer who drinks from barrels.'

'Convenient that your sensibilities do not prevent your taking their money.'

His mouth flashes up in a smile. 'I recall where I have heard of you, mademoiselle.' He thinks for a moment. 'Lord Morgan's bastard, is that right?'

He throws his head back and laughs, looking between Centime and me.

'Now I understand why you had the audacity to introduce yourself. My little slave girl must be fascinating to you, hmmm?' He turns to Centime, hooking his arm around her possessively. 'Let me warn you: Mademoiselle Morgan is not what she seems.' He pulls Centime closer, so she cranes back uncomfortably. 'Your English lady is a half-breed, born to a black slave in Virginia. Continues to be quite the scandal, living unmarried in Paris.'

Assuring himself of Centime's discomposure, he returns his attention to me.

'From what I heard, you escaped the slave plantation where you were born. Very clever, by all accounts, and some describe you as beautiful, for all that ungainly height.' He allows his eyes to roam my figure, suggesting he is not one of them. 'Not yet married though you are a few years over twenty now. Let me see, what else?' He fingers his chalice, then meets my eyes challengingly. 'Ah yes. There are stories you visit the taverns on the Marais.'

'They are the only places in Paris where a woman might enjoy herself without fear of the pox,' I tell him.

Centime looks at me in surprise. The Marquis notices and laughs loudly.

'You are interested, Centime? You have found one of your own in more ways than one.' He regards me, sneering now. I keep my emotions in check as I have been raised to do.

'I am afraid you English are gaining bad publicity on account of a certain criminal,' he adds. 'You have perhaps heard of the Scarlet Pimpernel?'

I bring my wine glass to cover my mouth, just touching my lips.

'Everyone has,' I tell him, taking a sip. 'The Pimpernel is famed.'

'Infamous, you mean?'

I give him a coquettish smile. 'You know how us ladies are, starved of adventure. This Pimpernel character seems the very epitome of a dashing hero, does he not? Stealing revolutionaries from under the noses of the authorities.'

'You should be more careful who you put your faith in, mademoiselle,' he says. 'I have heard you can be outspoken on topics unseemly for a woman to hold an opinion on. If you wish to continue in France you must be more prudent with your words. It is only a matter of time before the King reasserts himself.'

'Thank you for the advice. Though I fear I am a bad student,' I tell him. 'My uncle is of a similar mind to you. Women should be seen and not heard. I am rather hopeful times are changing.'

'Oh, no, mademoiselle. Your hopes are ill-placed. It is a little upheaval, that is all. This happens every few hundred years in France. A bad harvest. A little blood-letting. But the commoners know their place at the end of it all.'

'They have certainly made their feelings known in the Place de la Bastille.'

He studies me carefully, raising his golden cup to his mouth and sipping wine. 'I confess if you were my daughter, I should have you whipped for your insubordination, and married you to whoever I saw fit. But the English do things differently, don't they?'

I smile politely. 'We keep a great many more of our people from starving to death.'

His face flashes anger, then manoeuvres back into his strange smile.

'Centime's company is not complimentary,' he says, running a proprietary finger along her exposed arm. I notice her stiffen, but the painted smile never falters. Her fist is still closed around the scarlet pimpernel token. 'She will put on a little show for us later,' he says, looking at me now, with his hand sliding up to her shoulder. It rests on the place where I guess her branded skin is concealed. 'Such a pity you are not invited.'

Centime swallows.

'The men who I deal with expect the very best entertainments,' says Salvatore philosophically. 'The feeling has to be real.' His hand closes around the back of Centime's neck now. 'That is why Centime is very special. When I left the Bastille she was the first thing I came to collect. She loves her art, isn't that right?'

She turns her neck awkwardly in his grip.

'A noble is always right,' she says, her eyes glittering fiercely. I notice the hand holding the pimpernel token tighten.

Salvatore throws his head back and laughs. Then his face darkens. He raises two fingers to summon a servant, drains his wine and hands him his empty glass.

'I do not know how you got in this room,' he says to me, waving impatiently to dismiss the servant, 'but it is by invitation only, and you were not invited. I must ask you to leave.'

'An honest mistake,' I say, smiling pleasantly. 'Forgive me. I shall return to the party and leave you poor nobles to imagine you are still in power. God knows, you haven't much longer to play pretend.'

Salvatore's expression clouds. He raises a hand and instantly two armed men are either side of me. Instinctively my hand reaches for my knife and though I suppress the urge, Salvatore notices. As I turn to leave, he grabs my arm.

'*Parla Italiano*, Mademoiselle Morgan?'

With great effort I act as a startled noblewoman might, glancing at his fingers in surprise.

'A little,' I tell him, knitting my eyebrows in pretended confusion. 'Do you seek a translator?'

Salvatore looks me straight in the eye, fingers gripping me tight.

'In Italy, the moonlight men tell stories,' he tells me in thick Naples Italian, without breaking eye contact, 'of a woman who trained with the Sicilian Assassins. The best any had ever seen with a blade.'

For just a moment, I am back fighting for my life against my fellow trainees; cold, exhausted, ready to die. It's an effort not to shudder at the memory.

I move my mouth slowly as though trying to make out the words.

'I fear your Italian is better than mine,' I tell him, smiling politely. 'I am missing some of your meaning. My Russian is more accomplished.'

He releases my hand, still searching my face. Then his features switch suddenly into a charming smile.

'Forgive me.' He bows. 'My mother was Italian and I do love to speak the language. I had hoped for a worthy adversary.' He gives a little laugh. I return his smile.

'I am sure you shall find that wherever you go.'

His lips compress in rage and he returns his hand to grip Centime's neck tightly.

'Neither Centime nor I shall see you again here,' he says tightly. 'There would be consequences, if I did.' Centime flinches and I get the impression his words are for her rather than me.

'Come along now, Centime,' he says, turning and steering her away, his hand still locked at the base of her skull. 'We have business in the bedroom. Good evening to you, Mademoiselle Morgan.'

Centime regards me sadly as she is led away. She moves her closed fist up to my eyeline, then shakes her head sadly at me and lets her hand drop and open. As I watch, the Pimpernel token flutters to the ground, trodden amongst all the silken shoes.

CHAPTER TWENTY-FOUR

*I*T DOESN'T TAKE LONG TO LOCATE JEMMY IN THE TANGLE of overdressed people wandering the legitimate side of the arms fayre. He stands alone, examining the most ridiculous pistol I have ever seen. Extending from the butt is not one but four stubby barrels, splayed like four fingers of a hand.

'Tell me you haven't bought that thing?' I sigh.

'It's a volley gun,' he says proudly. 'Shoots four rounds at once.'

'I've heard of them,' I say wearily. 'In England they're called duck's foot pistols on account of the ridiculous shape. The Sealed Knot has decided categorically against their usefulness. There's no way to aim.'

'With this kind of fire power, who minds?' says Jemmy happily. 'And I just got a set of ruby-handled guns for less than the street price.' He twirls his purchases with pleasure and loads them next to his existing set of showy pistols.

'You'll run out of dandies to gun down,' I say, eyeing his bulging waistband.

He notices my dispirited expression. 'What's put you in such a long mood?'

'There is a room selling contraband to brigands,' I say. 'Easy enough to get inside using Salvatore's bullet as my invitation. I was able to discover Salvatore will meet his new associate in the Sun King's bedchamber. But then the Marquis arrived at just the wrong moment.'

Jemmy considers this. 'A man like Salvatore wouldn't lower himself to trading his best weaponry with commoners,' he agrees. 'He'll have something planned for the big players.'

'Nobles only, we assume,' I say. 'Highly secretive and unlikely to be accessed with nothing but a bullet. There are stories about the old King having a hidden room somewhere in the Louvre, away from his state bedchamber. A few more moments and I might have found out how to find it.'

'Ah.' He pauses to work it through. 'The girl in the carriage couldn't be turned? You win some, you lose some, eh? And,' he takes out a coin and flips it, 'as luck would have it, I just won some. These pistols you're so disapproving of—'

'I never said I disapproved.'

'It's written on every part of your face, Attica. In any case, they have bought me a little information.' He taps his nose. 'You high-ups might have your secret societies and passwords, but *someone* has to pour the wine. And the kindly fella who sold me these guns just told me something invaluable.'

'Which is?' The hope sounds in my voice.

Jemmy spins the gun and assesses the aim. 'Only that a room on the ground floor has been readied for some party or other. What are the odds that that is where Salvatore will hold his little private view?' He lowers the gun triumphantly.

I grin at him. 'I take it back,' I say, 'those pistols suit you very well.' I think some more. 'A secret apartment on the ground floor,' I say. 'Kept for the Sun King's mistress. There were rumours that no servants were allowed to enter.'

'Not like you to pay attention to court gossip,' observes Jemmy.

'There was talk of tables engineered to supply food anonymously,' I explain. 'I always wondered how such a thing could be done.'

I'm aware of a sudden musky-smelling presence immediately at my shoulder.

'Very true,' says a loud voice at my ear. 'Though it's not fitting for a lady to know of.' The volume and brash confidence of the speaker startle me, and I turn, half in surprise, half in annoyance.

The man is dressed as a French general, in a ludicrously tight navy coat, nipped in around the waist with several inches of gold embroidery and flaring to long tails down his close-fitting white breeches. He has a handsome face, with fine bone structure and an expression of indefatigable self-assurance.

'The Marquis de Lafayette,' he announces loudly, bowing low, 'at your service.'

CHAPTER TWENTY-FIVE

*T*he Marquis de Lafayette.

I recognise the name instantly. As a girl, I decoded some of Lafayette's letters and found the practice immeasurably dull in its simplicity.

I eye the Marquis distrustfully, having taken instant exception to the bold manner of his approach. I'm fully expecting him to try to corral me into a dance, and am ready with a refusal. Instead, he turns to Jemmy.

'Well, well, well. Do my eyes deceive me?' he continues in the same commanding voice. 'Little Jemmy Avery.' He slaps Jemmy on the back. To my great shock, they embrace fondly, staring into one another's faces in the manner of those who have not met in many years.

'You're all grown up,' says Lafayette, delighted.

'Thanks to you,' says Jemmy bashfully.

'You would have swum to shore without my help, I only hastened the conclusion.' Lafayette shakes his head. 'Those were the days. Now the King has named me Commander of the Royal Guard.'

'The Queen never did like you,' says Jemmy sympathetically.

'You should have dressed smarter for court.' He winks.

'It wasn't just the fashions,' says Lafayette. 'She always hated me. Never trusted I was popular with the common people. And then, of course, I wrote the Rights of Man and I dared suggest all men are equal. Can you imagine her wrath?' He gives a wry smile. 'Well, she's had her revenge now. Commander of the Royal Guard!' He shakes his head with a derisory expression. 'They might as well have pinned a target to my back for peasants to spit at.'

Jemmy laughs then turns to me, the smile still glowing on his face. 'This is Attica Morgan. You've heard of her, surely?'

'I've heard of him,' I interrupt, making the briefest of curtseys. 'Your military campaigns are the stuff of legend,' I continue. 'For the wrong side, of course. You tried to invade England with the Spanish. Hard luck.'

Jemmy winces, but the Marquis doesn't rise to the jibe.

'I've grown more measured since my youthful impetuosity,' he replies good-naturedly. 'Surely an Englishwoman doesn't hold a grudge? And if I'm right in thinking your father is Lord Morgan, he would have been on the side of the French in that affair.'

'My father might agree with you,' I draw myself up straighter, 'but I am loyal to my country.' A look passes between Lafayette and Jemmy that I don't like. The kind of thing you might see when adults indulge a child. 'I will concede that retreat at the Battle of Brandywine was inspired,' I mutter petulantly, trying to salvage a semblance of impartiality. 'And the Rights of Man was a well-written piece. If your King ever signs it.'

'She's a little peculiar for a lady,' says Jemmy amiably. 'Bore you for hours on troop movements and the like, so she will.'

'Is that so?' says Lafayette. 'I have heard you do great things for the abolitionist movement, Mademoiselle Morgan. Though I think France will soon be ahead of you English.'

'Not at all,' I say, bristling. 'England began the debate, and we send our best speakers to educate the French at great personal risk. You only turned to the case after your time in America, and waste your time with words, when you should be taking action.'

He smiles lightly. 'I have learned patience with age. If the document is signed, Mademoiselle Morgan, I shall have done more for the abolitionist movement than a hundred slave rebellions.'

He casts a final look at me, then seems to decide I am too strange to dally with. 'And what brings you to French waters, Captain Avery?'

Jemmy shrugs, hands in his pockets, appearing suddenly boyish. 'Few new shooting pieces, nothing more.' His eyes slide to me nervously.

'Nothing I can help with?' suggests Lafayette, taking a measured look at his expression, then looking back and forth between Jemmy and me with interest.

'Not unless you know where to find the King's secret bedchamber,' I tell him.

Lafayette guffaws, in what I interpret as a grossly overdramatic gesture, leaning forward and slapping both hands on the white fabric of his breeches.

'She's keen, I'll give her that!' he says, reverting to his infuriating habit of talking only to Jemmy. Too late I realise he imagines Jemmy and I are in some tryst and trying to locate the bedchamber for amorous reasons. A slow heat rises in my cheeks.

'I am engaged,' I tell him sharply. 'To a very good man. The wedding is in a few days.'

For some reason, Jemmy stiffens then makes some business of adjusting the new pistol at his belt.

'Forgive me,' says Lafayette, wiping tears of laughter from his eyes and not quite managing to recompose his features.

'My husband-to-be was foremost in halting your ill-planned attack on the English,' I say haughtily. 'You may have heard of Captain Atherton?'

Lafayette's humour fades away, though not entirely. He glances at Jemmy, hoping for camaraderie at the joke, but Jemmy is keeping his face tactfully neutral, despite a traitorous glow of amusement in his hazel eyes.

'I apologise,' says Lafayette, straightening his features with effort. 'You mentioned you were looking for a bedchamber.' He opens his hands to Jemmy, imploring. 'You know how men think.'

'It is no business of yours why we seek that room,' I tell him. 'But it is for no low reason, I assure you.'

'Well, I'm afraid I cannot help you,' Lafayette continues, glancing at my furious expression. 'It's a very secret room. There were even rumours the Sun King commissioned some very complicated engineering so tables fully set with meals could rise up through the floor.'

'If you recollect, I was explaining it when you interrupted us,' I reply, but Lafayette talks on as though I hadn't spoken, addressing only Jemmy.

'No servants needed, you see? Meant the meals and so forth could be set out below stairs and raised without a soul seeing what His Majesty was up to.' He eyes me. 'It spurred all kinds of stories about debauched orgies. We all agreed he must be up to something utterly abandoned if not even servants were permitted to bring food and drink. The engineering was advanced enough to inform cannon mechanism, I believe.'

'Fascinating,' I reply drily. 'I had no idea French military strategy owed so much to a greedy old adulterer. If you might excuse us, Monsieur Lafayette.'

He bows graciously, giving no indication I have offended him, then turns to Jemmy.

'Good to see you, Captain Avery,' he says. 'I am sorry not to assist you better, but if there's anything you need, do come to me. I am back in Paris for the duration now, it would seem. Her Majesty is keen to get good value from her new commander.' He smiles ruefully.

Jemmy smiles back.

'And don't let your usual vices get you into trouble,' warns Lafayette, nodding in my direction. 'Oh,' he adds, before I can reply, 'there is one thing.' He brings his hand to his forehead in memory. 'If it's a map of the palace you want, you might try the kitchens below stairs. They often have one. Many staff, big palace, all that. All those maids and footmen need to know which room needs them. Helps keep things efficient.'

He winks at me. 'The French know a thing or two more than the British about good service.'

CHAPTER TWENTY-SIX

*J*EMMY AND I CREEP ALONG THE LONG CORRIDORS OF THE Louvre, careful to avoid being seen. We're following the most likely route to the kitchens, which will be deep below stairs.

'I can hardly believe it,' I say, shaking my head in wonder. 'You know the Marquis de Lafayette. You might have told me. I've been wanting to meet him for years.'

Jemmy is looking at me incredulously. 'You were rude to him!'

'Naturally I have my loyalties to England. How do you know him?'

'Lafayette pulled me out of Boston harbour a few years back.'

'So you were privy to his campaigns? His troop actions are inspired.'

Jemmy is shaking his head. 'Sometimes I don't understand you English at all. Call me a simple pirate, but friend is friend and foe is foe.'

'Technically, Lafayette and I are on opposing sides,' I agree. 'But one can admire one's enemies.' To my surprise, Jemmy's expression twists to annoyance.

'Lafayette is just a man, Attica,' he says gruffly, as though something constricts his throat. 'A good man, to be sure. But there are many such without the lace and fancy titles.' And he stalks ahead, leaving me staring in his wake, wondering what on earth could be the matter.

'What is it?' I ask, walking fast to catch him up. 'You're angry I was rude to your French friend?'

His head snaps towards me. 'We share an oath to be loyal as shipmates to each other. You never told me you'd be married in a few days.'

'I did!'

'No. You told me your beloved Atherton was allowing us one last mission before your wedding. You didn't mention we only had days together … Days to complete it. When exactly do you plan to marry?'

'Monday.'

'*This* Monday?' Jemmy retains his breakneck stride, shaking his head. 'Saints alive, Attica. You really think you can find out the reason behind these deaths and match the tide back to England in two days? It will take you that time to arrange for your dress and trousseau, a fine lady like you.'

'I won't be needing anything like that,' I assure him, confused by his apparent interest.

'Your husband is a lucky man,' he says drily.

I ignore his tone. 'What did Lafayette mean by your old vices?' I ask. It's a trick to steer him from the subject of my marriage, and I don't expect him to fall for it, but incredibly he does.

'I had a penchant for dangerous women back when I knew the Marquis,' he mutters, looking straight ahead. 'Don't concern yourself,' he adds, 'I've long grown out of it. Let's get on with finding this secret bedchamber.'

We walk on in uncomfortable silence.

Paintings of classic scenes hang on the walls. We pass a large Raphael of an angel slaying a demon.

'Why are the French royals so fascinated by Greek myth?' asks Jemmy.

'Education in the classics is a way of keeping themselves distinct from commoners. You rather prove their point,' I add. 'That is a Roman depiction.'

Jemmy tilts his head all the way to the side, as though trying to work out the logistics.

'The King was considering allowing members of the public to view the royal art,' I tell Jemmy, 'but he has dithered for years.'

'By members of the public,' says Jemmy, 'he doesn't mean the likes of me.'

'The bourgeois,' I say, nodding. 'Property owners.'

Jemmy's jaw tightens slightly but he says nothing. We pass a row of portraits of the Sun King, each grander than the last.

There's a clanking of porcelain and a servant emerges suddenly from the end of the hallway, bearing a large tray of bread rolls. Jemmy grabs my waist.

'Giggle,' he hisses, 'pretend we are at sport.'

'Oh no,' I hiss back, dragging his hand free. 'You'll not get your hands on me that way, Jemmy Avery.'

'If he thinks us suspicious, he'll tell Salvatore.'

'Well, he'll never believe a fine lady would cavort with the likes of you.' For all his glittering weaponry, Jemmy's plain dress and boots make it clear he is no noble.

'Commoners will believe anything of the aristocracy,' he shoots back. 'Trust me. And do not flatter yourself I am in such a hurry to lay hold of you,' he adds in a furious whisper. 'If I want a lady I win her fair and square.'

The tray-carrying man is nearing our part of the long corridor.

Realising our limited options, I narrow my eyes at Jemmy, pursing my lips in annoyance.

'Get your fan out,' says Jemmy. 'Conceal us behind it and he'll assume the worst.'

It's a good suggestion, and I grab at where my matching red fan hangs at my waist, but the clasp is tight from lack of use and I can't easily free it. The servant nears, openly regarding us now.

Jemmy puts a hand at the top of my dress, where the velvet squeezes my bosom. Glowering, I rip my fan free, tearing the fabric, and rap him hard enough over the knuckles to crack the ivory casing.

'You naughty man!' I say in a high-pitched voice. He pulls his hand back, shooting me an aggrieved look.

'Just a little fun, your Ladyship,' he says, pushing me against the wall hard enough to bang my head. 'Before your husband arrives.' I put a hand behind my bruised scalp and glare at him.

The servant is in close range now. Jemmy looks meaningfully at me.

'Ha ha ha,' I manage unconvincingly. Jemmy lets a hand drift down my lower back and squeezes a handful of flesh behind my thigh. 'Unhand me,' I whisper, staring daggers at him.

'All part of the show.' He winks.

The servant walks on, shaking his head disapprovingly.

'You see?' Jemmy says, still clutching me as the tray-bearer walks out of sight. 'Servants will believe anything of ladies. I only just realised,' he adds, taking in my malevolent expression and then dropping his gaze to where I keep my knife, 'you are all restricted by your fine dress. I think I like you better this way. Less lethal.'

I twist my arm up, freeing my knife, and setting the blade at Jemmy's throat.

The rapid movement causes the thick fabric of my sleeve to tear loudly. Jemmy swallows, looking down at the blade.

'No need for that,' he manages, his tone a degree higher than usual.

I lower the knife and straighten my clothing. 'Have I upset you? We are quits then. It will take a very expensive seamstress to repair this velvet.'

I stride off down the hall, letting Jemmy follow behind, rubbing thoughtfully at his throat.

'The servant came from that door,' I say.

I glance back at Jemmy, who has recovered himself.

'Ready?' I ask. 'Below stairs must be that way.'

CHAPTER TWENTY-SEVEN

ROBESPIERRE WALKS QUICKLY INTO THE SECRET apartment, hands twitching at his sides. He pauses for a moment at the large door before beating out the complicated tattoo.

The door is opened by a large pockmarked guard, who beckons Robespierre inside. The room is every bit as decadent as he'd imagined, a veritable shrine to hypocrisy and greed. With effort, he prevents himself from shaking his head in contempt.

At the back of the room, on a large table, is the showpiece Salvatore boasted of. The poor girl from the brothel, stretched out like a provocative piece of meat. She is dressed – or rather, partially dressed – in the Roman fashion, and the corruption of Robespierre's democratic ideal brings a hard feeling of rage to his stomach.

His fury at her ill-treatment delays him a full few moments in placing the familiarity of the girl's pose. She has been styled to mimic a famous painting.

Robespierre has heard of the tasteless obsession of the nobles for acting out famous paintings with half-naked women. The hypocrisy of disguising lechery as high-minded art appals him beyond words.

He stands awkwardly, as though wondering where to place himself. His eyes drift again to Centime, exposed in torn robes. His small mouth is set hard, a flash of pain flares in his pale eyes.

Salvatore turns from his business dealings to eye his visitor. He still holds a rifle he has been showing laid across his arms. Noticing the lawyer's nervousness at Centime's display, he laughs unpleasantly.

'Here he is,' says Salvatore to the room at large. 'Our little rat.'

Robespierre's discomfort at the semi-naked woman falls away, replaced by something unreadable behind the round glasses. The Marquis, Robespierre cannot help but notice, has a dead quality to the eyes. A void – or perhaps, a *hunger*. Yet there is also something very corporeal about Salvatore, with his disturbingly red lips and smatter of dark chest hair peeking above his snowy collar. Something *fleshy*.

'You disapprove of the art, *monsieur*?' continues Salvatore, emphasising the lack of title. 'Naturally a man such as you does not make a business of studying paintings. Perhaps we can find you something a little more low-brow. Wait …' He extends an accusing finger. 'Now I recall. The lawyer is unmarried. Bathhouses are your vice, perhaps?'

He shares a smile with his fellows. There are rumours about the virtuous Robespierre.

'As a boy I was fortunate enough to receive a scholarship from the local monks,' says Robespierre. 'We studied the classics. This is *The Rape of Persephone*, is it not?' He nods to Centime's display. 'I was unsure at first because the original depicts laurel bowers and you have used linden.'

Salvatore's dark features cloud.

'Be careful you do not forget your station, monsieur,' he says.

Robespierre bows elaborately. 'I only seek to understand the greatness of my betters. Naturally I lack the sentiment to perceive art as you do.'

Mollified, Salvatore nods. Then his expression darkens again. 'Search him.' Salvatore gestures to his guard.

'As you can see,' says Robespierre in his nasal voice, 'I am unarmed.' He holds his slender hands in the air.

Ignoring this, the men approach Robespierre and proceed to pat him down. He bears this affront calmly, but there is a hint of rage deep in his light blue eyes, if you cared to look for it.

'You will not take it amiss,' says Salvatore, 'if I do not trust a man who has turned on his own kind.'

The Marquis' expression changes completely as he addresses the aristocrats in the room, bowing courteously.

'My noble friends,' he says, placing the rifle in his hands on a nearby table, 'please allow me and the commoner a few moments' privacy. The adjacent room has been laid out for your enjoyment. Food, wine and girls selected by Centime.' He allows himself a smile. 'As you know, she has an expert eye.'

He opens a door on the far side of the room, offers a glimpse of a chamber beyond where candlelight glistens on naked limbs and tables of sweetmeats.

The nobles file out, leaving only Salvatore, his guards and Robespierre, whose eyes drift back to Centime.

Frowning, Salvatore clicks his fingers at her.

'What are you waiting for, Centime?' he demands. 'Go entertain our guests. We have several large consignments arranged and I want those men to leave happy or you'll have me to answer to.'

Snatching up her robe, Centime gets to her feet and trips quickly from the room, covering herself as best she can as she leaves. Salvatore watches her with a greedy expression, the corner of his mouth turned faintly upwards.

He turns back to Robespierre.

'You are braver than I thought to come here in person,' says Salvatore. He removes a gleaming knife from his belt. 'It would be in my interests to kill you now.'

Robespierre's expression doesn't change. 'One such as I am beneath the notice of a great Marquis,' he says. 'The deer-hunter does not waste a bullet on a stray bird in the field.' There is the barest hint of a smile playing at his pale lips.

'Very good.' Salvatore nods. 'And you are correct. Not to mention, your information has proved useful. I shouldn't like to be in your skin if your fellow republicans discover you have been betraying them.'

Robespierre makes a strange little half-bow.

'I have more information for you,' he says in his high, clipped voice. From his neat coat he removes a piece of folded paper and holds it out. Salvatore takes it, opens it and his dark eyebrows lift.

'*Mon Dieu*,' he says finally, 'you are quite the snake.'

Robespierre doesn't reply.

Salvatore takes a breath, looking hard at the picture.

'You are certain?' he asks.

Robespierre only nods.

CHAPTER TWENTY-EIGHT

*J*EMMY AND I ARE NOW DEEPER UNDERGROUND, BELOW THE main rooms of the Louvre. There is an aptly subterranean feel both in layout and smell. A warren of damp, low-ceilinged corridors with no thought to decoration or appearance, in complete contrast to the grand rooms above.

'A map of the palace for servants,' says Jemmy, looking around the dimly lit tunnels ahead. 'Surely it would be in plain view.'

'You're assuming your friend Lafayette knows what he's talking about,' I snort. 'He may be gifted at inspiring men to charge in, all guns blazing. But his military campaigns have always lacked finesse when it comes to strategic map work.'

Jemmy rolls his eyes. 'How about here?' he says, turning on his heel and pointing to the way we came in.

To my annoyance, as Lafayette predicted, there is a large simplified map of the palace, just by the entrance. Above it a long plank holding mounted bells has been placed, each bearing a number.

'Right where servants could get their bearings,' says Jemmy. 'And match it to whichever room is ringing for them.' He whistles. 'Most bells I've ever seen in one place,' he adds, letting his eyes run to the end of the array, where the number '40' is etched into the wood.

I glance up at the thick iron bells, then back down to the map.

'Hard to read,' I say, trying to form letters from the strange shapes.

'That's because it isn't words,' says Jemmy. 'Those are symbols. For staff who can't read. We have something similar aboard my ship for hanging the rigging.'

Now I know they're not letters, the shapes transform themselves. There are forks and flags, saucepans and something that could be a bucket.

Each is next to a number – presumably matching the room to the bell.

'A crown here, and here,' I say. 'These could be the King's chambers.' I think for a moment. 'But that can't be right,' I add. 'Those are the rooms we just came from.'

'State rooms,' says Jemmy. 'There's something like a bed here,' he adds. 'Here too.'

I peer over his shoulder. 'Those are the official bedchambers,' I say. 'For the King and Queen. They act more like meeting rooms than private bedrooms. Very public places. I remember the same from Versailles.'

'I didn't realise you'd been granted an audience in Versailles.' Jemmy sounds hurt.

'Not recently,' I assure him. 'I came as a girl with my father. He was outwardly conducting a torrid affair with one of the courtly ladies. Looking back, I suppose he must have been gathering information.'

Jemmy is shaking his head. 'And I thought my family was mad.'

We spend a few more moments staring at the map, our mutual frustration growing.

'Whatever meeting Salvatore had planned will be under way by now,' I say, chewing a finger. 'If we don't solve this quickly it will all be over.'

Jemmy brings his face very close to the wall, then far away again.

'I suppose if it was a secret bedchamber,' he suggests reasonably, 'it was kept secret.'

I purse my lips, then something occurs to me, my eyes drifting back up to the study set of bells at the top of the doorway.

'The bells,' I say. 'They match up with all the rooms, don't they?'

My finger follows the various thin metal strands, leading deep into the bowels of the servant quarters. 'If one of these doesn't match,' I say, 'that is likely to be our secret room, is it not?'

Without waiting for an answer I begin the complicated process of working through the wires, associating each one with its bell. Matching each bell to its room.

'They all pair up,' I say, disappointed. 'There is something strange, though.' I point. 'Here. This bell is for below stairs. The only one, see?' I look closer at the mysterious match.

The bell itself is no different to the others. But the room is very oddly placed: below stairs, right in what would be one of the darkest and least pleasant parts of the servants' quarters.

'This can't be the secret apartment,' I say. 'It's too small, see? More like a large cupboard.'

'Doesn't connect to any other rooms either,' Jemmy points out. 'It's a dead end, with only the one small entrance. A pantry?'

'That would fit,' I agree. 'Or a confectioner's room to house some delicate pastries or sugar work prior to a feast. But why on earth should it have its own bell? This would be a servants' place.'

I'm aware of the minutes ticking away, of Salvatore somewhere in the Louvre, plotting, and us missing all of it.

Willing myself to break the code, I look back at the map, trying to imagine myself inside the rooms. A possibility occurs.

'Above this pantry,' I say, 'look. There's a set of three interconnected rooms. Grand in scale, for they must have the same proportions as these other chambers on the same level. But these have no bell. And no way in.'

We consider this.

'So we have some grand rooms with no door, no bell, and right beneath them, a mysterious bell where it shouldn't be.'

'There must be somewhere in to those rooms from down here,' I decide. 'I'm sure of it. The pantry is the secret entrance.'

I concentrate on the map, committing to memory the path we need to take to get there.

'We can be there in a few minutes,' I say. 'We've not a moment to lose.'

CHAPTER TWENTY-NINE

W E FOLLOW THE WINDING CORRIDORS, TAKING CARE TO keep out of sight of servants.

As we near our target, the air changes.

'Smell that?' says Jemmy.

'Roasted game,' I say. 'Salvatore's choice? No kitchens nearby.' I note the lack of clanging pots and plates, turning spits and woodsmoke characteristic of food preparation.

'If I remember correctly, the secret room is around this corner.'

We follow the passage through a low archway and into a strange little underground space, a close-walled cave of sorts.

'This is it,' I say slowly, hope fading away. 'It must be. Not what I was expecting.' I can't see anything that could lead to the King's secret apartment. The place seems to have been set for a fabulous dinner. Only everything about it is wrong.

The floor is flagstone, set in a circle. Arranged on top are three highly decorated tables looking so out of place in this dingy cavern, they might have been spirited from another time entirely.

'What is it for?' breathes Jemmy, taking in the set tables.

'Why would someone have a dinner down here?'

The tables are round, with snowy tablecloths, each heaving with gold-rimmed plates of food. The nearest holds roasted bird, steaming sauceboats and bowls of artfully styled fruit. The centrepieces are elaborate works of flowers, fruit and marzipan.

'It's like a ghost ship,' murmurs Jemmy, eyeing a second table, which groans with decoratively arranged fish, meats, cheeses, salads and sweetmeats.

'Of course,' I breathe. 'The tables. The tables that raise themselves. Food fashioned so guests might easily serve themselves.' I look up. 'This whole room is devised to deliver the meal without the use of servants.'

The ceiling of the cave-like room is made of overlapping metal plates in a flower-like pattern, starkly more decorative than the unadorned lower chamber.

'So it was true, then?' says Jemmy, tilting his head to the ceiling. 'The King really did engineer some system to bring fully set dinner tables to the room above.'

'Rather beautiful, isn't it?' I say, admiring the complex interlocking structure. Slivers of light show through from the room above, giving the space over our heads the appearance of a large glowing flower. 'As though two worlds collide at this point.'

'If that's the case, we're in the lower realm,' says Jemmy. 'And the only way out is through the roof.'

It's a good point, and one that needs solving. I had expected this room to allow us a way up into the secret chamber, but it doesn't.

'There must be another entrance on the ground floor, not shown on the map,' I decide morosely.

'Could work for us, even so, if we want to listen in,' Jemmy points out. 'If the secret chamber really is up there.'

'You're right. The ceiling must open somehow,' I decide, 'the plates.' I kneel to examine the tables. 'And these rise,' I say, lifting a tablecloth to observe the unusual construction beneath. 'They revolve upwards, I think. Like a screw.' I turn my finger in explanation. 'There. This is the mechanism.' I walk towards a part of the room in dark shadow, where an elaborate assortment of cogs and levers can be made out.

'Just be careful you don't send the tables up,' says Jemmy nervously.

'I doubt that's possible,' I reply. 'I imagine this whole configuration is controlled from upstairs.' I point. 'Which means they're likely up there now,' I add, taking in the distance between the food and the low ceilings.

Carefully I step up on to the nearest table, trying to avoid the close arrangement of plates and food.

'Attica!' says Jemmy. 'What if they summon the tables?'

'Dinner is not served until midnight in noble houses,' I tell him. 'Salvatore is not a man to corrupt decades-old protocol.'

The table wobbles and my foot narrowly misses a cheese sculpted to represent a crown.

'Hold it steady, would you?' I ask Jemmy.

Dutifully Jemmy moves to secure the edge, and I pick my way across the table, ducking at the low ceiling. In the centre I straighten. My fingers brush the ceiling.

'If we could somehow turn this table a little higher,' I say, 'I might be able to look into the room above, between the gaps in the metal.'

'I wouldn't play around with the cogs,' advises Jemmy. 'You'll serve yourself up to Salvatore and his men on a platter.'

'Very funny.' I frown in the direction of the cogs. 'There must be a way to twist the tables without opening the ceiling. The two things will be different mechanisms. Try turning the table counter-clockwise.'

'I've not had this many orders since I was a deckhand.'

'Don't be petulant. You know I understand engineering better than you.'

Frowning, Jemmy leans forward and begins to turn the table, grunting with effort.

'I don't think it is meant to turn this way.' There's an ominous clang, as though a spring has given way. Then I hear Jemmy's boots skid beneath him.

'It's turning by itself!' he shouts, grabbing hold of the edge with both hands and stopping the movement with effort.

'Sounds like a ratchet has been released,' I say, looking up at the ceiling. Jemmy's efforts have levitated me half a foot upwards, but I'm still not quite near enough to see. 'Probably best not to risk any further turns.'

'And what does the engineering master recommend I do to stop this table spinning?'

I look down distractedly and nudge a golden fork towards him.

'Wedge the underside with this.'

Jemmy lets go with one hand and takes the fork with bad grace. There's a scraping of metal on flagstones and some distant muttering about the waste of gold, and then Jemmy re-emerges.

'I don't know how well it will hold,' he says, watching me as I scan the ceiling, trying to work out how to get higher.

'Might I venture a suggestion?'

'What?' I'm still looking up.

'Only an ignorant pirate idea, you understand, the foolish notion of a humble sailor …'

'Just tell me.' Jemmy is insufferable sometimes.

'Might you just turn that big platter there upside-down?' he asks with a smirk. 'Would that not give ye enough height, without all the cogs and levers and table turning?'

I look down at my feet to see he is right. The large silver fruit bowl, if overturned, will close the distance between the table and ceiling sufficiently for me to peer through the plates above.

'Very good,' I say, leaning down to dump aside the heavy bunches of grapes and highly polished apples. 'Quite right.'

'I cannot claim your book knowledge,' says Jemmy, picking off a purple grape and tossing it high. He catches it in his open mouth with a smug wink. 'Only the school of life, your Ladyship.'

'Just hold the table steady,' I say. 'Be certain that fork doesn't give way.'

I tilt my head to see I now have a sliver-like view directly into the room above. Craning my neck I try to get a better view.

'I think we were right,' I call down to Jemmy. 'This looks very much like a King's boudoir. All velvet and nude paintings.'

I hear voices now, soft but unmistakable. Then, straining to an unnatural angle, I am suddenly confronted with a pair of familiar and highly decorated shoes.

Salvatore.

My head is only inches from his feet. If he was to look down he would see my eyes. My heart beats faster. If I listen very carefully I can make out a great deal of what is being said.

CHAPTER THIRTY

$\mathcal{F}$ROM MY UNNATURAL POSITION ON THE TABLETOP, I HAVE to remind myself not to move. The table has not been well secured and any noise could alert the men above to my presence.

I squint upwards to see Salvatore's silk-clad feet stride away, making clicking sounds. His low voice becomes indistinct. I realise if I move a little backwards I've a better view of the entire room.

There is a closed door on the far side. If this is the Sun King's private apartment, it will have several private rooms joined together. I calculate what that might mean. There might be many guards stationed on the other side of that far door.

'Have a care,' says Jemmy. 'You're rocking the table.'

I'm only half listening, mesmerised by the spectacle. I see Centime, laid prone on her side, bordered by huge swathes of fruit and flowers. She is naked apart from a torn white toga, arranged artfully across her hips. Her curling hair is loose in a dark cloud and her expression is pained and lost.

'What is it?' asks Jemmy, noticing my distress.

'It's a *tableau vivant* with Salvatore's courtesan,' I whisper down to him, fighting the instinct to prise apart the ceiling and pull Centime to safety. 'An aristocratic pastime,' I explain, catching his confusion. 'Real-life women mimic classical paintings. Mostly nude ones. This one is *The Rape of Persephone*, but they haven't got the bower right. It should be laurel leaf.'

'Never mind the art,' growls Jemmy. 'What else is happening in there?'

I drag my eyes reluctantly from Centime and across the room. The first thing I notice is that this is a very noble gathering. No bourgeois or rich merchants. Only landed men, with dress and manners to match. Different entirely from the gathering of cask wine and gambling sailors who comprised the earlier private event. It seems Salvatore reserves his best trade for nobles.

The Marquis stands towards the centre with a huddle of men, discussing and passing very lethal-looking guns around. One man raises a sleek barrelled weapon and examines a new kind of sighting development with obvious pleasure. Another smiles over a handful of large bullets with the latest detailing to make them twist in the air.

'Looks like an elite kind of gathering,' I tell Jemmy, 'the best weapons, only for nobles.'

Unexpectedly, Salvatore claps his hands. The trade ceases, and the noble guests depart. I frown, trying to get an idea of what's happening. They pass through the far door and out of sight, leaving only Salvatore and a few men who I assume to be his personal bodyguard.

'Something's taking place,' I whisper to Jemmy. 'A few of the traders are leaving.'

'Private meeting?' suggests Jemmy.

'I don't know. It looks like only Salvatore and his guards ...'
I peer closer. 'Perhaps there is some further entertainment in another room of the apartments. Wait ... someone is coming in.'

Another set of clipped heels approach my vantage point. A pair of rather plain-looking shoes – albeit immaculately polished with no trace of the usual street dirt – and white stockings of the cheaper kind a bourgeoisie might wear.

Something about the legs seems awfully familiar. I stretch up, trying to get a better look.

'Attica,' whispers Jemmy, 'you'll give yourself away.'

But I can't help myself. Something about the visitor is compelling.

'It isn't a noble,' I hiss back. 'That doesn't make any sense. Salvatore is wedded to aristocratic privilege. Why would he give details of his secret meetings to a commoner?'

The mysterious man turns and I catch full sight of his retreating back and neat lawyer's wig. It isn't much, but it's enough.

Robespierre. I knew it!

Shock and triumph factor in equal measure, washed away almost immediately by confusion. Because why should Robespierre want those women dead?

'It's Robespierre,' I tell Jemmy. His face flashes through the exact same emotions I've just experienced.

'What does it mean?' asks Jemmy.

'It means I was right all along,' I say grimly. 'Robespierre *is* involved in Salvatore's sudden predilection for assassination.'

'Betraying his own cause,' says Jemmy, shaking his head. 'I thought better of him. Even a snake like Robespierre.'

'He never would betray the republican cause,' I say. 'If you stuck a knife in Robespierre, he'd bleed red, white and blue. But it doesn't make sense. They're politically opposed on every issue.' I am trying to work it through in my mind. 'Robespierre is the kind of man Salvatore would kill for sport.' I think some more. 'One thing is for certain,' I decide. 'If Robespierre is involved, those women were part of a bigger plan.'

A thought occurs to me.

'Hand me a glass, would you?' I call down.

'Don't make too much noise,' replies Jemmy, correctly deducing my intention to use it as a listening device, and handing up a stemless crystal drinking glass. I put it to the ceiling gently, avoiding any loud sounds on the metal. As I rest my ear to the base, magically the conversation above becomes audible.

'I must commend you,' Salvatore is saying. 'You truly think it possible?'

I hear his heels walk up and down the room, and switch from listening to watching. There is something in his hand. A piece of paper with what looks to be a drawing. Only I can't see what it is. I put my ear back to the glass.

'I do not work in possibilities,' says Robespierre. 'The thing shall be done. Men loyal to the cause are now on every customs gate. No one enters or leaves the city without the Society of Friends knowing.'

Robespierre says something else that I can't make out. I stand on tiptoes, straining to hear. Then Salvatore's voice booms out, loud and clear.

'That is all? Very well. You may have it now.'

There is a faint rustling of cloth. I abandon the glass, hoping to catch what has been given over, but I'm too late. Salvatore has already handed him something I can't see.

Robespierre's smile appears to take effort. He straightens his clothing carefully.

Something else is said that I do not hear. I go back to the glass, straining to make it out, but it seems their conversation has come to an end. When I go back to watching, Robespierre is brushing down the sleeves of his coat, something in his hand that I can't quite see. Desperately, I move to look through another crack in the ceiling, and as I do so, Robespierre turns, obscuring my view again.

He is leaving the room, tucking whatever Salvatore gave him inside his coat.

Something gleaming. Golden.

I need to see what. As the door closes behind Robespierre, I step back and my foot presses on something yielding, and suddenly the ground beneath me shifts.

'Attica!' Jemmy's voice is urgent. As I look down I see his shocked face. Then the world spins, taking him with it. My hands fly out to steady me.

'You've unhitched the mechanism!' calls Jemmy. 'Jump!'

But now the table is turning so fast I can't get control of my balance. I only have time to see him draw his sword and plunge towards the spinning cogs.

My last thought, as the ceiling shoots towards me at terrible speed, is that Jemmy is doing just the wrong thing. If he breaks the system, the twisting riser will speed out of control, smashing me against the metal plates. But just before I hit the roof, the interlocking leaves fly apart, folding into one another to reveal the room above.

For a moment I cannot make sense of the switching scenes before me. Then the orbiting world slows. I am spun up into the room above. That's when I realise. In his bid to save me,

Jemmy has inadvertently left me trapped, sabotaging any chance I have of escaping back the way I came.

But before I can think through any of this properly, the spinning table comes to a halt and I crouch dizzily in the centre, trying to stop my whirling vision.

In the turning images in front of me I clearly see Salvatore's face, furious and cruel, and four very unpleasant-looking guards.

'Mademoiselle Morgan, I thought I explained you were not welcome.' Salvatore is gritting his teeth in fury. 'At least now we know what you really are. How much did you hear?'

I hold up my hands. 'An honest mistake,' I tell Salvatore. 'A wrong turn on the way to the salon.'

Salvatore turns to his guards.

'She is a spy,' he says, making to leave. 'An English one. I have business with the other nobles. Do what you like with her. Only be certain she is dead at the end of it.'

CHAPTER THIRTY-ONE

THE GUARDS UNSHEATHE THEIR SWORDS AND CLOSE IN ON me, grinning. As I draw my knife their smiles only widen.

'A lady with a blade?' says one. 'You should have been better with a pistol from upstairs, darling. There might have been a chance of hitting one of us.'

He approaches, sword held out. And as he reaches the table where I stand, I kick a plateful of roast meat at him. He falters, and as he does I drop to my knees, grab his hair and sever the artery at the back of his neck. Blood cascades downwards as the other guards watch, open mouthed.

'If you care for your lives,' I tell them, wiping the blade on my dress, 'come no closer.'

The truth is I'm praying they don't come all at once, since Jemmy was right about my dress. It is dreadfully heavy and restrictive.

'She's all talk,' says one of the guards. 'That was a lucky blow with the knife.'

Even so, he approaches me with caution, sword outstretched.

'I should rather not ruin my evening gown,' I tell him, holding out the curved blade. 'But I will if I must.'

His face darkens and he lunges. I dodge the blade, feeling the dress rip at the hip now. Cursing, I straighten. Something in my face causes him to back away.

'Now, now, sweetheart,' he says, holding his hands up. 'There are three of us. No sense making it harder on yourself.'

Another guard comes from behind.

'She is just a woman,' he tells his fellow. 'What is the matter with you?'

He strides towards the table and lifts the edge, sending it cascading to the floor with me on it. I am thrown back in a storm of fine foods and crockery. A dish of peach syllabub splatters across my skirts.

'Have you any idea,' I say, rising to my feet while I brush fruit from the folds of my clothing, 'how hard it is to get cream out of velvet?'

The guards charge and I duck low, slicing upwards to kill the first before he reaches me. Another grabs me from behind, and I kick my legs out, further tearing my fine dress, to send him flying backwards.

I am mourning the chance of keeping the bloodstains from my lacy collar as the men regroup with surprising speed. I anticipated Salvatore's having an excellent eye for guards, but the resilience of the attack is beyond what I would have thought possible.

Holding my knife aloft, formulating a strategy to pick-off the weakest. But the calibre of my attackers is such that I can't distinguish between them. As I accept my overwhelming disadvantage, there is a shrieking of metal from the other side of the room.

As we all turn to watch, the metal rose in the floor opens, and Jemmy emerges, spinning violently atop another table, sword outstretched. Relief floods through me. With Jemmy, I have a fighting chance. My hope clouds as Jemmy staggers, the motion of the table rising seems to be giving him trouble standing.

'Attica!' Jemmy tries to regain his balance, then makes an ungainly leap from the table, landing uncertainly.

'You're too late,' I tell him, elbowing the guard behind me. 'My skirts are ruined.'

Jemmy puts a hand out in front of him, trying to dispel the dizziness. 'Just a moment, so.' He presses a palm to his forehead and squints at the guards. 'Unless there are two of you, I'm seeing double.'

'You're too dizzy to fight,' I tell him. 'Stand behind me before you get killed.'

'I'm a sailor,' he replies, shaking his head and regaining his composure. 'Well used to shifting decks. I'm well enough.'

He seems to have miraculously dispelled his unsteadiness.

'If you make haste,' I tell him, as a guard comes at us. 'My shoes can still be saved.'

The guard grabs at my sleeve, and I turn, driving my knife up to its hilt into his stomach. He folds over in pain, pulling free a handful of Flanders lace.

'Two to go!' I call, turning in horror to see Jemmy, his ridiculous duck's foot pistol in hand, pointed at my attacker and the other guard.

'Don't shoot!' I shout in alarm. 'Those things have no aim at all …' The multiple barrels of the gun fire and I dive for the floor, covering the rest of my clothing in spilled food. I sit up to my elbows, taking in the complete destruction of my outfit.

'You were right about aim,' says Jemmy cheerfully. 'Sprays everywhere.' He looks happily into the smoking barrels of his pistol, and then back to the guards, lying dead on the floor with bullet wounds to the head and neck.

'There's no seamstress who can save you now,' he adds philosophically, taking in my tattered and cream-covered ensemble.

'You could have killed me,' I say, putting out a hand so he can help me up. 'And they would have heard your silly pistol in the next room.'

'Ah.' Already we can hear the party next door grinding to a halt. Shouts. 'Best be going, then.'

'Both exits are guarded,' I point out.

Jemmy hands me on to the table he rose up on.

'After you, your Ladyship.' He hops up next to me. 'Hold on tight,' he adds. 'And try not to let the nausea get to you. I think they go faster on the way down.'

CHAPTER THIRTY-TWO

*I*N THE LABYRINTHINE SERVANTS' CORRIDORS THAT LINE THE foundations of the Louvre, Jemmy and I are quickly lost.

The dark underbelly stretches on for ever, and it seems we've walked one giant circle. And since we don't want to lead anyone to us, we can't risk lighting the wall-mounted candles, spaced at convenient intervals for servants.

'I thought pirates could navigate,' I say, aggrieved, as Jemmy holds his compass beneath the light of his tinderbox, frowning in concentration.

'I can navigate well enough,' says Jemmy. 'Something is throwing the compass off. Lot of iron somewhere near here.' He frowns.

'Concealed weaponry?' I suggest, calling to mind the earlier meeting. 'What do you think Salvatore could have given Robespierre?' I add, the puzzle of it dogging me.

'Something small, you said?'

'Small enough to fit inside a pocket. 'But the way he held it … made it look heavy.'

'Something valuable, perhaps. Poor men always carry things of worth as though they weigh a great deal.'

'Just a few inches to one side, and I would have seen it,' I sigh. 'Whatever it is, Robespierre has some plan that Salvatore is on side with. Something the nobles want done, and cannot do themselves?'

'You can hardly be sure Robespierre was telling the truth,' Jemmy points out.

'He was telling the truth about the customs gates,' I say. 'I was right about his influence there,' I add with satisfaction, thinking back to Lord Pole's scepticism. 'And he is too cautious to risk the vengeance of a man like Salvatore.' I ponder some more. 'If all Robespierre wanted was to assassinate two female abolitionists, there are dozens of men he could have used, at far less personal risk.'

'Salvatore has knowledge of the execution methods,' Jemmy says.

'So do a good handful of men who are for the revolutionary cause.' I'm shaking my head. 'There is something about the murders that doesn't fit at all. Why kill two abolitionists in such a way? Robespierre has no interest in the colonies. He is against slavery. It must be something involving Salvatore's weaponry connections, surely?'

Jemmy considers this, still peering at his compass as he begins walking. 'Robespierre has no knowledge of armaments,' he says. 'He's never fought in the army. The man doesn't even carry a pistol. You saw the kind of men who deal in arms, Attica.' Jemmy shakes his head emphatically. 'I'm a betting man, and I'd wager every coin in my purse that your man Robespierre makes sort of trick.'

'Whatever it is, Robespierre is playing a very dangerous game. A game I'm not even certain he'd want his own people knowing about.'

'An aristocrat willing to do his dirty work,' agrees Jemmy. 'Hardly likely to go down well with the revolutionary boys.'

'That's just it,' I say. 'Robespierre is a man of conscience. This runs entirely counter to his principles. He must have something big planned or he should never stoop to such measures. I need to find out what.'

I'm running through possibilities and counting them out. Incendiary devices. Explosives. None would be small enough to fit in a coat.

'Good news for your husband-to-be, in any case,' says Jemmy, squinting into the middle distance and re-checking his compass. 'If we get out of here alive, you can sail back to London on tonight's tide.'

I furrow my brow in confusion. 'Why should I do that?'

Jemmy snatches a look at me. 'Isn't your mission to discover who Salvatore is working with, then sever the connection? You need only put a knife through Monsieur Robespierre and you are complete.'

I shake my head in annoyance. 'It's also my mission to serve the English crown. This is bigger than we ever suspected. It's a chance to find out what La Société des Amis' plans are. Assassinating Robespierre would waste our advantage.'

'You're certain it isn't that you cannot bring yourself to kill Monsieur Robespierre and return home?'

'I—'

Jemmy comes to a halt, interrupting me. 'We've found our iron,' he says, pointing towards a door hanging slightly ajar.

To my disappointment, it's not a cache of secret weapons, only a large neglected kitchen, hung with the largest array of cast-iron pots, pans, cauldrons and hanging tongs I have ever seen.

'Salvatore must know we're down here by now,' says Jemmy. 'Any ideas on which direction leads out?'

'Kitchens are usually close to a servants' entrance,' I say. 'Though that might also be a sound place for Salvatore to deploy his guards without alerting anyone upstairs.'

On cue we hear muttered voices from a corridor beyond. They don't sound friendly. There's a glimmer of light, as though candles are headed this way.

'This way,' hisses Jemmy, abandoning his compass. 'Press back against the wall.'

'You seem very certain. Pirate instinct?'

'Sometimes a man must navigate by his wits,' agrees Jemmy. 'But if those men have come from above stairs, we need only wait until they pass and follow the candles back the way they came.'

He points to a glow of light, where the men have used wall candles. Sometimes, Jemmy's self-satisfaction can be very tiresome.

We follow the little row of flames, and just as Jemmy predicted, it isn't long before we reach a narrow staircase. What he didn't account for, however, was reinforcements. A second pack of guards appears at the top of the steps.

'Double back!' I tell Jemmy. We run in the other direction.

'There must be more than one way out,' pants Jemmy. 'This place is enormous.'

'At least six exits on ground level,' I tell him, breathing hard. 'But we've missed all of them so far. And there are guards coming from both directions.'

We hear shouts up ahead and come to a halt. Voices from the other direction confirm we are surrounded, trapped underground with bloodthirsty men to either side of us. I pull out my knife. Jemmy draws a sword in one hand and a very plain-looking pistol in the other.

'No duck's foot pistol?'

'I listen to you on occasion, to be sure,' he says, noticing me staring at it. 'This one is for when I need to aim true.'

'Reassuring to know we're really in danger.'

He doesn't answer, only turns with his back to me and faces the approaching guards.

Before they appear, however, there's a movement in the shadows. A dark figure, moving in a doorway.

I can't work out how a guard could have got ahead of us, but this doesn't look good.

'Jemmy,' I whisper, directing my thumb to the movement and drawing my knife. He nods, standing back to let me lunge for it, blade high.

But as I bring the knife down, a familiar face rises out of the gloom, the whites of the eyes flashing in candlelight.

'Centime?' I lower my blade just in time.

In reply she raises a finger to her lips, then beckons. Now I can see her better, I realise she is no longer in her toga, but wearing the same dress she arrived at the party in. I can't work out how she might have got down here to find us, and can only assume it to be another trick of Salvatore's.

'There's another way out, back here, hidden,' she whispers. 'Follow me.'

CHAPTER THIRTY-THREE

I STARE AT CENTIME, WONDERING HOW SHE GOT DOWN HERE unaccompanied – and whether she can be trusted.

'How did you know we were down here?' I demand.

'I overheard Salvatore,' she says. 'He's covered all the escape routes. I … I didn't want you dead.' Her eyes sweep across my face and then down again. I still can't decide if she's trying to trick us.

Centime sees my hesitation. 'There's a secret way out,' she says. 'An exit he doesn't know about.'

'How do you know?' I ask.

'I used to work here,' says Centime. 'A long time ago, as a younger girl,' she adds, swallowing. I get the impression Centime's employment beneath the palace was more than just ferrying plates and washing dishes.

I glance back at Jemmy, who is staring into the shadows.

'Is she who I think she is?' he manages finally, staring at Centime.

'She knows a way out.' This at least I believe.

'That is Salvatore's courtesan?' he whispers. 'Why do you think we can trust her?'

'Because you have no choice,' says Centime. 'There are armed guards in either direction. You could never overwhelm them, just one man and a woman.'

'I wouldn't be so certain of that,' says Jemmy, adjusting his sword.

Footsteps are coming closer now. It sounds like there are a lot of them.

'Why should you want to help us?' I ask.

Centime takes a breath. 'Is it true what you said before?' she asks. 'You could save me? From him?'

'Yes.'

She looks hard into my eyes.

'I give you my word,' I tell her. 'You will be taken to England. To safety.'

'Then we have an agreement.'

Something tells me she is not telling us everything, but she is right about one thing: we have limited options.

'Show us the way out,' I say, 'and I will keep my promise.'

Centime leads the way, and Jemmy and I follow a little distance behind.

'Do you know what you're doing, helping that girl?' whispers Jemmy, pulling me by the arm so we fall back far enough that Centime can't hear us.

'She knows something about La Société des Amis and Robespierre's plans,' I say with certainty. 'We just need to persuade her to tell us.'

'That girl is courtesan to the deadliest arms dealer in Paris. In case you had forgotten, there has been a lock-down on customs gates, and Robespierre has infiltrated the guard.'

'I thought you liked a challenge.'

Jemmy makes another sidelong glance at Centime, her dark hair bobbing in front.

'Challenges I like,' he whispers. 'Impossibilities, less so. Unnecessary danger to the boys, not at all.'

'We have saved far riskier victims,' I say. 'What have you against Centime?' Privately, though, I am calculating the delay to my return to London. Rescuing Centime will cost a full day at least. But I cannot let the chance to uncover La Société des Amis slip through my hands. Atherton will understand if I miss the pre-wedding dinner. I'm sure of it.

Jemmy's mouth twists. 'I think you are lured by her beauty, Attica. I know girls like her. Centime has learned to live as a kept woman. You cannot simply take her from that life and expect her to adapt. She isn't like you. Better to let her vanish into the streets and fend for herself. She's a gutter rat. A survivor. Trust me. It takes one to know one.'

I stand, slightly agog. 'You'd leave her to fate?'

'I don't think she's telling us the truth. And if she's truly run away from Salvatore, she'll be looking for another protector. Do you really think she can simply slip into polite English society without a murmur? She was raised in a Paris brothel, Attica, and her dark skin will mark her out wherever she goes.'

'That doesn't matter to me.'

'It might not matter to *you,* but it matters to everyone else in your country.'

I frown, trying to choose the right words.

'There is more to Centime than meets the eye,' I tell him. 'She may have been raised to be the property of a brothel owner, but there is a strength to her, something deserving of our help. All I ask is for you to trust me.'

Jemmy sighs deeply. 'I was afraid you would say that. I do trust you, Attica.'

He makes one final glance at Centime, who has sensed how far we have drawn back and slows.

'I just don't trust her,' he says, so quietly I can barely hear him.

CHAPTER THIRTY-FOUR

Centime follows Jemmy and me silently as we reach the base of the hill. This is where the warrens of Parisian streets come to an end and the grassy fields of industry begin. At the summit are a number of fat-bottomed little windmills, their sails turning in the breeze.

'Montmartre?' Centime lowers her voice.

'I told you I would put you safe,' I explain. 'There are women rioting in the city, press-ganging any women they find into the march. We can't risk your getting swept along in it.'

I don't add that Salvatore has spies everywhere, and Centime is very conspicuous. I put a hand on her arm, trying to reassure her. 'Tomorrow the customs gates will be open,' I say. 'There is one just past Montmartre which is less guarded than the rest. We can smuggle you through, and from there on to a boat bound for England. Until then, we must hide you and hide you well.'

'People here are desperate,' she says, her eyes scanning the other structures of Paris's industrial outskirts.

On one side of the hill are urine-filled tanning pits; the other side is pocked with the smoking beehive-ovens of charcoal burners. These are trades too noxious to be allowed in the city.

Centime looks again at the whirling sails. 'Now there is so little flour to grind, those windmills are low brothels,' she says.

'That's why it's so safe,' I assure her. 'These people are for the common cause, and detest aristocrats like Salvatore. Their loyalty is easily bought and I pay a good purse.'

'You have hidden people here before?'

'A number of times.'

Jemmy glances sharply at me because we have only used this safe-house once. And the revolutionary youth we secreted was already known to the young prostitutes of the mills.

'Let's climb the hill,' I say. 'I have an understanding with one of the brothel-keepers. She won't betray us.'

I catch Centime's expression, taking in the sparse summit, the stinking refuse trench that runs carelessly down the hillside, the tanning fumes that catch in the back of the throat. 'It's only one night,' I remind her.

Centime chews her lip. 'Even if we survive the night, we shall never get through the gate,' she says. 'Since the Bastille fell the guard has doubled.'

'Not on the Montmartre gate,' I assure her. 'Trust me. It is open only to millworkers and the guard leaves it alone. No one wants to slow wheat coming into the city when people starve.'

Centime accepts this, looking up at the windmills. 'Which shall we be hiding inside?'

'Let's climb the hill first. We can come to particulars later.'

We take the well-trodden path up the hill, populated by a thin stream of traffic in either direction: farmers taking their sacks of grain to be milled; bakers bringing flour to be baked. With bread in such short supply, there is a suspicious atmosphere. The dirt track and surrounding hedgerow are dusted white, like a snow that will not settle. A nutty smell of ground wheat and hot tallow from the windmill axles fills the air.

We reach a trio of plank-clad mills on the crest of the hill, their sails creaking loudly in the wind. I approach the middle one and knock loudly on the door, since the grinding stone is deafening. A woman answers, dressed in the usual garb of Parisian low-class prostitutes: naked to her waist with a ragged selection of skirts on her lower half.

Her weary face jolts with something close to surprise, then avarice settles at the corners of her eyes. She all but rubs her hands with the expectation of profit, eyeing Centime's black skin and expensive dress.

'Mademoiselle Morgan,' she says, dipping her head in greeting.

I hold up a fat purse of coins. 'Double your usual sum,' I say briskly, before she can begin bartering, 'and we shall only stay until morning, so that is half the time. You may have your girls back up in the hayloft by dawn.'

The sight of the coins sees any negotiation she was planning die on the brothel-keeper's lips. She turns, beckoning us to follow. We move inside the dark interior, which smells of flour and hot grease from the turning parts.

Inside are three semi-dressed girls sat on wooden stools, looking bored. They barely glance at us, as the brothel-keeper shows us to a ladder leading to the back of the windmill. Behind the heavy sacks of grain is a hidden ladder leading to a hayloft. We ascend to a barn-like room, with wide planks letting the light and air through. The creaking windmill sail is loud inside, and we can see the oily mechanism turning on the far wall.

'I'll tell the girls not to come up,' says the owner. 'You'll not be troubled up here.'

She pauses at the opening, her eyes swinging back and forth between us all.

'Is this to do with the women causing trouble in the city?' she asks, staring full at Centime now. 'You are part of it?'

I shake my head.

'Shame,' she opines. 'Good luck to 'em, I say. About time the girls stood up for themselves.' She turns on her heel. 'I'll be keeping out of their way,' she adds, without a hint of acknowledgement to her own hypocrisy. She exits unceremoniously.

Around the dusty plank floor, straw has been arranged in mounds as makeshift beds. Centime is staring at one and it occurs to me she might have once worked in a place like this.

Jemmy catches my expression and makes for the ladder down.

'I'll find us a little bread and meat,' he says. 'Maybe some wine.'

'We're going to need provisions for the gate,' I tell him, reaching to my hip and tossing him a pouch of gold. 'A large sack that has been patched.'

He nods and descends, but before he is fully out of view, he catches my eye and mouths something. I don't quite hear the words, but it looks like.

Have a care.

Jemmy still doesn't think Centime can be trusted.

CHAPTER THIRTY-FIVE

*C*ENTIME HAS SUNK TO THE FLOOR OF THE HAYLOFT, AND IS raising and dropping handfuls of straw.

'If we are to sleep here, we should check for rat nests,' she says, not looking at me. 'I'll do yours if you like.'

In answer I kneel beside her and lay a hand on her arm.

'I am sorry,' I say, 'to bring you back to a place like this. You must have spent your whole life trying to get out.'

Centime goes back to lifting and dropping straw, throwing handfuls back on to the dusty planks.

'I never knew much else,' she says. 'I was nine when I came to Paris. Traders had brought my mother to sell to a brothel. She died on the crossing. When they arrived empty-handed, the brothel-keeper took me instead.'

'It was Salvatore who took you from that place?' I ask, wondering what the arrangement was.

She correctly reads my mistrust. A lifetime of learning cues, I suppose.

'I thought I loved him once,' she says. 'Before I knew what he was. He offered me a way out and I thought …' She looks at the floor again. 'It doesn't matter,' she says. 'There it is.

Now you know. I am even more wretched than you imagined. I was fool enough to give my heart to a worse villain than any of the rough comers I had before.'

'Do you love him still?'

She turns to me. 'Why should you care?'

I opt for honesty. 'Salvatore made schemes with a lawyer named Robespierre,' I say. 'I know you must have heard much of what they discussed.'

She swallows, shakes her head, a bitter smile on her face.

'I cannot tell you,' she says. 'He will kill me.'

'He will kill you anyway, if he finds you.'

She shakes her head. 'Disloyalty,' she says. 'That is what he hates the most. If he catches me, he may be kind and forgive. But that would never be if he discovered I had told secrets. You don't know what he is capable of. That is why this revolution is nothing but a dream,' she adds bitterly. 'The nobles will crush the common people as they always have. They do dreadful things to anyone who stands in their way.'

'Your people are starving,' I say quietly. 'The aristocrats are afraid, because their time is ending. I do not believe you are as hopeless as you pretend.'

She shakes her head and tears spill.

'Not with men like him,' she says, her voice catching. 'There is no sanctuary for me. You understand in part, I think.' Her grey-blue eyes are on mine. 'Salvatore said you are known in the bars on the Marais,' she says quietly. 'Are women your affliction, or merely a pastime?'

'That depends on the woman.'

She smiles slightly, then looks at her hands. 'So you may be married one day, perhaps happy.'

'I am due to wed soon.'

She considers this sadly. 'For myself the poison runs too deep. It is something I can never be free of. So you see, you cannot save me, Attica Morgan. But perhaps you can make me happy for a time.' Her eyes are back on mine now.

She moves a hand to the top of her dress, which she slides down at the shoulder, flinching as the branded flesh is revealed, and looks at me in part challenge, part something else.

Tentatively, I step forwards, then run my thumb slowly across her raised scar. A fleur-de-lis – the mark of the crown – imprinted on thieves and whores.

'We were caught on the dockside, soliciting men,' she says, holding my gaze. 'Uusually they turn a blind eye, but that day we were unlucky. It was me and another girl that had been sent out because the house was not busy enough.'

I don't ask how she felt, because I can imagine. From the plantation I remember the screams of people being branded, the terrible smell of burning flesh.

'I will always be a low thing now,' she adds in a whisper, looking at the lump of knotted flesh.

'Salvatore could have bought any courtesan he wanted,' I tell her. 'And yet he chose you. A girl from a street brothel in Paris. A place where three hundred men a day take a ticket to stand in line. Why do you think that is?'

Her lips twitch but she doesn't answer. Her eyes flick uncertainly to my hand on her branded shoulder.

'Because he is weak,' I tell her. 'For all his cruelty it is just a gilded shell that will break with the smallest tap. He thinks you vulnerable – a foil to make him look strong. But he underestimates you.'

There is something unreadable in her eyes.

'How could you know that?' she asks finally.

'People underestimate me too.'

It is the wrong thing to say. Her face closes down instantly. 'We are not the same,' she says. 'You are a noble and can do as you please. Do not pretend to understand me, Mademoiselle Morgan. You understand nothing.'

Her hand is at the top of her dress, pulling it back up over the scar, retracting the unspoken invitation.

'I understand if you live this life with him, dead inside, you might as well be dead,' I say softly. 'I understand some things are worth a little courage.' I move closer. Put a hand on her arm.

I'm wondering how to stop her pulling away when unexpectedly she kisses me. It's halting, uncertain, and before I have time to respond she draws away, fingers at her lips, head shaking sadly.

I take her wrist and pull her back towards me.

'You have nothing to lose, Centime,' I tell her, as her eyes leap across my face. 'Why don't you find out what it is like, when the show is real?'

CHAPTER THIRTY-SIX

*O*UTSIDE THE HÔTEL DE VILLE, THE WOMEN ARE BLEARY-eyed. Several have slept in the dirt. Others have not slept at all. Their petition has fallen on deaf ears, and the doors of the City Hall are firmly locked against them.

Ovette sent a message to Robespierre. *The fight has gone out of it. The women despair.*

And now something has happened under cover of night. Several barrels of wine have been dotted amongst the women, apparently without them noticing. As dawn breaks the round shapes become clear.

A thin-legged woman with a grossly bulbous stomach rises unsteadily to her feet. She is known as Drunk Greta, and spends her days in an inebriated slumber, drool-slick chin bobbing on her chest, or pissing where she shouldn't with the exasperated market women steering her to gutters. At night she vanishes to the streets famed for providing the cheapest fucks in Paris, where elderly women clutch at men in the dark, trying to drag them into alleys.

The fish-sellers are understanding, kindly even, of her malodorous presence, since many remember Greta from happier times. Besides, she's obviously dying. In recent months her stomach has popped outwards in a disturbingly jelly-like mass that has nothing to do with food, and the whites of her eyes have turned yellow.

Greta is first to approach a mysterious barrel, seizing hold of a flapping piece of paper tacked to it with a little nail. She rips it free, frowns at it, and hands it disinterestedly to Ovette.

'No bunghole,' says Greta, returning her full attention the barrel. 'Anyone got a hammer?'

'We don't know why it is here,' says a scrawny woman with a baby at her breast, sounding nervous. 'Could be a trick to have us break the law. Get us all put in prison.'

Murmurs of agreement ripple around the group. But Ovette, who has been reading silently, now speaks.

'This paper says the wine is for us,' she says. 'A token of appreciation, is what it says. "To the lion-hearted woman of Faubourg Saint-Antoine",' she adds, grinning wide enough to reveal her missing back teeth. She looks down. "If you find no bread in Paris," she continues, her finger following the words as she reads, "go to the baker and the baker's wife."

She looks all around at the women, wondering at the riddle of it. Greta, meanwhile, has found a heavy stone and is smashing it with dogged concentration into the barrelhead.

'Who is the baker and the baker's wife?' asks Ovette.

'It is the King and Queen, you dunce,' says another waking woman, rubbing the sore side of her face that has rested on stony ground. 'The baker and the baker's wife. It is said all over the city. They are the ones with the bread.'

There is a pause as the women absorb the statement. Then the silence is blasted by Greta's renewed attempts on the wine barrel, this time successful. The stone splinters through the wood, sending up a single jet of red wine.

'Breakfast!' shouts Greta with a grin, angling the barrel so cups might be filled.

A cheer breaks out.

As the liquid hits their stomachs, the fish-sellers are seized with something like euphoria. Suddenly it seems possible. Simple even. They will go to the King, demand to be fed. What could be fairer than that?

The only problem is not a single one knows how to go about it.

'We should ring the bell,' suggests Ovette. 'Sound the tocsin. Get all the market women in Paris with us!'

Eyes slide to Ovette's stained face and away again. No one is ready to take her suggestions, despite Robespierre's good word. Not to mention, no one is brave enough to enter the church and risk a beating from the priest.

The women fall to talking amongst themselves, shouldering Ovette out.

Greta is lurching towards them, slurping wine, and Ovette turns on her angrily.

'I have worked here alongside you,' she says, failing to keep the petulance from her voice. 'I do the same work as you, live in the same squalor.'

'Ah,' says Greta, casting her yellow gaze over Ovette in vague recognition, 'but you're not the same, are you? We're a family.' She points to several thick-armed women. 'I'd die for those girls there if I had to. And they for me. That's the part you don't understand.'

Ovette says nothing. She doesn't believe Greta. It sounds more like drunken chatter.

Greta shakes her head. 'You bourgeoisie are cold. Put money before people. That's why you are not liked. We see you, labouring for your own coins for your own self. When did you last bring food to a new mother? Or help sew a winding sheet for a dead child?'

Ovette cannot answer. She never has.

'I didn't think it was my business,' she replies finally, struggling to define why she excused herself from these community endeavours, and feeling ashamed. 'I didn't think the women would accept my presence.'

'It is all our business,' replies Greta evenly. 'And no woman in the Faubourg ever refuses help.'

'If you are truly family,' says Ovette, the birthmark on her face flushing deeper, 'then prove it. Fight for them. Ring the bell.'

Greta's head turns towards the nearest church, only half a street away. She drains her tankard.

'Very well.' She shrugs with the ease of a drunk who has had her first drink. 'I'll go ring the bell,' she says, loud enough for the market women to hear.

There is a murmur of hope from the group. They can see how Greta might terrify the priest into compliance with her strange swaying belly and general stink. 'I only need two big girls with me,' she adds, pointing to the fishermen's wives responsible for hauling in the nets. A couple of thick-armed women stand.

'This way, then,' says Greta, with the air of a military general. 'Follow me.'

A surge of excitement ripples through the marketplace as the bell-ringing contingent departs. Women begin talking earnestly to older children, arranging for them to guard pitches, make sales if necessary. Messages are to be relayed. But at the heart of it, no one is yet entirely sure. It is like the first drifts of smoke, before you know how quickly a fire may catch.

There is a sound of breaking glass and a shout from the church. Then Drunk Greta emerges, grinning, with a jug of Communion wine clutched to her protruding stomach. The priest is giving chase, but not very convincingly.

Then they hear the bell. A smile breaks out on every face.

The big-armed women emerge from the church, victorious. Greta reaches the market woman and the wine is passed around. The priest has prudently made himself scarce.

It is the first rule to be broken, but the effect on the women is pronounced. A drunken mirage of possibilities unfolds, in which they have the power to demand what is fair.

'To the baker!' roars the previously timid woman, with the unmoving baby strapped to her. 'And the baker's wife!'

The chant is taken up and the mood is joyous. It is all so simple, how could the men not have seen it? The King loves his people. All they need do is knock on his door. He will provide them with bread, and that will be that.

Greta has an idea.

'The Marquis de Lafayette,' she tells Ovette. 'He hates the Queen, does he not?'

Ovette nods slowly. 'She threw him out of court for wearing the wrong coat.'

Marie Antoinette's reasons for disliking the Marquis have filtered down to the masses in Lafayette's favour. If *she* doesn't like him, the people think, then *we* do.

'We should ask Lafayette to lead us,' says Greta. 'And if he doesn't, we'll string him up.'

CHAPTER THIRTY-SEVEN

*R*OBESPIERRE SITS IN A BUMPING CARRIAGE, CRUSHED IN next to Georges Danton's large frame on the hard wooden seat.

'This riot of women is your doing, Max. You've been riling them up for months.'

'I cannot take credit,' replies Robespierre. 'The King and Queen's spectacular indifference to their own starving people must take that honour. And it is not a riot,' he adds. 'They protest against injustice.'

'Even so,' rumbles Danton, 'the thing is well played. Those women ...' He squints at the raging scrawny people. 'I really do believe they might run her through. *Mon Dieu.*' He wipes his forehead with a handkerchief. 'I have hardly seen men on the battlefield look more bloodthirsty. I should not like to be in Her Majesty's silken shoes.' He barks a short laugh.

'They believe the Queen responsible for starving their children,' says Robespierre. 'One can hardly blame their anger. I tell them there is virtue in poverty. They seem to like it.'

'So you made certain this Pimpernel will not interfere with our business at Versailles?' Georges asks. 'He is caught?'

'Not yet,' says Robespierre. 'But the thing is imminent.'

He looks out of the window.

'Don't be coy with me, Max,' says Danton. 'I can see you're dying to tell me your cleverness. Let's have out with it, then.'

Robespierre withdraws from the window and turns to his friend. 'Ciphers, puzzles, problems of wit and logic. I have always enjoyed them. And then, the strangest thing of all. The tokens. A code I could not break.'

He pauses for effect.

'So you unravelled the code?' Danton slaps his back. 'By God, I knew you would! You always were a clever fellow.'

Robespierre frowns at the interruption.

'I did not break the code in the way you might imagine,' admits Robespierre. 'I looked at the problem from another direction. Perhaps you were correct and the tokens tell me nothing. Pah. So then what about the man himself? What if I regard *him* as the code?'

'Go on.'

'A code must be poked and pushed and turned about to make it reveal itself. And so I determined to study the people the Pimpernel aids, looking for a pattern.' Robespierre's fingers move lightly in the air, as though conducting an unseen orchestra. He closes his eyes for a moment, a smile on his lips. 'It was an enjoyable practice,' he says. 'Something I had not done before. I had what a religious man might call an epiphany, Danton. I did not need to find the man. I only needed to find the *person* who would draw the Pimpernel out. His favourite prey, if you will.' He manages a thin smile.

'Oh ho, so that is why you were making terms with the arms dealer. Put two rats in a box and they will eat each other, is that not how it is? Paris rats, at least,' adds Danton.

Robespierre smiles thinly, but makes no reply.

'We'll make a politician of you yet,' says Danton.

Robespierre bows slightly, accepting the compliment.

'It is a kind of politics, isn't it?' he says thoughtfully. 'In any case, I broke the code. Slavery was the connection. But he has another weakness I had not previously considered.'

Danton's eyes have glazed over. 'So long as he cannot bother our plans.'

'Since I have discovered his code,' says Robespierre, 'I was able to bait the hook. He will soon try to leave Paris. When he does, he shall be caught.'

'That is why you were so adamant about keeping the customs gates manned?'

Robespierre smiles widely. It is such an unusual expression that Danton draws back, a little disturbed.

'The Pimpernel has taken the bait. Now all that remains is to reel him in.'

CHAPTER THIRTY-EIGHT

CENTIME AND I LIE ON THE STRAW, HER ARM DRAPED ACROSS my naked belly. She is watching my face.

'There are stories,' she tells me, dark eyes gliding to mine, 'of an Englishman. A rescuer, who goes by a flower symbol. The token you gave me, at the weapons fayre … It is you, isn't it?' she asks. 'You get people out of France.'

'What makes you say it?'

'Just a feeling.' Her mouth twists. 'The lawyer, Robespierre. He wants to find out who you are. I heard him talking about you with Salvatore.'

I turn in the straw. 'What was said?'

She frowns. 'Only that Robespierre wanted Salvatore to tell him about a slave dock that burned down in Lisbon. He thought the Pimpernel was involved somehow.'

My stomach turns. Robespierre knows far more than I thought. I try to deduce what this could mean for Robespierre's using Salvatore but the answer eludes me.

'He has big plans, though, the lawyer,' says Centime. 'Salvatore told me so. He said the lawyer had a crazed idea that would soon get him killed. That is why he wanted the key.'

I sit up a little, as things fit together. Salvatore passing something hard and gleaming to Robespierre. The lawyer tucking it in his coat.

'What does it unlock?' I try to keep my tone casual, but something in Centime's face tells me she sees through it.

'Oh, something at the palace, I believe,' she says disinterestedly. 'As a commoner, Robespierre is permitted in a few areas with the other politicians. He wanted access to the Princes' Court where the soldiers enter to guard the royals. Salvatore was in the army so it was simple for him to get a key.'

'Why should Salvatore help Robespierre break into that part of Versailles?'

'I don't know.' She shakes her head slowly. 'Only that Salvatore thought it was in his interests, whatever Robespierre was planning.'

I try to think this through, but it's like a snake with a tail I can't catch.

What shared interest could Robespierre and Salvatore possibly have?

The two men are as diametrically opposed on every principle as it is possible to be. Salvatore is surely capable of buying anything he likes and putting his empire of arms traders to any dark work he would like done. He has military connections, friends in high places. It is unimaginable that a middling lawyer from Paris would have anything Salvatore wants. Yet somehow, Robespierre convinced Salvatore to commit murder.

How? Why?

Something snags in my mind, then slips away again.

I cannot connect the facts and, as usual, when faced with problems beyond my reckoning, I'm caught by a mad desire to be with Atherton. The only person who understands me properly. With whom I can discuss things rationally. I miss him, I realise. Dreadfully. When this last mission is over I shall give it all up and be a proper wife to him, I decide.

Something in Centime's face changes, as if she knows what I'm thinking.

She shifts to look at me. 'Has Salvatore underestimated Robespierre?' she asks.

'I don't know,' I answer truthfully. 'Probably.'

Something is occurring to me. Why didn't it strike me sooner that Robespierre's ambitions would go far beyond a few assassinations? And there is trouble now in the city, isn't there? The women revolt and petition the town hall. Are these things connected?

'The end justifies the means,' I say aloud, thinking of Robespierre's aims and feeling distinctly uneasy.

Centime reaches across the makeshift bed and, to my extreme discomfort, lifts my corsetry, loaded with its compliment of concealed weaponry.

'Heavy,' she says, weighing it with a grin. 'What have we here?'

She is examining the amber locket hanging around my neck now.

'Don't touch that!' I snap, closing it in my fist. Her eyes follow me wonderingly.

'Whatever can you be hiding?' She rests her chin on her hand, not the least bit perturbed by my outburst. 'I have guessed your identity now,' she points out. 'You may as well tell me everything.'

I relent slightly, not least because I don't want her harming herself with equipment she doesn't understand.

'The locket has poison inside,' I say.

Her eyes widen. 'No! Not really. You would poison someone?'

'If I had to,' I reply. 'But the poison is not for assassination. It is something passed out to spies who work in perilous circumstances. Pills to offer a quick death with no risk of telling secrets.'

It takes Centime a full second to realise what I mean. Her eyes widen, caught between horror and awe.

'You are really the one they're all looking for, aren't you?' she whispers, shaking her head in wonder and reaching out a hand in the same way one might pet a dangerous dog. She glances again at the locket. 'Would you ever do it?' she asks. 'Poison yourself, I mean.'

'If I thought I was likely to endanger others under torture,' I say, 'or was held under threat of terrible execution and could not escape. So no,' I conclude. 'Never. But my uncle wanted me to have it.'

Now Centime's face creases in a strange expression of disbelief. Finally she laughs out loud.

'Now I know you tease me,' she decides, moving back on to the bed and smiling a little as she gazes into my eyes. 'Tease me some more.'

CHAPTER THIRTY-NINE

THE DAWN SUN HAS NOW FULLY RISEN IN THE HAYLOFT.

There's a noise from the ladder and I see Jemmy's dark hair emerge, followed by the rest of his black-clad form.

'I got the sacks as you asked ...' he begins, then pauses, taking in Centime's state of undress, our proximity to one another on the straw bed. 'Don't let me interrupt,' he says, shaking his head as he climbs fully to the upper level, then heads to the little makeshift balcony where the huge windmill cogs grind.

Pushing myself up, I follow him, motioning to Centime she should stay inside.

I find Jemmy stood picking at his nails while staring moodily out on to the city rooftops.

'What is it?' I demand. 'You do not approve?'

He turns to look at me, seeming distracted. 'To find you in bed with that girl?' Jemmy shakes his head again. 'I wouldn't have imagined anything less of you, Attica. Did she tell you everything?'

I hesitate, trying to understand his mood. 'Robespierre was given a key by Salvatore,' I say, speaking fast and low. 'It opens the gate to the Princes' Court at Versailles.'

Jemmy absorbs this. 'Does Centime know who you are now?'

'Yes,' I admit, surprised at his discerning it.

Jemmy turns on me, eyes flashing. 'I knew it!' he says furiously. 'You've put us both in danger!'

I hold up my hands, placating. 'All is well,' I say. 'As soon as she is put safely on the boat, there is no more risk.'

'And until then? You want me to ferry around Salvatore's courtesan when there's a price on her head?'

'Can you think of an alternative?' I demand.

For a moment the other possibility hovers above us. The choice of sensible men like Lord Pole, men who live to fight another day. The world where we leave Centime to her fate, because her death will ensure our safety just as certainly as her escape, but with less risk to Jemmy and me.

Jemmy hesitates. Then sticks both hands into the pockets of his coat. 'Why don't you just be honest, at least with yourself?'

'I have no idea what you are talking about.'

Jemmy glances at me, frowning. Then he heaves a huge sigh.

'It is your wedding on Monday.'

'Yes. I will return with Centime on the ship tomorrow,' I say, assuming he thinks I do not leave sufficient time. 'Be married the next day.'

'For a love-struck bride, you are leaving things a little close, don't you think?'

'No. I think it rather efficient. The wedding will be a simple affair in the family chapel.' I am wondering if he still expects me to engage in some lengthy dressing or trousseau ritual.

'That isn't what I meant.' Jemmy rakes his hands through his dark hair. 'You have discovered that Robespierre is working with Salvatore. Your mission is complete. Then you appoint yourself the vital task of getting information from Centime. So now you have it. Robespierre has obtained a key to the Princes' Court at Versailles. Salvatore's business with him is done. Go home. Be married.'

'I must get Centime to safety. It is important I see the thing done personally.'

Jemmy only shakes his head. 'You do not want to finish this mission, Attica. It is clear to me, if not to you.'

'How useful to have you on hand to tell me what I feel and think,' I reply drily.

He scuffs his foot on the dusty floor, sending a little straw fluttering out of the hayloft and to the ground below.

'For all your talk of patriotism, I think the injustice of the mission sticks in your throat. Not to mention,' he continues, 'with your mission complete, you must return and be an English wife.'

'I will return and be married in any case,' I tell him crossly. 'How can you doubt it?'

'Just a feeling,' he says maddeningly, adding, 'You wouldn't have accepted the assignment if you truly had no reservations.'

'I accepted the mission *before* Atherton proposed.'

'Oh, so he actually proposed, now? Because from what you told me it sounded like more of a business arrangement.'

I shrug. 'I am not a person for grand declarations of love. Atherton knows that.'

'Are you not? In my experience, woman *say* they do not want grand declarations of love, then make you live to regret it for ever when you give them a tin ring and a yard of ale in the dockside tavern.'

'You're confusing me with one of your mad harlots.'

'All I mean to say is in your heart you want to stay an adventurer,' says Jemmy. He inclines his head towards the hayloft. 'That girl in there proves it. You delay by dragging her over the border.'

'Why should I endanger her life unnecessarily?' I am tight-lipped with indignation.

'It's your own life you're seeking to save. But Attica, if you do not wish to wed there are better ways of doing so than using this poor girl. Not to mention,' he lowers his voice and glances in the direction of Centime's room, 'has it occurred to you, she might be working with Robespierre?'

'Now you are ridiculous.' I sigh, remembering Centime's fragility. 'I know something of this girl, Jemmy; you misjudge her. She deserves our help.'

Jemmy looks unconvinced. 'She is lovely to look at, and I've no doubt her trade gives her certain skills. Let us see if she is willing to give up Salvatore's plan,' he says, a cynical set to his features. 'But if you ask me, Attica, you're just another gull to her. When she realises you can't offer her all she wants, she won't take it well.'

'And what does she want?'

'I warned you already. A girl like that always looks for a protector. Which isn't you. Unless you're planning on throwing over the love of your life for our little Centime now?'

'If I didn't know you better, Jemmy Avery, I'd think you jealous.'

Jemmy walks away, muttering something I don't quite hear. But it *might* have been: 'If I didn't know myself better, so would I.'

As Jemmy returns to the windmill interior I stay looking out, thinking through his words. It isn't true, of course. I need to stay because the mission is not completed. I am turning over how best to achieve this when I see a cloud of dust at the base of the hill. For a few moments I can't quite discern what it is. A large wagon, perhaps, or a spilled bag of flour. Then I put the shapes together.

Riders on horseback, galloping much too fast up the hill. From this distance it's hard to be certain, but they look to be in livery. The colours of Salvatore's house.

How did they find us so quickly?

The coiling uncertainty in the pit of my stomach hits a sudden jarring reality.

The slave dock in Lisbon. Robespierre's questioning Salvatore.

I close my eyes, unable to bear how wrong I had it all. Now it makes sense, I cannot believe I didn't deduce it before.

I almost laugh out loud at my stupidity. All Robespierre needed to do was persuade Salvatore to commit a murder. But it was never about those abolitionist women. Their murders were only to bring Salvatore to the attention of the Pimpernel. I had never been able to understand why Robespierre would use Salvatore of all people, when there are a dozen other assassins with revolutionary zeal.

But of course, Salvatore goes everywhere with his courtesan.

Centime.

Somehow, Robespierre knew enough of me to understand I should never be able to resist bringing her to safety. The liaison with Salvatore, the murder, all of it was to bring her to my attention. And it worked perfectly.

Centime was bait. And I fell for her hook, line and sinker.

CHAPTER FORTY

*R*OBESPIERRE STEPS DOWN FROM THE CARRIAGE ON TO the suspiciously clean road.

'You like it, eh, Max?' asks Danton. 'No shit, no rotting rubbish. They have it good in Versailles. This is the back way in,' he adds. 'No hoards of nobles to spy on us.'

'Very clever,' agrees Robespierre. 'I didn't know your geography of the palace was so adept.' There is the slightest hint of criticism, Danton perceives.

'Ah, well.' Danton adjusts the waistcoat over his protruding belly. 'Know your enemy.' He waves a thick-fingered hand. 'This way.'

He leads Robespierre to a gate, on which a single bored servant lounges. Danton pays him a stack of coins, which is pocketed with a nod of thanks. Without waiting to be asked, Danton strides past, on to a well-swept pathway between sapling trees.

'These are young,' says Robespierre, lifting the leaf of a tender sapling.

'The Queen plants them,' says Danton. 'Wants to make this back part her own private kingdom.'

Robespierre lets the leaf drop with no reply, but something behind his round glasses suggests he is noting Danton's knowledge.

'This way,' says the large lawyer, leading Robespierre through a tiny gate – the kind of rustic wooden thing one might find deep in the countryside.

Just for a moment, Robespierre thinks he is in a land of his own imagination. Something he has dreamed of countless times. A well-kept hamlet, with clean thatched cottages, and neatly tended vegetables. A smart little waterwheel turns in a babbling brook of sparkling water winding along the outskirts. There are no filthy beggars, no desperate mothers with scraps of babies wrapped at their bony chests. All is clean, tidy, wholesome.

Robespierre closes his eyes, and when he opens them again, tears cloud his vision. This is his pure society, his new France.

'What place is this?' he whispers to Danton, as they troop through the little village. 'Is it part of the town of Versailles?'

Danton shakes his large head disparagingly.

'This is the Queen's hamlet, Max. A little toy-land for her to play at being a peasant.'

Robespierre has heard of the Queen's hamlet, of course. Most Parisians have. The pamphlets run hot with the scorn of it – Marie Antoinette starving her citizens so she might build a strange little country idyll and play at being a farm girl. Most are convinced it is part of some depraved sexual fantasy of the Queen's, since she comes here in private with only her favourites. But he never imagined it would look so … wonderful.

Now he knows the truth, however, he is forced to notice the hamlet is deserted. No people at all. Additionally, the vegetable garden grows lusher than ordinary irrigation can account for, and the bordering hills have been landscaped into picturesque undulations that are unnatural.

The tearing of the illusion awakens something in Robespierre, some latent fury he cannot quite explain. When a little perfumed sheep, with an artificially snowy fleece, ambles up to him and pushes its velvety nose into his hand, Robespierre aims a kick at it.

Danton laughs as Robespierre's impeccably polished shoe misses.

'Steady there, Max. The injustice of the royals finally making a man of you, is it?' He puts a comradely arm around his small companion. 'Save your anger, my friend. It's because of this place we have a little base here. The servants are friends, hmm?'

He approaches a small cottage and performs a complicated knock on the door. It is opened by a man dressed as a peasant farmer – the cleanest Robespierre has ever seen – in a long cream-coloured smock, buttercup-hued breeches and incongruously plump cheeks.

The farmer looks right and left ostentatiously, then signals they should enter.

'All is well for you to stay awhile,' he says. 'It is just as you said. The Queen will not come today. Fears for her safety.'

He pauses as Danton and Robespierre enter the low-ceilinged little dwelling. A cauldron bubbles prettily on a small fire, and it's hard to know if this is a functional item or just for show. It feels a lot like wandering on to the stage set of a very impressive play.

The farmer makes another exaggerated glance around the room. 'It is really happening then?' he asks. 'They are coming.'

Inside his coat, Robespierre can feel the gold key pressing against his heart.

'We have news that they shall—' begins Danton, but Robespierre interrupts him, to the larger lawyer's obvious surprise.

'They will come,' says Robespierre. 'Everything is in place. By tonight, the thing will be done.'

CHAPTER FORTY-ONE

$\mathcal{A}$T THE BASE OF THE MONTMARTRE HILL, ARMED MEN ON horseback have begun the ascent.

I watch from the windmill balcony, possibilities churning. I counted on Montmartre as an area safe from aristocrats. But I never factored Robespierre's information network. Of course he has spies here. It is a hotbed for his faction.

I'm trying to stay calm, but the truth is Robespierre's plan has worked perfectly. Our only chance of escape is to attempt a far more dangerous gate, when the guard is at its height. He has played it perfectly. I cannot help but admire the tactic, for all the peril we are now in.

As I stride back into the windmill, Centime and Jemmy pick up on my mood instantly.

'What is it?' asks Centime, rising to her feet.

'A slight change of arrangements,' I say. 'The Montmartre gate is no longer possible.'

I catch Jemmy's eye and he opens his mouth and shuts it again. As I pass him to collect up our clothing, I draw close enough to whisper.

'Guards on the hill,' I say. 'Salvatore's men. On their way here.'

Centime misses nothing, and the blood drains from her face.

'He's coming, isn't he?' she whispers. 'You must leave me here. I can talk to him. Persuade him to let you go.'

I shake my head, the comprehensiveness of Robespierre's plan weighing heavy. I'm remembering the plantation. How the strongest slaves would begin to identify with the owners, even justify their behaviours. Better that than accepting the cruelty they suffered was arbitrary and indiscriminate. Centime is thinking it would be easier to return to Salvatore than risk the unknown, I can see it in her eyes.

'I will sail with you,' I tell her. 'We shall take the boat together to England. I'll be sure you arrive safely.'

Confusion flickers on her face. 'Arrive safely?' Her voice is caught between disappointment and hope. 'You won't stay once we are landed?'

'I cannot,' I tell her. 'I am to give up this life. After my wedding my husband and I have business abroad. But you mustn't fear,' I add. 'I shall make sure you are safe and well looked to in England.'

Her face makes a very peculiar expression, like a knowing smile. 'You will be married so soon?' she suggests quietly.

I nod. 'The day after tomorrow.'

She flinches. 'So soon. But,' she says piteously, 'if it is an arranged marriage, are you not free to leave your husband to travel alone, like other fine ladies?'

'Why would you think my marriage is by arrangement?'

'Because you have the air of a condemned man, whenever ye speak of it.' Jemmy's voice breaks in.

I choose to ignore his remark. 'We don't have time to discuss my wedding,' I tell Centime, reaching out my hand.

'I gave you my word that I would get you to England and I don't intend to break it.'

'But you said the Montmartre gate is closed to us.'

'There are other gates,' I say, not looking at Jemmy. 'We shall get you through one of those.'

Centime looks down at my outstretched fingers, then takes them, but her expression is of bleak despair.

'This way,' I say. 'You first down the ladder. There is a back way out, and we have time.'

She obeys with the wordless acquiescence of someone used to being told what to do. When she is out of earshot, Jemmy turns back to me, lowering his voice.

'Attica, are you mad? How exactly do you plan to get her through? Those customs guards are out for blood.'

'Robespierre has been using Centime as bait,' I tell him. 'He's used his information network to track us here.'

A complicated array of expressions plays over Jemmy's face, starting in horror and ending with hopelessness.

'All this time I was trying to understand why Robespierre wanted to murder an English abolitionist,' I explain. 'It never occurred to me that my attention was being drawn to Salvatore. Somehow, Robespierre knew I would try to rescue Centime.'

I'm struck with an awful uneasy feeling. Robespierre seems to *know* me. I swallow it down.

'If Robespierre went to all that trouble,' I decide, 'he must be planning something. Something he fears the Pimpernel could disrupt.'

Jemmy and I are silent, considering options.

'If that's true,' he says finally, 'then Robespierre knows you will attempt to pass a gate. You said yourself he has been infiltrating them. You're doing exactly what he wants you to do.'

'Not quite,' I reply. 'He wants me to be caught at the gate. We're going to clear it.'

'They'll spot that girl a mile away, Attica. They check every box and sack.'

'What choice do we have?' I realise my voice has risen and consciously lower it to a hiss. 'Robespierre has told Salvatore just enough to put Centime in terrible danger. If he gets hold of her now, he'll torture her for information about the Pimpernel.'

'Then Robespierre has played it very well,' says Jemmy grimly. 'If Salvatore gets hold of Centime, she will not withstand torture. She will give you up. You shall have to go home and be married.'

'That is not my main concern.'

Jemmy's expression suggests he doesn't believe me.

'Maybe part of it,' I admit. 'But mostly I cannot let Centime fall into Salvatore's hands.'

'Be careful, Attica; you do not risk all to win at any cost.'

'How can you say that?'

'Just a look you get whenever Robespierre is mentioned.'

I ignore him, pushing past and descending the ladder.

At the base I find Centime has been cornered by the brothel-keeper, who is jabbing an accusing finger at her with narrowed eyes.

She swings around to confront me as Jemmy drops easily to the ground beside me, his soft leather boots deadening the sound of impact.

'Some fine lies you've been telling us,' says the brothel-keeper bitterly, pointing at Centime. 'That girl is whore to a noble. A bad one.' She narrows her eyes. 'A traitor to the people of France, that's what she is.'

'Who brought you the information?' I say, keeping my voice calm.

'I don't see as it's—' the woman begins.

I move in swiftly, and before she realises what has happened she's pinned to the wall with a knife at her throat.

'It matters to me,' I say evenly. 'I paid for your hospitality, madame. I'd be obliged to you.'

She glances down at the knife.

'Messenger,' she says.

'A sans-culotte?' I suggest. 'Striped breeches, tricolour cockade?'

She nods, setting her mouth.

'He knew we were here?'

She shakes her head. 'Only said he'd been given a duty by the cause to inform all us peasants of the traitor.' She nods towards Centime. 'And to be on the lookout.'

'He offered a reward?'

'Two francs.' She swallows. I release her, glancing at Jemmy.

'Robespierre,' I tell him grimly. 'He's sending out his people, trying to trap us with Centime.' I turn back to Madame. 'I am, as ever, obliged to you,' I say, pushing another few gold coins into her hand. Her eyes glitter. 'We shan't let this small unpleasantness come between us. As you know, my payment is always a great deal more than two francs.' She nods, not taking her eyes from the money. 'When the guards come, please tell them you never saw us.'

Grabbing Centime's hand, I make for the back door, with Jemmy fast on our heels.

'Think she'll keep her part of the bargain?' asks Jemmy.

'Perhaps not,' I concede. 'But if Robespierre knows we have Centime, our only hope is to move fast.'

'Where to?' asks Jemmy.

'The marketplace for a few more provisions,' I say. 'Salt to fill those sacks you got us. A suitably ragged-looking donkey. Then we go straight for Porte Saint-Martin.'

'That gate is in a revolutionary district,' says Centime. 'They hate the nobles there. I'll be torn to pieces.'

'It's a foolish choice,' agrees Jemmy. 'Of all the gates, Saint-Martin is the best guarded. All goods to the north pass that way.'

'The most dangerous, the best guarded,' I agree. 'Robespierre will never suspect it.'

CHAPTER FORTY-TWO

$\mathcal{T}$HE WOMEN FIND LAFAYETTE TRYING TO CONVINCE HIS large body of troops not to desert. It soon becomes apparent to everyone that the Marquis has two options: lead his own troops and the rapidly growing crowd of Parisian women, or face the wrath of the mob.

Wearily, he mounts his horse and heads the procession. The fish-selling women are drunk with joy, heady with the knowledge of their own power. Men have joined the throng now. Half of Paris has come out to watch.

'Join us!' the market women shout. Several do. A silk-clad woman shakes her head with a smile. 'It is not my business,' she says, 'but I wish you good fortune!'

Ovette wades into the crowd and grabs hold of the well-dressed woman.

'It is all our business,' she says, 'to help our fellow citizens.' And she drags the surprised lady into the scrum of marchers. The crowd of women promptly crowd around the reluctant recruit, preventing her escape. Her eyes flit helplessly around the rough-faced women and settle on resignation.

Ovette has started a movement. Tired and determined, the

women take their duties to heart. They are an army now, with a real leader. As the great swathe of people storms the road to Versailles, anyone in their way is press-ganged into service.

Greta, exuberant to the cause, drags a bourgeois lady in a velvet frock into their midst.

'We'll none of us stand by,' says Greta menacingly, clapping her hands together, 'whilst mothers and children starve. This is all of our fight.'

The well-fed lady, in a pair of hand-made gloves, doesn't look like she quite agrees. But one glance at Greta's glowering face is enough to convince her to take part. A kitchen knife is thrust in her hand and she waves it uncertainly in the air.

'That's right!' cries Greta. 'Long live the women who sell fish!'

A cheer goes up.

Greta falls into stride beside Ovette.

'I never liked you,' says Greta conversationally, 'but you're not so bad really, are you?'

Ovette manages a smile. The women have slowed. The march is a trudge, but a trudge with inevitability to it.

'It's a long way to Versailles,' says Ovette, looking at the muddy ground.

Greta nods. 'Why did you take a market stand?' she asks suddenly.

Ovette hesitates. She has not told a soul from the shame of it.

'My son,' she admits. 'He stole some fine linens from a shop. I spent all my money on a lawyer, but they put him to death anyway.'

'Your son's family were starving?' suggests Greta with sympathy.

'That's what he told the court,' says Ovette evenly. 'But no. He had an idea of bettering himself. Setting up a street cart and growing a business from it.'

Greta nods sagely. 'The starving children story never does work in the courts, does it?' she observes. 'You wonder why they keep telling it.'

Ovette nods sadly. 'Is it true what you said before?' she asks. 'That you would die for your fellow market traders?'

'Might have been the drink talking,' admits Greta. 'But I suppose we'll see, shan't we?' She eyes the long road ahead.

At the front of the growing parade, the Marquis de Lafayette looks back to see he is now leading an army of thousands. It swells with every street they pass. The air is filled with pitchforks and knives, spears and pikes: whatever sharp and threatening things the women can lay their hands on. Their mood is infectious.

He looks back to the road, wondering how the King will take this arrival of dreadful-looking women and their hangers-on. It occurs to him, in his black mood, that this might be the very thing to convince His Majesty to sign the Rights of Man after all.

Nursing this happy hope, Lafayette clicks his heels, spurring his horse on a little faster.

CHAPTER FORTY-THREE

*J*EMMY IS SHAKING HIS HEAD. 'IT IS A RECKLESS PLAN,' HE SAYS.

We are standing in view of the huge Porte Saint-Martin – an impressive arched gate of white stone, through which commoners with taxable goods must pass. There is a thick queue of slow-moving wagons and trudging peasants with weighty bundles on their backs. We are disguised as country peasants. Jemmy in ragged striped trousers. My tattered skirts hang a half-foot clear of my bare feet and the washed-out short-gown worn over the top is closed with rusty pins.

'You honestly wish me to approach a customs gate with smuggled goods?' Jemmy is shaking his head. 'It goes against every pirate instinct.'

'Which is exactly why it will work,' I tell him. 'Robespierre will be expecting us to go through one of these gates. They'll be on the lookout for anything out of the ordinary. What could be more usual than a brother and sister attempting to smuggle a little salt?'

'When you asked me what the most commonplace contraband was,' sighs Jemmy, 'I didn't expect you to use it against me.'

'I'm only glad you have stopped boring me to tears with talk on salt taxes and their outcomes.'

'So says the girl who studies forts and battlements for amusement,' says Jemmy wryly, annoyed at my lack of interest in his favourite topic.

Jemmy has a lively interest in smuggled goods, and spent the best part of an hour explaining the untenable French system of forcing peasants to make large mandatory salt purchases, the thinking being that they wouldn't then buy the smuggled variety. 'In actual fact,' Jemmy told me triumphantly, 'it has the opposite effect. The people all turn to smuggling to plug the deficit from the compulsory outlay. And the cheapest contraband they can get their poor callused hands on is salt, which is cheaper than dirt when bought at source.'

'If your plan fails,' says Jemmy, as we get closer to the gate, 'you'll leave noble Atherton at the altar.'

'When have my plans ever failed?'

'Even if you succeed you're leaving things close.'

'There is plenty of time to return to London,' I say tightly, although a sudden panic at not getting to Atherton grips me. 'Centime will be past the gate by morning.'

'Tell that to those customs men.' His eyes drift to the people shuffling towards the gate. A man with a huge sheaf of tobacco on his back reaches the guards and throws down his goods for inspection. The custom's men begin an overly thorough search, pulling apart the large oily leaves, looking for contraband.

'Those guards wear tricolour cockades,' Jemmy says pointedly. 'If they discover us trying to pass Salvatore's courtesan through the gate, they will tear us limb from limb.'

'True,' I say, glancing back at where Centime is concealed, sat low in the wagon. 'Just don't let her hear you say it. And what is it pirates say? There is no reward without risk.' I slap him on the back.

'Don't take risks that might get you caught,' mutters Jemmy. 'That is our motto, if you would only listen.' But he moves towards the front and adjusts the bridle on the worn-looking donkey we acquired from outside the Marché d'Aligre for an inflated price that put Jemmy in a black mood.

I knock quietly on the side of the small battered wagon and peer over to see Centime curled into a ball in the small confines.

'No one is looking,' I tell her. 'Time to fashion your hiding place.'

Centime sits up, looking about fearfully. 'I am dangerous to you,' she says. 'Leave me to try my luck alone and do not risk yourselves.'

I shake my head. 'Centime, you are known. There is a price on your head. You would not make it as far as the line for the gate before someone denounced you.'

She absorbs this. 'I am sorry,' she says finally.

'Don't be,' I tell her. 'We have done this many times. It is a sport for us.'

I glance across at Jemmy, who looks anything but enthused at the mission.

'To get you safely through, you must do everything I ask. Without question,' I tell Centime.

A smile plays on her lips. 'You sound like Salvatore.'

'Stay hidden, no matter what happens,' I say. 'Never lose faith I will come for you.'

She nods slowly. 'Then what should I do?'

In answer I unfurl a large dusty sack from the floor of the wagon. It is an old thing, patched and worn.

'You need to climb inside,' I explain. 'We will fill the rest with salt and disguise you.' I point to two smaller sacks in the wagon, stiff with salt bloom, and draw open the top strings to reveal the white granules inside.

'This is the great plan?' asks Centime uncertainly.

'Trust me. The weight is around the same. And this salt will hide your shape.'

'But it is illegal to smuggle salt,' hisses Centime, eyeing the patched bag she is to be secreted inside. 'If these sacks drop even the smallest amount …'

'The sacks must be old to fit the disguise,' I tell her. 'You must trust me, and promise you shall not say a word.' I take both her hands. 'I have never failed, Centime,' I tell her.

Slowly she climbs inside the sack. Once she is almost hidden from view I pour salt to pad out the sides, so only her head is free.

'Ready?' I ask. She nods. I tie up the top of the sack, then turn to Jemmy.

'It's a good idea,' he says, loud enough for Centime to hear. 'Certainly, you'll blend in. The way the French salt laws are, every man, woman and child is breaking the law in some way.'

I make a final check of my hair, tucking it under the grubby headscarf. Then, slapping the donkey, I move slowly towards the gate, joining the lines of others being questioned and dismissed by customs. The cart lurches dangerously from side to side, with the bagged contraband perched precariously on top.

CHAPTER FORTY-FOUR

ROBESPIERRE PACES AROUND THE LITTLE FARMER'S cottage in the Queen's hamlet. From the window he sees sculpted hillsides and a little waterwheel turning prettily.

Now he knows the trick of it, the fiction is obvious. Thin-legged boys with blistered hands built the lovely horizon. The farm animals have been bathed and scrubbed by women who buy cheap milk by the cup from overused cows. Yet he cannot deny the visage speaks to a part of his secret heart.

Inside the farmer's cottage is different, as though the owner has taken his own low aspirations behind the attractive exterior walls. The scant furniture is barely more than sticks of wood nailed together. A chair, a floor-frame with straw inside and a blanket thrown over for a bed. The kind of things desperate people are executed for stealing from the worst Parisian rented accommodation.

Laid out on the plain table are documents Robespierre brought with him. His map of Paris, sketches of the city gates. Occasionally he seats himself to ponder them, specifically, the city gates. He finds he is missing Georges Danton, who has now gone to the palace, where the National Assembly are gathered.

Distracted and unnerved, Robespierre is pleased when the door opens, to reveal the same farmer that let them in. Robespierre's face is impassive as the man creeps inside, face taut with the drama of his own subterfuge.

Robespierre stops pacing. He is unnaturally animated, his eyes glittering.

'It was done as I asked?' he demands.

'There are seven gates in the city,' says the farmer apologetically. 'We had not the men to police them all.'

'Then,' decides Robespierre, pacing again, arms clasped behind his back, 'you used my suggestions of the gates he is most likely to attempt.' There is an energy to him, a vibrancy.

'Porte Louis is the safest,' offers the farmer. 'Half of all Paris's goods leave that way—'

Robespierre holds up a hand to silence him.

'You will remember from my letters, I have put most of our number there.'

The farmer, who cannot read, nods nervously. 'Whoever this aristocrat is, he will not pass,' he offers.

'They were given a description of the girl he will travel with?' clarifies Robespierre.

Again the man nods. 'Don't mind my saying, monsieur,' says he, moving to the cauldron, which sways above the sad little fire, 'but you seem very sure this aristocrat you're chasing will attempt the gate this morning.'

Robespierre doesn't answer, instead moving to the plain wooden chair and throwing up his coat tails before seating himself. Once again he studies the map of Paris.

'The criminal will be caught in a pincer,' says Robespierre, without looking up. It isn't clear if he means these words for the farmer or is merely speaking aloud. 'He must run from

Salvatore's men with a very conspicuous prize.'

Now Robespierre looks directly at the farmer, pushing his round glasses a little higher on his nose.

'I have given the Scarlet Pimpernel a hot potato,' he explains. 'A courtesan by the name of Centime. The only way he may be rid of her safely is to leave the city. Keep her in Paris and he risks her being torn apart by the mob. Not to mention, she is … unstable. Liable to blab his identity in a fit of pique. Or run back to Salvatore, hoping to buy forgiveness with the Pimpernel's arrest. Whilst Centime stays in Paris, he risks all. Paid men will be combing the city even as we speak, and I have made it known that Centime is an enemy of the people. She is hunted by commoners and nobles alike.'

Robespierre looks particularly pleased with himself.

'His problem,' here Robespierre raises a thin finger in explanation, 'he is emotional and that is his weakness. The Pimpernel has no stomach for the business of warfare. A rational man would leave Centime to her fate. She likely knows his identity by now, after all, and is a risk.' He steeples his fingers. He takes a breath, eyes the glass of wine before him as though daring it to tempt him.

'But he shall not do this. He shall succumb to vicissitudes of the heart. He cannot bear to leave a chosen one behind, not he. It is his heel of Achilles.'

The farmer clearly doesn't understand the classical reference, but Robespierre doesn't bother to enlighten him. The lawyer begins arranging the papers on the table. 'I am almost disappointed,' he says, 'that the Pimpernel has such a commonplace weakness. Women.' His brow crinkles in disgust.

He studies the gates again, pleased with himself. 'Check mate. He must move or die. What he doesn't yet know is he runs fast to his own doom. Our men will be waiting to uncover whatever trick he attempts to smuggle Centime to freedom.'

His eyes drop again to the plan of Paris. A finger stretches towards a gate then curls inside itself.

'Not there,' he mutters. 'Surely not.' A strange look tightens his features.

'Porte Saint-Martin,' he says slowly. 'How many men have we there?'

The farmer shakes his head. 'None. Only a fool would attempt that gate,' he says. 'It is strongly manned, and in our staunchest stronghold. People there would gleefully tear the head from Salvatore's courtesan.'

'Ah, but I have applied myself to studying the Pimpernel,' says Robespierre. He holds a hand in front of his face, examining it. 'I see him as though reflected in glass. And he always does what I least expect,' adds Robespierre, lowering his hand. 'The most irrational and incautious of behaviours.' Robespierre breathes in deeply, his pale nostrils flaring. 'Get a message to our house on the Rue Saint-Jacques. Double the guard at Porte Saint-Martin. Search every sack, trunk and cart that comes through. Look closely on every face. That is where he will come.'

CHAPTER FORTY-FIVE

As WE TRUNDLE OUR CART FORWARDS ANOTHER PLACE IN
the line I look up at the imposing Porte Saint-Martin, the
carved faces of the stone sides seeming to stare down at me
and Jemmy accusingly.

Ahead of us is a village boy, fencing sticks bound in a roll
on his back. The guard waves him through and he walks
determinedly, sweating under the burden. Next comes a well-
dressed merchant with a neatly stacked cart of cambric cloth.

'What's this, then?' sneers the gateman. 'You off to dress
the wealthy at the poor man's expense, friend?'

'It is cambric only,' says the merchant. 'Poor stuff.'

The gateman pinches the cloth between his fingers and
rubs it.

'Don't seem like this will clothe any farmers,' he opines.

The merchant waits wordlessly for the decision. Sweat has
broken out on his top lip, I notice.

'Go on, then,' says the gateman, after a long pause. 'Next
time use the gate for your own kind, understand? I see you
carting that fine stuff this way a second time, I'll have my men
burn the lot.'

The merchant nods, his head hung low, and quickly mounts his vehicle.

'Wait!' The gateman raises a hand. 'What's inside the box?' He points to a small trunk tucked at the feet of the merchant's driving seat.

'Nothing.' The merchant is pained. 'Only my personal effects.'

'Open it. Nothing passes through without a search. We have word of aristocrats escaping justice.'

'This trunk is not large enough for—'

'Open it. Before I smash it.'

The merchant fumbles nervously inside his coat and removes a key. Fitting it into the lock he throws open the lid. I am too far away to see inside, but the gateman's whistle of admiration is clear enough.

'Fair bit of gold in your personal effects. That needs taxing.'

'It has already been taxed. At the City Hall. I have the documentation.' The merchant is fumbling again but the gateman holds up a bored hand.

'You've been taxed illegally, so far as we are concerned. By the aristocrats. You give them your money that is up to you. You have not paid the people of France.' There's a jingling as the gateman plunges his hand into the trunk and withdraws a handful of money.

'This should be enough,' he decides. 'You have an objection, friend? Take it up with my associates.' He jerks a thumb to the heavyset men lurking by the pile of confiscated goods. They are watching the events with interest.

'Be off with you,' says the gateman. 'On your way. And be grateful I didn't take the lot for your subterfuge.'

The merchant spurs his horses, and his cart takes off with a jolt.

Jemmy and I approach next, he at the rear of the wagon, me at the front, my expression timid.

'What's this, then, sweetheart?' asks the gateman. He takes in my dress. 'You look like you're from the borders. Come from the *pays rédimés?*' he suggests.

I nod.

The gateman eyes Jemmy skulking at the back of the wagon. 'Your husband?' he suggests.

'My brother,' I say. 'He never learned to speak.'

'Simpleton, eh?' says the gateman sympathetically. 'There's one in every family, my dear. The business falls to you, then.' He sighs. '*Pays rédimés* is a cheap place for salt,' he observes, rubbing his forehead and eyeing my wagon with its large patched sack. 'That your sack, sweetheart?'

'It is fruit, only,' I say, speaking quickly. 'Apples from the farm.'

'Funny shape for apples. Bag has been patched as well.' He takes in the seamed portions of the bag, stitched on to make it larger. 'Kind of thing people do when they're trying to get around the King's measures.'

I bite my lip, hold my head up high.

'You're not too good at this,' he says. 'Better leave smuggling to the men. First rule. Don't try to take something suspicious through in a suspicious sack.'

'I don't know what you mean.'

He shakes his head. 'Look at my back, do you see any feathers? I am no downy chick and these are not apple sacks,' he says. 'They are from the saltworks. You have a father or brother who digs in the mine?'

'A father.' My voice comes out as a whisper.

The gateman sighs. He removes a corkscrew from his belt

and plunges it into the sack. A little river of salt streams free. He raises his eyes to mine. 'Apples, eh?'

'I'm sorry.' There are tears in my eyes. 'It's only … We are so hungry.'

He nods. 'Your father put you up to this, did he?'

I swallow.

The gateman sighs. 'We're going to have to take your cargo. I'm sorry for it, truly. There is to be a fine, also, of twenty sous.'

'No!' I allow the tears to flow. 'Please. We cannot pay.'

He shakes his head.

'It is the law. Listen,' says the gateman, 'I'm sure you are a good girl and do no wrong. Your donkey and wagon can be sold. That'll raise enough to pay the fine.'

'My father will beat me,' I tell him pitcously.

'Better than what they'll do to you in the debtors' prison, believe me,' says the man. 'Pretty little country thing like you wouldn't stand a chance.'

'The cart is not mine to sell,' I tell the gateman sadly. 'It is in keeping to my brother.'

The gateman eyes Jemmy, who is staring inanely into space in a convincing expression of a witless country boy. He sighs.

'Hi there, fellow,' he says, waving a hand at Jemmy. 'We need to take this cart, so you and your sister mightn't be imprisoned as debtors.'

Jemmy says nothing. The gateman shakes his head.

'You cannot persuade him to sign it over?' he asks.

'He cannot write his name,' I say.

'If you cannot pay I must arrest you. You'll be put in the debtors' prison until someone can pay your fine.'

'My relations are all in the *pays rédimés*!' I protest. 'How should they know where I am?'

'If they are reading people, you might send them a letter, at the cost of a sous.'

'And if I do not have it?'

'Then you shall be imprisoned until the debt is paid.'

He jerks his head at two men who have been loitering to the side of the gate; they approach with meaningfully expressions.

'Put the salt in with the other contraband,' says the gateman. 'The girl might sell the donkey and cart for her freedom.' One of the men takes the donkey's bridle to lead it away.

He pats my shoulder with a consoling hand. 'You'll both be put in the gatehouse lock-up overnight. Think it over. By morning you might have come to a different opinion.'

The other guard moves in closer.

'Lock the girl and the simpleton in the gatehouse,' says the gateman. 'If she's come to a better way of thinking in the morning, we'll have the cart and donkey and think no more of the crime.'

He looks over my shoulder, frowning.

'Strange,' he mumbles, nudging his companion. 'Why do they send us extra men?'

I don't dare turn around. But I know without looking, that Robespierre has somehow deduced the gate we pass through.

'Wait!' shouts a rough voice. 'Hold that cart. We have orders to search every sack.'

CHAPTER FORTY-SIX

THE WOMEN TRUDGE ON THROUGH THE COLD RAIN, CHILDREN at their hips or tripping behind in the soft mud. They are soaked to the skin and frozen to the bone. But the march has something of fatalism about it now. They will reach the palace or die trying.

And there are so many of them. No longer just women, though they have joined in their thousands. Men too. They have even managed to acquire a cannon, the heavy weight of which they take turns in lugging along the dirt road, churning two deep troughs in its wake.

They have no powder or ammunition for the cannon, but they like the way it looks. As though they are a real army. Something to be reckoned with.

When the first wide boulevard of Versailles town comes in sight, a great cheer goes up.

But slowly, the jubilation settles to something else. A hush of uncertainty. Because the little town is like nothing these Paris folk have ever seen. The buildings are reminiscent of those in the capital. But the stone used to build them has a honeycomb-like appearance, exotic and unfamiliar. The streets are a similar construction. But it is all so *clean*. So orderly. And the people, who are fleeing to their smartly plastered homes and closing fresh-painted shutters, are round of limb and clean of dress. One imagines that if a child dies here, it is not flung on to a teetering pile with all the others.

At the noise of ten thousand tramping footsteps, a startled rat leaps from a nearby gutter and hurtles across the broad cobbled road. The women slow to watch it, a reverent hush amongst them.

'Look at the meat on that,' says Greta finally, voicing everyone's thoughts. 'If rats looked that way in Paris we'd feast off 'em.'

A shrill noise of rope on metal causes heads to turn upwards. One of the buildings employs a technological marvel unfamiliar to the market women. A winch device built into the eaves of the roof, which is currently employed manoeuvring a pianoforte through the first-floor windows. Now they notice many houses have this novel invention.

'Must be a lot of grand furniture goes in and out,' remarks Ovette, watching in wonder as the pianoforte sways gently on the ascent.

The woman with the baby strapped to her chest starts to cry. Later she will tell people the shock of the royal betrayal only hit home when she saw the town. 'It was the future,' she will say. 'They'd built it already, and not invited us. Not even *told* us about it. We would have lived our whole lives not knowing it was there.'

The great mass of protestors file upwards along the main boulevard, and now they can make out the palace itself, squat and magnificent, in the middle distance, flanked by mighty gold gates. The number of people has swollen so greatly that pockets of women are forced out into the side streets, like a river bursting its banks.

One of the tributaries flows past Versailles' tidy marketplace. It is more like a shopping arcade than the kind of pavement market found in Paris – a broad building with well-stocked stalls in its exterior arches.

'Bread,' says Greta, pointing accusingly. 'They got bread here.' The frightened market traders are only half packed away when the mob descends.

CHAPTER FORTY-SEVEN

At the gate of Saint-Martin i am frozen with fear as Robespierre's men approach, demanding to rifle each sack that passes through.

'We do our job well enough,' objects the gateman gruffly. 'What business have you here?'

'We've word of an aristocrat trying to pass through this gate,' says a man in striped breeches. 'A criminal with a courtesan who sells secrets to the English.' He eyes me and jabs a finger at the sacks loaded on the little wagon. 'What's in those bags?'

'Salt,' says the gateman, wiping his nose on the back of his hand. 'This poor little fool was trying to smuggle. It's off to the lock-up with her and the half-wit brother.'

Robespierre's man eyes my wagon, then unsheathes a wicked-looking dagger and plunges it into the nearest sack. Salt spills free. He moves to the next, repeating the process. Centime's sack is next in line. I hold my breath as he lifts his knife, ready to sink it deep.

'You seek an aristocrat?' I blurt. 'I've seen him.'

The man lowers his knife and turns to me.

'What's that?' He glowers at me. 'If you have information you'd best be quick about it.'

'I've seen him,' I continue. 'He passed a little way ahead of us. I could give you a good description. Only,' I let my eyes drift to the guard, 'you should have to settle our fine in payment.'

Robespierre's man shakes his head in disgust.

'I can tell you everything,' I say. 'What he looks like. How he speaks. He is from the south. A great tall man, he is.'

Robespierre's man spits on the ground.

'Get her away to the lock-up,' he says in disgust, 'before she drowns herself in her own lies.'

The guard, who has been watching the scene with amusement, jerks his head that I should pass through to the prison beyond.

'Wait!' I say. 'I have good information. I can help you.'

Robespierre's man has turned away from me now and busies himself examining other goods.

I watch as my wagon of salt is trundled to where confiscated goods are kept. Jemmy and I are taken roughly in another direction, towards a small cell with a single dark door.

'This is where you'll spend the night,' says a guard, leading us towards it. 'Tomorrow it's the debtors' prison for you both.'

CHAPTER FORTY-EIGHT

At the Queen's hamlet in Versailles, a strange electric energy is in the air. Even now, Danton may be speaking to the commoners at the National Assembly in the rooms begrudgingly afforded them by the King.

The men plan to debate how they might force the King to sign the Rights of Man. Robespierre will join them soon. He is waiting on an important message from Paris.

The hours have been long. He stands, sits, paces. Drums thin fingers on the simple table. Any moment now, any *moment*, he will receive the news he has been waiting for.

The true identity of the mysterious Scarlet Pimpernel.

Now he is certain he hears hoof beats and is beside himself with excitement. Just as he hoped, there is a knock at the door, and his spy from the customs gate enters.

'You have him?' Robespierre demands, a mad excitement gleaming behind his round glasses.

The man shakes his head. 'Whoever this Pimpernel is, monsieur, he has not tried to get past our fellows.'

Inch by inch, the expression on Robespierre's face changes, as though a set of whirring cogs are turning behind the pale façade.

'Impossible.' Robespierre pulls the documents a little too quickly from the man's hands. He sits, pushing his round glasses up, and begins poring over the papers.

His spy shuffles uncomfortably from foot to foot, with the distinct impression he has been entirely forgotten. He glances hopefully at the cauldron of soup bubbling on the peasant-style fire. It has been a wet cold ride from Paris, and he was forced to take a longer route to avoid the thick crowds of protestors on the road.

'Porte Saint-Martin,' Robespierre says finally. 'You doubled the inspections as I asked? Every vehicle searched?'

The man nods. Robespierre reads, a small smile on his face as he notes the most common contraband.

'Books,' he says aloud. 'Ideas. The King tries to keep them out, but still they keep coming. From Switzerland, mostly, ideas of equality he doesn't like.'

The spy nods uncertainly, the nuances of such matters lost on him. He is a simple man, a customs guard by trade, recruited to the Society of Friends after the price of bread doubled and his mother starved to death.

Robespierre sighs. 'Chestnut staves,' he says, 'wax. Nothing out of the ordinary?' he confirms. 'You are *certain*?'

The man shrugs. 'Nothing we saw. And the men were looking out for it.'

'Every sack was searched?'

'Every sack searched, every trunk opened.'

Robespierre flips pages in disbelief. 'Nothing, nothing, nothing,' he mutters. He stands suddenly, and begins pacing the room. 'It is not possible,' he says to himself, 'he cannot risk keeping Centime in Paris. She has no friends. Salvatore's men are everywhere.'

'If you please, monsieur.' The man is looking at Robespierre, who has sat down again to make another examination of the papers.

'What is it?' asks the lawyer, looking up distractedly.

'Tonight it will all be over,' says the man. 'We shall have won. The Pimpernel will have to flee France or be lynched or imprisoned along with all the other foreigners. It is a small matter, this thing, compared to the grand cause.'

Robespierre turns, very slowly, eyes unreadable behind his glasses.

'You think this man should simply retire to England with no recompense for his crimes against France?'

The spy hesitates, feeling a previously unseen net close around him. 'No, but—'

'I want him *caught in the act.*' Robespierre slams a small fist on the table with impressive force. There is a strange fury to him now, wholly at odds with his small body. 'I want these criminals who pretend themselves Gods *torn down.* Their despotic rule *obliterated.* So it might never threaten us again.' He is breathing hard. 'So you see why the Pimpernel must be arrested at the gate? I want people to see him for what he really is: a low criminal.'

The man nods slowly.

'Moreover,' says Robespierre, 'this noble Pimpernel has interfered with my plans before. Do not forget he is a noble and able to go where we cannot. If he were to discover the plan, he might easily seek an audience in the palace, and then,' Robespierre clicks his fingers, 'pouf, all our plans rent asunder.'

Robespierre reads on, every part of him singularly focused on the page of exported goods. He stops for a moment, finger hovering, then taps another list, made separate from the customs entries.

'These are confiscated goods?' he confirms.

His spy nods.

'Did you search these?' asks Robespierre.

'They are to be incinerated,' says the man, speaking slowly as though Robespierre is not in charge of all his faculties. 'Burned, according to the King's law,' he adds for good measure.

Robespierre ignores the tone, returning with renewed vigour to the list.

'Silk, salt, leather.' He leans back, thinking. 'A barrel of wine.'

His eyes lift to the man.

'White wine,' he says out loud. 'But the season is over. Why should white wine be coming through Paris at this time of year?'

'Late harvest?' The man shrugs.

Robespierre is shaking his head. 'The summer drought killed half the crops.' He draws the paper very close to his bespectacled face, as though hoping to read the answer there.

'Did anyone open this barrel?' asks Robespierre.

The man tries and fails to hold his nerve under Robespierre's steely gaze. 'Could be we tried a drop or two,' he admits.

Robespierre sags, disappointed. 'I was so certain,' he mutters. 'So certain he would choose that gate.' His fingers drift to the other documents on his desk. Tallies from the other gates. There is an expression on his face like a little boy trying not to cry. It passes. He looks back at the customs gate documents. His long finger taps a line of text.

'Three salt sacks?' he asks.

227

'Some girl and her idiot brother from the *pays rédimés*,' he says, 'trying her luck. Their father put them up to it.'

Robespierre winces at his compatriot's heartlessness. 'The Society thanks you for your service,' he says, with a long sigh at the failure of it all. 'It is time I joined the men in the National Assembly. One way or another, France will change for the better tonight.'

His spy bows, his eyes once again dancing towards the full cauldron of soup.

'Please,' Robespierre waves his hand, 'take some food. I eat sparingly myself and often forget that others get hungry.' He tries for a smile, but it comes out strangely.

Relieved, the spy walks to the cauldron, lifts the ladle, serves himself into a tankard, then liberally sprinkles the contents with salt from a dish on the mantel.

Something about the shape of Robespierre's eyes changes very slightly, as though a suggestion has come into his mind he is unsure of. He shakes his head as if to nudge it into clearer view, then frowns, looking back at the papers.

'Unusual for a poor girl to bring *three* sacks of salt,' muses Robespierre. 'The salt smugglers were sent back to Paris?'

The man shakes his head, his mouth now full of soup from the ladle. 'Couldn't pay the fine,' he says, swallowing. 'The brother is a simpleton. We put them in the little lock-up on the gate overnight. It'll be the debtors' prison for them in the morning.' He gives a rather heartless laugh.

Robespierre folds the paper and taps it on the desk. He stands, eyes flashing.

'The lock-up,' he breathes. 'It is ingenious. Get put in the lock-up and you pass the gate. All he needs do is break out, and it cannot be so secure.'

The man at the fire pauses in his soup-eating, uncomfortably aware he may have erred in some profound way.

'The lock-up is very secure,' he ventures. 'No escapes. Ever.'

Robespierre ignores him, victorious in his deduction.

'Get a message to Salvatore,' he instructs, the words spilling out almost too fast to be comprehensible. 'Tell him he will find Centime at Porte Saint-Martin. Hidden inside a salt sack. My price for the information is the pair of prisoners held in the lock-up.'

CHAPTER FORTY-NINE

*J*EMMY AND I ARE SAT ON THE TINY BENCH OF THE DARK little lock-up. The stone-walled room is just large enough to stand inside.

'That was well played,' he says as the guard passes out of sight. 'And your plan is working. I got a good look at where they store confiscated goods as we passed by and you were right in your thinking. It is far less heavily guarded than the second gate. You've had the guards deliver your salt sacks straight past it.'

'So long as Centime holds her nerve,' I say, 'we can pick her up at nightfall. Those men will be drunk on contraband wine by then.'

'So what is the second part of the plan, Lady Morgan?' asks Jemmy. 'How will you get us free from this cell? Something of Atherton's perhaps? More magic sticks that set themselves alight?'

'Better.' I pull free the little glass vial of acid given to me by Atherton. 'This will burn through the metal,' I explain, nodding to the thick bolt just visible through the crack in the door. 'Atherton's invention,' I add proudly.

'But that is liquid,' says Jemmy, peering suspiciously at the bottle. 'Liquid cannot *burn*, Attica.'

'I have seen it myself,' I assure him. 'It will dissolve away the metal bolt, wait and see.'

Jemmy crosses himself. 'Witchcraft, to be sure,' he says uneasily.

'It's science,' I explain happily. 'An alchemic reaction. Only a little is needed.' I pour a few drops on to the top of the metal bolt and listen for the tell-tale hiss. It doesn't come.

'Perhaps a little more,' I say, frowning as I tip half the contents of the little vial on to the chunky bolt.

I wait longer this time, willing the chemicals to react.

'It must be the wrong metal,' I say, disappointed. 'Some kind of pig iron, perhaps. The mix is impure.'

'Your fine Atherton made no allowances for poor smelting.' Jemmy sounds unnecessarily triumphant. 'I'll wager he has never seen the inside of a real prison.'

'It's all very well to consider yourself worldly,' I retort, 'but it does rather mean we're trapped.'

'Hogwash,' scoffs Jemmy. 'You've got enough equipment for seven prison escapes stuffed in your stockings, I'll be bound.'

'As is happens, I do have a device for digging out mortar,' I say stiffly, sliding free a claw-ended metal rod from my stays. 'This French lime plaster should be soft enough to dig free a few bricks, but it will take all night.'

Jemmy shakes his head and loops free the crucifix he wears around his neck.

'What are you doing with that?' I'm wondering whether he has some ingenious plan for pulling the bolt that will save my fingers from blisters.

'Pirate signal,' he says. 'Drop an upside-down crucifix outside your prison window, and if there's a brother-at-arms passing, he's bound by pirate lore to set you free.'

I shake my head at Jemmy's romantic notion.

'You've always had a mistaken faith in honour amongst thieves,' I say, turning to the wall, and scraping hard with my little tool. 'Not to mention, it is hardly likely a pirate will just wander past.'

'We're everywhere,' says Jemmy, tapping his nose and retreating to the narrow bench. 'A few hours, and some kind soul will slide that bolt. You'll see.'

I give him a pitying look and redouble my efforts, causing plaster to fall in a soft drift at the dirt floor of our cell.

'You could help me,' I add, as Jemmy reclines, tilting his hat over his eyes.

'No need,' he says, adjusting himself. 'I might as well get a little rest while I wait for a brother to release us.'

CHAPTER FIFTY

Several hours later I have almost worked free a single large stone and rest back on my heels, dusty and pleased with my progress.

'Another three like this and we'll have a large enough gap to crawl through,' I tell the slumbering Jemmy, who wakes with a grunting sort of start.

'I told you, Attica,' he says, yanking and sliding his boots to the ground, 'you're wasting your time.'

'It's been hours,' I point out, 'and not so much as a tap on the door.'

'We're only a few miles from port, at a customs gate,' replies Jemmy easily. 'We walk amongst you. You'll see.'

I turn back to the stones, ignoring the blisters on my hands, and begin chiselling another block.

'Wait.' Jemmy holds up a ringed hand.

'What?' I glare at him in annoyance. 'Is it the ghost of the pirate who will rescue us speaking in a language only you can hear?'

As if in reply, the crucifix string wound around the bars moves.

Jemmy and I look at one another.

'You see?' Jemmy springs upright, bouncing on his hands, and smoothing down his black coat.

In answer I draw my blade.

'I don't have a good feeling about this,' I tell Jemmy. 'Would a pirate be carrying a lantern? Only wealthy men can afford—'

The bolts slowly slide back. Jemmy's hand falls to his sword hilt. As the wide door creaks open, a strong smell of alcohol fumes rolls into the room.

Jemmy breaks into a grin.

'My old mate,' he says, slapping the shoulder of a reeling drunk man, standing in the doorway. 'You answered the code, true enough. The lady here will recompense you for your troubles.'

'What does he want?' I hiss to Jemmy, eyeing the drunken sailor, who is now openly leering in what he approximates to be my direction.

'Money,' says Jemmy. 'That's the other part of pirate lore. Whoever frees you earns ten gold pieces in ready coin.' He makes a deliberate show of patting his empty pockets. 'As I'm a little embarrassed for the amount, I shall have to loan it from you. Temporarily, of course.' He grins.

Rolling my eyes, I draw out my purse from its secret hiding place within my skirts, and slowly count ten pieces of gold into the drunken man's hand.

'Thank you.' He bows.

'Have a care with that lantern,' warns Jemmy. 'If you're caught with it, they'll string you up.'

'Hadn't you heard?' The man grins. 'There's no law at all in the city. The women have gone to Versailles, a great marchin' pack of 'em. Twenty thousand, so they say. While the cat's away, eh?' He winks and staggers off, the lantern light petering out into the dark.

'He'll have lost that money before the night is out,' I say, watching him go. 'Whoever he stole that lantern from will catch up with him.'

'True enough,' says Jemmy. 'But lore is lore.'

'Does it count with someone else's money?' I ask archly.

'Honour amongst thieves.' Jemmy grins. 'Open to wider interpretation than the regular kind. Do you think it's true about the women marching on Versailles? Twenty thousand?'

I try to imagine a group of women that large. 'An exaggeration, surely?'

'Makes you think, though, doesn't it?' says Jemmy. 'Did someone put them up to it?'

'Robespierre is planning something,' I consider. 'But surely even he—'

Jemmy puts out a sudden arm and pulls me back into the shadows. I turn in shock, but he raises a finger to his lips and slowly drags me out of sight.

Just as Salvatore's dark figure appears like a spectre.

CHAPTER FIFTY-ONE

SALVATORE STANDS MOTIONLESS OUTSIDE THE OPEN DOOR to the lock-up, taking in the empty blackness inside.

He is so still I could almost convince myself he is a dark statue. Then he moves sharply, fury evident in the tight stride, and makes for the compound where the smuggled goods are held.

'Centime,' I whisper, looking at Jemmy. 'He'll find her.'

Jemmy shakes his head. 'He can't possibly know where she is hiding.'

'He knew to come here, to look in the lock-up,' I say. 'If Robespierre deduced we were here, what else does he know?'

I draw out my knife.

'Don't,' says Jemmy. 'A man like Salvatore doesn't come alone.' He points to the middle distance and I see he's right. Human shapes lurk in the shadows. Salvatore has brought armed men to cover him.

Reluctantly, I put away my blade. We both move silently towards the large open-sided barn, in which all the confiscated customs goods are housed before the King's men come to take their monthly cut. It's a basic structure consisting of a large thatched roof suspended at intervals on long wooden staves.

'Salvatore knew what time to arrive,' observes Jemmy, eyeing the unmanned open door. 'There's a few minutes while the customs men change posts. Robespierre must have a great deal of information at his fingertips.'

We creep carefully to the open side of the compound, where sacks and trunks are laid out by the hundred beneath the rudimentary roof.

'We might be lucky,' Jemmy adds in a whisper. 'There are a hundred or more sacks in that compound. Salvatore cannot search them all before the guard returns. Not unless Centime gives herself up.'

'Why should she do a thing like that?'

As if in answer, Salvatore cups his hands over his mouth and shouts into the dark.

'Centime!' he bellows. 'If you are here you must reveal yourself. Whatever this Pimpernel has promised you, it is a lie. He cannot keep you safe. You know it.'

He waits. There is a long silence. 'You think this Pimpernel can save you?' demands Salvatore. 'He is English, Centime, and only cares for what England wants. He will abandon you, and what will you do, all alone?'

I close my eyes, willing Centime to keep still and silent.

'At midnight there is no way out of France.' Salvatore hesitates for effect. 'Every port and border will be closed.'

Jemmy and I exchange shocked glances. Is Salvatore telling the truth? I wonder if he has been privy to Robespierre's plan and what it could mean.

'You wonder if I tell you true?' suggests Salvatore, in the same loud voice. 'The little lawyer is making plans. I gave him a key to the Princes' Court. At midnight, a mob will swarm the palace. A rule of law will be declared and your Pimpernel will be powerless to help you.'

Again he waits and listens. 'All the foreigners in France will be hunted and imprisoned,' continues Salvatore. 'He has sold you lies, Centime. In a few hours, no one leaves the country. It is too late for you.'

Jemmy and I exchange silent glances. It makes no sense. Even if Robespierre could engineer the borders to be closed, how would that further his revolutionary cause?

'It is lies,' I whisper to Jemmy. 'It must be. Salvatore only tries to frighten her.' But I can't deny there is something very convincing about the way he tells it.

'The women go to Versailles,' Jemmy whispers back, a worried tone to his voice. 'That much is true. An army by now, the old pirate said. Could this be part of Robespierre's plan?'

Possibilities are whirling in my mind now. If it is women, not men, who attack the palace, they will not demand political change or votes. Parisian mothers do not care for such things.

'They will come for bread,' I say, thinking aloud. 'How can that benefit Robespierre?'

Then the other possibility dawns. Of all the people in France, it is the women who most hate Marie Antoinette. They loathe her, as the greedy spendthrift who takes food from their children's mouths to buy shoes and ribbons. Several thoughts come together in my mind.

It was the Queen who was responsible for Salvatore's family imprisoning him in the Bastille. Salvatore and Robespierre are political opposites in almost every regard. But in their dislike of Marie Antoinette, they are united.

Salvatore may be an aristocrat, patriotic to his King and country. But he hates the Austrian-born monarch. And the key he gave Robespierre is for the Princes' Court.

That quadrant leads directly to the Queen's staircase.

'Robespierre's plan,' I tell Jemmy. 'I might know it. If I'm right, we need to get to Versailles before midnight. If we don't a lot of innocent people will die.'

Jemmy sighs theatrically. 'You'll need to stop speaking in riddles, there, Attica.'

I turn to him, my eyes blazing. 'He's going to kill the Queen.'

CHAPTER FIFTY-TWO

A SMALL TROOP OF WOMEN ARE BEING LED INTO THE PALACE by a frightened-looking servant. They follow behind, open-mouthed, agog, eyeing the sumptuous table with a mix of awe and suspicion, as if the sculpted platters might be an illusion – a trick of paint and plaster.

Never in their lives have these honest fighters seen such ornamental food in such great quantity.

The National Assembly could hardly refuse them. King Louis greets them in his own apartment. The women's soaking shoes flap wetly on the glossy parquet floor. Several glance longingly at the bed – an impossibly high draped box of embroidered silk, fenced off by a chunky balustrade of carved golden posts.

Lafayette takes up the rear, hanging back to distance himself from the women who are not his troops, yet with an expression to suggest he is not unsympathetic to their cause.

The King stands to face the women, liveried in a suit of plush blue velvet and frothy white linens. His apartment, designed to inspire awe, makes him look small, kindly even, since he is making a concerted effort to smile at the women.

'Your Majesty,' says a delegate of the Assembly, 'these women have come from Paris. They forced themselves into the National Assembly Hall and demanded—'

'We want bread, Your Majesty,' interrupts Ovette, shivering in her wet clothes and encouraged by the King's diminutive appearance. 'Children starve.'

King Louis clears his throat and frowns. He raises his eyes to the women.

'Then you must have bread,' he says. 'I shall arrange ten wagonloads to accompany you back to Paris.' He turns slightly on his heel, hands behind his back. 'Will there be anything else?'

Ovette can only shake her head.

'Then I thank you for making the long journey to alert me to this grave problem.' As an afterthought, Louis walks towards the women. Several take an involuntary step back. He takes the hand of the nearest women, and kisses it. A collective gasp goes through the group as Louis walks along the line, raising female hands, brushing his lips on them. One of the women faints dead away.

The mood is cordial, convivial almost. No one dares criticise His Majesty, and the King himself seems rather to be enjoying his celebrity. Everything seems to be well. The women are led out, smiling with their victory.

As they vacate, Lafayette moves closer to the dazed-looking King.

'There are still a great many of them out there,' he says. 'Not all will be pacified with bread.'

The King tilts his head, waiting for Lafayette to continue.

'The Rights of Man,' says Lafayette meaningfully. 'It would send a very strong statement indeed, if you were to sign it now.'

CHAPTER FIFTY-THREE

*J*EMMY AND I WATCH WITH EVERY MUSCLE TENSED AS Salvatore stalks the compound of confiscated goods, kicking out at sacks in his fury. He paces between the bags and boxes, but to my mounting relief, looks to be giving up.

'So Robespierre intends to kill the Queen,' whispers Jemmy, his eyes still glued to Salvatore. 'Surely that is a good thing for England?'

'I have no love for Marie Antoinette,' I say, not missing the sardonic quality to his tone. 'But if she dies, there will be a bloodbath, and Robespierre could easily rise to power.' I catch Jemmy's eye. 'English subjects will be slaughtered too,' I add defensively. 'It is not that I have forgotten my loyalties. Parisians are crazed with fear of foreign attack at the best of times. If the Queen dies, rule of law is declared on the borders. Foreigners will be lynched.'

Jemmy's mouth twists. 'I can't pretend to understand this game between you and Robespierre, but I do know a little about winning at all costs. True, there's a pack of women marching on Versailles. But they are weak with hunger and only want bread. They don't have the strength of purpose to attack the royals.'

'He has seen an opportunity,' I tell Jemmy. 'If those women can be riled up to murder, they may just accelerate the whole revolution beyond Robespierre's wildest dreams. And you shouldn't underestimate women with starving children,' I say. 'With the right encouragement, those hungry women would gladly run a sword through Marie Antoinette's guts. That is why Robespierre was able to recruit Salvatore. He might be a royalist, but he loathes Marie Antoinette. She's the cause of his imprisonment. I'll wager the key Salvatore gave to Robespierre was to help him get those women to the Queen.'

Salvatore is backing away from the goods now, retreating to the outskirts of the large covered area.

Jemmy is still shaking his head. 'Attica, you cannot simply tell a pack of women to murder their Queen, and they run off to do it.'

'Robespierre is highly vocal on the subject of female emancipation. Women line up outside his office to make him gifts. If I am correct,' I add, 'and Robespierre's plan works, it would be as when you strike the head from a chicken and the body runs around madly. Austria will likely attack in revenge for their slaughtered daughter, and even if she doesn't the French people will be crazed with paranoia. It is as Salvatore says. Louis will invoke a rule of law. All ports and borders will be closed. And God help any foreigners trapped in the country.'

'Why should Robespierre want that?' demands Jemmy, keeping his voice low, as Salvatore begins a slow circuit of the sacks and crates.

'In such a state of terror, a driven man such as he could easily rise to the top,' I whisper.

'Sounds like someone is a little obsessed with his movements,' mutters Jemmy pointedly.

I take a breath. 'He has been clever,' I tell Jemmy. 'Robespierre has been making speeches in the marketplaces for months. He knows the women cannot read. The propaganda and pamphlets are lost on them. His influence is absolute.'

I have an image of Robespierre, his little body standing erect, as he spins alluring words to the half-starved women workers. Conjuring images of plenty in Versailles. Bread and corn sat ready to be taken.

'They are angry,' I hiss, glancing nervously in Salvatore's direction. He is far enough away now that our voices won't carry, but I'd rather not take the chance. 'Everyone thinks the Queen is to blame. There is hardly any guard at Versailles. If those women get inside the palace ...' I rub my temples. 'We have a few hours to warn the Queen and be sure she vacates Versailles,' I say. 'Or Robespierre could gain power.'

'Aren't you forgetting something?' says Jemmy. 'Your wedding is tomorrow. If you go off to Versailles and miss this tide, you will never make it to the altar. Or is that what you wanted all along?'

I shake my head, unwilling to admit I've cut things far closer than I ever intended. After waiting so long for Atherton, I can't bear the thought of jeopardising our wedding day.

'I can ... get a message,' I decide.

I can't let Robespierre win.

'Not in time to stop Atherton waiting like a fool at the church,' says Jemmy. 'I do not think even your mild-mannered spy-master could forgive such a humiliation.'

He paints a terrible picture, and my face twists with the pain of it. I realise I've been taking Atherton's kindness for granted. I picture my mild-mannered husband-to-be, his even features perplexed, hurt even. Of course he'd wait for me. Wouldn't he? I'm gripped with a fierce need to be back where he is, but I cannot leave France to Robespierre's machinations.

'There is still time,' I whisper. 'I could get a message using the Sealed Knot network.'

Salvatore is padding back nearer to where we're hidden now. I ball my fists.

'That a usual use of government resources, is it?' says Jemmy. 'Telling someone you'll be leaving them at the altar?'

He's right, of course. I can't use a highly privileged spy system for that purpose. Men risk their lives to get messages through.

Jemmy's expression softens. He shakes his head and speaks quietly. 'You must choose, Attica: England or France.'

Atherton or Robespierre. It's a strange thought and I dismiss it.

There's a long pause. I look back to Salvatore, who has completed his tour of the peripheries. He turns as if to leave, his coat swirling, then suddenly cups his hands to his mouth.

'You are nothing without me, Centime,' he shouts into the midst of smuggled goods. 'I took you from the gutters. You may have let this Pimpernel convince you of your fine sentiments and heart, but I know you better.'

I locate the patched salt sack with Centime inside. I feel as if I can see her in there, face screwed up in fear, not daring to breathe.

Hold on, Centime, I beg her silently, *don't give up.*

'Does he seduce you with kind words, Centime?' continues Salvatore. 'You know you would wither and die under such treatment. You have been raised to cruelty and cannot exist without a master. *I* know you. Have I not told you, we are two sides of the same coin? You cannot escape who you are.'

'Salvatore speaks like a madman,' I say, shaking my head. 'Centime is hardly likely to hand herself over to the promise of ill treatment.' But to my surprise, when I glance over to Jemmy, he looks stricken.

'For some women,' he says, 'it's all they know.' Something about his face tells me he knows, or has known, someone in that category very well. I'm distracted by a searing pity for him, remembering stories of his drunken mother. I return my attention to Centime's sack. Very faintly, it begins to shake.

No, no, no!

I send up a little prayer, begging Salvatore not to see it. But he has the eyes of a hunter, and he turns, detecting movement. In a moment I scoop a stone from the ground and throw it a few sacks away from where Centime hides.

Salvatore strides towards where it lands, then stands over the bag for a moment, before levelling a hard kick at it. The sack tips over, disgorging a heap of flour that rises in a puff of white.

I risk a glance at where Centime hides, and am relieved to see it silent and still.

I fire off another stone, this time striking a sack to the far corner. Salvatore wheels around, darting his sword, then lowers it.

From the middle distance comes the sound of drunken voices. The customs guard are making their return, rolling an ill-gotten barrel with them.

Salvatore's red lips press very thin.

'A curse on you, then,' he mutters towards the sacks of goods. 'Commit yourself to his care. When you repent of your folly you will find yourself dead to me.' He spits and taps a finger beneath his eye in an Italian gesture of warning. 'You will regret your disloyalty,' he says.

I watch, breath still held, as he returns to his horse, mounts and urges it away, digging his heels sharply into the animal's belly. There is a clatter of hoof beats as he exits. From the showy edges, Salvatore's men peel away, mounting their own steeds and following behind.

When the danger is passed, I run to where Centime is hiding.

'You are safe now,' I tell her as she emerges, white-faced and shaking. 'He is gone.'

But Centime is blank-eyed, as though still listening to Salvatore's words in a haunted replay.

I put an arm across her shoulder but she stands rigidly.

'It is not true, what he said,' I say. But my French is deserting me and I cannot find the words to say what I mean.

'How would you know?' she whispers. 'Raised in grandeur, betrothed to a lord. I am nothing to you. I am nothing to anybody,' she adds bitterly. 'Only him, and now he is gone.'

'Centime …'

'Is it true?' she demands, turning to face me. 'The ports will close at midnight?'

'I don't know,' I admit, feeling her falling away.

'If Salvatore was telling the truth,' says Centime, 'then you must leave me to my fate.' There is a dangerous note to her voice, as though she suspected all along I would betray her for my own cause. 'We will never get to a port before midnight.'

I'm searching for a way to reassure her, and finding none, when, to my surprise, Jemmy speaks.

'The royal port, just outside Versailles,' he reminds me quietly. 'Close enough. I know a captain there who'll help us.'

We exchange glances. A royal port will be crawling with Salvatore's men, and Centime seems in a mood to turn herself in.

Jemmy looks at me meaningfully. 'So long as you are both on the water, you will be safe.' I have not yet told him what my decision will be. Home to England or stay and attempt to warn the Queen and foil Robespierre.

'There is a nearer port we can leave by,' I tell Centime, possibilities uncoiling themselves. 'We have hours until midnight. Let us get you aboard a ship.'

'You will sail with me?'

I glance at Jemmy, and swallow hard.

I think of Atherton, waiting for me in England. If I get a message to the Sealed Knot, they can begin work, protecting English subjects in France, repatriating them.

'Yes,' I tell her. 'I will sail with you.'

It is the right choice, but my mind keeps leaping back to Robespierre. A fallen France.

This is not your country, I remind myself. *The mission is over.*

'Only take me from the city,' Centime mutters. 'I am not in my right mind and cannot think so well.'

We leave the compound of confiscated goods, headed to find stables for fast horses. And neither Jemmy nor I say aloud what we are thinking.

If we are right about Robespierre's plan, Versailles port will be one of the first to fall to chaos and looting. If Centime is to be made safe, we must set sail, and fast.

CHAPTER FIFTY-FOUR

*U*NCERTAINTY REIGNS OUTSIDE VERSAILLES. BREAD HAS been promised. But a great number of things have been promised to these hungry women over the past months. They believe things they can see with their own eyes. Not to mention they are exhilarated, charged with the power of their accomplishment. They have got what they came for, yet in a way they cannot define, they haven't.

'That's that, then,' murmurs Ovette, as they watch a large wagon of bread being trundled out of the palace to muted applause. 'The King is a good man, as we hoped. We can return home.' But somehow, none of them want to.

'The men would not do it,' they say, 'but we did. We came and asked, and it was given.'

A brave group of representative women are now back on the road to Paris, packed off with a token offering. Several wagonloads of bread. The rest stay, waiting for something else. What, they cannot quite say.

They cannot quite shake the feeling they have been tricked. Fobbed off. Certainly they are on the outside of the palace, with the huge golden gates very firmly closed against them.

Drunk Greta staggers around the courtyard and vomits copiously on the royal cobbles. A soldier approaches, trying to guide her out by the arm. She shakes him off.

'I don't give a fuck for your rules!' she tells him. 'We want Marie Antoinette!'

A small man walks to the front of the throng. Smartly dressed, which usually means a person cannot be trusted. But there is something about him that makes the women quieten down.

'If you have come to tell us to go back to our husbands, you can fuck off,' shouts one, over the growing hush.

The man smiles coolly. 'I do no such thing,' he says. 'I only come to greet you as equals. Lion-hearted citizens who have come to claim rightful justice.'

Some of the women recognise his voice. He is the same man who offered them kind words in the marketplace.

'Wait!' calls one. 'It is the lawyer. Monsieur Robespierre.'

'I hear you were granted an audience with the King,' says Robespierre. 'I commend it. You women have done what all the politicians could not.'

He gives a moment to let the words sink in. The women are listening now. The kind words resonate.

Robespierre tilts his head towards the palace.

'The men of the National Assembly meet in a hall in Versailles,' he says with a jerk of his thumb. 'A small hall, you might be sure,' he adds with a little smile. A few good-natured jeers go up, like cat-calls at a pantomime.

'The men talk of law for many hours, often late into the night,' continues Robespierre. 'And in the many months that have passed since the great storming of the Bastille, they have achieved not one tenth of what you ladies did today.'

A variety of broken and missing teeth are displayed in the crowd as several women grin. They like being referred to as 'ladies'.

'I only counsel you now with a warning,' continues Robespierre. 'The King is a kind man and has heard your pleas for bread. He has pledged to open the stores of Versailles.' He raises a finger to stop the inevitable glee from rising. 'But tonight he will go to his Queen, and tell her what he has done.'

There is a ripple now of discontent.

'You brave women well know how a husband in his bedchamber can be persuaded by a willing wife,' says Robespierre, waiting to see his words have been understood. A snake-like whisper begins in the crowd. The women's faces harden.

'She will make him take it back,' says one, loud enough for the others to hear. 'The Austrian bitch will make him go back on his word. She will starve us for her pretty ribbons and laugh as we drop.'

Robespierre holds up his hands.

'I will say no ill of the Queen,' he says.

'Of course you won't,' bellows a red-faced woman at the front. 'You're a man, like all the rest of 'em!'

This is met with jeers and taunts.

'All I say,' replies Robespierre, 'is be assured you have the King give you his promises in writing.'

'What good will that do us?' mutters a market girl with two broken front teeth. 'None of us can read.'

Discontent is growing now in the crowd. Fear of hunger is back in the faces.

Robespierre moves back. A marvellous feeling of power

surges in his chest. It was all so easy. He retreats to the discussion chambers, wishing for more such crowds, more such listeners. If only his words could reach those ears, the cause would be won in a day.

He walks quickly back to the main gate, where he is duly looked over and sneered at by the perfumed guard, before being admitted to the commoners' area, a part of the palace carefully demarcated to those without noble blood.

Hemmed in by high walls is the hall where the National Assembly meet. The stench of sweaty men in the small chamber is oppressive, and Robespierre raises a handkerchief to his nose as he insinuates his small body back next to Danton's bulky frame.

The large lawyer looks down at his diminutive friend.

'How is it looking out there?' he asks, moving aside slightly to afford Robespierre more room in the crush.

'I have always thought women were cleverer than men,' replies Robespierre. 'Those market girls will not be fooled by sugared words and a little bread. They distrust the Queen too greatly.'

'Very good,' grunts Danton. 'If they stay to put pressure on His Majesty, we might even get this thing signed today.'

His eyes drift back to the man speaking. So far he has been on the stand for thirty full minutes, speaking about the importance of a King on the throne.

'Lucky they can't get into the palace,' adds Danton meaningfully. 'If they hate the Queen as much as you say, they'll tear her to pieces.'

'Quite,' smiles Robespierre, looking pointedly to the speaker.

His hand drifts to his coat, feeling out the shape of the

tool Salvatore got for him. So simple for a noble to acquire these things.

Inside Robespierre's pocket is a golden key that will open the side gate at Princes' Court leading into Versailles Palace.

CHAPTER FIFTY-FIVE

With fast horses and a judicious choice of roads, we make short work of the miles between Paris and the town of Marly-le-Roi. Even so, it's a tiring journey, flat out, with Centime clinging to the back of my saddle. I am growing increasingly uneasy as to her state of mind. Since Salvatore's indictment of her character she seems to have closed in on herself, silent and brooding.

She agreed to be clothed in a disguise of a ragged peasant dress wordlessly. I have no idea what she is thinking. Her pensive silence has swollen to something more ominous as we reach the neat outskirts of the small royal town.

The rain is relentless, cold and running down our collars. Strands of Jemmy's dark hair are plastered to his face under his hat, which is rammed down low, and even his dark seafaring coat is showing signs of failing him. I can feel Centime shivering. She could easily have taken some dread contagion, hiding in the dusty windmill, then the damp customs compound and now soaked and shaking with cold. I promised her safety and exposed her to menace.

The road forks, and Jemmy and I slide from our horses to

examine the road sign. Centime waits, shivering, on my horse, her face blank and distant.

I brush mud from the wooden sign and dig my finger into the old letters.

'This way,' I say. 'Only a few more miles.' I hesitate, taking advantage of Centime not being able to overhear us.

'From Marly Port it is a short way to where your men are docked?' I confirm, not willing to admit out loud that despite my decision to return to England, I am leaving things extremely close, even by my own standards, to return for the wedding day.

Jemmy eyes me knowingly. 'Wedding jitters? Or have you finally realised it's not the best start to a marriage to arrive dirty from a channel crossing with a female lover in tow?'

'So long as Centime gets aboard, we shall be out of France before the borders close,' I say, as much to reassure myself as to convince Jemmy.

Jemmy shields his eyes and squints at the horizon through the downpour.

'You've read the sign wrong, Attica,' he accuses. 'There is Versailles Palace on the distance. Every bit as magnificent as they say, too,' he adds admiringly. 'I can see the great fountain they speak of.' He gazes at a vast marble-flanked crescent of water just visible in the middle distance.

'This is Marly-le-Roi,' I tell him, wiping rain from my face ineffectively. 'A country house for the Sun King. It's fallen out of favour so is mostly abandoned.'

'No!' He turns to me, half-smiling. 'You jest, surely? That great palace? You're certain?'

I smile. 'I told you, I came to Versailles before. I remember it well enough, young though I was. Listen,' I add. 'Hear that?'

Jemmy frowns, tilting his head. Rainwater streams off his hat to one side. 'That great booming noise? I thought it was thunder,' he says.

I shake my head. 'That is the great waterworks. Seven wheels, each ten times the height of a man. I have always wanted to see it,' I admit wistfully. 'It's held to be a marvel of engineering. Built to supply Versailles' fountains – there are at least fifty.'

We walk back to our horses and mount up. I glance at Centime, and she manages a wan smile.

'You'll have to come back and tour the waterwheels another time,' Jemmy tells me drily, urging his horse on.

'I do have an interest in fountains and waterworks,' I say, clicking my tongue for the horse to walk. 'The mechanics have always intrigued me. Versailles has some of the greatest, and Marly-le-Roi is the site of one of the greatest water pumps ever built. The Palace of Versailles is pitched at an elevation, you see, a great distance from water. A huge amount of power is needed to pump all that water to the grand fountains. And with every new fountain the task became more difficult.'

I sense I'm losing my audience, since Jemmy has turned his head back to the road with a glazed expression.

'Not without flaws, of course,' I add, moving my horse closer alongside his, and switching to an aspect of design I feel sure will interest him. 'It never worked as it should. One of my father's games for me was to hypothesise how the wheels and pumps might have been better configured. I always held the wheel should drive a piston horizontally. He thought the wheels should be larger. But that is often the answer of men.'

Jemmy is shaking his head. 'That's the problem with you

nobles,' he says. 'Did any clever soul ever think to build the palace closer to the water?'

We trot on, slowing as the tidy residences of Marly-le-Roi close around us. The little town hasn't lost its royal favour, and the residents still enjoy a little glamour, despite being eight miles from Versailles. To my great relief, the port is still operating as usual, with several likely-looking skiffs and boats being loaded with expensive supplies – gifts from the King of France's munificent advisers to royals from other realms.

'Should be easy enough,' says Jemmy, catching my mood. 'That ferryman by the little barge will help us, I shouldn't wonder.'

He slips easily from his horse, and I do the same. But I am shocked as I take in Centime's exhausted appearance. She seems near to swooning as I help her from the horse, and I fear the worst as she slumps to sit on the dirty cobbles.

CHAPTER FIFTY-SIX

*L*ETTING GO OF THE REINS OF MY HORSE I AM ABLE TO GET to Centime just before her head hits the ground. Her frail little body is ice-cold and shudders in my arms.

'Centime?' I say, as her eyelids flutter. 'Can you hear me?'

Jemmy is at my side in an instant, waving a little bag of smelling salts under her nose. She starts at the stench, and her eyes fly open wide.

'Centime.' I kneel beside her. 'Are you unwell?'

She waves away my concerns, raising her head. A baleful look goes in Jemmy's direction, I notice.

'It was a bumpy ride. I am only a little fatigued.' Her eyes settle on the decorated port before us. I glance up at Jemmy, who is hovering uncertainly, holding both our horses by the reins.

He motions me to come closer. I stand, hesitating for a moment. I drape my riding coat over Centime's shoulders then walk to his side, out of her earshot. Huddled down on the cobbles, she doesn't even seem to notice.

'I'll talk to the ferryman,' he says. 'You stay and look to her. Take care, Attica, I think the malady is more in her mind than her body, and this port trades arms.'

He doesn't need to say more. I am also concerned that Centime still bears loyalty to Salvatore. With her former master's vast criminal network, it would be all too easy for her to get a message to him here and alert him to our where-abouts.

Jemmy hesitates, looking at me.

'You're certain about this, Attica?' he asks quietly. 'Sailing to England? If you're right about Robespierre's plan, then tonight will be the end of France as we know it.'

'I promised Centime I would bring her to England,' I say, glancing at her.

Jemmy pauses. 'I only meant … You sure ye know what you're doing, marryin' this man?' he asks, his accent dropping several levels into New York Irish. 'If you were to be my wife, wild horses wouldn't—' He stops himself. 'I just don't know how he can be so rational about it, is all. Letting his bride to be off to Paris, when he could be bedding her.'

I wince at the vulgarity of the image. 'You don't understand,' I say, more harshly than I mean. 'People like me don't marry for hot-blood and fancy. There is too much at stake.'

'I don't see you as the calculating kind. Maybe you're more common than ye think.'

'You don't know anything about me,' I snap.

I glance up to see Jemmy looks wounded and regret saying it, but I won't take it back either. I've spent the last few hours wrestling with my conscience. The last thing I need is more doubt.

'Atherton and I are perfectly matched,' I say, avoiding Jemmy's eyes. 'We could hope for a good deal more happiness than most husbands and wives.'

'A fine aspiration, to be sure,' says Jemmy.

For a moment I allow myself to consider staying. Riding to Versailles, rescuing the Queen. Saving France from Robespierre.

I'm in a port. A message could be sent to reach Atherton by morning. Surely he would understand?

But he wouldn't, because it makes no sense. I am English, not French, and I have made promises that must be kept.

Jemmy shakes his head. 'Then go to our man, marry him. Don't miss the tide.' His voice sounds strained. 'I only thought … Maybe you'd be better suited to someone more able to meet your love of adventure.'

'You mean someone like you?' I say it jokingly, but see something cross his face and regret my tone. I open my mouth to take it back, but the right words don't come.

He looks away first, angrily.

'I would never flatter myself,' he says, 'that I could aspire to a fine lady such as yerself.'

His reaction jolts me clear of the temptation to stay a little longer in France.

'There is no question I shall return and marry Atherton,' I say, speaking more to myself than to Jemmy. 'Go talk to the ferryman,' I tell him. 'Ask for two people to cross.'

I shake my head, wrapping my arms about myself, since having given my coat to Centime, the rain falls on my bare arms.

'So long as you are certain you can handle our passage,' I conclude, trying to rub the goosebumps from my wet skin.

'You may be sure of it.' He glances at Centime, who is staring ahead with that same blank expression. 'Better get the thing done. If we wait, there might be no port for her to leave by.'

Centime's head turns suddenly towards us, and I wonder what she has heard. She presses a hand to the damp cobbles and raises herself to standing.

'Centime, you are unwell.' I walk to her side, helping her up, but she shrugs me off.

'I am not ill,' says Centime. 'I only need take a little wine, that's all.' And her voice is so void of feeling I am frightened for her. She swings towards a little clutch of seedy-looking riverside taverns, each with a table-mounted barrel of wine at the front to show their wares. 'Something to bring back my strength,' she adds.

I glance at Jemmy, who nods quietly.

'A cup of wine would be restorative,' he agrees. 'She'll be boarded within the hour. Get a good slug of grog into the girl, all will be well.' The look on Jemmy's face suggests otherwise, however.

'Not here,' I tell Centime, looking at the dockside taverns. 'Salvatore will likely have men on the local ports. You might be recognised. Let us go to a street back. Jemmy can meet us there.'

'Give me a little time alone with my thoughts,' says Centime. There is a steely set to her small jaw. 'It will be the last time I see French soil.'

I open my mouth to protest, but Jemmy puts a hand on my arm and draws me away.

'I can't see the harm in it, Attica,' he says. 'The folk that frequent these old drinking dens are so soused, they wouldn't know what day of the week it is, let alone recognise a fugitive.'

Against my better judgement, I let Jemmy lead me to the waterside, as Centime approaches one of the low drinking dens, looking entirely out of place, despite her disguise.

'They'll surely see through that tattered dress,' I mutter. 'She is far too well-fed.'

'In my experience,' says Jemmy, 'when a woman gets that

look, you leave her be.' He glances at the tavern she's headed for. 'She'll be safer there than with us,' he adds. 'Less to trouble her thinking.' Jemmy shakes his head, watching her go. 'A fine mess you've made, Attica. Did ye not think she'd have feelings for you?'

'I have feelings for her too,' I say, confused. 'I am bringing her to freedom.'

'And what if she does not want to be free?'

CHAPTER FIFTY-SEVEN

*A*s Jemmy predicted, making the deal with the ferryman is easily done. A passage is arranged far cheaper than I might have thought possible. Jemmy relays my message, so it will reach the Sealed Knot, warning them of the danger to their subjects. We retire to the cobbled waterfront, leaving Centime to one last tankard of foul dockside wine, though we're both uneasy about her state of mind.

With my head full of doubts, I've set to work whittling a stick with my knife, trying to distract myself. I cast the occasional glance at the tavern door, assuring myself Centime has not yet decided to come out of her own accord. I should go in. Console her. Somehow I can't bring myself to have that conversation just yet.

'Will there be any of that stick left when you're done with it, Attica?'

'I only hate the waiting part.' I push the blade deep and peel off a layer of bark.

'You and Centime will be loaded aboard within the hour,' says Jemmy. 'By my reckoning, that leaves us five hours until midnight. Time enough for a safe passage.'

He sits next to me on the dockside cobbles and eyes the rapidly diminishing stick.

'Still wondering over whether to make the crossing?' he asks gently.

'No,' I say untruthfully, halting my blade halfway down the skinned stick. 'Even if we rode now to Versailles, Marie Antoinette is blinkered and stubborn, by all accounts. Likely she'd refuse to believe the worst until it is too late.'

'True,' agrees Jemmy, frowning as I chip off more pieces of bark. 'Fortunately, there is no need to convince her of the imminent peril. All we need do is stop Robespierre from opening that gate.'

I shake my head fiercely. 'A few English subjects in France. What does it really matter?' My knife strips wood at high speed.

'Not a great deal, if that is really all you fear for,' says Jemmy. 'The problem is, I think it is the French people you care for. All those innocent women and children who will be slaughtered at Versailles if the Queen dies. Robespierre could rise to power.'

My blade slips on the stick. I reset my knife to continue stripping bark.

'There are things about being a noble you couldn't understand,' I say. 'A birthright comes with responsibilities as well as privileges. And,' I spread my hands, trying to explain, 'I might be a half-breed, born out of wedlock, so expectations of me are less. All well and good. But I'm still my father's only daughter. I have enjoyed great advantages from the family name, and now I must repay them.'

'Not to mention,' says Jemmy, 'you are deeply in love with your future husband.' He arches an eyebrow.

'That hardly needs saying,' I retort. 'Perhaps I do not know where I am supposed to fit,' I add. 'But I do know I am in love with Atherton. I have been for years. All my adult life.' I look down at the stick and begin peeling the length with my knife again. Great long shavings fall free.

'You always did think too much,' says Jemmy, watching the curls of wood drop. 'You have a pirate's heart, Attica, plain and simple. You are meant to roam, not be locked away as an English wife. Be true to your own code and worry not of anyone else's.'

'This isn't something to be solved by one of your ocean wisdoms,' I retort. 'It isn't the same for me. You were born free.' It's the nearest I've ever come to admitting aloud that I yearn for something other than the life that seems to be awaiting me.

'Everyone is born free, Attica. It's thinking we should be someone else that is the cage. You might rather you were a political person, writing speeches and making change that way. But the truth is you wouldn't be much good at it.' The corner of his mouth twitches. 'Like it or not, you're a lot more like me than them,' he says. 'We're the idiots who rush in, guns blazing, risking life and limb. Those high-ups pretend to admire our courage but secretly they pity us. What they don't know is that we love all this.' He waves a hand at some unseen thing and I know exactly what he means. The explosive uncertainty of our life here. The daring rescues.

'I can do more good—' I begin.

'In the drawing rooms,' interrupts Jemmy. 'So you keep telling me. But are you really made for such a task? Should it not be better filled by someone with the ability to sit quietly and listen? You cannot help who you are,' he says. 'You would not last a year at ambassadors' parties before you began picking locks and avenging justice.'

He's right.

Jemmy sighs and moves closer to me, lifting what's left of the whittled stick out of my unresisting hand. 'Shall I solve the problem for you?' he suggests.

I look distractedly to the stick, wondering if he has some clever trick for whittling. But he lets it drop to the ground.

I frown, confused. 'Why could you …?'

In answer Jemmy slides his hands on either side of my chin. It is such an assured gesture that I am momentarily frozen in surprise. When I was a girl, my father showed me how to tickle a trout under its belly, stilling it in the water. I always wondered how the fish felt, entranced. When Jemmy kisses me, it is salty ocean and wide-open skies, and the surprise of it has me momentarily mesmerised. Then he draws back, examining my eyes keenly.

'If that felt like nothing to you,' says Jemmy, 'you must go back and marry your Englishman.'

Then he raises himself to standing and walks smartly back towards the ferryman, leaving me sat on the cold cobbles with my mouth open. I want to hit him.

'I will go and marry my Englishman!' I shout after him, getting to my feet. He doesn't turn around, only calls over his shoulder.

'You do that, Attica.'

'It *did* feel like nothing!' I add, raising my voice higher, recovering myself from his earlier spell and feeling the fury rise. 'Less than any kiss from a girl on the Marais, you may be certain!'

'Then board the ship with Centime. With a good tide you might arrive in time to be married yet. But just on the chance you decide against it, I'll find us fresh horses.'

Jemmy continues walking without looking back, and something about the maddening swagger of his gait suggests he is confident I'll decide against sailing back to England.

'Bloody pirates,' I mutter. My fingers move to touch my lips, and I pull them away quickly, annoyed with myself.

The truth is Jemmy is right about everything. The fact I cannot stand by and let women and children die at Versailles. A traitorous part of my heart that is not ready to be married tomorrow. And at the heart of it all: *I cannot let Robespierre win.*

Perhaps I will stay. Ride to Versailles and defend the French Queen. Jemmy's crew will honour my promise to Centime.

I roll the idea around in my mind. The idea of boarding the boat to England feels grey and empty. I watch Jemmy's retreating back, his kiss still tingling on my lips.

I won't give Jemmy the satisfaction of telling him straight away.

First I should assure myself of Centime's state of mind, I decide. At the very least I owe her a goodbye. I will keep Jemmy waiting just long enough to give him cause for concern at his own arrogant predictions.

CHAPTER FIFTY-EIGHT

I FIND CENTIME IN THE FAR CORNER OF THE BARREL-BAR. It's a low-ceilinged room made from three mariner's cottages made one. A dirt floor is littered with broken stools and tables from old barrels. Greasy lamb-fat tapers fill the air with smoke.

Jemmy was right to think her striking looks would have little impact here. The little gaggle of customers are too drunk to notice anything, including the rat-faced landlady, who sways in her seat as she draws me wine from her tap.

Beyond is a small sparse room of crumbling plaster and visible wattle and daub peeking through at intervals. The only other customer, a dead drunk man, lies sprawled in a corner, snoring loudly enough to rattle the few remaining broken windowpanes.

My fears eased somewhat, I take a sip of wine. It is disgusting. The cheapest, most poorly cellared variety I've ever had the misfortune to drink. Most likely the landlady allows her barrels to sit on the street in full sun for as long as it takes to sell the contents. A mouthful of sediment catches at the back of my mouth and I take another swig to drive it down, examining the murky contents of my tankard accusingly.

Centime laughs good-naturedly. 'Not to your taste?'

'It is the bitterest wine I have ever drunk.' I draw the liquid over my teeth, wincing. 'And I have been to some low establishments in my time.'

'Try mine,' she says, adding a splash from her tankard. 'In places like this you pay the extra sous for a dash of clove. It helps sweeten the mix.'

I sip tentatively, and find she's right. The spice overwhelms the astringent sourness of the cheap wine.

'You learn such things in cheap brothels,' says Centime, with a faraway look. 'Places like this.'

A shadow falls on the doorway. A shambolic prostitute has staggered into view then retreats, disappointed on seeing the newest arrival is a woman.

'There's a system,' says Centime, watching her leave. 'A creaking plank or a bell. Lets the dockside whores know when fresh meat has arrived. I was arrested in a place like this,' she adds, not meeting my eye but looking through the peeling doorway to the riverbank beyond.

She glances at me, perhaps wondering if I'll divulge the truth of my own tragic past. The parting from my mother. The life she gave for my freedom.

'We sail to England soon?' she asks, when I make her no reply.

'It will not be long,' I tell Centime. 'By morning you shall be on English soil.'

'English soil,' she repeats, more to herself than to me. Her low mood seems to have taken another turn now. There is a strange energy to her beneath the layers of gloom. My guess is she has drunk a good deal too much wine during the wait, but bears deep drunkenness with practised aplomb.

'Shall I bring some water?' I suggest. 'Something to dilute the wine?'

'You do not like me drunk?' asks Centime, leaning forward to overfill her tankard and taking three attempts to match the rim with her mouth.

'I only fear for your safety. You must keep your wits about you.'

'Naturally,' says Centime, after a deep sip, 'you must take me away with all speed. I am a threat to you, is that not so? If I were to reveal you as the Scarlet—'

I catch her hand. 'Innocent lives will be lost. Centime, this isn't a game.'

She looks away from me with a small smile. Her inebriation makes her difficult to read. I'm wondering which version of herself she will lapse into next. As if in answer she draws her hand gently free from where I hold it.

'And when you are married to your fine lord?' she asks softly, replacing her tankard on the table and leaning both her elbows either side of it. 'Surely the game is over for you as surely as it is for me. One way or another,' she adds morosely, following my gaze to the bottle-panes of the window.

I don't reply, glancing to the doorway.

'You are as bad as he is,' accuses Centime. 'I thought, in the windmill—' She stops herself and gulps wine. 'The way you were,' she says quietly, shaking her head.

I reach across the table and take her hands. 'Things are complicated. I've made promises. This isn't about just me.'

She laughs bitterly. 'You English are all cold,' she says. 'You are as bad as the lawyer.'

'I didn't realise you had spoken with Robespierre.'

She tries to hide her slip, tossing her head as though unconcerned.

'Oh, we had a few words,' she admits. 'He wanted me to get him a map of Versailles Palace. I refused, out of loyalty to Salvatore.'

'He told you his plans, didn't he?' I accuse.

She swallows more wine, then meets my eye triumphantly. 'Robespierre means to let a mob into Versailles. If they enter by the Princes' Court gate, they cut off the entrance for the guard. The Queen shall be trapped in her bedroom.'

'Why didn't you tell me before?'

'It is a ridiculous plan, Salvatore said so. Besides, *you* can hardly scold me for keeping back the truth,' she adds, her eyes flaring. 'You came here to tell me you would not make the crossing with me.'

The shock of the accusation must show because she smiles triumphantly.

'I knew it all along,' she says, staring down into her wine, then taking another long draught. 'You are in love with him.' She gestures her arm towards the street, and Jemmy's face hovers in my vision.

'I am betrothed and he, Atherton, will understand,' I say, struggling to keep up with her leaps of logic. 'I will make certain you will be well looked to on the boat. But there are innocent lives at stake. Hundreds. Maybe thousands.' I take her hand, speaking quietly. 'You will be free, Centime, away from a monster who mistreated you.'

To my surprise she only laughs again, seeming suddenly a great deal more sober.

'I never expected you to understand,' she says. 'The monster is in here.' She strikes her narrow chest. 'I carry it with me wherever I go.' Centime looks suddenly very thoughtful, and desperately sad.

'You are right,' she says. 'I am too drunk. I am sorry. Might you bring me a little water? I must cause no trouble to the good men who will take me to the boat.'

She gives me such a vulnerable look of repentance that my frustration with her melts away. 'Of course,' I frown. 'You will be happy, Centime, only wait and see.'

'You are very good,' she says quietly.

I rise and leave her sitting at the table, wondering if I am doing the right thing at all.

CHAPTER FIFTY-NINE

WHEN I RETURN WITH A CARAFE OF VERY BROWN-LOOKING water, Centime seems to have recovered her old charming self.

'Tell me about him,' she says, as I reseat myself. 'The one who is to be your husband.'

I hesitate, wondering if this line of conversation will only draw out the less predictable side to her.

'Please,' she adds. 'I am calm now.'

'He is a good man,' I say slowly. 'In many ways, he made me the person I am.' I frown. 'It was he who suggested I train in Sicily,' I say, 'at an academy that teaches assassins knife-craft.'

She giggles. 'Nothing you ever tell me sounds true.'

I smile in acknowledgement of this.

'So this man,' she says, 'he sent you to school with cut-throats?'

'It was a dreadful place,' I admit. 'Atherton came out to see me there, and I told him he had made a mistake. He had overestimated my abilities and I would be dead within the week.' I smile. 'I was so certain.'

I think back. For the first time since I'd known him, Atherton had raised his voice.

'Do you think I sent you to Sicily to die?' he said. 'Do you think I would give my prized girl over to an Italian slaughterhouse, unless I thought her better equipped than any other there to defend herself? You have dexterity of a kind I have never seen before. You have a brain that can solve codes, puzzles. What is the human body, if not a code to de deciphered? Strength has nothing to do with it, Attica. So long as you are strong enough to plunge the blade where it matters, you have sufficient.'

Even so, it had taken a few days for his words to sink in. It was on the day of my first fight to the death and the third boot to my face, things had finally fallen into place. The delicate network of arteries and veins hiding beneath the skin. Slightly different in every person. The places if even lightly struck that would make a man gasp or bend in a particular direction. Things to put a person off balance so they might stagger left, right, down. Whichever direction would expose their most vulnerable pulse point.

It had all seemed easy then.

'He gave me valuable advice,' I conclude. 'Advice that kept me alive. And changed me, too. My way of looking at the world.'

'So you owe him something?' asks Centime, rolling her tankard around in her hands. 'The same as with me and Salvatore? He saved you from your old life.'

'It is not the same. I love him,' I say with feeling.

'Maybe there are different kinds of love.' Centime looks thoughtful. 'I am sorry for putting you to so much trouble,' she tells me. 'I shall be a quiet mouse from now on, I promise.' She tips a little water into her wine and slides my tankard to me.

'To England,' she says. 'A new life.'

We chink tankards, and I drink wine, still entirely disconcerted by Centime's lightning switches in character.

She upends all the liquid into her mouth, a dribble running down her chin.

'Sailors say you must drink it all for a lucky voyage,' she says, wiping her mouth with the back of her hand.

I follow the gesture sadly, thinking Jemmy is right. These little defects in formal manners will be quickly noticed in London circles. Pitying her, I throw back my own wine, gritting my teeth at the awful taste.

The minute I do, Centime's expression changes completely. The nervousness I had attributed to the upcoming voyage is replaced by something different. Guilt.

Dread spreads through the pit of my stomach.

'Centime,' I begin, 'what have you …?'

She is looking at my tankard. I stare into the empty vessel. There is a horribly familiar oily residence at the bottom. Something I have seen a hundred times in the darkened fusty residues of my father's study.

'The spices,' she says miserably. 'You couldn't smell it, with the spices.'

Laudanum. The sweet scent was disguised. Not so the brownish oil, which clings to the sides of the tankard. A terrible certainty strikes me, as I realise how much I must have ingested in one draught.

'I am so sorry, Attica,' she says. 'You never could understand. I cannot survive without him. And he shall never forgive me unless I bring him the Pimpernel.'

I stand quickly. Too quickly. The fast movement brings an immediate rush of blood to the head. I turn, placing a hand on the table to steady myself, and noticing in a slightly abstract way that the wood seems to shift unexpectedly beneath my fingers. Putting one foot in front of the other, I walk determinedly to the door, but before I'm halfway there, my legs are not behaving as I want them to.

No one bats an eye at the staggering Englishwoman as I pass through the mouldering doorway.

Something moves behind me. I try to turn, but now I notice the world divides into two. Centime's sad and guilty face is looking at me in duplicate.

'Attica,' she says, 'be careful. You will fall.'

My legs give out on the cobbles outside, and I lean on the doorframe, putting a hand to my head. The world spins, changes entirely, and I realise that I am now resting my head on the open door.

Then the wooden texture slides away, and I am on the ground, watching Centime's silken shoes walk lightly from the dockside tavern.

The last thing that crosses my mind, before the mouldering tavern interior closes into darkness, is Jemmy. He will assume I have boarded the ship to England.

CHAPTER SIXTY

*W*HEN I COME TO CONSCIOUSNESS I CAN'T MOVE MY ARMS and legs. I'm bowed backwards in a strange posture. It's loud, as though I'm onboard ship in the midst of a terrible storm. Spray is hitting my face. The whole world rattles and rumbles around me.

I turn my head and see my wrists are tied above my head. I guess my ankles are fixed the same way. I'm tied to a massive waterwheel.

I close my eyes. This isn't good. I'm struck by a sudden certainty that I'm in hell, subject to some bizarre torment for all eternity.

Then the shapes turning around me come into better focus and I realise.

I'm in the Marly machine.

The mighty set of waterwheels that send the immense body of water needed uphill to spurt through the Versailles fountains. I can feel the reassuring shape of my knife, cold across my chest. I can't get to it, of course. I am completely immobilised.

I scan the wooden confines of my immediate area. A man is

seated a little way back. Icy fear sweeps through me. Salvatore sits on a wooden stool watching me intently.

'You woke up far sooner than I might have expected, for someone who had taken such a large sleeping draught,' he says conversationally. 'Perhaps your father's tolerance for the stuff is in your blood.'

He stands, adjusting his green silk suit jacket. In the half-light of the mill his dark eyes and widow's peak have taken on an even more fiendish quality. My vision is still horribly blurred and it's hard to keep focus. There's an ache to my head that ebbs and flows.

'Centime,' I manage, my lips parched. 'Where is she?'

He shakes his head. 'You needn't concern yourself with her. Centime is a slave at heart and will always return to her master. She gave you up,' he adds with relish, 'to buy back her place at my side.'

I try to swallow, but my throat it thick. I cannot quite believe that Centime would bring me to Salvatore. But there is no escaping it. She drugged me, and arranged my capture. Hot betrayal flashes through me.

'Mademoiselle Morgan,' Salvatore stands, walking closer, 'you are a strange breed. I imagine you think yourself noble. But a cup of wine half-filled with brackish water is still a salty drink. You are no commoner. You may as well accept it. Yet you are no noble either. There is no place for you.'

'I have no delusions to my aristocracy,' I say tightly.

'Yet you do not know your place. You have been playing with my toys.'

The roar of the Marly machine is making it difficult to think. All around is tumbling water and groaning wood. I pull at the ropes securing my wrists and ankles, but they are bound so tight there is barely any blood left in my hands.

Salvatore doesn't take his eyes off me.

'As you know, I have an interest in old prison methods.' He sweeps a hand to the pounding water all around. 'The Marly machine is quite the marvel,' he says. 'But not all the elements first envisaged worked as the engineers hoped. This smaller wheel, for example, is now wholly dormant. Unless, that is, someone cares to turn it manually.'

I try not to look down into the dark waters beneath.

Salvatore comes back into view, scrutinising my expression.

'I considered very deeply which punishment would best apply to you,' he says. 'Here in France we burn witches. But you are English, so I thought something from your own country more appropriate. I am told you English use a ducking stool for women who go beyond their place.'

He gestures to the waterwheel.

'I could not replicate the exact same as you have in your native country.' He gives a little smile. 'But I believe this is close enough for the desired effect. The thing about cold water,' observes Salvatore, looking at my face, 'is it doesn't take long for it to start stripping your faculties. I have watched men – very brave men – fall to pieces very quickly under its influence. Something to do with blood flow, I believe.'

'Blood rushes to the heart,' I tell him, 'away from the hands and other extremities. One quickly loses the ability to coordinate the muscles, to swim.' I manage a smile. 'Fortunately, in my present condition, this is not a concern.' I meet his eye. 'Anatomical knowledge is a little more advanced in England than in France. We dissect our criminals for science, rather than pull their bodies apart with horses.'

Salvatore's expression darkens.

'Ah yes, your insufferable English superiority,' he sneers. 'Look at you, in your ridiculous unfashionable clothes, all straight and stiff and full of your own importance. I imagine you think yourself very clever indeed, running around, playing at spying for your country.' He pauses. 'Yet they keep things from you,' he says. 'The escaped slave.' He smiles wolfishly. 'You really think your countrymen would have troubled themselves to inform a half-breed – female at that – of English plans in France?' He leaves a deliberate pause, then moves closer.

'Did they tell you the English are mad to acquire French slaving routes?' he enquires. 'I imagine they left that little detail off the briefing when they sent you to spy on me?'

I say nothing, keeping my mouth tight shut.

'We French own a great many lucrative plantations,' he muses. 'That kind of wealth is very tempting to an English King.'

'It isn't true,' I say. 'England advises France on how to end slavery.'

'And why might that be?' Salvatore grins. 'Because if France ends slavery our economy will collapse. England will be free to pick and choose which coastal routes they like. Do not fool yourself, Mademoiselle Morgan. It is all about money. There is not a drop of sentiment to your country's seeking abolition in France.'

Lord Pole. I feel my hands ball into fists. This is exactly the kind of plan he would construct.

It would be a means to an end, of course. Gain the routes, overtake the plantations. Allow a degree of trading that could be controlled and finally phased out. I remember how Atherton was tight-lipped about the exact plans for our upcoming mission and it hits me like an assassin's knife in the ribs: Atherton must have known.

A means to an end.

A livid despair blooms on my heart like a bloodstain. It occurs to me in a flash of clarity: I have been fighting for men who are no better than Robespierre.

The pain must show on my face because Salvatore's smile widens.

'So you see, your country is not so very noble after all,' he says.

A chasm seems to open up between the Atherton who is to be my husband and the man who keeps national secrets. In the depths of the void, everything I knew has been turned upside-down. I do not know what to think or what to believe.

'I know how you feel,' says Salvatore philosophically. 'Everything you have believed in is a lie. I thought the same myself, shortly after the Queen had me imprisoned. You cannot imagine how many ways I plotted killing Marie Antoinette.' He smiles cruelly. 'Then came the little lawyer with his plans to have her torn apart by the mob. Naturally I was happy to help.'

'You plot the destruction of your own kind,' I spit. 'If the Queen dies France will fall to chaos and the commoners will wipe your noble bloodlines from the earth.'

Salvatore chuckles. 'You think me as silly as the lawyer. This is not England, mademoiselle. France has had kings and noble blood for centuries.' He pauses, to be certain I am listening. 'There is another way out of the Queen's bedchamber that a commoner such as Robespierre would not expect. A passage that connects her chamber to her husband's.' He smiles broadly. 'Marie Antoinette will have a nasty fright, but she will escape. I am sensible enough, Mademoiselle Morgan, to salve my revenge with such. The idea of our Queen running through a cobwebbed corridor in her undress,' he chuckles. 'She will probably die of the humiliation.'

'What if the Queen doesn't do as you expect?' I say. 'There is every likelihood she won't understand the danger she is in.'

Uncertainty flashes across his face.

'Not even she would be so foolish,' he mutters, but I can see from his face he thinks she might. 'The people love the King,' he decides. 'Even if something were to happen, he would retain the throne.'

'It sounds as though you have underestimated Monsieur Robespierre,' I tell him. 'The lawyer plans for everything. I doubt he would have risked his schemes on something as obvious as your betrayal.'

Salvatore tilts his head to consider my expression. His eyes narrow cruelly. 'I must confess, Monsieur Robespierre's *fixation* with a mysterious English spy piqued my interest.' He comes close enough to be only inches from my face. 'Which is why you are going to tell me all about the Scarlet Pimpernel.'

CHAPTER SIXTY-ONE

THE MARLY WATERWHEELS POUND LOUDLY, CHURNING A constant spray of water into the air.

I close my eyes, letting Salvatore's words sink in. Centime must have told him everything.

'Poor little Centime,' continues Salvatore. 'She would do anything to buy back my good favour. Including betraying your little secret.' I open my eyes. He is smiling malevolently. 'Imagine what the lawyer will say when he discovers I have captured you. He is obsessed. I have already sent him a message, telling him that I have the Pimpernel in my possession. Monsieur Robespierre will doubtless arrive with us, as fast as his cheap old mare can carry him.' Salvatore scoffs at his own joke.

I turn over what this might mean. In the short term, Salvatore is more likely to keep me alive, so he might show Robespierre his prize. In the long term ... Even if I do escape, it is all over.

'Naturally,' he continues, 'no woman could have master-minded the kind of escapes and plots this Pimpernel masterminded.' He reveals white teeth in a partial smile. 'You weren't working alone.'

It's as much as I can do not to shake my head at the ridiculousness of it all. The thing would be funny if I did not know what was coming next.

'The pirate,' continues Salvatore. 'Jemmy Avery. You will tell me how to find him.'

'Jemmy can barely sign his own name,' I say. 'He is a fool, with a love of jewelled pistols. Nothing more than a pirate drawn to gold.'

'Tell me where he is.'

I shake my head.

Salvatore smiles cruelly. 'I thought you would be difficult,' he says. 'Hoped, rather. It is always more entertaining to win a lady, rather than her be too willing, don't you think?'

'Our notions of winning women are very different.'

Salvatore walks away. His being out of sight is more frightening than anything. I close my eyes, trying to drive the fear back, then feel the wheel jerk hard downwards. My feet are submerged, then my legs and torso.

I try to stay calm, not to panic and gasp. But as I'm plunged under the icy water all orderly thoughts flee and the cold takes my breath away. I shut my mouth, only just managing to catch a scant gasp of air before I'm plunged into the depths. The wheel is turning a full rotation, taking me all the way down.

The wheel is pulling me so I am inches from the riverbed, and back up out again. For a moment I am upside-down, blood rushing to my head. Then I am face to face with Salvatore once more, nausea and despair hitting me in equal measure. I cough out water, involuntary shivers convulsing my entire body.

'I imagine you are enjoying your time in France rather less now?' suggests Salvatore, as I gasp for air.

'On the contrary,' I say, coughing out water. 'It's long been an ambition of mine to see the Marly machine mechanisms. I must thank you for the opportunity.' I drive back another shiver.

This gives me an idea. I have studied the great waterwheel. Surely I must have some knowledge that might help me escape. None comes to mind. Jemmy's scorn at the over-engineered construction drifts into my frozen brain.

Did any clever soul ever think to build the palace closer to the water?

Jemmy would tell me not to make things so complicated.

Salvatore eyes me keenly. 'The lawyer will be very angry,' he says. 'He has a fascination with you. Imagine his expression when I tell him how you died.'

'You should be careful, monsieur,' I say. 'Robespierre will soon be a powerful man. Torturers of the ancient regime such as yourself will not be part of his vision.'

'I? Torture?' His eyes lower laconically. 'I only perform His Majesty's justice. A little sideline, albeit a very pleasant one. The lawyer hasn't the stomach for it.' His fleshy lips widen in a smile. 'The very notion that little runt might become powerful. You are very amusing, mademoiselle. But enough pleasantries. Let us get on with discovering what you know.'

This time he cranks the wheel slowly, submerging me to the chest in water. The cold is such that my head aches beyond rational thought. I cannot seem to piece together something that could help me escape.

I try to fix my gaze on anything but Salvatore. There is an unexpected movement at his shoulder. For a moment I think it is Jemmy, come to rescue me.

Then the shape comes into focus and I see it is Centime. Despite it all, my heart twists to see her, standing at Salvatore's side.

'You said you wouldn't hurt her.' Centime's sad voice does something to me I can't explain. It is worse than the cold water. I wonder if she really is here. If it is perhaps some trick of the cold and shock.

Then she looks at me, and something passes between us. Salvatore sees it and his dark eyebrows knit together in fury.

He strides back to the mechanism, and turns it fast. This time when I go under, I'm not quick enough to take a breath of air. Instead, I inhale a gulp of water somewhere in the freezing dark world beneath.

When I break the surface I am upside-down, entirely disoriented, and choking on cold water. Slowly I am turned the right way about, and am once again brought level with Salvatore's face.

There is a horrible expression of excitement to his wolfish features, the close-set eyes hard and bright, the fleshy lips red and hungry.

I am coughing, trying to breathe, and shaking uncontrollably from the cold. My heart is pounding; my forehead feels swollen, like a cold mask. I find I cannot move my fingers. It is as though my body no longer knows how to order itself.

'Tell me where the pirate is,' demands Salvatore.

I shake my head. The world is sliding in and out of focus. He smiles thinly. 'Then let us use some more persuasive tools,' he decides. 'Something from Monsieur Robespierre's execution assignments, perhaps.'

He retreats to the back of the platform, where I notice with an abstract kind of dread that he has a leather bag, similar to what a doctor might carry. As I'm weighing up the terrible possibility of what might be inside it, Centime walks closer to me.

She extends a hand, her face screwed up in pity, and strokes a tendril of soaking hair from my wet face.

'Poor Attica,' she whispers. 'You must not be so brave. He won't stop. Tell him what you know.'

I shake my head. She leans in closer, and now her eyes are at my chest. I am still wearing the amber locket given me by Lord Pole. With the suicide pill.

Gently, she eases it open and removes the tiny glass vial.

'Take it,' she urges, lifting it to my mouth.

I shake my head.

'Please. The things he does ...'

I shut my mouth tight, and look away from her.

Centime rests her head on my neck and a little sob escapes her. She thinks I will break under torture, I realise, and cannot bear to see it.

'If it ends for me here, it will not be as Salvatore hopes,' I tell her. 'I will never give Jemmy up.'

She raises her head, looking into my eyes.

'You are brave,' she whispers. 'But it will do you no good.' Centime shakes her head.

She places a hand on my chest and jerks the locket free in her closed fist.

From a few feet away Salvatore laughs. 'What a venal creature you truly are, Centime. Surely you can wait until she is dead to rob the corpse?'

She backs away, keeping her eyes on mine.

Then she turns in a whirl of skirts, and returns to Salvatore, who is clutching a wicked-looking set of pincers. Centime holds the necklace aloft.

'A spy device?' she suggests, letting the empty compartment swing.

'Perhaps.' Salvatore barely looks at it. 'You shall have to work harder for my forgiveness.'

She bats her lashes and gives him a dazzling smile.

'My darling, it will be the business of my life.' She leans up and kisses him softly on the mouth. Salvatore winds his hand into her hair, pulling her head back. He finally releases her with a self-satisfied expression, looking at me.

'You can never trust a whore,' says Salvatore, gazing down at Centime. 'They will always follow the money.'

Centime turns to me. 'Adieu,' she says softly. But there is something in her eyes – a sadness. As swiftly as a card sharp, she moves her closed fist to her mouth. When she brings it down again her fingers are outstretched, empty.

The poison pills. She was holding the capsules in her palm.

Centime turns back to Salvatore, who is still gloating at his prize.

'One last kiss,' she says, 'before I go.'

'No! Centime!' I close my eyes, trying to find the words. I am struck by an awful childlike fear of her leaving me here. It shames and surprises me all at once.

Misinterpreting my horror, Salvatore throws his head back and laughs victoriously. He pulls Centime close to him. She moulds her body to his and kisses him passionately.

'Centime,' I say, helplessly straining at my bonds. 'Don't.'

When she breaks away from Salvatore, her lips are already contorting strangely.

She brings her dark fingers to them wonderingly, following the spasms of her mouth.

'You were right,' she says in a strange voice. 'It is so quick.'

Behind her, Salvatore's smile of victory does a bizarre jig, as though the muscles have their own agenda. There is a fraction of horror in his expression as he realises something strong is burning him.

'Centime,' he croaks in utter disbelief. 'What have you done?'

Centime wheels away, panting, then falls to the ground, eyelids fluttering.

'She got the stronger dose,' I tell him, watching as Centime fades away.

Salvatore's fury at the unexpected betrayal could burn through walls. But it is too late for him. He tries to lurch towards me. Then it all happens so quickly, I can hardly believe it.

Within two rapid breaths, Salvatore falls to his knees, his whole body gripped in sudden spasm. His arms wing out, as though jerked by invisible strings, then he gasps and slumps unmoving on the ground.

CHAPTER SIXTY-TWO

*L*AFAYETTE SLIDES FROM HIS HORSE AND LEANS FOR A moment, pressing his head to the sweating flank. He has not slept now for two days. And still there is work to do. The King has inadequate guard. Grossly inadequate. Barely enough to form a colourful parade, far less defend a palace of the proportions here.

The best he can do is dig in and await the breach. Because this flimsy palace cannot withstand even the most half-hearted attack by starving women. Seven long decades have lavished millions on broadening the doors, widening the windows and painting it all gold. He must only hope the King has dug some vestige of charm from his strangely mannered demeanour.

Lafayette turns these things in his mind, when a strange little man approaches, apparently from nowhere. He is a pin-neat fellow, with the ink-stained fingers of a book-man. Likely one of the men from the National Assembly, considers Lafayette, with a lurch of unease. One of the lawyers. Though this man looks so pale and small as to be almost ill, with a disturbingly burning glint behind his round glasses.

He bows to Lafayette. 'A good evening to you,' he says. 'I am Monsieur Robespierre.' He pauses and the next words seem to cost him some effort. 'It is a good thing you did for France today,' he says. 'We were told you helped guide those women and stop them from tearing apart the palace. It seems you are popular with the people.'

Robespierre makes a smile which is odd in the extreme.

Through his exhaustion, Lafayette notices the lawyer holds a decanter of wine, clasped incongruously to his spotless shirt, as though the hand of a drunkard has been strangely grafted to the body of a pedant.

'How did you get up here?' demands Lafayette, attempting to shake back his tiredness and stand straighter.

'Forgive the intrusion,' says Robespierre, ignoring the question. 'The men at the National Assembly thought you should take some comfort after your long ride.'

'Yes?' Lafayette finds himself thinking he has seen this man before, but cannot bring to mind where.

'Only to say, your watch is over,' says the man. 'There is no danger to the Queen. Most of the arrivals are asleep, or falling down drunk. The rest have returned to Paris, well satisfied with their King.'

Lafayette nods. He is relieved, though a part of him feels there is something not quite right about this tidy little fellow, with his spotless suit.

'You are one of the Assembly men?' he asks finally, rubbing his forehead. 'One of the lawyers?'

The man nods politely. 'No one of importance,' he replies. 'Only a messenger. But be assured, you may rest now. Your duty to the King has been accomplished.' He raises the decanter like a peace gesture, then places it on the ground. 'For your thirst,' he says. 'No glasses could be found. Food is being sent. The guard are under orders to alert you if any women make an attempt on the palace. But this seems unlikely. They are simple market people, exhausted and sleeping where they fall.'

Lafayette accepts this with relief as Robespierre turns to leave. With a great sigh, he lifts the decanter, and tips an appreciable measure down his throat.

He slides to sitting, running through the outcomes of tonight. The King and Queen are in their apartments. A scant guard is assigned to their protection. Enough, surely, to repel hungry women, should the need arise. He formulates other possibilities, but sleep is overcoming him. The situation is under control. The lawyer told him so. Guards will come if things change.

Before he knows it, Lafayette is lost in slumber.

Out in the grounds, the guard retire to their beds. The usual night watch come on duty – a handful of men to keep an eye on the glittering fairyland of Versailles, deep in sleep.

CHAPTER SIXTY-THREE

𝓑OTH CENTIME AND SALVATORE LIE ON THE GROUND. HE is on his back, prone, features stretched in an unnatural expression, horror in the dead eyes.

Centime lies sideways. Her lifeless face is peaceful. Blood seeps from her nose.

My situation dawns on me by degrees. There's no easy way off this waterwheel. And now the immediate threat is passed, my painful position, stretched backward and soaked in icy water, is more apparent.

I set about trying to work my hands free, but it's an impossible process, made even more so by the compulsive shivering that racks by body every few seconds.

At some point someone will arrive, I decide, trying to ignore the seeping cold that clings to my sodden limbs. The waterwheels must be maintained. I'll be set free and I'll have to explain the presence of a dead aristocrat and his courtesan. The shaking grips me again. So long as the cold doesn't shut me down before then.

I make another futile pull with my wrists, gritting my teeth as the rope cuts into my trembling wrists. Just when I'm ready to give myself up to despair, I see a movement. Someone is climbing down from a gantry that supports part of the turning mechanism.

I'm hopeful it's an engineer. Preferable a naive one. But then to my overwhelming relief, I see Jemmy, moving down the overhanging structure with the rapid alacrity of a seasoned sailor.

'Attica!' His voice echoes above the turning wheels. 'Attica?'

But at the sound of his voice, something seizes tight in my throat and for a moment I can't speak at all.

I watch Jemmy's slight figure climbing fast over the wooden edge of the wheelhouse.

'Attica!' he calls. 'Jesus and all the saints, girl, just tell me you're alive!'

'I'm here,' I manage weakly, fighting the constriction in my voice. 'I'm well,' I add. 'No injuries.'

'Thank Jesus above,' he says, his voice shaking with emotion as he runs to where I'm confined. 'You gave me a good scare there.' He looks into my face, and begins untying the ropes.

'You are not hurt?'

'Not at all.' I shake my head, but he purses his lips, unconvinced.

'I know a bluff when I see one,' he says. 'You're half frozen to death. Let me get you down.'

I wait as he works at the ropes, drawing his sword and cutting away the cord with more care than I might have credited him with.

'Can you stand?' he asks, as one of my hands comes free, and he grasps it in his. 'Mary Mother of God, you're cold.'

I try to answer, and find my jaw frozen. He cuts free the rest of my bonds without further comment. He catches me as I fall from the wheel, and suddenly I am able to talk.

'I'm sorry to be a bother,' I say, trying and failing to stand on my own two feet. 'I cannot seem to make my limbs work.'

He laughs in relief. 'Cold water can have strange effects,' he says, carrying me to the far side of the wheelhouse. 'I've seen it before. You'll be right in a few moments.' He takes off his coat and wraps it around my shoulders. Then he stands and walks over to the bodies of Salvatore and Centime.

I pull the coat around me. The cold is abating, but for some reason I can't stop shaking.

'One thing's for sure,' observes Jemmy. 'Your spy handler won't be pleased with this day's work. You were supposed to keep Salvatore alive.' He seems pleased by this.

'I didn't kill him,' I point out, through chattering teeth. 'Centime sacrificed herself. Managed to feed poison to Salvatore, but had to take it in the process.'

'I did wonder how they both died.' Jemmy scans around the wheelhouse and then fixes on a pile of hessian sacks laid up in a corner. He lifts a few then lays them over the bodies.

Relief washes through me, to have them out of sight.

'I'm sorry I didn't come sooner,' he says. 'I couldn't risk failing. And I wasn't sure what side Centime was on.'

'Her own, for the most part,' I admit. 'But she rallied at the last. How did you know where to find me?'

'You mean, how did I know you hadn't sailed back to England as you'd threatened?' He smiles. 'Like I said before, just a feeling I had. I figured you'd be too stubborn to come on your own, so I went to find you in the tavern. Only took a few pieces of gold to persuade the drunk old landlady to tell me everything. How Centime had drugged you. Some noble man had arrived from nowhere and taken you away.'

His expression darkens at this last part.

'They told her you were an errant noble bride, who'd run from your wedding. True enough in a way, I suppose.' His eyebrows lift. 'In any case, I tracked you here and listened in to some of what happened,' he adds conversationally. Jemmy returns to where I'm sitting, and drops to one knee to look into my eyes. He peers intently then draws back, not entirely satisfied.

'So, I'm a fool and a showy pirate who cares only for gold, eh?' he asks.

I shudder involuntarily. 'I was only trying to keep you safe.'

'I'm teasing, Attica. I was about to come in, guns blazing, when your girl there did my work for me. Lucky she did,' he added. 'I didn't fancy my chances against Salvatore. But I would have tried. For you.'

'For me?' I try to smile, but my face muscles are working against me. 'Didn't you think I'd run back to England?'

'I've a little more faith in myself.'

'Your arrogance always was your worst quality.' I'm smiling now.

'*Perseverance* and arrogance are often confused.'

'Salvatore sent a message to Robespierre,' I say. 'Telling him the identity of the Pimpernel. It is all over for me now in France.'

'Never mind all that.' He stands, raising me with him. His previous concern has been replaced by something more workmanlike.

'How are your legs?' His tone is brusque, awkward even.

'Getting better.'

'Then we must get you aboard the ship,' he says. 'With a little luck and a fair wind, we might get out before midnight.'

'But …' I try to stand alone, and this time am more successful. 'Then we still have time.' My eyes are blazing. 'We can get to Versailles, stop Robespierre using his key to open the gate. Perhaps even delay Salvatore's messenger …'

Jemmy is shaking his head.

'Salvatore told me there is another way into the Queen's apartments, where her bedchamber is,' I insist. 'One that a commoner like Robespierre would not know of. I doubt Marie Antoinette would demean herself to use it, but if someone could get to her that way …'

'It is perhaps a few minutes until midnight,' says Jemmy gently. 'We are miles from Versailles and you are in no state to go up against a mob of fearsome women. Even if you could ride faster than time, which you cannot.'

I frown, trying to make sense of it all.

'I'm sorry, Attica,' he explains softly. 'The thing is done. We tried but we lost.'

CHAPTER SIXTY-FOUR

FROM THE EAST SIDE OF THE PALACE, ROBESPIERRE SLIPS out quietly. It is dark and no torches are lit. The soldiers are asleep. All about, women are snoring, sleeping off the wine. A few are picking around looking for better places to sleep than under the relentless rain.

Robespierre can hardly believe it. There are *thousands* here. His heart swells a little. He is proud of them, these bold women. The simple purity of their message had so much more impact than the meandering politics of the men. Bread. Only bread. And here they are, with what seems like half of France alongside them.

Robespierre looks out on the sleeping masses. They are so thin, so tired, wet with rain and ragged with exhaustion. Some have found barns or porticos to shelter under. Others have drunk what wine they could steal and collapsed on the open cobbles. He is struck by an urge to leave them here, sleeping. To save them an ugly fate at the hands of the King's soldiers.

Robespierre's fingers linger of the lock of the gate – a preposterously gold-latticed thing. He has almost decided to turn back when he hears a high-pitched scream. It takes him a moment to realise it is a child. A small boy, perhaps three or four, though age is a tricky thing to discern in situations of desperate poverty. Robespierre has met seven-year-olds who don't yet speak, and young women who look like old crones.

The little boy writhes and kicks, fighting an unseen assailant. He is having a nightmare, Robespierre realises, and the realisation is more like a memory which blindsides him with its familiarity. A slumbering woman rolls next to the boy and tries to coax him back to sleep. Robespierre lets his gaze wander across all the sleeping children. The babes in arms. He wonders how many are here with their mothers, and how many had mothers who did not wake up.

Preposterously he realises his cheeks are wet. What would Danton say, to find him weeping for the boys of France? Robespierre wipes his face with the edge of his sleeve, taking great care not to smudge or wrinkle the linen. He adjusts his clothes, straightens the coat, neatens the neckerchief. Order is restored, along with his purpose.

If the gate is left locked, the knot of explosive tension will have been brought to the brow of the hill, only to tumble harmlessly back again. This he cannot bear.

Carefully Robespierre turns the key in the filigree lock. Then he pulls back the gate. Versailles is now wide open, for whosoever might care to wander in.

A moment later the gate swings open. Robespierre curls his fingers around the iron gate and clangs it loudly. Several sleepers open their eyes. One of the pacing women begins making for where the entrance to Versailles now hangs curiously ajar.

Robespierre slips away over the courtyard. When he returns to the room of debating men, he is barely noticed. Only

Danton turns curiously to his small friend.

'Call of nature?' growls Danton, sleepily rubbing the emerging stubble on his broad chin.

Robespierre nods, pretending to be very interested in what the speaker is saying.

'The piss-pots are through the other door,' observes Danton, eyeing his friend. 'Never known you not to use one.'

There's a pause.

'I pissed against the velvet curtains,' says Robespierre finally.

Danton takes a long look at his friend, then throws back his big head and laughs.

'You never cease to surprise me, Max,' he says, slapping Robespierre's back hard enough to pitch him forward. 'Just wait until I tell the others.'

Danton turns back to the speaker smiling, then he presses his meaty hand to his forehead.

'*Mon Dieu*, I nearly forgot,' he says, 'there was a messenger for you.' His eyes slide to his friend, waiting for an explanation.

'A messenger?'

Danton nods meaningfully. 'Well dressed. Lace, all that. Servant of a noble, I should say.'

Robespierre is white. 'Where did he go?'

'Oh, he went looking for you a few moments past. If you go fast enough to the gardens, you should find him. He shall have to ride out that way, since the front is packed thick with bloodthirsty women.' Danton adjusts his coat. 'Are you going to tell me what this is all about? Saint's blood, Max. Are you well? You're sweating.'

'The Pimpernel,' hisses Robespierre, his eyes feverish. 'The *Pimpernel.*'

He sets off at a run for the vast palace gardens.

CHAPTER SIXTY-FIVE

At Marly-de-Roi, possibilities are falling away from me, like the water tumbling from the mighty waterwheels. Time has run out. The courtyard door will be opened and the women will swarm into the palace. I press my palms into my eyes, trying to keep track of the many, many bad things that are about to happen.

'We can board a boat,' says Jemmy, putting a hand on my arm to urge me away. 'Get to safety. Time enough to decide what to do after that.' I shrug him away.

'That is always your answer,' I say. 'Get out to sea. You belong on the ocean. I do not fit anywhere. I am too dark to be English, too fair to be African. I love women and men both. But Paris ...' I sigh. 'Paris was the perfect flux. No one demanded I be anyone. And by the morning it will be destroyed. Every foreigner will be hounded from France. All those women and children slaughtered ...' My voice catches. 'Robespierre has won.'

'Then return to England,' says Jemmy quietly.

I walk to the edge of the wooden platform, where a rail guards the edge of the tumbling flow, and look down to the churning depths. After a moment, Jemmy joins me with a weary look.

'England is trying to win France's coastal slaving routes,' I say quietly, staring down on to the churning water. 'Atherton must have known and kept it from me. How can I marry a man like that?'

A pained look passes across Jemmy's face, as though he is trying very hard not to blurt something out. He takes a breath and frowns deeply. Seemingly from nowhere, a flask of rum appears in his hand.

He unscrews the top and passes it to me. I take a long swig. It burns, reminding me of the cheap rum I always drink with Atherton. From nowhere, embarrassingly, tears rise up in an involuntary sob.

'You mustn't be too hard on your man,' he says. 'There is some truth in what the politicians say, Attica. Europe is in deadlock. Like it or not, the first country to stop trading slaves will be at a disadvantage to the others.' He sighs. 'Your Atherton seems like a clever fellow. Kind, too, I'll wager.' He sighs, lifting his eyes to the Heavens. 'He is probably trying to do the best thing in an impossible situation.'

'It's not like you to defend him.' I wipe at my eyes and take a juddering breath.

'No.' Jemmy takes the flask from me and takes two large gulps, wincing.

'Salvatore was right,' I tell him. 'I don't belong here, fighting this cause. Someone like me only confuses things.' I lift my eyes to Jemmy. 'My uncle has been telling me since I was a girl that my sex was a great blessing – I could do more for slaves in drawing rooms than wielding a knife like a man.' I shake my head and tears fall. 'I was too proud. I should have listened to him.'

'You think you would have impressed those people, with manners and a fancy accent?' says Jemmy. 'I think you may have been fooling yourself there, Attica. I never met a girl less suited to eating fine dinners in uncomfortable dresses.' He pats my hand. 'Some people are born to talk and flatter, others are bred for action. You may take it as a curse, or work with what you have. Attica, you have done great good in France. You have rescued worthy people – speakers and radicals who would have been assassinated.'

'How many have we saved?' I demand. 'Ten? Twenty?' I wipe tears away fiercely. 'Everywhere,' I say morosely, 'are men with the same idea. The end justifies the means. My whole life I have resisted it. Now I find I have been fighting for those people all along.' I turn to Jemmy. 'But now I come to realise something even worse. What if they are right?'

Jemmy is silent for a moment.

'They are right,' he says finally. 'But they are wrong, too. There is a place for all of it.' His mouth twists. 'Leading a crew of men into deadly places, you sometimes have to make decisions for the good of all.' He breathes out. 'But there is always one man,' he says, 'who goes against that. There is always one man, who will not leave others behind, who will fight to the death for what is right, and never give in. Every crew needs a sailor like that, Attica.' The serious look slides away and he grins and takes another tot of rum. 'Only one, mind,' he concludes with a wink. 'More than that and you won't get enough loot.'

I smile, despite myself.

'When I left America,' says Jemmy, 'it used to play on my mind, too, that I was rootless. Then I came to realise this was my advantage. Same as you.' He slaps my back. 'You do not

303

fit anywhere. Very good. Then perhaps you are a hero of two worlds. Go where others cannot.'

A memory rises up, seemingly from nowhere.

'My mother used to tell me a story about that,' I say. 'An African legend. A girl who could walk between realms. Through fire and water.'

Something about that image speaks to me. We are divided from Versailles Palace by a river. As the crow flies, the distance is far less than by road. If I only could walk through water, like the girl in the story, there might yet be a chance to save the Queen.

I picture the water, churning uphill, powered by the wheels. And then a real possibility strikes me.

'Jemmy,' I say slowly, 'how good are you at building rafts?'

'I can build a mighty fine raft, if you want to know,' says Jemmy proudly. 'Me and a few men once had to get through some rapids in a pinch and I—' He stops talking suddenly, his eyes tracking to the white water bubbling beneath our feet. 'Attica,' he says, 'you are not seriously suggesting what I think you are?'

CHAPTER SIXTY-SIX

*J*EMMY IS FASHIONING A RAFT FROM PLANKS AND BARRELS, whilst I work on a system to get the waterwheels at maximum capacity.

'Flow rate is height of the wheel multiplied by the length of the turning arm,' I mutter. 'But here the energy goes horizontal rather than vertical ...'

'No need to talk me through it,' says Jemmy. 'I've calculations of my own to make here.'

'Shall I give you five buttons to count it out?' I suggest. 'Or will it confuse you?'

'Very funny. This is numbers of a different kind, is all. Street learning rather than the book sort.'

I return to my calculations, walking around the massive structures. I have a memory of discussing the failures of this particular invention with my father many years ago, but can't bring to mind what the solution might be.

Jemmy glances up as I walk to a set of levers and pulleys that operate the enormous turning structures.

'If the wheel height is fixed,' I say, 'the turbine cannot be adjusted. Which only leaves the flow.' My eyes wander to where the water enters the Marly machine, diverted through a huge wooden dam.

'I think I have a solution to make the machine work faster,' I tell Jemmy. 'But I don't think your little raft will withstand the pressure.'

'Oh ye of little faith,' says Jemmy, putting a booted foot on the makeshift raft, teeth gritted as he pulls a cord tight. 'I've taken a raft like this over a waterfall before.'

'The flow will increase at least tenfold,' I say, looking at the already pounding water, the spray that hangs on the air.

Jemmy takes a moment to eye the giant grinding waterwheels. 'With a current like that, the water will split two ways,' he says, eyeing the water moving uphill. 'We will steer a path between the main flow streams.'

'A raft can do that?'

'Not usually. Fortunately, this one will be captained by the best sailor on the seven seas.'

'Lest I forget.'

'Attica,' Jemmy looks pained, 'what we are about to attempt … You must decide. Are you English in all this? Because there are many in your country who would consider rescuing the French Queen to be treason.'

'I am growing to be more of your mind,' I tell him, 'when it comes to ideas of nation. Cups from the same ocean, is that not how you say it?'

Jemmy doesn't answer, but his expression is conceding.

'Does this mean you want to stay in France?' he asks finally.

The question takes me completely by surprise.

'I mean to say,' he puts his hand to his mouth, coughs in an unconvincingly casual way, 'if you were to marry and go back to England, it hardly matters what happens here.'

'I want to stop Robespierre,' I say truthfully. 'I haven't thought much past that.'

The hope in his expression clouds and I feel guilty, though I don't know for what.

'Perhaps I do want to stay in Paris,' I counter. 'But first I must be sure there is a city to inhabit.'

His mouth tilts up. 'Then I must help you, to be sure,' he replies. 'For I am of the same mind. It's impossible, the thing you suggest, but we might as well try or be damned. I've grown fond of Paris these last months.' His eyes linger slightly too long on my face before looking away. 'Whatever happens, it is a momentous day when the women of Paris march on their King,' he says philosophically. 'If we are timely, October fifth may even be remembered as bloodless. Sorry,' he adds, catching my expression, 'it would have been your wedding day.'

My face feels tight. 'It is no matter,' I say, not liking the brittle tone to my voice.

Jemmy gives the raft a friendly pat. 'She's all set. How are you planning on increasing the flow?'

I bring Atherton's little grenade from my hanging purse.

'I'm going to blow up the dam.'

CHAPTER SIXTY-SEVEN

*J*EMMY AND I ARE EACH SAT ASTRIDE A PLANK ON HIS RAFT, which strains at its mooring like a dog on the leash as the water tugs us upwards.

'It's all about balance,' Jemmy explains. 'You ride it a little like a horse. I've given you extra ballast,' he adds, 'since you're heavier than me.'

I rock about on the plank, testing the structure.

'It doesn't feel solid enough,' I say. 'When I blow that dam, an extra ten thousand gallons of water is going to start turning those wheels.' I tilt my head up, taking in their looming enormity. 'That's a lot of extra current.'

'I'll be honest with you there, Attica. I don't think it very likely you'll blow that dam. No insult to your man Atherton, but that little ball of metal can't possibly be powerful enough. Not to mention, any momentum will be swallowed up the moment it hits water.'

I shake my head. 'That is a common misconception of grenades,' I explain. 'In actual fact, water magnifies the charge.' I wink at him. 'Book learning over street learning.'

'It first has to explode,' says Jemmy grudgingly. 'Your Atherton doesn't have a perfect history there.'

'The problem is where to place the grenade,' I admit. 'I must have time to get back to the raft and climb aboard. The only solution is to throw it, which is not as accurate as I would like.'

'Explosions are never perfect,' says Jemmy.

'Shall we give it a try?' I pull the pin and heft the grenade as far as I can towards the back of the Marly machine. It drops into the water near the dam and vanishes in a very unprepossessing ripple.

'It takes a few seconds,' I tell Jemmy. 'If you untie the mooring—'

My suggestion is drowned out by a cataclysmic explosion. A tornado-like torrent surges upwards, then rains down wide enough to soak us to the skin.

'The mooring ...' I gasp, but the explosion has already driven a great burst of energy to the enormous wheels, turning them full circle in a matter of seconds. There is a deafening boom of screeching wood and metal as the structure begins working at an unprecedented velocity.

'You might have warned me,' says Jemmy, eyeing the tidal-wave coming our way. 'I'd have built a stronger raft.'

The water sweeps us up like a giant hand, and surfs us along at breakneck speed.

'Steady!' shouts Jemmy. 'Keep your balance! If you tip, this water will shred us!'

He's doing something I can't see with the makeshift tiller, his face a mask of concentration.

'I thought you said you'd taken a raft like this over a waterfall?' I scream above the surging flow.

'More of a rocky rapid,' he admits. 'Hold tight, there's another surge.'

A second wave hits, more scattered than the first, and the raft rocks crazily from one side to the other. I plunge towards the frothing water just as Jemmy grabs my wrist.

'Too much ballast,' he says. 'I am sorry for it. You are heavier than you look.'

The third wave hits, a broken mass of water, buffeting us so badly that even Jemmy's sailing cannot keep the craft afloat. The raft flips completely, hurling us both into the water. I manage to catch hold of the mooring rope just as an icy tide closes over my head. In the tumult that follows I lose complete track of up and down, as the undercurrent drags me about. Then a jerk at my shoulder reminds me I managed to keep hold of the rope, and suddenly I break above water. I can see the upturned raft, dragging me upstream.

Then a great black wall appears, blocking the way ahead. For a moment I can't understand what I'm seeing. Then I make sense of it. I'm at Versailles' outer wall. The current has driven us full upstream in a matter of minutes.

This is the tributary that divides the water through its various fountain routes beyond. Four massive tunnels swallow up the water. I'm trying to deduce which one I'm being sucked towards, when a ringed hand closes on my wrist and drags me to the side.

I let go of the rope, kick with my legs and turn to see Jemmy, perched precariously on a half-submerged ladder that is affixed to the canal-like bankside.

'I've got you, Attica,' he says. 'Plenty of foothold here.'

My feet hit the bottom rung, and I grab a secure handhold, relieved to be out of the tumultuous water. We climb to safety just as the raft smashes to pieces against the black stone wall.

Jemmy takes off his hat.

'May she rest in peace,' he says.

'That surge must have taken us at over twenty miles an hour,' I enthuse, looking at the breaking water smashing against the dark stone wall. 'The power of the grenade is above even what Atherton predicted.' I am humming with the excitement of it all, making calculations in my head. Then I remember. Atherton kept vital parts of the mission from me. I'm not sure if I can ever feel the same way about him.

Not that it matters. I remind myself. *When he arrives at church tomorrow and you are not there, he shall never forgive you.*

I push the dark feelings away.

'The original engineers must have planned access to this part,' I add admiringly, taking in the clever way various ladders are placed. 'And this almost a hundred years ago. The whole system really is a marvel. Enough capacity to withstand a ten-thousand-gallon surge.'

Jemmy replaces his hat.

'Plenty of time to make a mathematical study later,' he says. 'We have a Queen to save. I take it you have a plan?'

I nod. 'Find the way in to the passage. Rescue the Queen.'

'You don't know where the passage is?'

'Most of these buildings follow the same kind of architecture.'

'We should find Lafayette,' says Jemmy. 'He will be at Versailles. Likely he knows the ways in and out very well.'

'You are not in earnest?'

'He is in the palace, he must be,' says Jemmy, ignoring my tone. 'For all your contempt of him, you are now fighting for the same side.'

'This may not be entirely an English mission,' I tell Jemmy, 'but the day I need to call on the help of French militia is the day I die.'

'Good to know your pride doesn't interfere with your judgement.'

'It's not about pride,' I say crossly. 'Finding Lafayette would do nothing but slow our pace. Our best hope of preventing Marie Antoinette's death is getting to her apartments fast.'

CHAPTER SIXTY-EIGHT

*R*OBESPIERRE DESCENDS THE MANY SHALLOW STEPS INTO the great gardens of Versailles. Excitement is growing in his chest. He can see the messenger Danton spoke of. The man is walking, not especially fast, along the tree-lined boulevard that passes the Versailles canal.

Naturally the gardens are of a preposterous scale. Robespierre has had his fill of the outsized environs as surely as a man who has lived on sweetmeats for days. His feet, in their smart buckled shoes, ache with the distances. The cross-shaped canal, stretching long enough to be entirely out of sight, can house hundreds of boats. It is said the Sun King decorated the expanse of water with enormous vessels rowed by teams of sweating convicts hidden away in the hull.

Trying not to look as though he is running, Robespierre hurries after the man in a strangely jogging stride. He passes large fountains, several of which depict famous classical scenes: the vanquished giant Enceladus being consumed by the lava of Mount Etna, Neptune rising from the deep, Apollo riding his chariot.

Robespierre noted the irony of this to Danton earlier that

day. Rome and Greece with their democracies and senates hold a model of virtue that all societies might follow, yet naturally nobles idolise the tyrannical gods, the wars and the victories. He has no time for such observations now.

'Hi there!' Robespierre raises a hand, shouts up the lantern-lit path. He notices a gaggle of women have waded into one of the fountains on the far side, the one with the golden turtles. Robespierre shakes his head briefly and readdresses his efforts.

'You there!' he calls, his nasal voice raising a few octaves. The messenger is just vanishing around the corner of the first great canal, at the point where it extends to a majestic cross of flat water. Then he turns, the pale oval of his face now visible in the middle distance. It is all Robespierre can do not to sob with relief.

'You are the messenger?' Robespierre calls, moving at the same jerky stride. He is closing the gap. It is difficult to tell, but it looks as though the man nods. As Robespierre gets closer, the messenger lifts his arm, and in it … a paper.

'You are Monsieur Robespierre?' he confirms, as the lawyer closes in.

Robespierre bows in acknowledgement, the anticipation unbearable now.

'From Monsieur Salvatore, yes?' he demands, moving closer.

'From Marquis de Salvatore,' says the messenger pointedly, jerking the letter slightly higher like a school-boyish game.

'Yes, yes,' says Robespierre tersely. Then noting the servant's expression, he rearranges his features with effort. 'Forgive the omission,' he says, bowing even lower. 'I have been with blunt and mannerless men in the National Assembly and their lack of grace must have rubbed off.' He manages a smile.

Appeased, the messenger lowers the note. 'Just so long as we don't forget our places,' he says haughtily, as Robespierre's fingers close gratefully on the missive. 'The King is still the King, for all the disruption.'

Robespierre is no longer listening. He is opening the letter.

'I'll inform the Marquis the letter has been delivered, then,' says the messenger.

Robespierre turns his back. There are shrieks from the far fountain. Several women are trying to disengage the head of a golden turtle. Robespierre doesn't look up as the messenger retreats, scanning the writing as fast as he can.

He crushes the paper to his chest, lips moving in disbelief, then brings it to his eyes again. The low lantern light of the grounds make it hard to read, but the meaning is certain.

Salvatore has done it. That brutish despot has actually captured the Scarlet Pimpernel.

Robespierre lowers the paper, his heart beating fast. Part of him doesn't want to believe it. That nasty aristocrat with his hideous arrogance has succeeded where Robespierre couldn't.

Such things aren't important, Robespierre counsels himself severely. *The humble man serves France.*

He permits himself a glimmer of sheer glee, imagining the country that will emerge from this night's work. For surely now, everything is perfect.

One thing, however, is missing. Robespierre's lips curl into a thin smile. *How like Salvatore.* The ruffian has omitted to *name* the Pimpernel in the paper and only given the location as the waterwheels at Marly-de-Roi as the place where Robespierre might finally discover the identity of his nemesis.

Robespierre taps the paper to his chest, deciding the next best course of action.

It could be a trick. Salvatore might have understood the real implications of assassinating Marie Antoinette, and is luring Robespierre to his doom.

He turns over these thoughts, walking back towards the palace, when a strange noise attracts his attention. An ugly sound, like the hissing of steam. It is the nearest fountain, he realises, stepping towards it, in a kind of a daze.

Something is wrong. It fits and starts as though the pressure is being tampered with. In fact, now he looks around, it seems the same thing is happening with *all* the fountains.

What could it mean? His eyes switch back to the women, who had previously been gallivanting with the golden turtles. They have vacated now, and stand frightened at the edge of the far side, watching the water buck and rear unnaturally. The women look at Robespierre as though he might have the answer.

Perhaps some crucial business has not taken place with the running of the water, Robespierre theorises. An order missed.

As he is considering this possibility, a great jet of water erupts from the mouth of a golden water nymph, who stands in the centre of the fountain. Then one by one, each gilded turtle's small mouth explodes. The dainty sprays become jets, then a surge, shooting straight out horizontally.

Robespierre stands back, appalled, brushing water drops from his coat, then retires even further to be free of the spray. All around the grounds he can hear the sound of tinny explosions as fountains erupt and fall apart, water breaks its bonds.

This, Robespierre thinks, surely cannot be a simple matter of faulty overseeing. He dismisses the strange event with a slight shake of his head. But as he is about to leave, something strikes him.

The Marly machine. That was where Salvatore claims to hold the Pimpernel.

A horrible thought dawns.

The Pimpernel. The Marly machine. The destroyed fountains.

There is something about this he doesn't like at all. Turning on his heel, he makes for the palace.

CHAPTER SIXTY-NINE

Outside Versailles Palace, the word is spreading. A door has been opened. There is a way inside.

It went something like this: Ovette had fallen asleep for a few exhausted moments, on the cold cobbles of the Versailles courtyard. She awoke to a clanging like a tocsin. Initially, she assumed an alarm had been sounded, they were under attack. Then Greta knelt unsteadily beside her.

'Psst,' she whispered, breathing wine fumes. 'Get up. The door is open. Someone is letting us in.'

Ovette rises, rubbing her stiff legs. Her gaze falls on the gate. Greta is right. Women are drifting through it, trancelike, as if they, like her, have not fully woken up. It feels so much like a dream that Ovette doesn't think to feel afraid.

She follows along behind. At first it is innocent. They enter in awe, gazing up at the specular ceilings, the marble floor, the incalculable wealth that put it all here. The women fan out, uncertain which direction to go. It is inevitable that they will eventually find a guard.

When they do, he stands between them and a large door, a young man with a nervous air, despite his Versailles finery.

'Hold!' His voice rings out along the corridors. It does not have the effect he hoped for. The uncertainty in his tone seems to galvanise the disparate group. Women begin to linger behind Ovette and Greta, wondering what is happening.

Sweat breaks out on the young man's brow.

'Get back, I say!' he announces. 'This is the way to the Queen's apartment. Not for the likes of you.'

It is, of course, exactly the wrong thing to say. Women begin to crowd in now. The uncertain drifts have a focal point. Not to mention many have awoken to empty bellies, thick heads and cold bodies. They are spoiling for a fight, and this foolish young man is in the wrong place at the wrong time.

'Stand back!' says Greta. 'We have business with Madame-Fucking Deficit, who will not deign to meet her own subjects.'

The young guard, compounding his ill luck, makes a badly judged attempt to reply.

'The Queen has been very concerned about the situation in Paris,' he says helplessly. 'She loves all her subjects.'

'Oh *ho*!' booms Greta. 'So she knows we starve, then? Knows and does nothing but buy more pretty ribbons?'

The guard is unable to answer.

'Stand aside,' says Greta. 'Stand aside or you're a traitor to the people.'

The guard adjusts his sword, but does not look confident.

'I cannot let you pass,' he says. 'The royal children are sleeping. It is unthinkable—'

He stops speaking and looks down in horror. A pikestaff has been insinuated between his ribs. At the other end is Ovette. She stares into the guard's face, a hard look of pain in her eyes.

'If only my son might be awoken,' she says.

They stand there for a moment, no one quite able to believe what has happened. At the back of the crowd, women are clambering, wanting to know what's going on. It is only when Ovette pulls the pike free that the guard sinks to his knees, and a great river of blood pools out on to the marble floor.

It floods past the feet of the market women. Barely shod feet. Bare feet. Feet with missing toes.

'Who is it?' mutter the ones at the back. 'Is it one of ours?'

Then they hear Greta's roar.

'A blow for the revolution!' she screams. 'Death to the aristos!'

The young guard, not yet dead, drops glassy-eyed to the cold marble. The blood-soaked feet form a circle around him.

A frenzied woman in grisly rags drops to his side. He registers the hatred in her eyes as she grasps his hair and exposes his neck. Vaguely he notices she carries a rusty-looking kitchen knife, with several notches where it has been badly sharpened.

He would like to tell her she should use a better steel. His own father was a butcher, and he knows some of the trade. But he feels too warm and absent to trouble himself. The crowd of scrawny women is fading away.

Workmanlike, the squatting woman sets her blade to his neck, and roughly hacks away his head. She lifts it to a final cascade of blood, and roars of approbation from the crowd.

In the bloody frenzy that follows, something changes in the attitude of the women. Greta sums it up. She the bloody pikestaff from Ovette and issues an awful screech that reverberates around the gilded corridors.

'Where is Marie Antoinette?' demands Greta, loud enough to rattle the carved windows. 'I'll cut out her liver and have it for a fricassee!'

CHAPTER SEVENTY

*J*EMMY AND I HAVE TRACKED AROUND THE VAST GARDENS AT a run, to reach the great Palace of Versailles.

Protestors and rioting people have spilled out on to the grounds, and are attacking the fountains and topiary.

There is an impossible number. People are crammed in the fountains, stampeding the manicured lawns and walkways.

The stark incongruousness of these thin-legged ragged people romping in the finest gardens of Europe is like an impossible dream. It's joyous and awful at the same time, this huge-scale invasion of the privileged site.

A man has climbed a perfectly clipped orange tree and is tearing out the branches one by one. A young woman with a gleeful expression is smashing a statue of Apollo with a heavy stone. Two boys, old enough to know better, stand at one of the long, long palace windows, hurling stone after stone through the outsized glass panes and laughing as they break in turn.

Jemmy is staring up at a vast building. He appears completely lost for words. It is gloriously lit by lanterns, every side of the white stone bathed in warm orange flame.

'Well now,' he manages eventually. 'They said it was grand. But nothing prepares you for seeing it, does it? All that stone. All that *gilding*. No wonder it took a hundred years to complete.'

I follow his gaze, over the glittering candles that flicker on the carved white stone.

'This is the stables,' I tell him. 'Versailles Palace is over there.'

Jemmy turns to where the palace is set a little way back. The thousands of candles and torches that illuminate the windows and exterior like stars lost in a vast night sky. His mouth drops open.

I have to admit, it is an impressive sight. From left to right, as far as the eye can see, are the mighty white wings of Versailles, fanning out as if to envelop the town beyond in a proprietary embrace.

Jemmy is muttering, trying to take in the scale of it, then shaking his head when the attempt defeats him.

'It's their own kingdom they've made here,' he manages finally. 'A different country to France entirely.'

'Not much of a kingdom with no guard,' I point out.

Our eyes switch to the long run of windows. Lights flash. Candles.

'We need to get to the front,' I tell Jemmy.

'Attica,' Jemmy is shaking his head, looking at the devastation, 'we are much too late.'

I shake my head. 'See how large it is? The palace is overwhelming. It doesn't look like they have reached the royal wing yet.'

I point to one side of the palace, the internal lighting of which suggests an altogether more sedate and royal affair than the frenzied jiggling flames in other parts.

'This way,' I say, tracking the candlelight.

We round the half-built structure of an orangery and make it to the front of Versailles. The expanse of cobbled courtyard alone, lined by gate after wrought-iron gate, is large enough to hold Notre Dame.

The courtyard I remember as a girl has been emptied of its coaches and sumptuously dressed guests. But unlike the thickly populated gardens, the protestors have mostly dispersed from here, drawn to the alluring depths of the palace.

Instead, pockets of ragged drunken people stagger about. But there is no large mob, no army of protestors. I estimate a hundred or so people, too old or crippled or drunk to join the main force of the attack.

The front gates, towering structures that run to twenty feet of decoratively wrought iron, hang ominously open.

'Through the Princes' Court,' I say, leading Jemmy to a side entrance. 'There's a reception room and I think the Queen's staircase is beyond.'

A drunken woman is propped against a wall.

'Fucking aristos!' she slurs. 'Burn in hell, the lot of yers.'

'I am a sailor,' says Jemmy, offended. 'Whore for a mammy and mystery for a daddy. You'll not find any lower.'

The woman eyes me, but must see something in my stance, for she says nothing more, only muttering to herself.

A blood-curdling scream sounds from somewhere near.

We break into a run.

CHAPTER SEVENTY-ONE

*J*EMMY AND I ENTER THE PRINCES' COURT TO COMPLETE chaos. It's an elbow-deep scrum of people, pushing and shoving to get through the wide door beyond. We shoulder our way in, into the first marble reception room, only to meet with an even denser wall of thickly packed peasants, a heady stink of rain-soaked sweaty wool and ill-gotten wine humming on the air.

There is a bizarre carnival feel to it all, with people chanting and singing. The strains of the Parisians' revolutionary favourite, '*Ça Ira*' –'It'll Be Fine' – break out intermittently, accompanied by a new tune. Something about the women who sell fish, and hanging nobles from lamp-posts.

But through all the seeming disarray, the crowd are of one mind. They want to find the Queen. It is announced in every song and every war cry from a pitchfork-waving market trader.

The marchers assure themselves of the route, call back directions, and are moving as one great wave towards the back, where the Queen's staircase has been identified.

'It's no good!' shouts Jemmy over the mêlée 'We can't walk a step in here. There's no way we can get ahead of this crowd.'

'We don't need to,' I tell him. 'We only need to break free

of it. The King's apartments are in another part entirely and these people care only for finding the Queen. Over there!' I point to a corner that seems less thickly populated and we make for it. As we get nearer it becomes clear why this part is not well attended.

On the white marble floor is a great pool of blood, dappled with footprints that have trodden it outwards. It runs in a wide circle, stretching many feet in either direction. In the centre of it is some kind of strangely shaped dog or bear, lifeless and grotesquely dressed in human clothes. Then I realise. It's a corpse. The head has been hacked off at the neck, giving the sad remains an oddly animal appearance.

I swallow, glancing at Jemmy. 'They took his head,' I say, feeling unexpectedly grief-stricken by this act of barbarity. 'Like a trophy.'

'Against pirate lore, to be sure, to desecrate remains,' says Jemmy, holding his hat to his chest, his voice unusually gravelly. 'He's a mother's son, whatever side he chose.'

'The crowd have not moved beyond him,' I say, pointing to the corridors that run east. 'We can go that way to the King's apartments.'

We step around the pool of blood, moving deeper inside the palace. Shrieks and chants rent the air, and the sound of footsteps pounding stairways echoes around the corridors. In this part are barely a handful of rioters, only opportunists or falling-down drunks, who pay us not the least mind as we pass through.

'There are a lot of people above us,' I say, as the ceiling shakes. 'There may be time yet. The mob could have assumed the Queen's apartments are to the front.'

'They aren't?'

I shake my head. 'That is for the bourgeois. Royal bedchambers are public places.'

We turn a corner deeper into the palace and I make an involuntary cry, running to where a bloody set of skirts is huddled in a doorway.

It's a woman, her dead face screwed up in fright, intestines lolling in her lap. She lies at the end of a long blood trail, as though having been pulled to the end of a ragged red road.

'She is so young,' I whisper, my mouth tugging down at the corners. 'They *butchered* her.'

I gaze up at Jemmy, whose expression is similarly stricken, though he is trying not to look at the sad remains. 'Why was she moved?' I add, looking back to the blood trail.

'The guards would have been frightened out of their wits,' says Jemmy. 'One of them slashed out at the mob at random, and likely moved the body in some attempt of decency.' He sighs. 'The people came for a fight, Attica. They got one.' But he looks devastated, all the same.

I shake my head. 'They came for *bread*. And have been misled and manipulated. These are simple women whose children are hungry.'

A bubble of dark hatred for Robespierre rises up. He must have known this would be a consequence of his plans. Innocent women slaughtered. More like he *wanted* it. Brutality fuels fear. Better be sure the mob are good and riled up.

Past the terrible remains is an emptier part. The dead girl has acted as a deterrent. Even the petty thieves and inebriated wanderers are unwilling to tread over bloody skirts and explore beyond. It is deserted.

Hope swells as we reach a set of broad double doors.

'The way to the King's stair,' I say, taking in the scale and the decorations.

Jemmy reaches for the golden handle.

It suddenly occurs to me that the placement of the dead girl might not have been some act of decency. I never properly considered that Robespierre would not just unleash a mob into the palace and hope for the best. He is a planner in all things, leaving nothing to chance.

I manage to grab Jemmy's hand just in time to stop him opening the door.

He turns to me, a questioning expression as I raise my hand to my lips.

Very slowly, I move to look at the crack between the doors. I breathe out, my worst fears confirmed.

'Armed men,' I whisper, backing away and pulling Jemmy with me.

The men are dressed in simple peasant clothes: the striped long trousers known disparagingly to the nobles as sans-culottes – workman-like breeches rather than knee-length silken breeches in decorated shades and trimmings.

'I should have known better,' I tell Jemmy as we retreat. 'Robespierre hasn't taken any chances. Unless we can get up that staircase there's no way to get the Queen out. There are at least ten men. Prime position on that stair. Higher ground and the only way in from the front.'

I think back to the dead girl with her exposed guts. Her placement there would prevent the mob veering off towards the west side of the palace, away from the Queen.

'Robespierre is ruthless,' I spit, a wave of hopelessness washing over me. 'We have no such advantage. He will do anything to accomplish his ends.' I give Jemmy a small smile. 'We are encumbered, my friend. He will slash and burn anyone who stands in his way.'

Jemmy looks thoughtful. 'Ruthlessness can be useful, right enough. Most of us pirates would have one such on our crew. But ruthless men are not good leaders, Attica. They want all the glory for themselves. And battles are won by the crew, not the captain.'

'All well and good,' I say distractedly, 'but we are low on crew members.'

'Are we, so?' Jemmy grins. 'It seems to me we are in need of Lafayette.'

The horrible truth of this dawns.

'Lafayette is Commander of the Royal Guard and will have men at his disposal,' continues Jemmy. 'Might even spare us a few if we ask nicely. Clear the stair for us.'

I am silent, knowing Jemmy is right, though the idea of asking Lafayette for help is unpleasant.

'We don't know where he is,' I point out truculently.

'He'll be defending the King,' says Jemmy unhesitatingly. 'Doing his duty. We only need follow the troops.'

'We'll have entirely different strategies on how to get those sans-culottes off the stairwell,' I protest. 'He won't listen to me.'

'That he won't,' agrees Jemmy. 'But he'll listen to me.' He takes my shoulder. 'Come on, Attica,' he says, 'you've already decided to help a foreign queen against the wishes of your countryfolk. Why not help the English army's worst enemy to boot?'

CHAPTER SEVENTY-TWO

WE FIND LAFAYETTE EASILY ENOUGH, JUST AS JEMMY SAID we would. He is positioning a body of men in an outer courtyard, issuing instructions and mounting a plan of defence with his pitiful guard.

'His Majesty is safe in the Guards' Room,' he tells them. 'The people only want the Queen.'

Lafayette is dishevelled and dazed looking, as though he has only recently woken up. Nevertheless, much as I hate to admit it, he is an impressive sight, calm against the mayhem of being on the losing side.

He isn't pleased to see us, shouldering through the ranks of his neatly lined troops.

'What the devil are you doing here?' he demands of Jemmy, blinking as if he might have dreamed us. 'Get your lady out of the palace. There's women roaming around who'd tear her limb from limb.'

Jemmy tilts his head in my direction. 'Attica here thinks there's more to this than meets the eye. A plot to assassinate the Queen.'

Lafayette frowns. 'Why should an Englishwoman care for our Queen?'

'I have no love for your Queen but,' I sigh, 'she is a pawn in all this. Women usually are. If she dies, there will be a great terror, a lynching of foreigners. Many of my countrymen will die.' I hesitate. 'Many of yours, too.'

Lafayette's gaze flicks between Jemmy and me. He looks even more weary. 'You always did have a blind spot for troublesome women,' he says to Jemmy. 'The people who have broken into the palace,' he tells me, 'they are gutter poissards, armed with knives and blind hatred of the aristocracy. There is no plot here,' he looks at me pointedly, 'just a lot of women who don't know their place.'

I'm so offended I am momentarily stunned. In answer, I reach into my pocket and unfurl the silken handkerchief given me by Lord Pole, with its spy-map of Versailles Palace.

'There are armed sans-culottes defending the King's small staircase in the east wing,' I tell him sharply, pointing. 'The mob took the Queen's stair, on the west side. Did you once think that those two groups could not be in entirely different places by chance?'

He hesitates, looking confused.

'You did not,' I confirm, without waiting for a reply. 'And as a military man you should have. I would have hoped, that even with French battle strategies, you would be aware of a fortified defence strategy,' I add haughtily.

'There are men at the King's stair?' asks Lafayette finally, and I can see his mind working, closing off possibilities to get Marie Antoinette out safely. 'We were to go to the Queen's apartment next,' he admits. 'Though God knows, we haven't enough men ...' His voice drifts off. 'The Queen doesn't understand the seriousness of the situation,' he says, shaking his head. 'She has no notion of the danger she is in. Knowing Marie Antoinette she will insist on being fully dressed before she will even consider leaving her chamber, and by the time she realises the mob is at her door it will be too late.'

'Why didn't you secure the palace when the mob first broke through?' I'm rather enjoying the failure of the smug general, though I know I shouldn't.

'I … I fell asleep,' he admits, flushing.

I feel a little sorry for him. He looks devastated and confused. I have to admit it is out of character for Lafayette. He is famed for sticking fast to his post while others sink from exhaustion.

'There is a passage,' I tell him, 'connecting the Queen's apartment to the King's on the first floor.'

'There is a way in through the Hall of Mirrors,' says Lafayette. 'Her Majesty would never deign to use it,' he adds wearily. 'It was something of the last King's and she thinks it a vulgar practice. And it is treason to set foot there without Her Majesty's permission.'

'It is not treason for me,' I say. 'With your help, I can get inside the passage entrance and bring the Queen to safety.'

'Mademoiselle, I admire your bravery,' he says. 'Those women are thirsty for blood. They will not spare you, even though you are a woman. Worse, they might mistake you for a companion of the Queen. Have you ever fired a pistol?'

Slowly I pull out my knife. I see his eyes grow large as the curved black blade emerges. 'I am not an assured shot with a pistol,' I say, 'but find this serves me better.'

'*Sacré bleu.*' He leans forward. 'A Mangbetu. There are stories in the Americas of a knife such as this. Legends. Where did you get this?'

'A family heirloom.'

For a moment he appears to be scouring what he has heard of my chequered family history.

'Part of my mother's dowry,' I fill in. 'The other slaves worked together, passing it around, keeping it safe for her.'

He relaxes at the mention of a dowry. 'Yes,' he says, 'I suppose savages might make dowries of such things. Well,' he passes a hand through his hair, 'I suppose you could point it forward and wave it around if someone comes at you.'

With effort, I make no reply.

'There is another problem,' continues Lafayette. 'How do you propose getting in, if the stairways are blocked as you say?'

I swallow my pride. 'I had hoped you might help me there.'

There's a long pause. Lafayette rubs his chin thoughtfully.

'Two staircases to His Majesty's apartments,' he says finally, 'a grand one and a smaller back stair. If I sent men to the larger, it would draw away any troops defending that part. Give you time to get up without being seen. It would be a risk to the King if the mob turns,' he adds. 'I have precious few men as it is.'

'How long do you imagine the Queen has until the mob breaks down her door?' I ask.

'Her Majesty's apartment is defended by a guards' room, then an antechamber where Her Majesty dines.' Lafayette reels off his mental map without hesitation. 'We must anticipate they are already inside the guards' room. In which case, they must storm the antechamber, then get through the two thick doors beyond that. You should have time enough to get to the Hall of Mirrors,' he concedes.

'I can find it.'

Lafayette sighs, then appears to come to a decision.

'I shall clear your path,' he says. 'Put what guard I have to securing the King's apartments. If you succeed, bring Her

Majesty to the Grand Chamber. I can defend the King and Queen there well enough for a time.'

His face clouds. 'Even if you are successful, Mademoiselle Morgan, it would take a miracle to change the mood of the crowd. *C'est la vie,* I am ready to die at the feet of my King.'

'How very French.'

CHAPTER SEVENTY-THREE

*L*AFAYETTE'S MEN ARE POSITIONED AT THE GRAND STAIR, and Jemmy with them.

I ready myself for the back stair, and the troops follow their orders perfectly. They aim a volley of gunfire at the double doors separating the main staircase from the rest of the palace. Within moments there are shouts from the other side as the sans-culottes collect themselves for attack.

As I wait in hiding near the smaller staircase, I see men in striped breeches run past me shouting, ready to defend their brothers. After a moment the way is clear, though it cannot be long before the men realise their guard formation is broken and race to fill the breach.

I hurry up the wooden stair, broad despite it's being the smaller of the two, and emerge on a long corridor at the top.

Lafayette has given me directions as to how to find the famous Hall of Mirrors and locate a secret door there.

In contrast to the thick crowds in the east wing, the emptiness is eerie, as though the mob had a natural aversion to the palace's most important diplomatic areas. The usual battalion of cleaning maids, chimney sweeps, floor polishers and wick trimmers have fled. I run through chamber after chamber, flock-lined walls in deep hues. All around the empty corridors, though, is an unnatural booming sound. Drumbeats and chants, as though the great body of people are mobilising to something more organised.

As I near the heart of Versailles, there is evidence of a recent stampede. Guards lie dead, their bodies plundered for weapons. But the famous Hall of Mirrors is deserted.

For a moment, I barely recognise the wide corridor, robbed of its usual dancingly reflected courtiers, who crush in daily, hoping for the ear of the King.

I came here once, as a girl, with my father. I remember crowds so thick you could barely see the fine furnishing and gilded decorations. I put a hand on the cold glass, remembering how my father bent low to whisper to me in the throng of people.

Kings once built castles to show their power, Attica. Now they make wonders, to have us think them gods. Be not fooled.

I catch my own reflection, and hesitate, taking in the round-eyed girl in the glass. I hadn't quite realised how *English* I look, dressed in London fashion, with Atherton's patriotic cockade pinned to my dress.

Slowly, I wrap my fingers around the circle of ribbons, and tear it free. The black cockade flutters to the ground. As the dark fabric splays on the parquet, I sense another movement, deep in the darker spaces ahead. A familiar voice rings out from the crepuscular gloom.

'Mademoiselle Morgan.' The nasal tone strikes at some powerful fear, deep within me. I spin, knife in my hand in an instant.

There he is, Robespierre, pale as a spectre. He trains a small pistol in my direction.

CHAPTER SEVENTY-FOUR

For a half-moment, Robespierre and I face one another.

On instinct I throw my knife, aiming to disarm and knock the gun from his hand. Instead, the butt of my Mangbetu blade strikes glass, sending a long crack splintering out.

A mirror. Robespierre is only a reflection.

He appears again. This time further away, towards the back of the long hall.

'You needn't trouble yourself, Mademoiselle Morgan,' he says. 'I have spent a good deal of time in this hall, these past weeks. Since the fall of the Bastille, His Majesty has deigned to allow commoners to witness his exalted parade of wealth.' He pauses, allowing himself a smile. 'The King doesn't actually *speak* with us, of course.'

He vanishes and reappears in the middle distance.

'To amuse myself I devised a little system, deducing where I could be seen and not seen if I used the reflections against themselves. No one pays much attention to a strange little lawyer.' He tilts his head slightly. 'I should imagine you have the opposite problem,' he decides, absorbing my height. 'You are quite striking. Not really the best choice for a spy.'

His smile widens at my expression.

'Ah, you think I could not deduce it, Mademoiselle Morgan? I know enough about you now to be wary. The Pimpernel does not choose defenceless companions. You are part of his league, are you not? I know he does not work alone.'

I bite my lip, wondering if he is baiting me to reveal my identity. Certainly he seems to be watching my face very closely, but in the reflection his glasses glitter strangely, hiding his pale eyes almost completely.

'You certainly seem very at home in the shadows,' I observe. 'Do you not seek any glory for your carefully set plans?'

Robespierre turns on his heel and begins to walk, disappearing and reappearing in the line of mirrors. I watch closely, looking for some kind of pattern that could reveal his whereabouts, but I can't for the life of me work out how he has managed to use the mirrors in this way.

'Glory is for men like Lafayette,' he says. 'He loses as many battles as he wins, and yet the people love him. I fear I should never enjoy such popularity. For I only like to win.' He allows himself a small smile. 'Yet brave Lafayette is strangely sleeping, leaving his King and Queen undefended. Most unlike him.' Robespierre clicks his tongue in admonishment. 'The long ride tired him out.'

In the corridor of glass, I still can't work out where Robespierre is in the flesh.

'Lafayette has woken up,' I reply. 'I suspect he has a stronger constitution than you counted on.'

Annoyance dances on his features. 'No matter. It is too late. Marie Antoinette cannot survive this night.'

'If she does, it will be you who saved her, monsieur,' I tell him. 'For you have told me how to get into her bedchamber.'

The first flicker of unease plays across his features, as though he is the victim of a joke he doesn't yet understand.

'Your strategy betrays you,' I tell him. 'I am certain you planned to be far away by now, removed from any possible blame. But then you remembered a weak point. Something you couldn't entirely dismiss. A rumour about a passageway. And you could not help but guard the place most vulnerable to attack.'

He blinks fast and takes a few steps back.

'You knew where to come, but not which mirror to protect,' I tell him. 'People raised in such homes know to look for where the run of skirting board does not match.'

My eye drops to the gold-painted carvings decorating the bottom part of the long hall. The workmanship is exquisite, with every join seamed so as to be invisible. Except for at the base of one large mirror.

I take a step towards it. Robespierre raises the pistol.

'This is not your fight, mademoiselle,' he says. 'Go home.'

I shake my head. 'If Marie Antoinette dies, the King will declare rule of law. Every border will be closed and foreigners trapped in France will be lynched.'

Robespierre considers this, nodding slowly.

'Now I see the problem,' he says, sounding every bit the serious lawyer. 'But it is not, I think, insurmountable.' He spreads his hands wide, amicable, accommodating. 'I have friends in Lille. I can be certain any of your English friends get through the border there. It only takes a letter.'

'What of the other foreigners?'

He frowns. 'I had you as a patriot, mademoiselle. Why should they concern you? But … if you feel so strongly, I suppose I can make arrangements to keep foreigners under protection for a few days. Enough time for them to leave France.'

He bows his head low, a diplomat, offering ever such reasonable things.

'What of the market women,' I say quietly, 'who will be slaughtered if the Queen comes to harm?'

His lips press tighter. 'Now you are unreasonable. I only request that you leave French matters to the French, mademoiselle. Is that too much to ask? Look to your own affairs. Your countrymen will be safe. You have what you want.'

I find myself shaking my head.

'If you had asked me yesterday,' I say, 'I might have agreed. I might have left you to your war. But things have changed. I have changed. You might say I have become a little French, despite myself.'

The friendly nature drops away. 'You are saying you won't do as I ask?' His jaw tightens.

'If your Queen is murdered tonight, the thing falls apart. Any chance you have of a sensible system is lost. You fall into a dark age. An endless terror.'

Something glimmers behind his round glasses.

'You and I have different notions of terror, mademoiselle. Fear can be a useful tool when directed appropriately.'

'You are a villain.'

'*I*, a villain? Do you see a mob of angry women accusing at *my* door? The villain you seek wears a crown.' He waves towards the King's apartments. 'Vacillating, dithering. With every decision he allays, my people suffer. I only wish to make fast and sensible arrangements to alleviate hunger and injustice.'

'With Salvatore,' I accuse, 'your pet aristocrat, set to enact all the terrible penalties you are so set against?'

Robespierre's assured expression falters. 'There was

some … collateral damage. I had to be certain the Pimpernel was out of the way.'

'By breaking women on the wheel? Crushing their bones?'

Robespierre's hand trembles very slightly.

'Mademoiselle Morgan, you are an abolitionist. If I were to tell you two slaves could be brutally killed so as to prevent hundreds, thousands of future such deaths, surely you would see the need?'

'I am not encumbered by your military acumen,' I tell him. 'I should fight for those people to my dying breath, and never give up hope there was a better way.'

Robespierre looks away.

'Salvatore played his part,' he says quietly. 'He is dead now?' he asks, a childlike expression on his face.

I nod.

'Then the thing is done,' he says. 'The rotten core must be swept aside by any means.'

'If you really believe that,' I tell him, 'then kill me.'

His face registers shock, but he raises the gun.

'Go back, Mademoiselle Morgan. I shall not ask you again. My terms are reasonable.' He tilts his head slightly. 'I am not an accomplished marksman,' he adds. 'But at this distance I don't imagine that matters a great deal.'

I move out into the centre of the hall, holding my hands wide.

'I don't suppose it does,' I tell him. 'But allow me to make the thing easier. You may shoot me as I stand.' I meet his eyes. 'Only I do not think you will.'

CHAPTER SEVENTY-FIVE

$\mathcal{R}$OBESPIERRE'S REFLECTION SHIFTS IN THE HALF candlelight. His reflection vanishes and he steps out into full view.

'You cannot do it,' I tell him. 'I know you cannot. You are no cold-blooded killer, Monsieur Robespierre. You couldn't bear the stain on your perfect conscience.'

'You think me a coward?' he asks. 'You are wrong. I have done things … Things I never thought possible I should do.'

He holds my gaze, waiting for me to jerk back, to flee. But when I stand firm, his hand holding the pistol begins shaking. He grips it with both hands.

'France cannot continue as it has done,' he says. 'A monumental shift must occur to begin our new virtuous society.' He blinks fast, as though remembering something he would rather forget. 'I will not go back now,' he says, his voice almost a whisper.

Robespierre's finger tightens on the trigger, his decision made. 'The women will find the Queen in her chamber,' he says, calmer now, 'and rest assured, I have no low view of your sex. They will do what they set out to do. Naturally I shall not be here to see it. There is much work to be done in Paris. Our new dawn must begin with the correct documentation.'

He has assured himself of things now, put his thoughts in a kind of order. A flicker of madness glimmers behind the glasses, deep in his pale eyes. He is a man who has come too far down a strange road.

'I wish you adieu.' Robespierre's voice is breathy, as though his heart beats too fast for him. He raises a skinny finger. 'Please send my regards to the Pimpernel. And my commiserations. I'm afraid his perfect record is about to be tarnished. This is one life he will not be able to rescue.'

He looks genuinely sorry.

'Monsieur Robespierre,' I say, 'can you really be so certain I am not the Pimpernel himself?'

Robespierre seems to shrink in on himself, as though a complicated mechanism of thoughts is rolling beneath the pale surface of his face.

'You have played a long game,' I continue. 'Cleverly, to be sure, but you have lost. The Pimpernel's identity eludes you yet. The only victory would be to catch him in the act. A public trial. You would never risk your chance to defeat your enemy by a single ill-played move.'

I can see Robespierre working this through, deducing, speculating.

'It isn't you,' he says, shaking his head as if to dislodge a troublesome thought. 'When I meet him, I will know. I will *know*.' He is speaking to himself.

'If you are truly convinced, then kill me.' I step a little forward. Robespierre doesn't move.

I approach where I have identified the hidden door, run my hand along the length. Halfway down, where a handle might naturally be, is an inset piece of wood. I close my fingers around it, and pull.

'Stop!' Robespierre's voice has taken on a strange high-pitched quality. 'Go no further!' he shouts. 'I will shoot.' He waves the pistol.

I shake my head, unafraid. 'No. You will let me live, monsieur, because you want to play another round, with better odds.'

I pull hard. The great mirror peels away, becoming a massive door.

Robespierre raises the pistol high, his hand shaking again, then turns his head from me, closing his eyes. Then in a moment, he lowers the gun, breathing heavily, an expression of disgust on his pale features.

Robespierre steps back, and once again become a reflection in one of the mirrors. Then he vanishes completely. There is an expression of abject misery on his face just before it clears from view. As though he has entirely failed his own expectations. For a moment I feel almost sorry for him.

'*Au revoir*, monsieur,' I say, before stepping forward and walking through the mirror.

CHAPTER SEVENTY-SIX

THE WEALTHY WORLD OF VERSAILLES SEEMS TO DROP AWAY as I pass through the mirror. On the other side of the glass are black shadows. I can just make out stately decorations, velvety shapes and a large desk. But older, more muted than the extravagant interiors of elsewhere.

This is where the King signs state papers. A private adjunct to the ostentatious Hall of Mirrors, designed by the Sun King to intimidate visitors. Where outside is light and frilly, the heart of it all is heavy, with solid furnishings.

There are no candles still burning. But on the far side of the room is a sliver of light. A flickering rectangle marking out a further hidden door.

'Candlelit throughout the night,' I say to myself, wishing Jemmy was here to witness my discovery. 'I'd wager that's the way to the Queen's chamber.'

Since I don't have time, or the lamplight to work out whatever clever hidden opening gains entry, I pick up my skirts, and aim a strong kick at where the lock would be. I hear the expensive wood split then yield, wondering what other devastations are being wrought by the mob to the decades-old workmanship of the palace.

As anticipated, the door construction is flimsy, relying on the completeness of the hiding place. The thin door smashes open with two more kicks. Wall-mounted candles in the passage beyond bow at the sudden draught of air.

The corridor is lined with cobwebs and dust. Presumably the King hasn't made a midnight trip to his wife's bedchamber for some time. I reach another square outline of light – candles shining from a room on the other side. Taking a breath, I hook my fingers around the door and drag it open.

The scene on the other side is of blind panic. A spectacular bedchamber is crowded with large-skirted ladies and servants, all of whom are grouped around a single figure.

Ladies-in-waiting are racing around the outskirts of the huddle, white with shock, dresses and stockings in their hands. At the creaking hinges of the secret door opening, everyone turns to look in my direction, expressions slack with terror.

Only one face appears unconcerned by the general mayhem.

Marie Antoinette is in the centre of it all, looking surprisingly unconcerned. She is a small woman with a large chin. I imagine she was pretty as a younger girl, but she is rather ordinary-looking without her finery.

I realise I am covered in cobwebs, and brush myself down self-consciously.

'Madame,' I say, looking at the Queen.

Marie Antoinette's eyes widen fractionally at the affront of being addressed like a commoner. 'Who is she?' she mutters to one of her ladies. 'How dare she?'

'I am … a friend,' I say, as politely as I can manage, 'here to help. If Madame wishes to avoid being caught in her bedchamber, you might dispense with putting on stockings.'

A distant shout can be heard beyond her door. I glance at it. The mob have breached the inner sanctum.

'They will be at the door in moments. Better just run,' I clarify, motioning to the entrance to the tunnel.

There's a fraction of a second where they all look at me, open-mouthed and appalled. Then the Queen turns her back, slowly, like a ship in full sail. With an air of inevitability, the ladies slowly rotate inwards around Marie Antoinette, and resume their fussing over her dress.

It's such an impressive snub, I am momentarily stunned. From outside, cheers ring out from the corridor beyond. It sounds as though the mob are through the final door.

Very deliberately, Marie Antoinette motions for one of her ladies to begin rolling her stockings, ready to put on. 'My guard will defend me to the death,' she tells one of her ladies.

I close my eyes.

'Madame!' I bark at her. 'If you stop any longer the mob will tear you to pieces.'

She turns to look at me, a sharpness in her eyes, then addresses one of her ladies.

'Anne-Thérèse, would you tell this,' she hesitates and looks me up and down, 'strange *woman*, to whom she speaks?'

Taking the cue, a lady-in-waiting turns to me furiously. 'You show disrespect to the Queen of France!' she hisses.

I ignore her, addressing the Queen. 'My name is Attica Morgan. I am here to rescue you. But we must leave now.'

There is a pause. The voices beyond the door have amplified.

'You are a foreigner?' replies Marie Antoinette, holding a hand up to her lady-in-waiting. 'I do not trust you.'

I hesitate in my reply.

'I am English in the same way you are Austrian,' I say eventually.

Several gasps of affront ripple around the ladies.

'I have grown to love France, just as you have,' I continue. 'And I know, as Your Majesty does, that this palace is not France. You must open your eyes, madame,' I conclude. 'The bubble has burst. They are coming for you, and it is not to kiss your skirts.'

Uncertainty shows in her round face.

'If you value your life,' I say, 'leave your stockings and follow me.'

'Your Majesty must be properly dressed,' whispers a lady, her eyes wide. But Marie Antoinette holds up another chubby hand and addresses me.

'Prove to me you are loyal to France,' she demands.

'There is no time …'

'A single curtsey,' she says, a small smile on her lips, 'will suffice.'

For a moment I mean to refuse. Then I remember the starving desperate women in Paris. The cruelty they will suffer if the Queen dies today.

I try not to roll my eyes, grateful only that Jemmy is not here to bear witness.

Then keeping my eyes fixed on Marie Antoinette, I drop her a curtsey.

'Very good.' She nods, turning to a servant. 'Shall we go? Anne-Thérèse, you might bring the stockings with you. I think it might be best if we run.'

Behind us is a splintering of wood. I grab the Queen's arm and pull her towards the open door of the secret passage.

'In here!' I shout. 'Now! We cannot let them see the door!'

Blank with shock, Marie Antoinette doesn't protest. The other ladies are suddenly mobilised and run like clucking chickens for the open door.

A roar of fury sounds from the other side of the door.

'Bring me the Queen!' screams a woman. 'I'll cut her to pieces!'

The bedroom door is breaking ajar as I push the last of the ladies into the opening of the passage. I catch a glimpse of a livid-faced peasant women, brandishing a red-tipped pike. Then I pull the secret door shut, just as an army of angry women descend on the Queen's empty bed.

I watch through the crack in the door as they attack the mattress, stabbing and slicing. Feathers float in the air. For just a second, I imagine what might have been. If the Queen had waited a moment longer … If she had followed protocol and put on her stockings.

It would be a very different France. Turning back to the gloom of the corridor, I follow behind the Queen and her ladies as they make their way to the King's chamber.

CHAPTER SEVENTY-SEVEN

WE BREAK OUT INTO THE KING'S APARTMENT, THE QUEEN, her gaggle of frightened ladies, and me bringing up the rear. In contrast to the dark tunnel linking the royal chambers, the candlelight is dazzling. Bright as daylight, with every great chandelier lit with a hundred candles. It is a strange feeling to be in this stately room of exquisite privilege, with only a few doors between us and the ragged bloodshed of the mob.

'Your Majesty.' The Queen curtseys to her husband. The King is deathly pale, and looks as though he might vomit. Behind him I recognise Lafayette, and then my heart soars to see Jemmy tucked behind him, face grim.

'They have swarmed out in the courtyard below us,' says the King. 'They seem to have … lost interest in the palace interior.'

He glances towards the wide windows of his first-floor apartment, from which the loud noise of an angry crowd can be heard. Having found the Queen's bedroom empty, they have come into the area below the King's balcony to demand he hand her over.

I glance at Marie Antoinette, who is astute enough to realise what has happened.

'It was me they wanted,' she says quietly.

No one replies.

'Where are my guard?' asks the Queen, in a voice that suggests she knows the answer.

The King steps forward. 'Those brutes murdered your guard,' he says. 'Have no fear, they will be punished.' His eyes drift to Lafayette. 'Fortunately,' continues the King, 'we have our great general to protect us.'

The Queen's eyes settle on Lafayette, the General she ousted from court for his bad dress sense. She swallows and straightens her back.

'I am obliged to you ...' she begins, but her voice catches.

Lafayette moves forward and bows graciously. 'Your Majesty,' he murmurs, avoiding her eye. 'It is my pleasure to serve you.'

Humiliated tears run down the Queen's face; she brushes them away angrily and walks to the window. Musket fire whistles from outside, and she steps back quickly, shocked.

The door opens and the royal children are shepherded in, tearful and frightened. They run to their mother and cling to her. The Queen's face softens, the vacant look replaced by something infinitely sadder.

'Can you help us?' she asks Lafayette. 'Might we leave the palace unseen?'

Lafayette glances at the King then back to Marie Antoinette. 'I am sorry, Your Majesty,' he says. 'It is too late. The mob have surrounded the entire palace. They will easily notice a carriage leaving.'

'They would dare chase a royal carriage?' Two pink spots appear in Marie Antoinette's cheeks.

'Your Majesty, they will drag you from the vehicle and kill

you,' says Lafayette bluntly. 'There is no sense in leaving your children motherless.'

The princess begins crying at this and clings tighter to Marie Antoinette's skirts. Her brother tries for a frightened stoicism.

The Queen's mouth opens and shuts wordlessly, as though a reality she has long dismissed is suddenly, awfully real. The King says nothing. The Queen glares at Lafayette, as though he is to blame for unsettling her children.

'Perhaps we could get the Queen and the royal children to safety,' suggests an advisor. 'A disguise could be engineered. The King would follow later.'

'I shall not sneak away like a fugitive, without my husband,' says Marie Antoinette, as her children continue to wrap themselves into her skirts. 'I have done nothing wrong, only love my people.' She rubs at her temples. 'How long until the men are here?' she asks. 'Lafayette's soldiers?'

The minister opens his mouth and shuts it again.

'I ... Your Majesty,' he says, 'they are already here. This is all we have. There is no rescue, Your Majesty. We are impossibly outnumbered. If we do not find a way to calm the mob, this is the end of it for all of us.' He glances at the balcony. 'Perhaps the King might go out to speak on the balcony,' he adds. 'The people like the King.'

As if in reply, another missile shatters glass, and the ugly shrieks begin to consolidate into a clear chant.

'Bring us the Queen! Bring us the Queen!'

Marie Antoinette's daughter begins to cry afresh, putting her mother's hand to her lips. The Queen puts an arm around her and distractedly strokes her hair, whilst simultaneously drawing her son closer.

'You,' she says, addressing me. 'The Englishwoman who claims to love the French. What does the friend of France think I should do?'

I hesitate, wondering for a moment if she really is addressing me. For a moment I am conflicted. It is hard to match the Marie Antoinette of the pamphlets with the mother standing before me. Perhaps she could change.

'Your Majesty,' I say, 'those women are starving. They are angry. You are no Queen if you will not face your own subjects. I say, face them.'

Marie Antoinette turns to Lafayette.

'What say you?' she demands. 'Shall I walk out to my execution?'

'I think it the only chance you have to save your children,' he says matter-of-factly.

Marie Antoinette swallows hard. She kisses her daughter's tear-streaked face.

'Be brave, *chérie*,' she whispers. 'You are a princess.' Then Marie Antoinette straightens. She kisses her small son on both cheeks, and suppresses a sob.

'Very well,' she says. 'I shall not hesitate. I will go.'

CHAPTER SEVENTY-EIGHT

A DEADLY HUSH HAS FALLEN OVER THE NOBLES ASSEMBLED in the King's apartment.

'If she goes out on to that balcony,' says Jemmy, leaning in so only I can hear, 'anything could happen. Those people are exhausted, hungry, and they hate her. She only need walk a little too straight or seem haughty, and they'll open fire.'

The chant for the Queen has got louder and clearer now, a steady morose chant.

Musket fire twangs against the wrought iron of the balcony balustrade, and another pane of glass shatters.

The Queen begins to walk slowly towards the window. No one tries to stop her. But as she comes into view of the crowd, just before the balcony opening, a volley of bullets is unleashed, pattering dustily into the stucco of the exterior.

A servant tries to place himself in front of the Queen to shield her from the bullets, but she moves him back.

'The King cannot afford to lose such a faithful servant,' she tells him. 'Open the doors.'

Behind her, the white-faced princess cries silently. The prince stands a little apart, his small face white with shock, glancing to his father who looks at no one.

The great glass doors are moved apart, exposing the interior of the royal bedchambers to the angry crowd. There is a hush from outside. Gunfire and stone-throwing stops. They are waiting to see who will come.

'Mama!' the princess runs to her mother's side, clutching at her hand. She is quickly followed by her brother, who takes the princess's break in protocol as permission. They grab the Queen's hands, the girl and smaller boy, holding tightly. When she tries to disengage herself they cling on. The young boy erupts in loud tears.

Lafayette steps forward.

'They will not fire on children,' he tells her. 'It is a good idea to let the people see you with the Dauphin and his sister.'

She looks down, an uncertain smile for her children. Then white-faced Marie Antoinette steps out on to the balcony.

For a moment, there is a deadly hush. Then the jeers and the shouts begin again.

'No children!' shriek the mob. 'No children! Away with them.'

Marie Antoinette turns and calmly leads the children back inside the palace, then steps out once again, her arms folded, eyes lifted to the heavens.

A hush falls across the crowd once more. She stands for some minutes. The Queen's cheeks flush. Her lip trembles. She reaches a hand to steady herself on the balcony.

The tension in the King's apartment is unbearable. It would take only one stone thrown to break the temporary deadlock. Everyone is waiting for the inevitable. The crowd will only watch for so long before someone takes action. Some brave soul is about to go down in history for killing the Queen of France.

We're all wondering what is to be done, when Lafayette walks calmly towards the balcony.

'What is he doing?' I whisper to Jemmy.

'Perhaps he has a plan to order them away,' suggests Jemmy. 'Tell them they break some law. He is a trusted commander.'

'He'll only succeed in making them furious.'

Jemmy says nothing, but his face reflects agreement. The last thing this crowd needs is someone to start laying down the law.

But Lafayette does not start issuing orders or edicts. Instead, he walks serenely to the Queen, and lifts her unresisting hand. Dropping to one knee, he kisses it ceremoniously.

The effect on the crowd is immediate. A ripple passes through the women, like a sigh. The sea of weapons, bristling in the air, loses some of its aggressive uprightness.

Lafayette stands and a look passes between him and Marie Antoinette. I cannot see her face, but the stiff line of her posture suggests she hates him.

Then from somewhere deep in the crowd, a woman's voice rings out.

'Long live the Queen!' she shouts. 'Long live the Queen!'

Incredibly, the cry is taken up. And suddenly Marie Antoinette faces a crowd of admirers, royalist subjects come to lavish regard on their sovereign.

'I can't believe it,' I say, shocked. 'Lafayette has done it.'

Marie Antoinette turns back to the apartment now, gliding graciously back over the threshold. But as soon as the doors close behind, her foot gives way and she staggers. Her lady-in-waiting takes her arm, staring into her face. The Queen convulses, a hand covering her mouth, then leans over, holding her stomach, breathing hard.

'I am well,' she manages, waving down any attempt to fuss around her. 'A moment of feeling unwell is all. It has passed.'

Her eyes seek out her children, then fill with tears as she collects them to her.

'It is well,' says her lady. 'You did well, Your Majesty. Surely their bile is passed now. You showed them—'

But another shout comes from outside. It is taken up en masse.

'What do they say?' The Queen turns to Lafayette, suddenly all ears as to his judgement.

He coughs into his hand. 'They want you and the King to go to Paris, Your Majesty.'

Marie Antoinette turns to the King, her eyes wild.

'But they will murder us! They will murder us if we go to Paris.'

'They will murder you if you do not go,' says Lafayette calmly. 'That is for certain. We haven't enough guard to protect you.'

The Queen's features work through the facts of the situation. If she didn't realise before that she should have left when Lafayette advised it, she realises it now.

'You must defend us,' she protests weakly.

'Your Majesty, there is no guard,' says Lafayette wearily. 'There is nothing to protect you from a mob of ten thousand people. You have won their good grace. The only chance you have is to retain it.'

'But it is twelve miles to Paris,' she whispers. 'I cannot ...' She puts a hand to her forehead, then rearranges her features, looking to her children again. 'Very well,' she says hoarsely. 'We must give the people what they want.'

I glance at the King. He has a distant look in his eye, as though he has withdrawn from things completely. I wonder if he really understands what he has cost his family today.

Servants begin making arrangements, issuing orders for carriages to be readied, clothing to be fetched.

Marie Antoinette watches them. Desperately, she swings towards me.

'I did nothing wrong,' she says. 'I never harmed anyone.'

'You had a duty, a great power. You were careless.' I shake my head. 'I am sorry, madame,' I tell her. 'You have been saved from the mob, but you cannot escape justice.'

CHAPTER SEVENTY-NINE

𝒯HE DRIZZLE HAS BEGUN AGAIN AS THE ROYAL CARRIAGE IS readied to depart Versailles for the last time.

We all watch quietly – commoners, servants and nobles alike – as the King and Queen are packed silently into the carriage with their children. His Majesty sits tight-lipped and brooding, while Marie Antoinette strokes her daughter's hair, and tries to pretend the trip is not enforced.

'She is so brave, so courageous,' says a minister, leaning towards me as the carriage jolts into motion. 'She has had no sleep, no food.'

'Every one of those women who marched,' I tell him, 'did so with not a crust of bread in their bodies. Marched miles in driving rain and cold, with children on their hips. Risked the worst kind of tortures as traitors, only to ask that their children might not starve. Yet you speak not of those women's courage?'

'She is the *Queen*,' says the minister, white-lipped in outrage.

'Let us see for how much longer,' I tell him. 'Certainly, she is the Queen of Versailles no more.'

The slow-moving carriage suggests it is to be a long, awful march back to Paris. Lafayette rides alongside, every muscle in his body tensed for the twelve-mile parade, expecting at any moment that things might take a turn for the worst. Part of the procession, moving at the same dismal pace, are citizens touting the severed heads of two royal guards, waving on pikes in the air.

The Queen catches sight of one and flinches, before setting her features to a stubborn look of outrage. The King, bearing a distant, haunted set to his eyes, gives no indication he has seen, whilst his children sit, pale with fear, and sneak terrified looks at the haggard commoners. It must be the first time the young royals have seen the emaciated people on whom their vast wealth depends.

The mood of the crowd is erratic, one minute shouting 'Long live the King!', then veering to bad-natured taunts about the royal guard.

'You could have saved her, couldn't you?' observes Jemmy, watching Marie Antoinette's squared jaw. 'Why didn't you?'

I watch the Royal carriage roll away from us, with the white-faced captives inside. Marie Antoinette sits straight-backed, not acknowledging her husband.

'Her dress,' I say. 'The printed cotton. It's picked from the slave plantations in Virginia. The Americas were on the cusp of disbanding them, for cotton was not profitable enough. No one wanted it. Then the Queen began her whimsy for informal floating things. Naturally the court ladies followed along, and soon every bourgeois lady in Paris wore cotton dresses.'

I look steadily at the King and Queen's carriage departing. It is being driven inexpertly by a commoner, and the jolting wheels periodically jerk the royal occupants forward, but they are in no position to complain.

'That woman's thoughtlessness tripled the number of cotton slave plantations, just at the point they were falling from favour,' I say. 'Thousands of people owe their miserable enslavement to her alone. She could have done things differently. She didn't.'

Jemmy absorbs this. 'That is why you won't wear the French-style chemise dress? I thought you were wedded to English fashion.'

I consider. 'It is one of the reasons. But it's also true the English style is better for wearing weaponry.'

Jemmy laughs. 'They're a funny kind of nation, the French,' he says finally. 'Think they'll take the royals back to Paris and do for 'em there?'

'I don't think so,' I say. 'They're too tired. I imagine they'll keep them under an unofficial house arrest in the Tuileries and make a fist at a constitutional monarchy. With the King they have it shall never work.'

Jemmy turns to me. 'You sound quite the revolutionary,' he observes, 'and yet *I* heard you curtseyed to a French Queen. I should have liked to have seen it.'

'Who told you that?'

'Lafayette got it from one of the ladies-in-waiting. Is it true?'

'Absolutely *not.*' I glance at his smiling face. 'Never tell anyone of it.'

'Pirate's honour.' He winks.

We're both silent, acknowledging the momentous events.

CHAPTER EIGHTY

When we arrive back in Paris, the mood in the city is peculiarly subdued. A victory and a defeat. No one can decide what to feel, but they know they are still hungry.

Jemmy and I enter our favourite little tavern of the same mind. We have succeeded and failed all at once.

'Shall we sit inside?' I suggest, not able to bear our usual outside table, with the view of Porte Saint-Martin. The memories of Centime are too difficult.

Almost as soon as we pour wine, I am confronted with what I was dreading. A letter is already waiting for me from Atherton. It feels very strange to see the familiar handwriting outside of the usual Sealed Knot coding and blue wax.

I open it quietly, already predicting the accusations and hurt. Part of me wants to fold it back up without reading it and throw it on the burning embers under the nearby kettle of meat stew.

'Better to face the music,' says Jemmy, who must have noticed my glance towards the fireplace.

I read the note once, then twice, hardly believing the contents. Without meaning to, I laugh, shaking my head at the news. Then I fold the note back up and slip it into my pocket. Seeing Atherton's writing has confirmed everything I have felt since leaving Versailles.

'Bad news?' suggests Jemmy, eyeing me cautiously over his tankard.

'No,' I say, although that is not entirely true. The new world that had been expanding before me has just been turned on its head.

'He forgave you, then,' he asks, 'for leaving him at the altar?' Jemmy takes a swig of wine. 'If he writes so quickly he must have.'

'Atherton wrote a day ago, asking to postpone the wedding,' I say, giving Jemmy a baleful look. 'He thought I might need more time for my wedding trousseau, so I might buy clothes in Paris. I must have … missed the letter.'

Jemmy suddenly seems very interested in the contents of his tankard.

'You'll be going back, then?' He continues speaking before I can answer. 'You beat Robespierre,' Jemmy is looking everywhere but my face. 'Stopped his plans for chaos. I thought you might stay and finish what you started.'

I smile thinly, watching the ghoulish march of citizens with their bloody trophies.

'I would say,' I tell Jemmy, 'this was very much a draw.'

'Don't tell me you're giving up, Lady Morgan.' The words are light, but there is something pleading in his expression.

I smile, but make no answer. The truth is, I made a decision back in the King's apartment, long before I received this letter.

When the Queen stepped on to the balcony, I finally realised something. It is time I faced my own fate and stopped running.

CHAPTER EIGHTY-ONE

London, One Week Later

MY FAMILY HOME FEELS DIFFERENT IN EVERY WAY, NOW it is intended for my wedding. The ancestral manor near King's Cross has its own private chapel, and I had been hoping for a quiet affair. But my father's latest wife was quite adamant the marriage of Lord Morgan's only daughter be aptly celebrated.

For my own part, I'm hoping Atherton and I might slip away after the ceremony, and leave all the old people to congratulate themselves. But I can't quite formulate the image of Atherton and me alone in a carriage, as husband and wife.

It feels ridiculous to be in the bedroom I slept in as a girl, with a lady's maid hired especially for the occasion to fuss around my dress and finish my hair. And much as I wish I could deny it, a sick feeling has sat in my belly ever since I came back to England. Jemmy and I didn't part on good terms, and I can't make my peace with it.

There is a knock at the door.

'Shall I send them away, miss?' suggests the maid.

I glance at my rather plain wedding dress and shake my head. A silly notion grips me. An image of Jemmy with some urgent message. Even as I dismiss this as impossible, the urge to see his scarred face expands like a bubble in my chest. But Jemmy is far out at sea; he refused the invitation to my wedding for reasons I still don't understand.

'We could work together,' I told him. 'In Africa. There's bound to be a requirement for someone with a fast ship.'

Jemmy had been positively haughty in his rejection. 'Work for your men in London, Attica? No thank you,' he replied. 'Me boys and I are a pirate crew, with plenty of smuggling work to occupy us. We don't take orders from government. And your fancy people won't take kindly to a ruffian like me at a society wedding, no matter how clean me boots are.'

'It will be a small wedding,' I told him. And he shook his head and laughed.

'If you think your fine family will let you marry on the quiet, then more fool you,' he said, more bitterly than seemed appropriate. Though it transpires he was right. The Morgan manor has not seen such spectacular preparations since I can remember – not even for my father's wedding to his American wife last year.

Then, for all his chagrin, Jemmy had still insisted on sailing me to England, his face making some complicated mixture of expressions all the while, as though he wanted to say something but couldn't find the words.

I sigh to myself as the maid walks to open the door. If I live a hundred years, I shall never understand pirates.

The door opens and the exciting prospect of seeing Atherton is quickly replaced by the reality of Lord Pole.

'Attica!' For the first time in my life, my uncle's smile appears genuine. This marriage suits him well enough, of course. But it flashes through my mind that perhaps, beneath it all, Lord Pole has a glimmer of sentiment for his niece. He has even dispensed with a few of his heavy furs in honour of the joyous occasion, though he still wears his black parliamentary robes. Without the musky animal hides to bulk out his shoulders, he looks smaller and older.

'Your dress is rather continental,' he says with a frown, killing dead my fleeting optimism in his character. 'For an English bride.'

I glance at the dress. 'Fashions have simplified,' I say.

'In Paris perhaps,' he retorts, 'every French lady wants to look as though she's stepped out of ancient Greece. In London things are rather more formal.' He coughs into his closed fist. 'No matter. You'll lose such affectations soon enough.'

I am beset by sudden uncertainty, since I'd felt sure my future husband would favour my choice. Missing nothing, Lord Pole backtracks.

'You must be comfortable, of course,' he mutters. 'It is your wedding day, after all.' There is a pained look in his hawk-like eyes, as though such conventions of sentiment are inconvenient to him.

'You are anxious?' He's trying to read my face, peering at me.

'Why should I be? I have known and respected Atherton since I was a girl.'

'Yes.' Lord Pole eyes the maid, drumming fingers on his chin. 'But he was not a cripple back then, Attica.'

'He is not a cripple now.' I'm outraged on my future husband's behalf.

'I only mean ...' For once Lord Pole seems entirely out of

365

his depth. 'You have made things right between you? Atherton had nothing to do with those trading routes. You must have understood that. If it was down to him, he would have continued his sugar -beet experiment. Created our own supply of sugar.'

There's something about his expression that I would attribute to guilt, if I thought Lord Pole capable of such things.

I take a deep breath and let it out. 'I understand that his loyalty to the Crown occasionally demands Atherton go against his own ethos,' I say. 'That is the nature of a monarchy, I suppose. Sometimes the end justifies the means. Perhaps France will do things differently, so more reasonable men have a say.'

Lord Pole considers, not seeming entirely convinced. His brows knit together. 'You do intend to have children? It is important for appearances. Though your issue couldn't be expected to inherit any of your father's estate, naturally.'

'Of course.' I make a smile that is a little too bright, too brittle.

'You will arouse suspicions in Africa if you and your husband remain childless. Little point in sending you to infiltrate foreign embassies if you cannot give the appearance of a normal married couple.'

'I intend to fulfil every part of my wifely duties,' I tell him through gritted teeth. 'Shouldn't you be with Atherton?' I add pointedly.

Lord Pole nods. 'I only came to wish you joy.' He hesitates. 'And to be sure this is really what you want.' His eyes search mine, then dart away before I can answer. 'You served your country, and of course we are grateful.' He waves his hand, dismissing my four years' service, risking life and limb, as a little sideline, a whimsical hobby. 'Now a new life awaits you. The chance to do greater good.' He takes a breath, as though making a speech he's rehearsed. 'More changes are made …'

'In the drawing rooms than on battlefields,' I fill in.

Lord Pole fixes me with a long look, then seems to come to a conclusion.

'In any case,' he reaches inside his coat, 'I brought you the latest news from France.' He untucks a sheaf of letters.

My beaming smile seems to take my uncle aback. 'That was very thoughtful,' I tell him.

'I have my moments.' He passes the papers. 'If I may summarise,' he adds, as I track through the dense spy-report, 'the King and Queen were escorted to the Tuileries Palace in Paris. No one is yet admitting they are imprisoned, but it is clear they cannot easily leave. On the few occasions the Queen has taken the air in her carriage, she has been subject to some very gross impertinences.'

'They are still legally recognised as King and Queen?'

'Yes. Though no one is quite sure of the terms of the new arrangement. Only that power has shifted vastly. The Rights of Man, now signed, seems oddly redundant.' Lord Pole looks thoughtful. 'There is something else,' he adds. 'Your pirate friend tried to conceal a message for you in the correspondence from our man in Paris. Rather artlessly done, though I give him credit for low cunning. What I don't understand is why he felt the need for secrecy. Here it is.'

He passes me a page of dense text, overlaid by scrawling decoding ink, and the insignia of the Sealed Knot.

'Jemmy wrote me a letter?' I stand up to take it, disconcerting the maid, who'd been holding some decoration thoughtfully above my hair.

'I hardly think your pirate capable of putting pen to paper in any comprehensible way,' replies Lord Pole sniffily. 'He sent you some badly coded thing from a slave colony. We broke it in minutes. Why he tried to conceal it is a mystery. I can only imagine he suspected we wouldn't deliver it.'

'Thank you.' I'm only half aware of Lord Pole making to leave, since I'm pulling apart the code in my mind, trying to understand why Jemmy wanted me to see it.

'I wish you well,' says Lord Pole with grave sincerity, bowing. 'When I next see you, you shall be a married lady.' I glance up to see his expression uncertain, concerned even, but I am more concerned with my letter.

'Attica …' he says.

I look up, frowning at being distracted from the code. 'What?'

Lord Pole hesitates. 'Never mind.' He shuts the door behind him.

CHAPTER EIGHTY-TWO

I'M STILL WORKING ON JEMMY'S CODED MESSAGE AS I WALK down the stairs to the chapel. People seem to be buzzing about me, but I hardly notice.

The paper is something to do with a secret uprising in Haiti. A plan among the slaves to free themselves. The last line is something about France and the revolution. I am just making sense of it when I see Atherton, standing at the foot of the stairs. Nerves flutter in my stomach.

I hadn't expected to see him until we met at the altar in a few hours. It is so good to see him. Suddenly, all the doubts I had are rushed away. Of course I will marry this man. It was all I was ever destined to do. We make perfect sense.

'You look beautiful,' Atherton says, with feeling. 'I hope you don't mind,' he adds quietly, as I descend with a quizzical expression. 'I know it's bad luck. Only I wanted to see you.'

I have no idea what he's talking about until he adds: 'People like us aren't wary of old superstitions, are we?'

'No,' I say, and the words come out as though they belong to someone else. Because unexpectedly, Jemmy's missive has made sudden sense in my mind.

The revolution. The uprising. It came about because of the women's march on Versailles. Slaves are looking to France as proof that they can stand up to their cruel masters. That all men are equal.

'There was a slave rebellion,' I tell Atherton, 'in Haiti.'

'Yes.' He nods. 'The only successful uprising ever. The enslaved people took inspiration from the bravery of the French women,' he adds, smiling at me. 'Other French colonies are following suit.'

'You realise, I was there?' I tell him. 'When the marchers reached Versailles?' I'm not saying what I mean to say, and it is confusing. Why does this development feel so personally significant? I can hardly take credit for the actions of the French, after all.

'Naturally, I was aware,' Atherton says. 'A very dangerous business it sounded, all those strong-armed women with pitchforks. I am very, very happy to have you back safe, and embarking on no more undertakings in France.'

But for the first time, perhaps ever, Atherton hasn't taken my meaning at all.

'Surely, we might yet return to Paris?' I say. 'You know how much the slave cause means to me,' I finish lamely, realising this doesn't exactly make sense.

'How could I forget?' Atherton's voice holds just the smallest shade of sadness. 'Isn't that what our future life together is all about?' He comes closer, in the way that people of my class are practised at doing, so the servants don't overhear. For some reason, my thoughts fly to Jemmy, who airs his grievances at full volume.

'Do not imagine I am under any illusions, Attica. You would never have agreed to become my wife if it had not come with the position in Africa. And if you wish to visit the Paris salons, and debate the slave cause, then of course we shall.'

I'm stung, realising how selfish I sound.

For the first time between Atherton and I, all the words go away, and we're left in an awkward silence.

He takes my hands in his and clasps them to his chest. It's such a heartfelt, innocent gesture, it very nearly has me cast aside my fears. Only just at that moment, another wave of realisation hits me.

'Do you mean to tell me,' I ask quietly, 'that you took the position in Africa because you thought it meant I would agree to become your wife?'

Atherton doesn't reply, but I can see from his face it's true.

'You don't have a great interest in breaking the slave rings,' I ask, 'do you?'

'Now you are unfair,' he says hotly, my hands still clasped in his. 'Of course I care, of course I do. But my life, my work, is here in London. And more than anything I care for *you*. I care for you more than any of it. The politics, the work. Isn't that what you want in a husband?'

He looks so desperate, so defeated, that my heart goes out to him.

'Yes, it is,' I say, and I know it with my whole heart.

CHAPTER EIGHTY-THREE

*M*Y FATHER STANDS WAITING IN THE FAMILY GROUNDS, as the maid escorts me outside. He looks so different these days I can't help but smile to see him. The once bloodshot eyes are now a sparkling blue, and there is an energy to him that was previously lost in laudanum fug. He wears a perfectly tailored suit in muted colours, and no wig over his neatly combed dark hair.

'Your new Lady Morgan is good for you,' I tell him. 'You look like a handsome edition of your brother.'

He laughs. 'More fashionably dressed than Lord Pole, I hope. Hello, Attica.' He kisses me on the cheek. Takes my arm, a little too tightly.

'How are you feeling?' he asks, his eyes searching my face.

I manage a smile. But I cannot help the sick feeling in my stomach. I yearn to marry Atherton, but the reality of life beyond that – an ambassador's wife – now crowds around me like prison walls.

'The Sealed Knot is broken-hearted to lose you,' says my father, 'but it is a new adventure you embark on now.'

I nod resolutely, glad of my father's sturdy arm to lead me

across the wet autumn lawn. My new situation is the price I pay to become Atherton's wife. I would pay it ten times over.

'I always hated the wedding ceremony,' my father remarks conversationally, as we approach the church. 'Seemed a lot of nonsense to me, to make a public declaration of it all.'

I smile in agreement.

We're nearing our family chapel: a small, rather ramshackle affair. A tiny building constructed a hundred years ago, when worship was a more sober practice. Since there is only space inside for ten or so people, the ceremony at least will be mercifully small.

'Best not keep your future husband waiting. Time to deliver him his bride. I almost forgot ...' He stops walking suddenly, tapping his fingers to his mouth. 'I have a message from your pirate friend.'

I had no idea my father even knew about Jemmy, but of course he was a spy himself.

'Jemmy is well?' I confirm hastily.

My father nods. 'I extended him a family invitation to the wedding,' he adds in a suspiciously neutral tone. 'In light of the services he has done, keeping my daughter safe.' He casts me a sharp little smile. 'He wouldn't accept,' my father says. 'Strong-minded fellow. I liked him. Good to have at your side in a crisis, I should imagine. He refused under any circumstances to attend. Any thoughts on why that should be?'

I shake my head, thinking Jemmy must be the only person my father has been unable to bring around to his point of view.

'He's a pirate,' I tell my father. 'They are impossible to understand.'

'I don't doubt it,' says my father, smiling at the unintended frustration in my voice. 'In any case, Jemmy said that should you *want* to see him, he's waiting at the Prospect of Whitby in Wapping, until the next tide. There is a person to be rescued from the machinations of some lawyer fellow, and he thought you might be game.'

For just a moment, I allow myself to imagine a final mission might be possible. One last Pimpernel adventure, snatching an innocent life from Robespierre's grip.

But of course, it is impossible. I have already put Atherton through too much to abandon him on the day of our wedding. I am racked with sudden fury at Jemmy for being too stubborn to come to my wedding.

My father catches my expression.

'If I might offer you a little unsolicited advice,' he says, 'from a man who has made more than his share of mistakes?'

'Go on.' I eye the chapel.

My father heaves up a world-weary sigh. 'I've had three wives, Attica. The first, your mother, I loved very dearly. The second, well, you know about her. My current wife, I am happy to say, has woken a hope, long since buried, that a man and woman might live in convivial happiness. I only wish I had been braver earlier. It would have spared you all those years … Well, you know it all.' He frowns. 'I was a coward, Attica, and it cost you a great deal. But you have always been better than I. You have your mother's good qualities. She had a fearsome temper, you know. Quite ferocious. The bravest woman I have ever known.' He smiles at the memory.

'Thank you for the compliment, though it hardly counts as advice.'

'What I am trying to tell you is that I think Atherton understands your rather unconventional character. I think he loves you for it.'

I am sure of it too, and a rush of affection for Atherton suffuses me.

'So I expect he will understand,' continues my father, 'when you inevitably act in ways that ordinary members of society might find unusual.' He pats my hand. 'If you wish to be happy in your marriage, you must start as you mean to go on. Be yourself, Attica.'

I consider what he is suggesting.

'Even if Atherton were to agree to a final mission,' I say, 'I have about a hundred relatives to greet after the ceremony.'

'Hmmm,' says my father. He eyes the church ahead. 'Then perhaps as a little wedding gift, you might accept my help.'

I stare at him, trying to take in the magnitude of what he's saying.

'You spent a good many years fretting for me,' says my father. 'I am better now. More than capable of appeasing a few relatives, should my daughter wish to slip away early from her wedding reception.'

'But your wife has invited half of London,' I say weakly, the prospect of a reprieve from the formal reception like golden water pouring through me.

'Then we shall have a very jolly party. All the jollier for knowing you are happy.' He smiles at me. 'I've designed entire military campaigns, Attica, completed impossible spy missions. I can be rather persuasive, even where my indomitable American wife is concerned.' He winks. 'Shall we get you to the chapel?'

CHAPTER EIGHTY-FOUR

THE PROSPECT OF WHITBY IS AN ATMOSPHERIC OLD TAVERN on the banks of the Thames. Just the place to watch ships coming and going. It's filled with drunken sailors, returning captains and prospectors eager to trade off the latest voyage.

For a moment I don't see Jemmy, and then I make out a dark figure skulking at the back.

'You look rather plain,' I observe, closing in on him, 'for an adventurer.'

Jemmy stands, disbelief and pleasure lighting his features.

'Attica?' He moves towards me, taking me by the shoulders as though to assure himself I won't vanish away. 'I didn't believe you would come.'

We're beaming at one another. Jemmy's hands are still at my arms and he seems reluctant to take them off.

'Oh ye of little faith,' I say. 'Where are your jewelled pistols?'

'You don't wear fancy pistols in a place like this,' he explains. 'Not if you're alone without your crew.' The smile slips from his face. He withdraws his hands. 'I am sorry for how we left things.'

Our last ugly conversation leaps painfully to mind. Jemmy

sits back at his table and I slide in next to him, remembering the last time we spoke.

Jemmy had told me in no uncertain terms that Atherton and I were ill-suited.

'He could have asked you to marry him three years ago,' Jemmy had fumed, seizing the ship's wheel with unnecessary force.

'He thought I would refuse.'

'A man thinks nothing of such things. He was decent enough to know you deserve more. He knew he had no business marrying a spirited young wife, when all he could offer is a slow limp around the world, shaking hands with perfumed old men.'

'And what should he be offering me?'

Jemmy's green-brown eyes had taken a pained expression.

'You come to it like one of your codes, Attica, a problem to be solved. Love is not like that.'

'Should I come to it like you, then? A broken heart in every port?'

To my great surprise he had look offended.

'You have me all wrong, Attica,' he'd said. 'I was wed and when it did not take I was broken-hearted.'

We had been silent after that, for the remainder of the voyage, and I had disembarked to a frosty farewell from Jemmy, and open glares from his shipmates.

I have the strong impression Jemmy is thinking of the same conversation. To break the silence I take out my tankard and pour off some ale from Jemmy's vessel into mine.

'I am sorry too,' I tell Jemmy. 'We weren't ourselves on that voyage.' I try for a smile. 'Something in the ship's rum.'

He shakes his head. 'I never get drunk aboard a ship,' he

says. 'Perhaps I was sad you were leaving.'

We're both looking at one another, and deep in his eyes is a story I never want to stop reading.

I've missed him so badly, I realise, with a shock.

Then Jemmy's eyes slip from my face to my hand, and his face puckers in confusion.

'You are married?' he asks, and whatever was just between us vanishes like smoke.

I nod, looking at the gold ring on my finger.

'Moved the day, did you?' The false lightness resounds in his voice.

'There is no need to dwell on the details.'

'Did you ever consider,' suggests Jemmy, 'that Atherton knows you well enough to make a delay? Just to be certain you'd make it?'

'I …' I never had considered it, but now Jemmy says it the possibility seems rather obvious. Not nice either, I consider with a frown. The kind of manipulation Lord Pole would engineer.

'I'm only teasing,' says Jemmy quickly. 'A lucky coincidence. Fate at work.' He studies my face. 'If you are married,' he says, 'why are you here?'

'Fortunately my new husband is a very understanding man.'

'But …' Jemmy frowns deeply, trying to make sense of this. 'Your wedding night,' he manages.

'We've postponed it,' I say lightly. 'Atherton knows the mission is important to me. If Haitians are inspired by events in France, then we have a chance to do real good.' I force a smile. 'I will only be gone for a week. That was the arrangement.' My eyes lift to Jemmy's, and his earlier joy has been replaced by something more complicated.

'A week,' he murmurs. 'Well, better than nothing,' he adds, brightening. 'And perhaps you shall make another delay.'

'I won't,' I say. 'Not for a second time.'

'Even so, your Atherton takes a risk,' he says, looking happy. 'Unconsummated is not yet wed, is it?'

'That isn't how I regard things.' I eye him in amusement. 'If we are to continue to work together, you shall have to give your word to respect my arrangements with Atherton.'

'The marriage that isn't yet a marriage? I'll make no such promise.' He grins.

'Now you are impossible,' but I cannot keep the smile from my face.

Jemmy drains his tankard, stands and wipes his mouth with the back of his hand.

'How about it then, Lady Morgan,' he says, offering me his arm. 'Another adventure with your pirate crew. Our ship awaits. What shall you say to it?'

I thread my arm through his, feeling the solid dependableness of him like an anchor.

'Captain Avery,' I say, 'I do.'

ACKNOWLEDGEMENTS

I love every minute of writing these adventures, and I have so many people to thank for helping me along the way. My editor Poppy Mostyn-Owen for being such a great support throughout, and the same goes for my agent Piers Blofeld who has been my champion for many years now. Susannah Hamilton deserves thanks for cheering from the sidelines, as well as Kirsty Doole, and those at the publicity coal-face, Aimee Oliver-Powell and Sophie Walker, thanks so much for getting behind the book. The entire Corvus team, headed by the able Will Atkinson are a dream to work with, and so much fun besides.

At home, my amazing sister, Susannah Quinn, is always the first reader and critique of my books and is my favourite author besides. I am also blessed with a partner who is also my best friend, Simon Avery, and is just as entertaining as when we first met. My two children, Ben and Natalie, are my best little bringers of joy, and robbers of author snacks – and I wouldn't have it any other way.

Finally, my biggest thank you, as always, goes to my readers, who never fail to amaze me by liking the books, sometimes, quite a lot. What a great time we have together. I'll keep writing them, if you keep reading them.

Truth is stranger than fiction.
Which of these events really happened?

One of the following facts is false. Do you know which? Go to www.atlantic-books.co.uk/scarlet to find out which, and unlock a secret history to *The Scarlet Code.*

1. The women of Paris's market organisations (a kind of early trade union) marched on Versailles and brought about the royal family's enforced move to Paris.

2. Marie Antionette missed being set upon by a mob in her bedroom by mere moments, rescued only by the suggestion she flee through a secret back door without her stockings on.

3. Pencils were an emergent and exciting technology.

4. King Louis XIV commissioned the design of 'automatic tables' that could be set with food and rotate upwards into his apartment, without servants impeding his legendary seductions.

5. Spy weaponry of the time included maps on handkerchiefs.

A Revolution Spy

The thrilling historical crime series from C. S. Quinn

Read book one, and find out how the revolution began…